MYSTERY SCIENCE THEATER 3000®

THE COMIC

DEVELOPED FOR COMICS BY
JOEL HODGSON
HAROLD BUCHHOLZ

D1160949

Illustration by TODD NAUCK

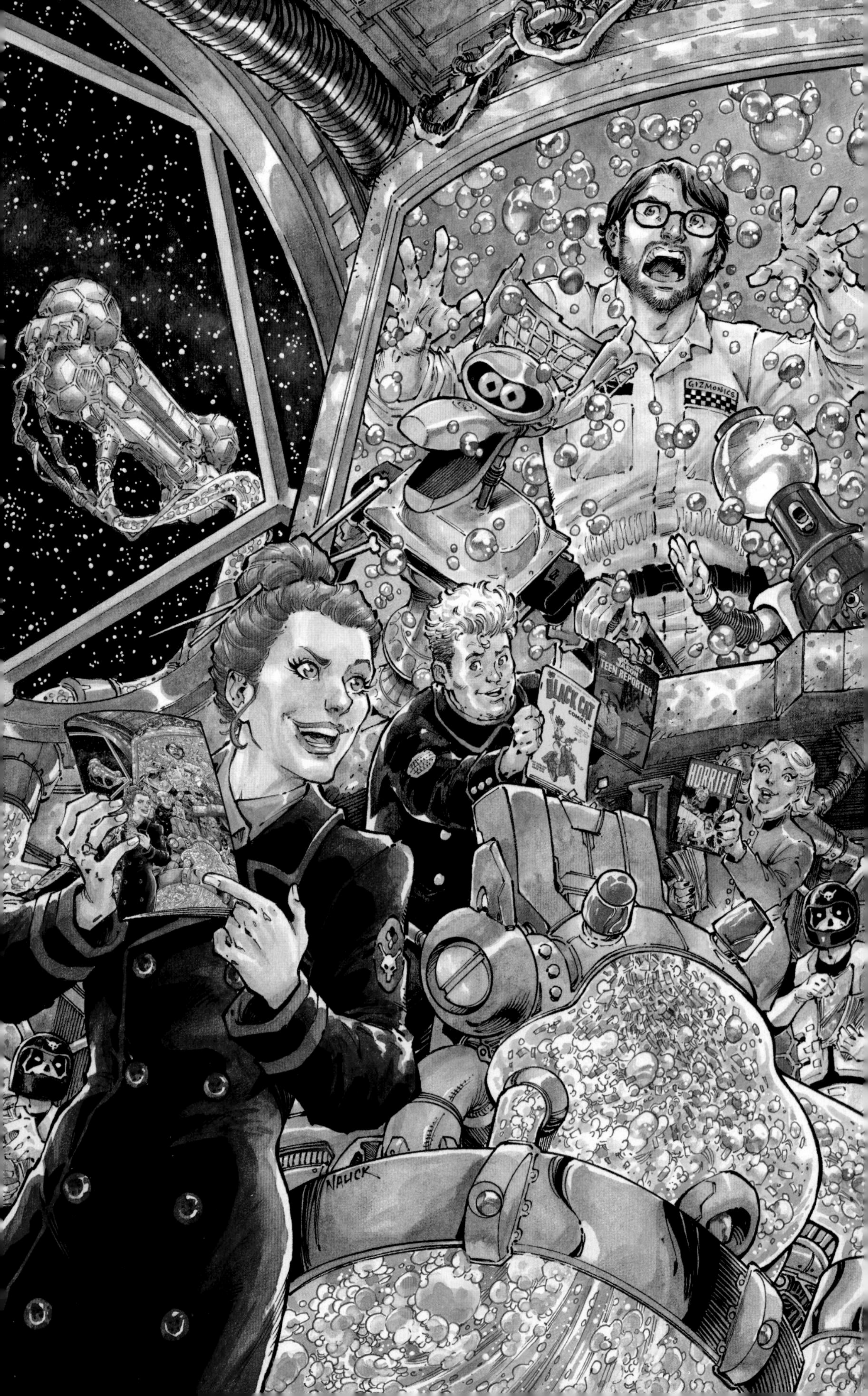
GIZMONICS
BLACK CAT
COMICS
TEEN REPORTER
HORRIFIC
NAUCK

MYSTERY SCIENCE THEATER 3000®

THE COMIC

WRITERS
JOEL HODGSON • HAROLD BUCHHOLZ • MATT McGINNIS
SETH ROBINSON • SHARYL VOLPE • MARY ROBINSON

ARTISTS

HOST SEGMENTS
TODD NAUCK
colored by WES DZIOBA

TEEN REPORTER AND "TERROR ON HIGH"
MIKE MANLEY

BLACK CAT AND "TAIL OF DEATH"
JACK POLLOCK

"THE CLAY COFFIN," "IRON DOOM," AND "DEVIL CLAWS"
MIMI SIMON

LETTERER
MICHAEL HEISLER

FRONT COVER ART
TODD NAUCK
colored by WES DZIOBA

BACK COVER ART
STEVE VANCE

DARK HORSE BOOKS

PRESIDENT AND PUBLISHER
MIKE RICHARDSON

EDITOR
RANDY STRADLEY

ASSISTANT EDITOR
JUDY KHUU

PROJECT COORDINATOR FOR ALTERNAVERSAL
MATT McGINNIS

DESIGNERS
ETHAN KIMBERLING
PATRICK SATTERFIELD

DIGITAL ART TECHNICIAN
ADAM PRUETT

Special thanks to **TOM ROGERS, ERIC KILKENNY, JAKE NYBERG,** and to **MSTies** everywhere.

GO WATCH THE SHOW ON NETFLIX RIGHT NOW!
CHECK OUT CLASSIC EPISODES FROM SHOUT! FACTORY.
MST3K.COM

Advertising Sales • 503-905-2315
To find a comics shop in your area, go to www.comicshoplocator.com

MYSTERY SCIENCE THEATER 3000: THE COMIC
Published by Dark Horse Comics LLC, 10956 SE Main Street, Milwaukie, Oregon 97222. Mystery Science Theater 3000 ® & ©
2020 Satellite of Love, LLC. All rights reserved. Totino's® and Pizza Rolls® are Registered Trademarks of General Mills. Used
with permission. Dark Horse Comics® and the Dark Horse logo are trademarks of Dark Horse Comics LLC, registered in various
categories and countries. All rights reserved. No portion of this publication may be reproduced or transmitted, in any form or
by any means, without the express written permission of Dark Horse Comics LLC. Names, characters, places, and incidents
featured in this publication either are the product of the authors' imaginations or are used fictitiously. Any resemblance to actual
persons (living or dead), events, institutions, or locales, without satiric intent, is coincidental.

This volume collects the Dark Horse comic book series *Mystery Science Theater 3000: The Comic*,
originally published September 2018–May 2019.

Published by Dark Horse Books
A division of Dark Horse Comics LLC
10956 SE Main Street • Milwaukie, OR 97222

DarkHorse.com • Facebook.com/DarkHorseComics • Twitter.com/DarkHorseComics

Library of Congress Cataloging-in-Publication Data

Names: Buchholz, Harold, writer. I Hodgson, Joel, 1960- writer. I McGinnis,
    Matt, writer. I Nauck, Todd, artist. I Manley, Mike, artist, colourist. I
    Pollock, Jack (Comic book artist), artist, colourist. I Simon, Mimi,
    artist, colourist. I Dzioba, Wes, colourist. I Heisler, Michael, letterer.
Title: Mystery Science Theater 3000 : the comic / writers, Harold Buchholz,
    Joel Hodgson, Matt McGinnis [and others] ; host segments art, Todd Nauck ;
    'in-comics' art, Mike Manley, Jack Pollock, Mimi Simon ; colorists, Wes
    Dzioba, Mike Manley, Jack Pollock, Mimi Simon ; lettering, Michael Heisler.
Description: First edition. I Milwaukie, OR : Dark Horse Books, 2019. I "This
    volume collects the Dark Horse comic book series Mystery Science Theater
    3000 #1-#6, originally published September 2018-May 2019."
Identifiers: LCCN 2019017037 I ISBN 9781506709475 (paperback)
Subjects: LCSH: Comic books, strips, etc. I BISAC: COMICS & GRAPHIC NOVELS /
    Media Tie-In. I COMICS & GRAPHIC NOVELS / Science Fiction. I FICTION /
    Science Fiction / General.
Classification: LCC PN6728.M978 B83 2019 I DDC 741.5/973--dc23
LC record available at https://lccn.loc.gov/2019017037

First edition: September 2019 • ISBN: 978-1-50670-947-5
Digital ISBN: 978-1-50670-956-7

1 3 5 7 9 10 8 6 4 2
Printed in China

Illustration by STEVE VANCE

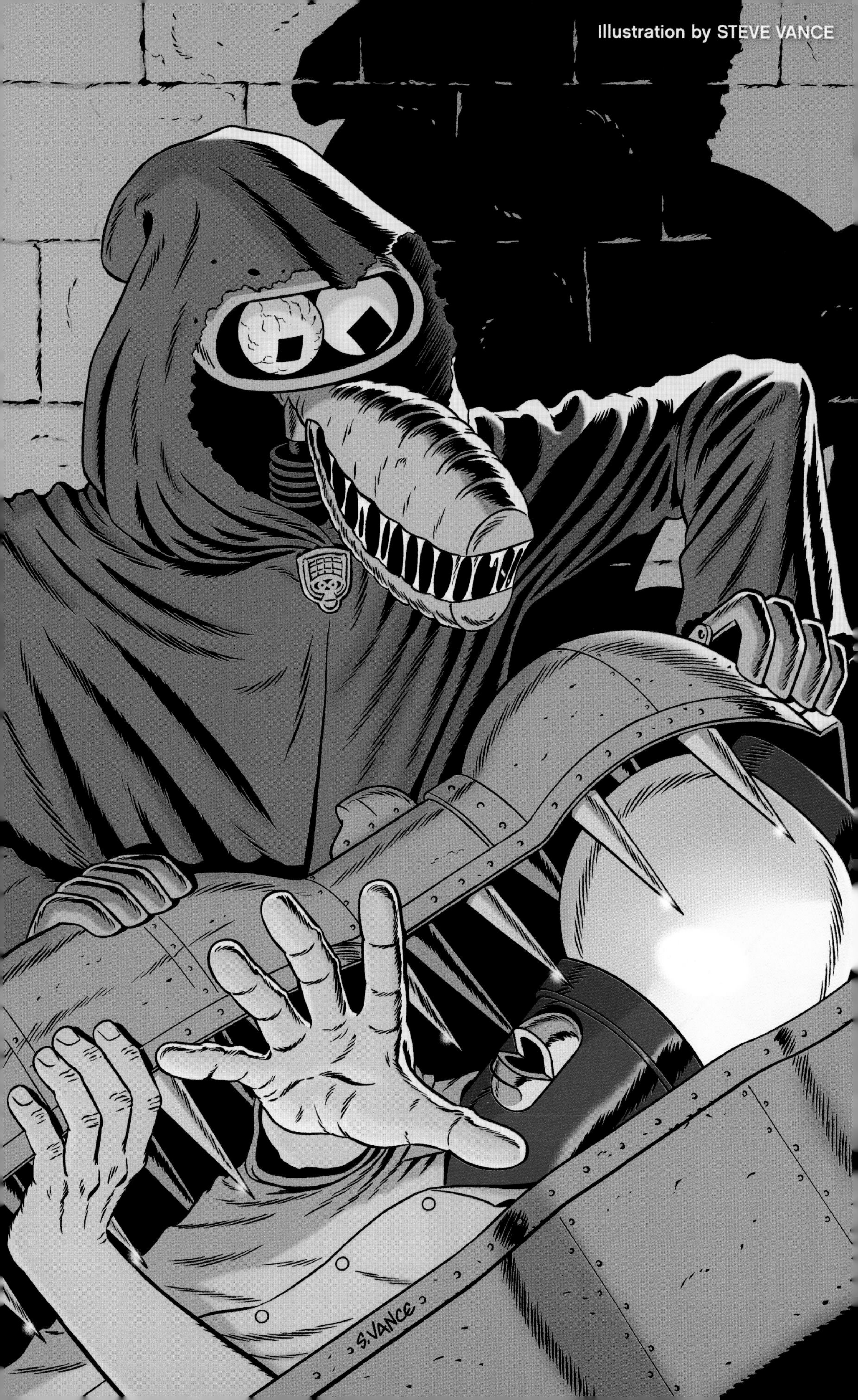
S. VANCE

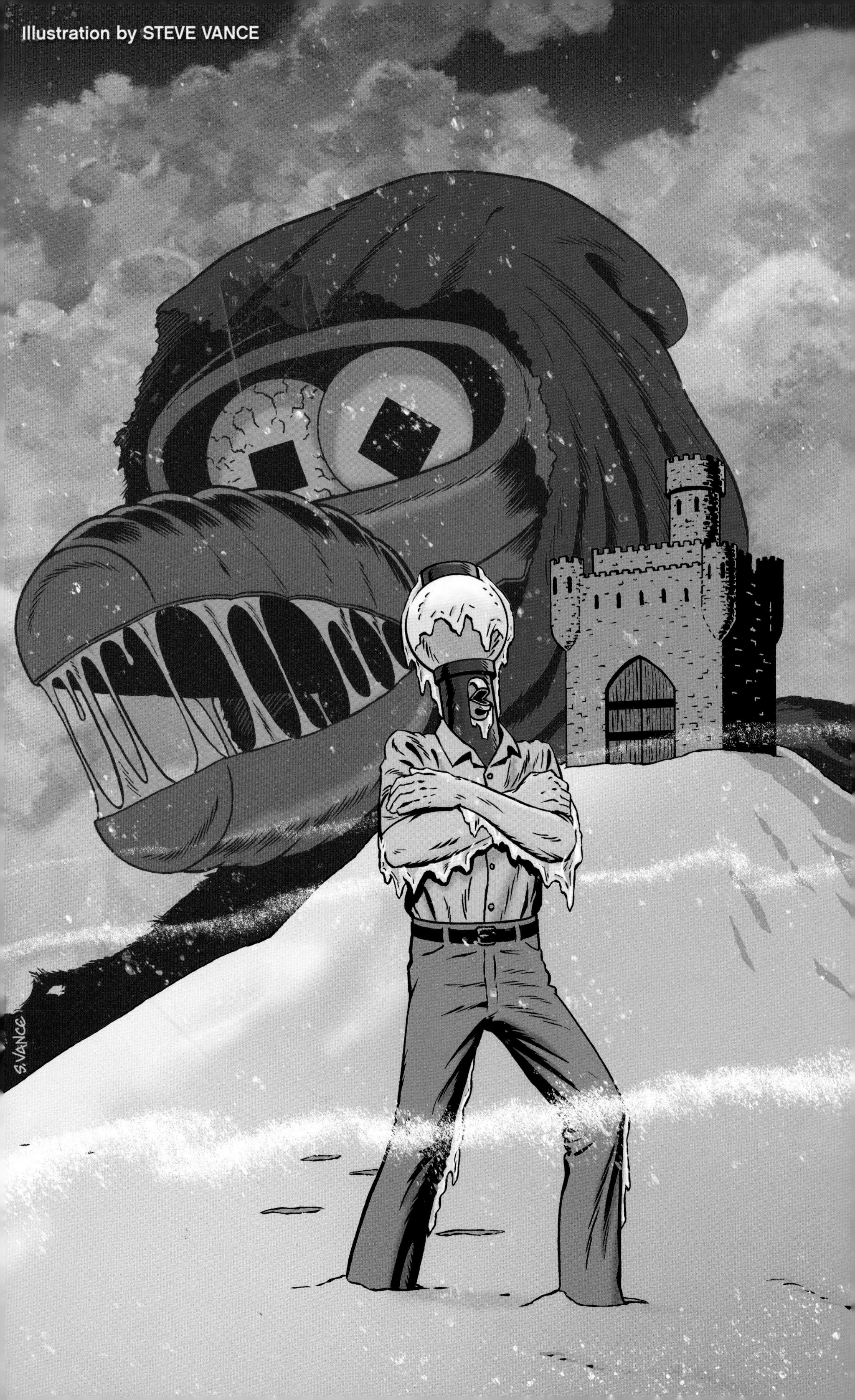
S.VANCE

Illustration by STEVE VANCE

Illustration by TODD NAUCK
Colored by WES DZIOBA

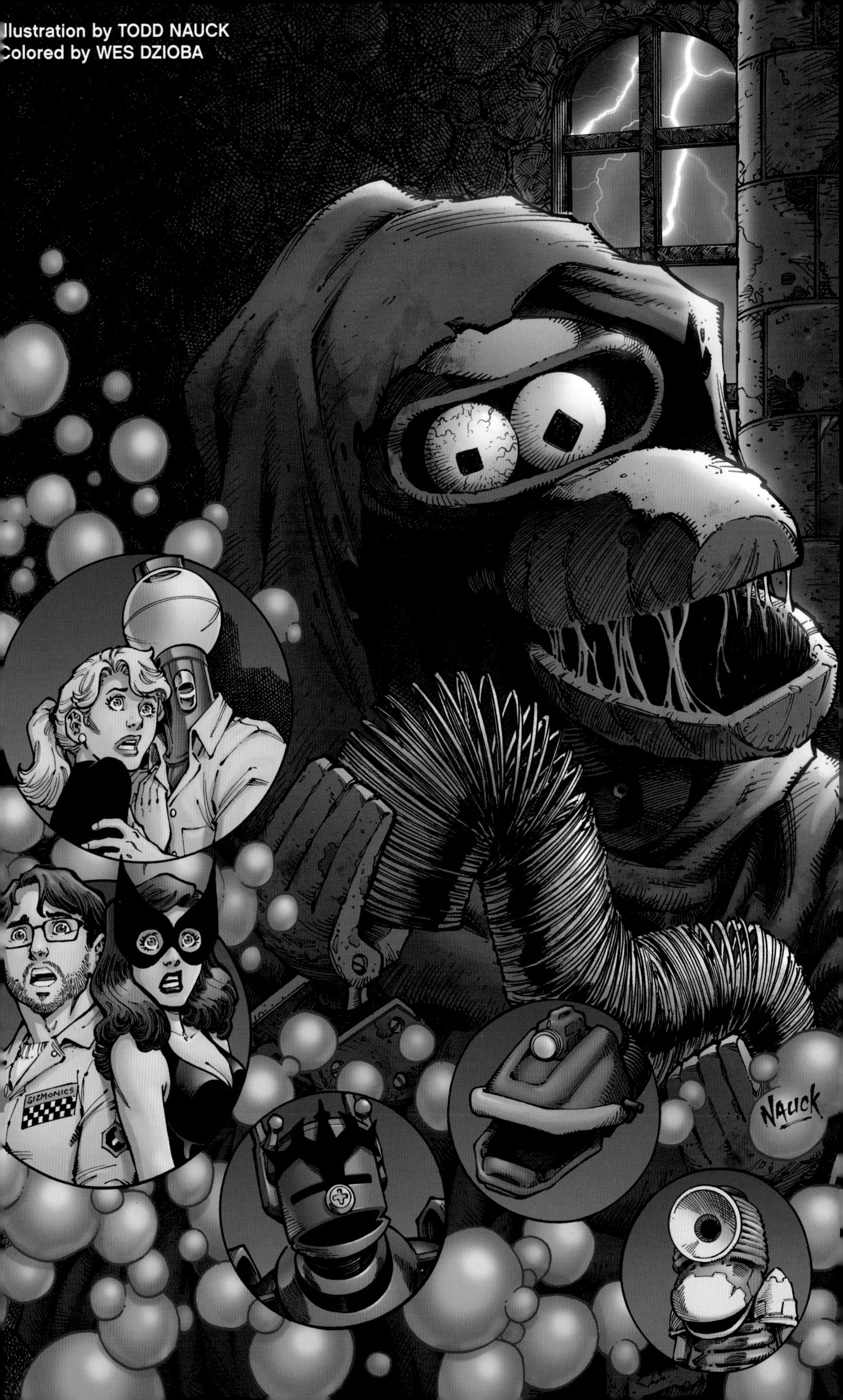
GIZMONICS
NAUCK

INTRODUCTION
by JOEL HODGSON

As I prepped to write this introduction, I readied myself by reviewing all six issues of *Mystery Science Theater 3000: The Comic*. And I have to admit, it's pretty rock solid.

In fact, I'm going to encourage you to stop reading this introduction and go ahead and read the rest of the book, and then circle back. Go ahead. I'll wait.

All done? Great.

Let's go.

Here's what I think, and this might sound blunt, but I'll just let it fly.

Good art inspires us, bad art shows us a path to make our own art.

Sui generis? Yeah. Sure.

And I have an example to help explain why, and it's germane since it's a comic book story.

I say this because of the very first comic I ever owned. It was *Adventures of the Big Boy* #174. That would be the *Big Boy* comic series that was offered at the Marc's Big Boy in Green Bay, Wisconsin, and in Big Boy Family Restaurants all over the country. It said "15¢" on the cover, which was crossed out by a stamp that read Free to Our Guests. I remember picking it up, rolling my eyes and thinking sarcastically, "Yeah, right. Lucky us. We're guests. At Big Boy."

Adventures of the Big Boy #174 didn't have that glossy comic book cover. It was just newsprint. It didn't have ads for the Johnson Smith catalog, or Hostess snack cakes, or Olympic Greeting Cards either. Everything in Big Boy's world seemed slightly off-model. Big Boy's girlfriend, Dolly, was often half the size of the Big Boy and didn't even appear to be from the same species. Big Boy's dog, whose name escapes me now, kind of looked a little like Snoopy but remained in the same expressionless stance throughout the entire comic. And then to add even more cognitive dissonance, the size of Big Boy's head would vacillate wildly from panel to panel. It was a mess.

I've often tried to describe *Adventures of the Big Boy* #174 as a bit like Ernie Bushmiller's *Nancy*, if Nancy and Sluggo had no sense of identity, were completely unmotivated, and faithless.

Also, over time these *Adventures of the Big Boy* issues became one of my favorite things to read. Seriously. I would look forward to making it back to Big Boy to see what new-yet-bland scenarios the Big Boy had coming. I would often read it aloud to my parents and my siblings while we waited for our meals. I'm pretty sure I laid it on pretty heavy too, putting a real sardonic spin on it for a ten-year-old in Wisconsin while we waited for our strawberry waffles (a dish, I might add, that the Big Boy in Green Bay does very well).

I've got to level with you, in an act to defend myself against the people who believe that they must defend the Big Boy in this easily-triggered pop culture landscape—not all *Adventures of the Big Boy* Comics were bad. In fact, I recently learned that comics luminaries like Stan Lee, Bill Everett, and Dan DeCarlo worked on them in their early iterations.

But I wasn't seeing any of that Golden Age of the Big Boy stuff. I was seeing the issues that were coming out in the early Seventies, and by that time Big Boy, Dolly, and that little black and white dog had completely lost any sense of their original canon.

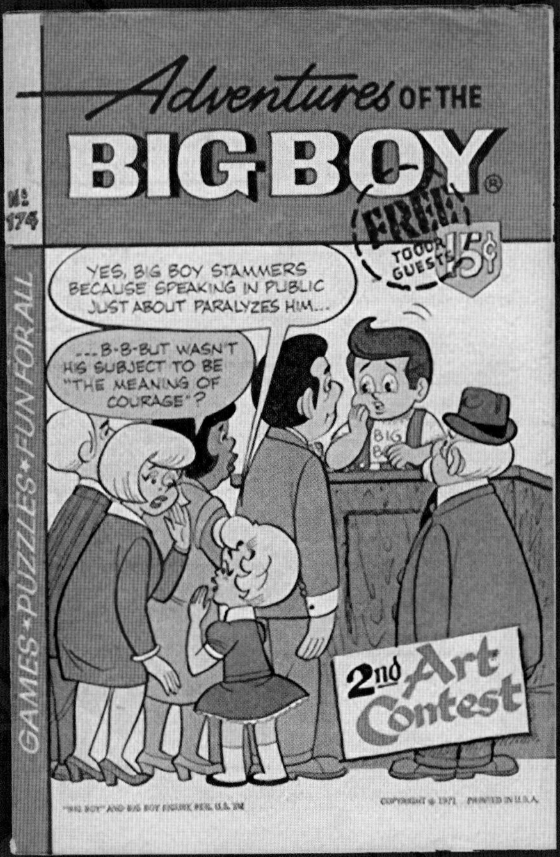

Adventures OF THE
BIG BOY®
No. 174
FREE! TO OUR GUESTS
15¢
YES, BIG BOY STAMMERS BECAUSE SPEAKING IN PUBLIC JUST ABOUT PARALYZES HIM...
...B-B-BUT WASN'T HIS SUBJECT TO BE "THE MEANING OF COURAGE"?
GAMES ★ PUZZLES ★ FUN FOR ALL
2nd Art Contest

I understand too that the comic was really just a PR product and was never intended to be sold in a comic book store. No one really expected them to compete on that level. It was free, after all. And they simply could not afford to create engaging plots and surprising, inspired gags along the way. That kind of work takes time and money. Or extraordinarily talented people. Or sometimes all three.

But here's what I want to say. Seeing this cheesy comic at the age I was may have been my first invitation to really participate with the medium. Everything prior to that was really well-done, seamless—and a complete mystery to me how it even worked.

Good art inspires us; bad art shows us a path to make our own art.

Thanks, Big Boy.

So, yeah, basically, ever since the *Adventures of the Big Boy* #174, I've wanted to participate with comic books. I'm grateful for the chance to make this book, and I'm proud of the outcome.

First and foremost, I'd like to thank my friend and collaborator Harold Buchholz, who is writing the afterword, and is also responsible for helping me bring *MST3K* back to life in TV form through our Kickstarter campaign and our twenty episodes on Netflix, the two seasons of the MST3K Live tours, and now this—MST3K's first comic series! Thanks, Harold—I simply couldn't have done it without you. Also, my co-workers and writers at Alternaversal: Matt McGinnis, Mary and Seth Robinson, and Sharyl Volpe. And, of course, everybody at Dark Horse Comics, especially Randy Stradley, Todd Nauck, Mike Manley, Jack Pollock, Mimi Simon, Steve Vance, Wes Dzioba, and Michael Heisler.

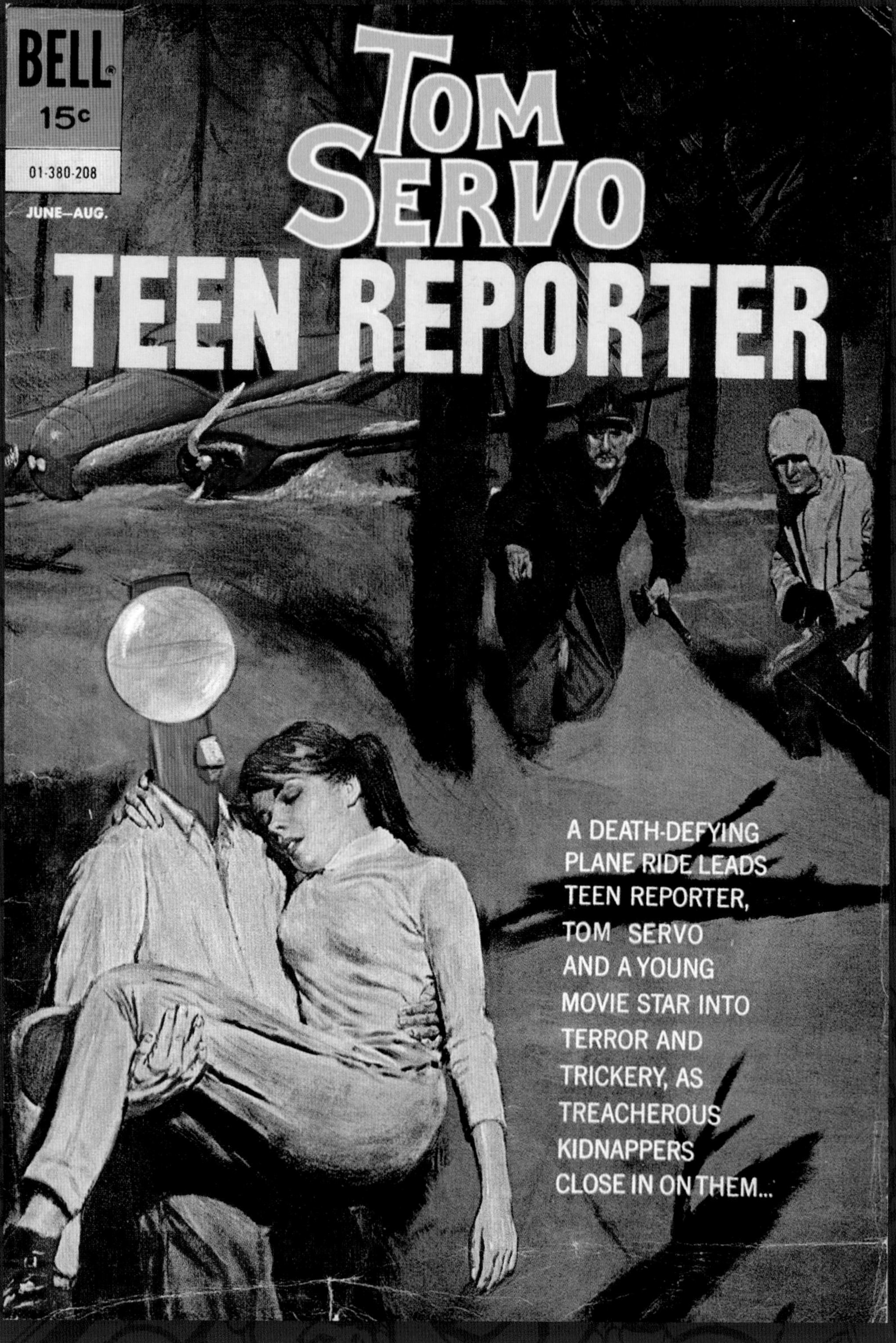
BELL
15¢
01-380-208
JUNE—AUG.
TOM SERVO
TEEN REPORTER
A DEATH-DEFYING PLANE RIDE LEADS TEEN REPORTER, TOM SERVO AND A YOUNG MOVIE STAR INTO TERROR AND TRICKERY, AS TREACHEROUS KIDNAPPERS CLOSE IN ON THEM...

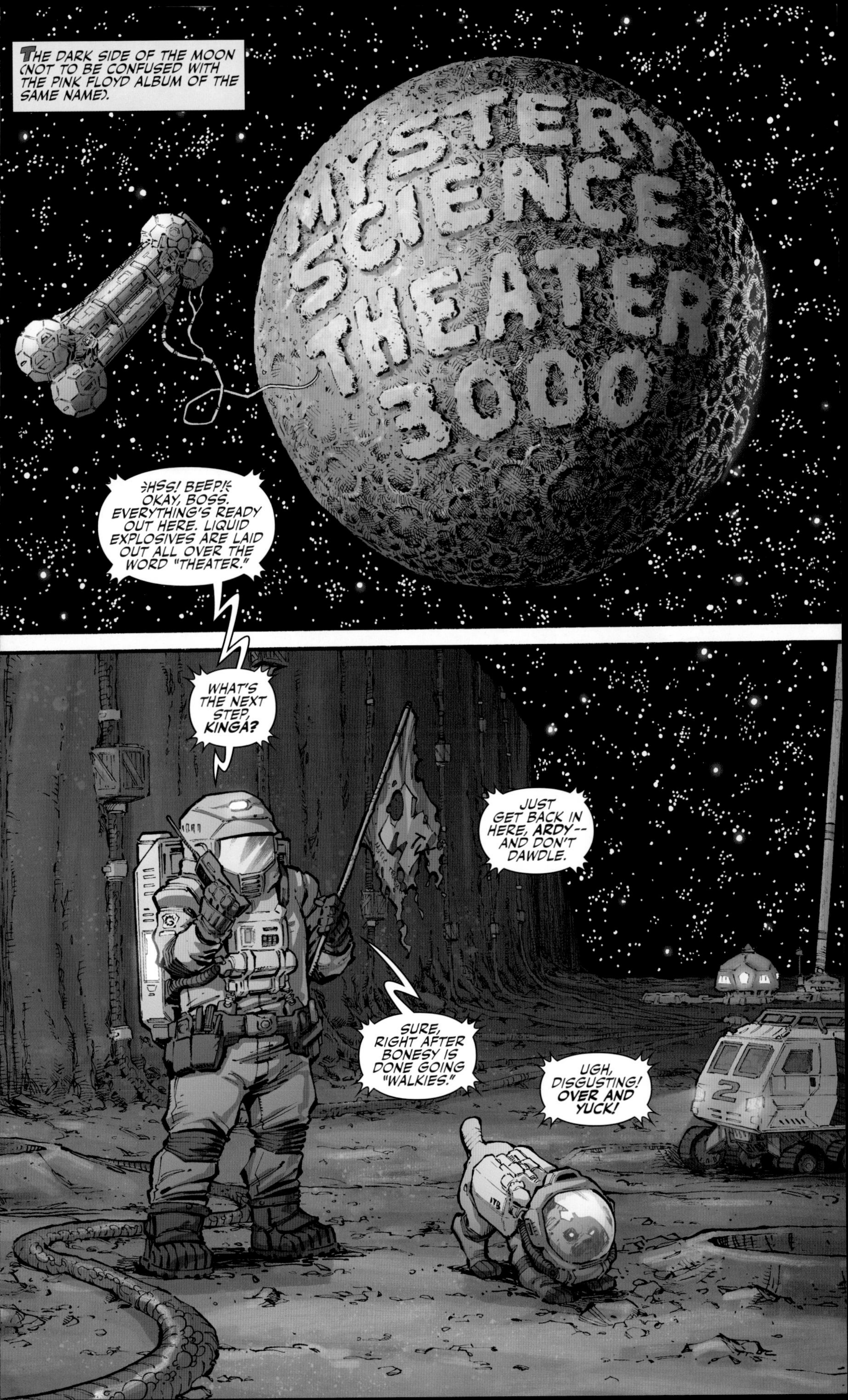

THE DARK SIDE OF THE MOON (NOT TO BE CONFUSED WITH THE PINK FLOYD ALBUM OF THE SAME NAME).
MYSTERY SCIENCE THEATER 3000
HSS! BEEP! OKAY, BOSS. EVERYTHING'S READY OUT HERE. LIQUID EXPLOSIVES ARE LAID OUT ALL OVER THE WORD "THEATER."
WHAT'S THE NEXT STEP, KINGA?
JUST GET BACK IN HERE, ARDY-- AND DON'T DAWDLE.
SURE, RIGHT AFTER BONESY IS DONE GOING "WALKIES."
UGH, DISGUSTING! OVER AND YUCK!

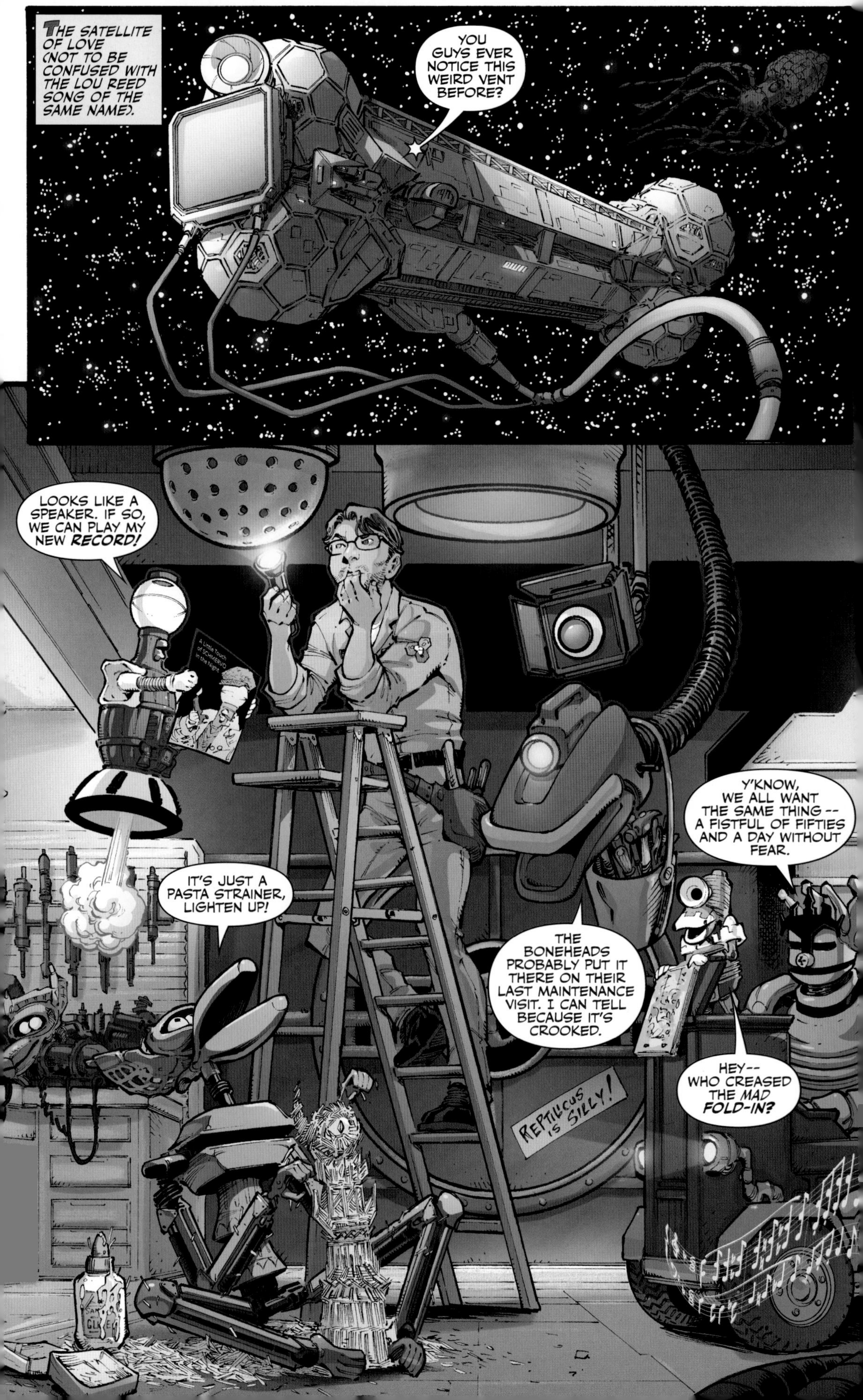
THE SATELLITE OF LOVE (NOT TO BE CONFUSED WITH THE LOU REED SONG OF THE SAME NAME).
YOU GUYS EVER NOTICE THIS WEIRD VENT BEFORE?
LOOKS LIKE A SPEAKER. IF SO, WE CAN PLAY MY NEW RECORD!
A Little Touch of SCHMERVO in the Night
IT'S JUST A PASTA STRAINER, LIGHTEN UP!
THE BONEHEADS PROBABLY PUT IT THERE ON THEIR LAST MAINTENANCE VISIT. I CAN TELL BECAUSE IT'S CROOKED.
Y'KNOW, WE ALL WANT THE SAME THING -- A FISTFUL OF FIFTIES AND A DAY WITHOUT FEAR.
HEY-- WHO CREASED THE MAD FOLD-IN?
REPTILICUS IS SILLY!

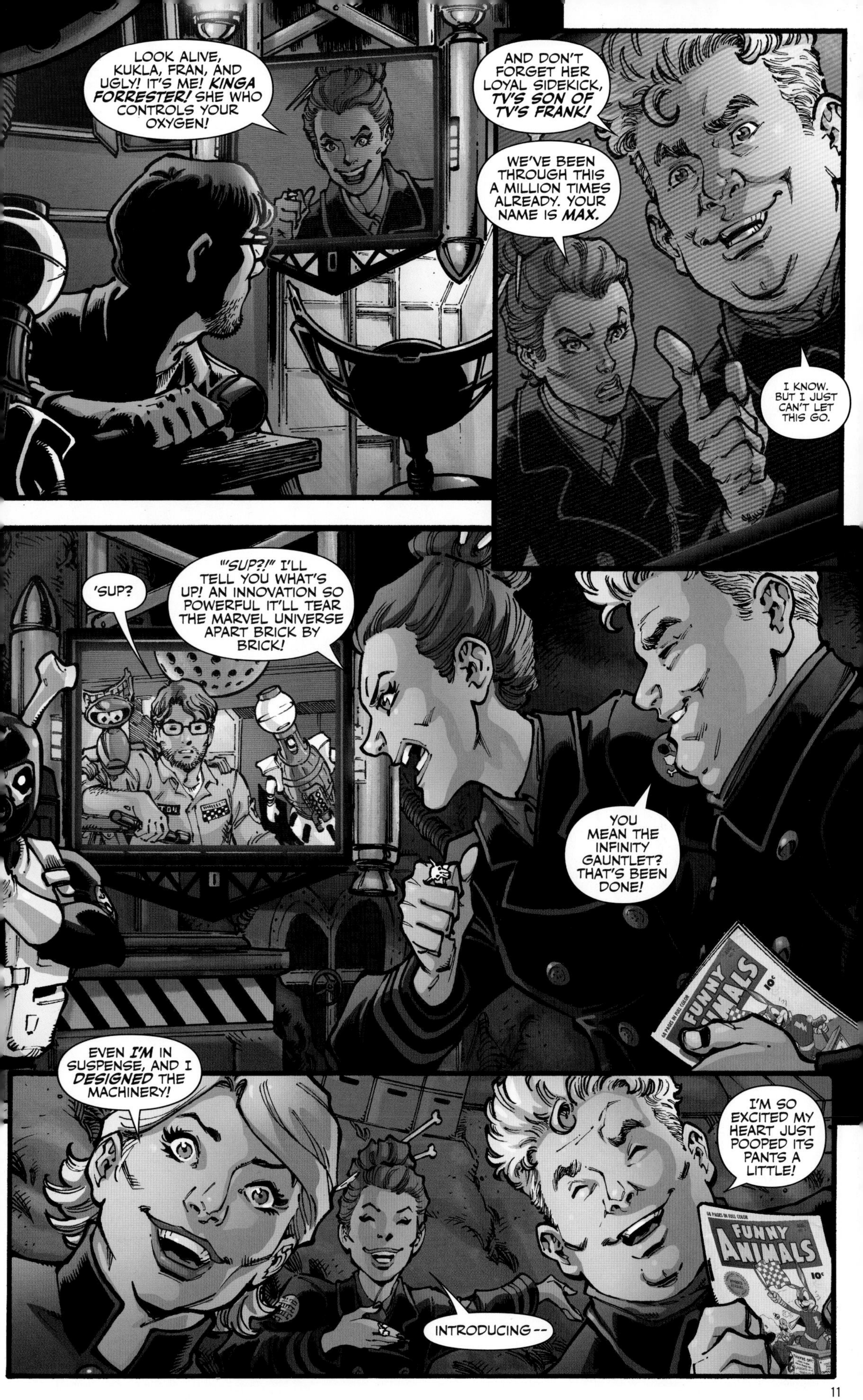
LOOK ALIVE, KUKLA, FRAN, AND UGLY! IT'S ME! KINGA FORRESTER! SHE WHO CONTROLS YOUR OXYGEN!
AND DON'T FORGET HER LOYAL SIDEKICK, TV'S SON OF TV'S FRANK!
WE'VE BEEN THROUGH THIS A MILLION TIMES ALREADY. YOUR NAME IS MAX.
I KNOW. BUT I JUST CAN'T LET THIS GO.
'SUP?
"'SUP?!" I'LL TELL YOU WHAT'S UP! AN INNOVATION SO POWERFUL IT'LL TEAR THE MARVEL UNIVERSE APART BRICK BY BRICK!
YOU MEAN THE INFINITY GAUNTLET? THAT'S BEEN DONE!
FUNNY ANIMALS
10¢
EVEN I'M IN SUSPENSE, AND I DESIGNED THE MACHINERY!
I'M SO EXCITED MY HEART JUST POOPED ITS PANTS A LITTLE!
INTRODUCING--
FUNNY ANIMALS
10¢

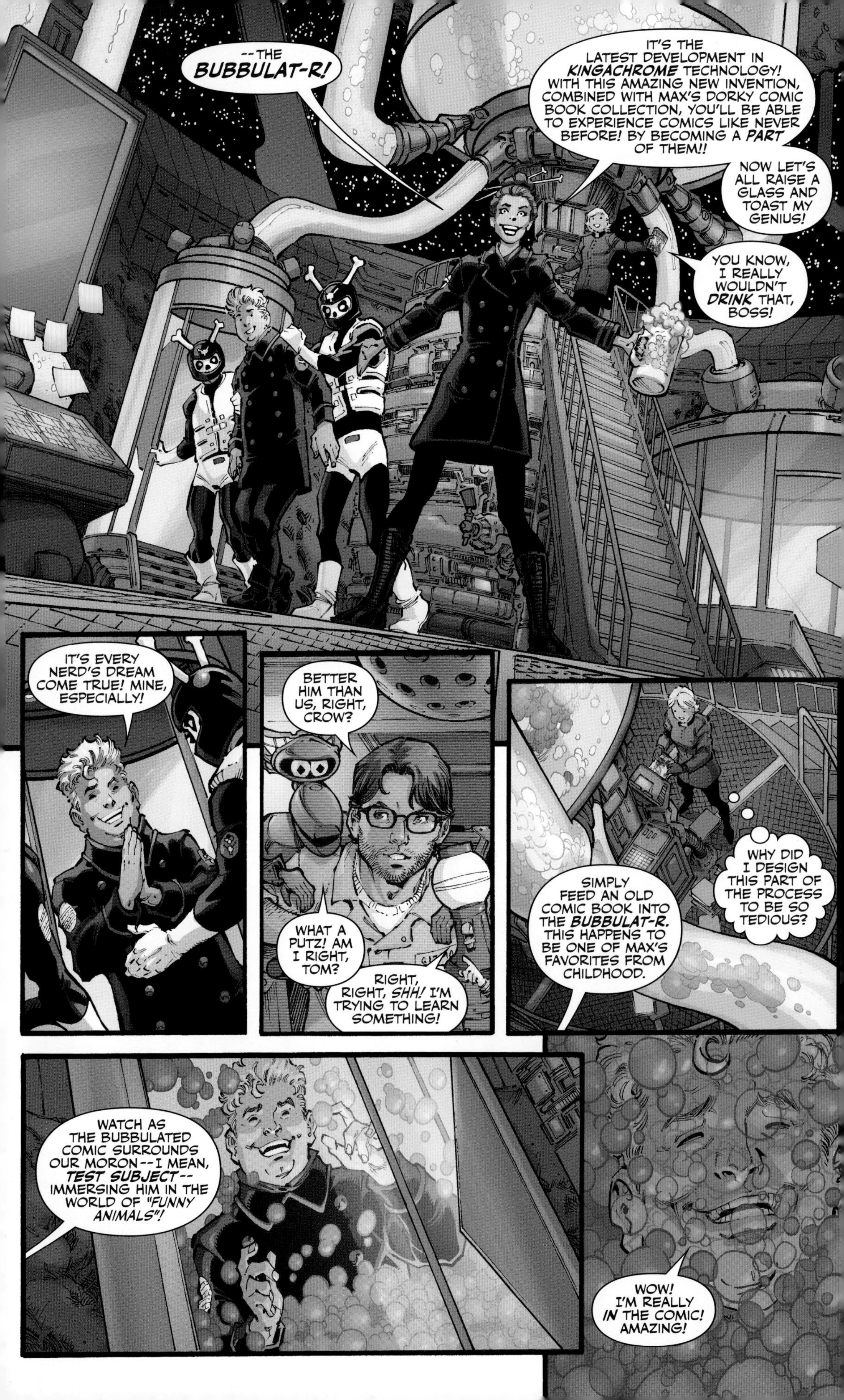
--THE BUBBULAT-R!
IT'S THE LATEST DEVELOPMENT IN KINGACHROME TECHNOLOGY! WITH THIS AMAZING NEW INVENTION, COMBINED WITH MAX'S DORKY COMIC BOOK COLLECTION, YOU'LL BE ABLE TO EXPERIENCE COMICS LIKE NEVER BEFORE! BY BECOMING A PART OF THEM!!
NOW LET'S ALL RAISE A GLASS AND TOAST MY GENIUS!
YOU KNOW, I REALLY WOULDN'T DRINK THAT, BOSS!
IT'S EVERY NERD'S DREAM COME TRUE! MINE, ESPECIALLY!
BETTER HIM THAN US, RIGHT, CROW?
WHAT A PUTZ! AM I RIGHT, TOM?
RIGHT, RIGHT, SHH! I'M TRYING TO LEARN SOMETHING!
SIMPLY FEED AN OLD COMIC BOOK INTO THE BUBBULAT-R. THIS HAPPENS TO BE ONE OF MAX'S FAVORITES FROM CHILDHOOD.
WHY DID I DESIGN THIS PART OF THE PROCESS TO BE SO TEDIOUS?
WATCH AS THE BUBBULATED COMIC SURROUNDS OUR MORON--I MEAN, TEST SUBJECT--IMMERSING HIM IN THE WORLD OF "FUNNY ANIMALS"!
WOW! I'M REALLY IN THE COMIC! AMAZING!

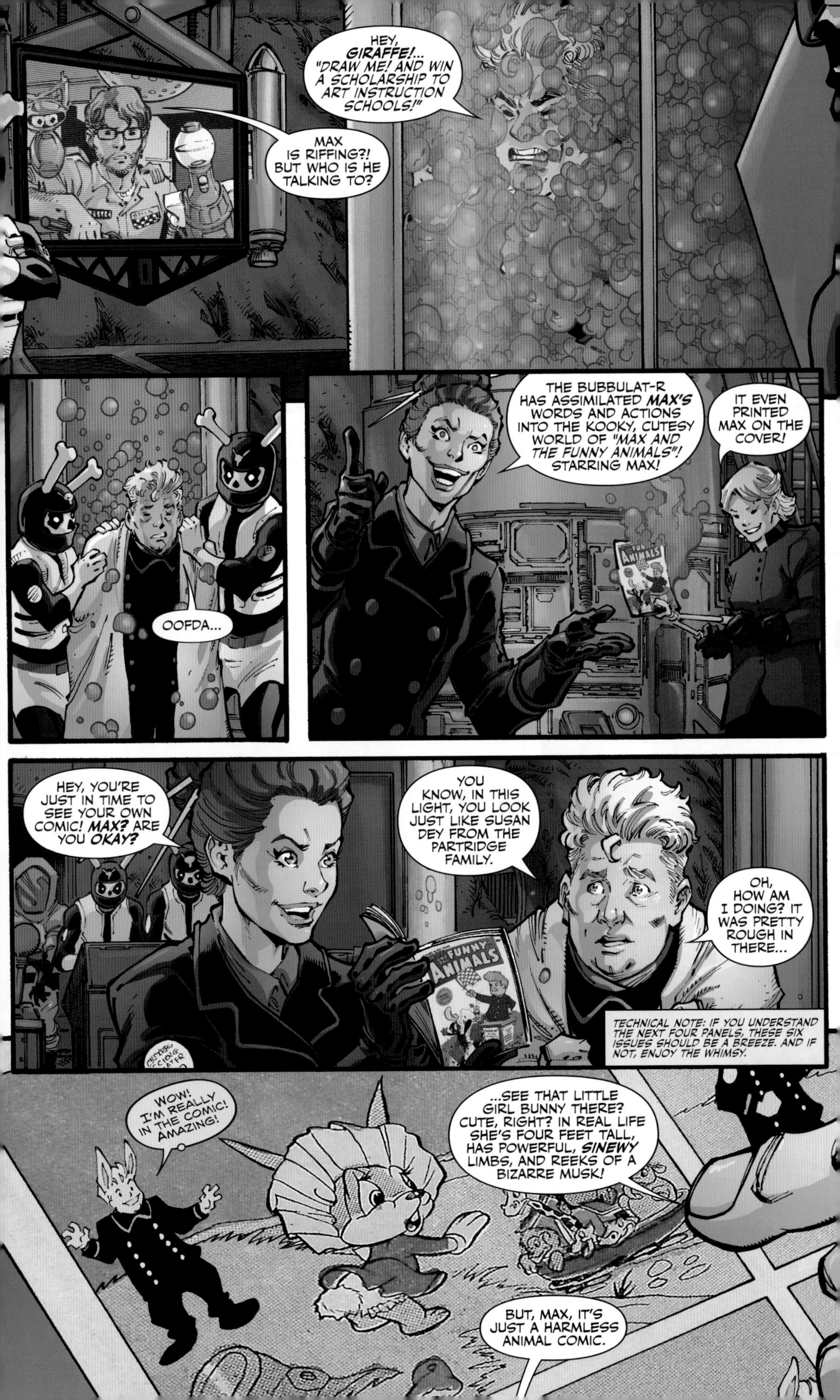
HEY, GIRAFFE!... "DRAW ME! AND WIN A SCHOLARSHIP TO ART INSTRUCTION SCHOOLS!"
MAX IS RIFFING?! BUT WHO IS HE TALKING TO?
OOFDA...
THE BUBBULAT-R HAS ASSIMILATED MAX'S WORDS AND ACTIONS INTO THE KOOKY, CUTESY WORLD OF "MAX AND THE FUNNY ANIMALS"! STARRING MAX!
IT EVEN PRINTED MAX ON THE COVER!
HEY, YOU'RE JUST IN TIME TO SEE YOUR OWN COMIC! MAX? ARE YOU OKAY?
YOU KNOW, IN THIS LIGHT, YOU LOOK JUST LIKE SUSAN DEY FROM THE PARTRIDGE FAMILY.
OH, HOW AM I DOING? IT WAS PRETTY ROUGH IN THERE...
TECHNICAL NOTE: IF YOU UNDERSTAND THE NEXT FOUR PANELS, THESE SIX ISSUES SHOULD BE A BREEZE. AND IF NOT, ENJOY THE WHIMSY.
WOW! I'M REALLY IN THE COMIC! AMAZING!
...SEE THAT LITTLE GIRL BUNNY THERE? CUTE, RIGHT? IN REAL LIFE SHE'S FOUR FEET TALL, HAS POWERFUL, SINEWY LIMBS, AND REEKS OF A BIZARRE MUSK!
BUT, MAX, IT'S JUST A HARMLESS ANIMAL COMIC.

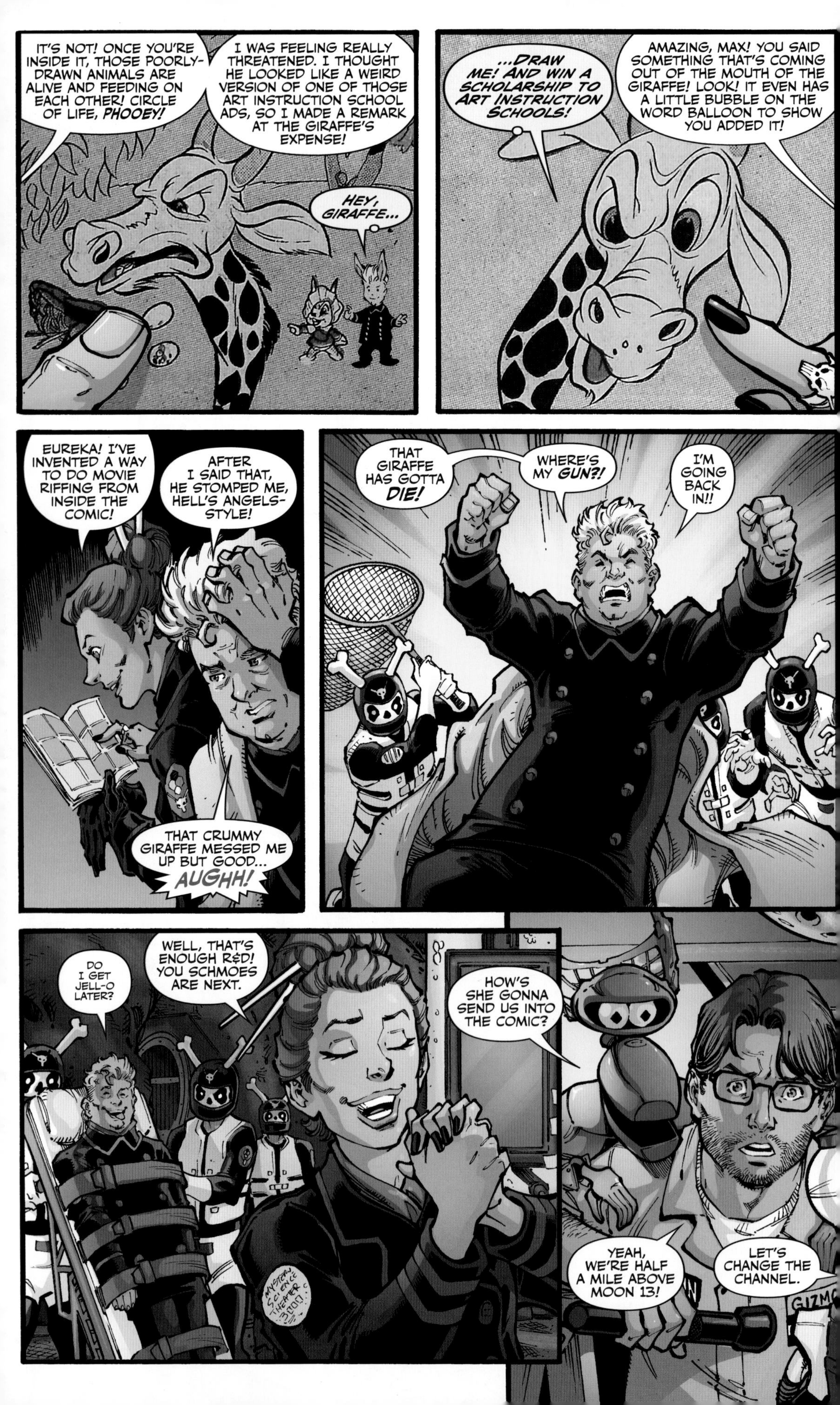
IT'S NOT! ONCE YOU'RE INSIDE IT, THOSE POORLY-DRAWN ANIMALS ARE ALIVE AND FEEDING ON EACH OTHER! CIRCLE OF LIFE, PHOOEY!
I WAS FEELING REALLY THREATENED. I THOUGHT HE LOOKED LIKE A WEIRD VERSION OF ONE OF THOSE ART INSTRUCTION SCHOOL ADS, SO I MADE A REMARK AT THE GIRAFFE'S EXPENSE!
HEY, GIRAFFE...
...DRAW ME! AND WIN A SCHOLARSHIP TO ART INSTRUCTION SCHOOLS!
AMAZING, MAX! YOU SAID SOMETHING THAT'S COMING OUT OF THE MOUTH OF THE GIRAFFE! LOOK! IT EVEN HAS A LITTLE BUBBLE ON THE WORD BALLOON TO SHOW YOU ADDED IT!
EUREKA! I'VE INVENTED A WAY TO DO MOVIE RIFFING FROM INSIDE THE COMIC!
AFTER I SAID THAT, HE STOMPED ME, HELL'S ANGELS-STYLE!
THAT CRUMMY GIRAFFE MESSED ME UP BUT GOOD... AUGHH!
THAT GIRAFFE HAS GOTTA DIE!
WHERE'S MY GUN?!
I'M GOING BACK IN!!
DO I GET JELL-O LATER?
WELL, THAT'S ENOUGH R&D! YOU SCHMOES ARE NEXT.
MYSTERY SCIENCE THEATER 3000
HOW'S SHE GONNA SEND US INTO THE COMIC?
YEAH, WE'RE HALF A MILE ABOVE MOON 13!
LET'S CHANGE THE CHANNEL.

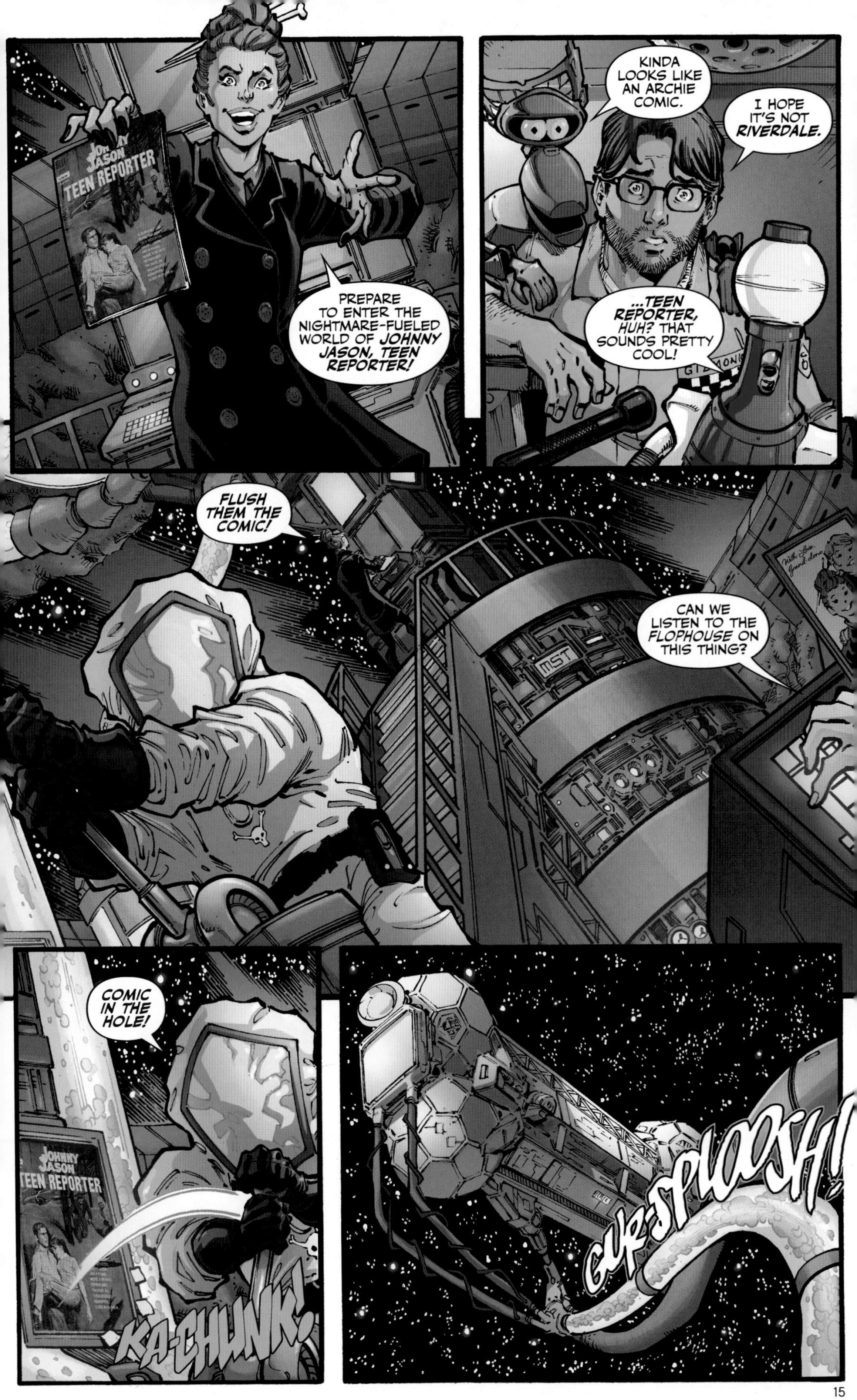
JOHNNY JASON
TEEN REPORTER
PREPARE TO ENTER THE NIGHTMARE-FUELED WORLD OF JOHNNY JASON, TEEN REPORTER!
KINDA LOOKS LIKE AN ARCHIE COMIC.
I HOPE IT'S NOT RIVERDALE.
...TEEN REPORTER, HUH? THAT SOUNDS PRETTY COOL!
FLUSH THEM THE COMIC!
MST
CAN WE LISTEN TO THE FLOPHOUSE ON THIS THING?
COMIC IN THE HOLE!
JOHNNY JASON
TEEN REPORTER
KA-CHUNK!
GLP-SPLOOSH!

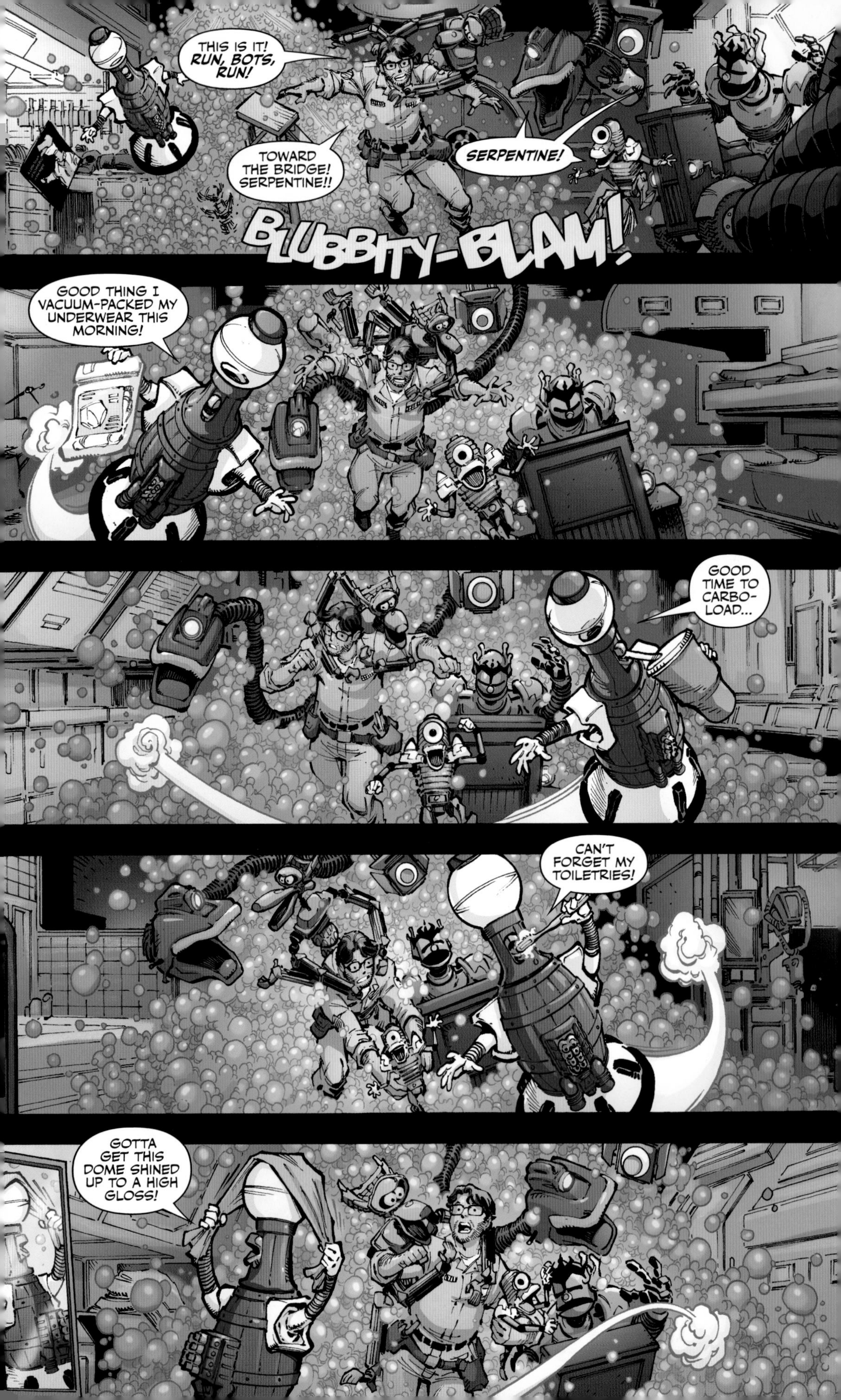
THIS IS IT! RUN, BOTS, RUN!
TOWARD THE BRIDGE! SERPENTINE!!
SERPENTINE!
BLUBBITY-BLAM!
GOOD THING I VACUUM-PACKED MY UNDERWEAR THIS MORNING!
GOOD TIME TO CARBO-LOAD...
CAN'T FORGET MY TOILETRIES!
GOTTA GET THIS DOME SHINED UP TO A HIGH GLOSS!

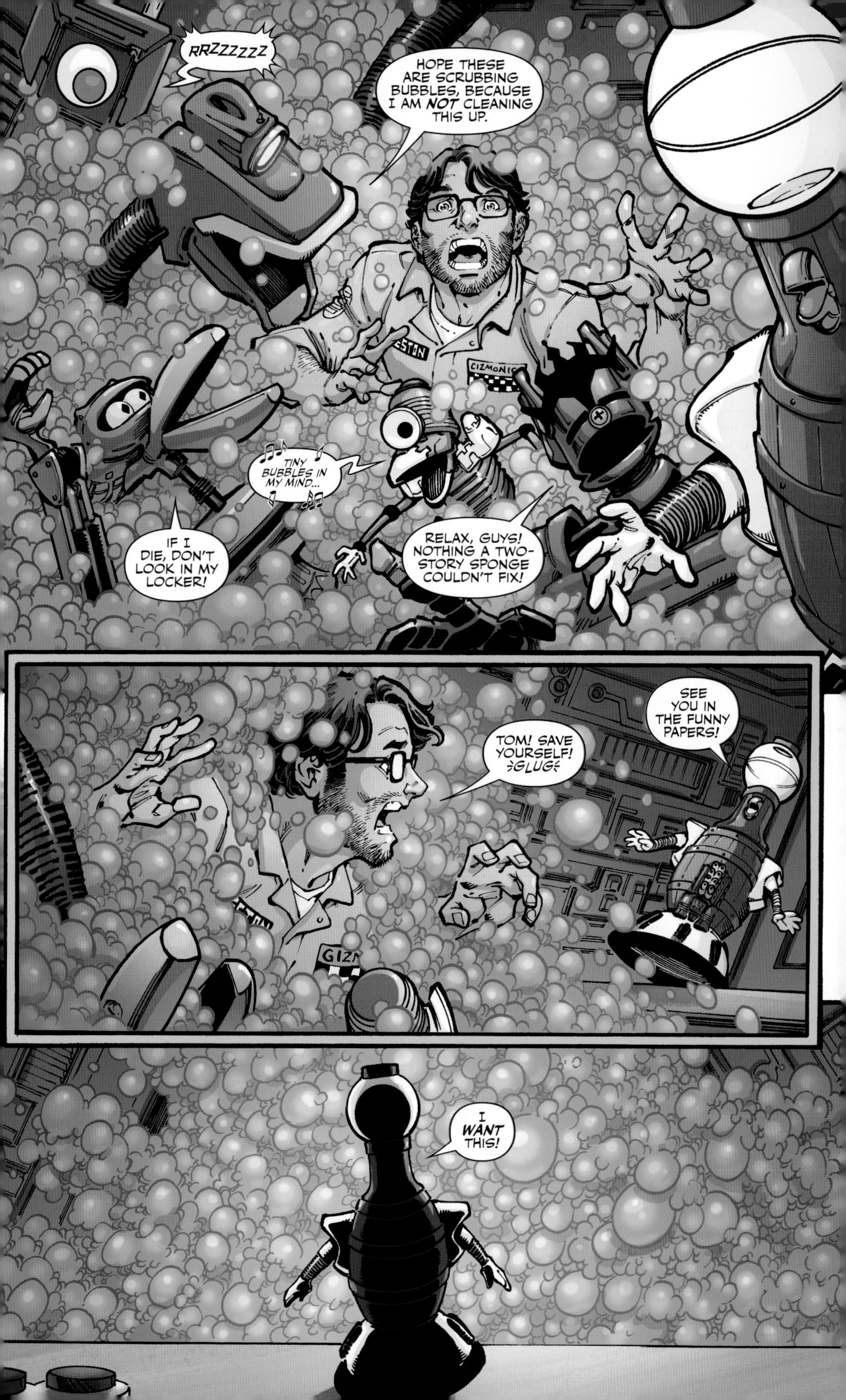
RRZZZZZZ
HOPE THESE ARE SCRUBBING BUBBLES, BECAUSE I AM NOT CLEANING THIS UP.
WESTON
GIZMONIC
TINY BUBBLES IN MY MIND...
IF I DIE, DON'T LOOK IN MY LOCKER!
RELAX, GUYS! NOTHING A TWO-STORY SPONGE COULDN'T FIX!
SEE YOU IN THE FUNNY PAPERS!
TOM! SAVE YOURSELF! GLUG
I WANT THIS!

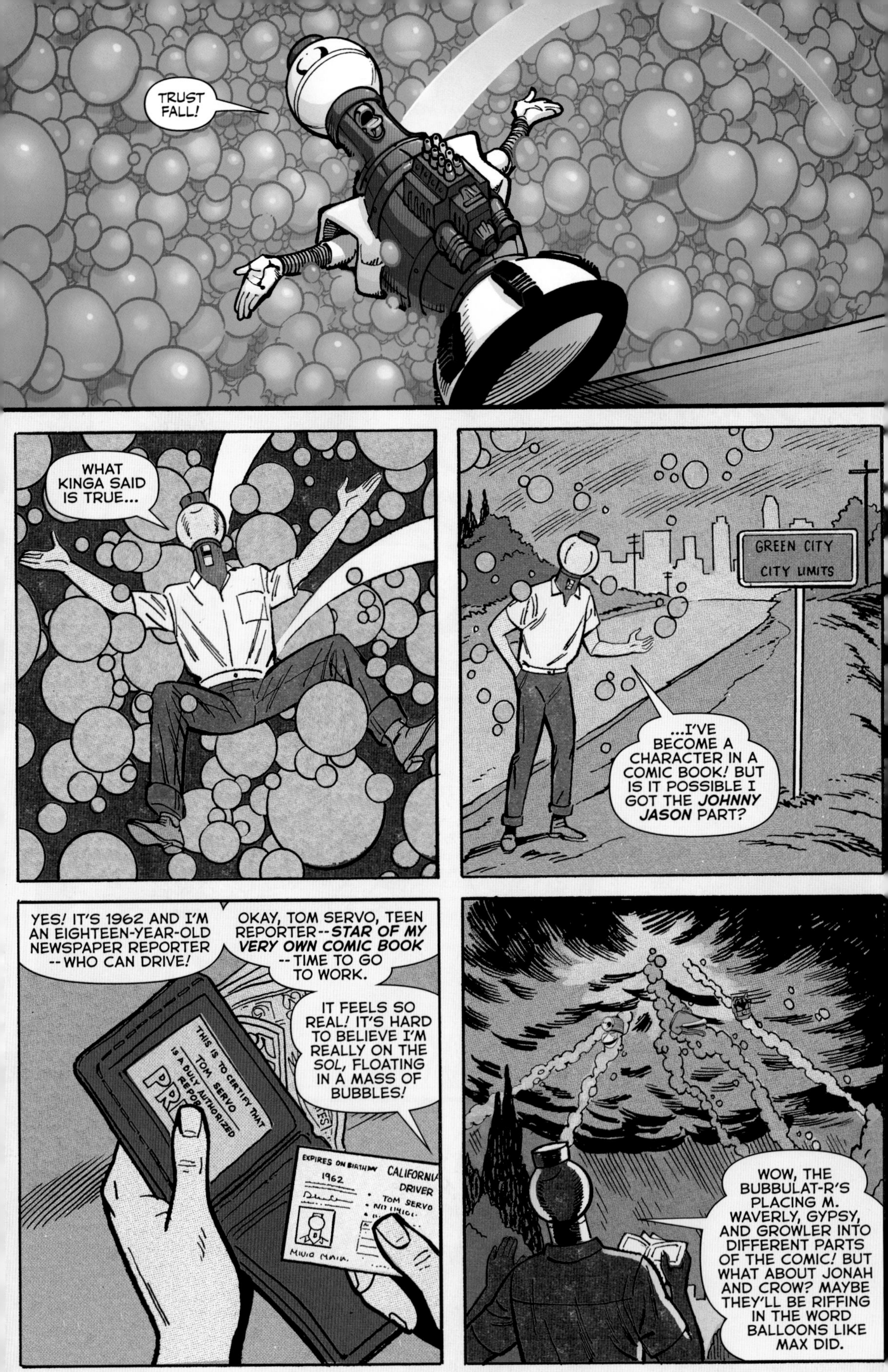

TRUST FALL!
WHAT KINGA SAID IS TRUE...
GREEN CITY
CITY LIMITS
...I'VE BECOME A CHARACTER IN A COMIC BOOK! BUT IS IT POSSIBLE I GOT THE *JOHNNY JASON* PART?
YES! IT'S 1962 AND I'M AN EIGHTEEN-YEAR-OLD NEWSPAPER REPORTER --WHO CAN DRIVE!
OKAY, TOM SERVO, TEEN REPORTER--***STAR OF MY VERY OWN COMIC BOOK*** --TIME TO GO TO WORK.
IT FEELS SO REAL! IT'S HARD TO BELIEVE I'M REALLY ON THE *SOL*, FLOATING IN A MASS OF BUBBLES!
THIS IS TO CERTIFY THAT
TOM SERVO
IS A DULY AUTHORIZED
EXPIRES ON BIRTHDAY
1962
CALIFORNIA
DRIVER
TOM SERVO
WOW, THE BUBBULAT-R'S PLACING M. WAVERLY, GYPSY, AND GROWLER INTO DIFFERENT PARTS OF THE COMIC! BUT WHAT ABOUT JONAH AND CROW? MAYBE THEY'LL BE RIFFING IN THE WORD BALLOONS LIKE MAX DID.

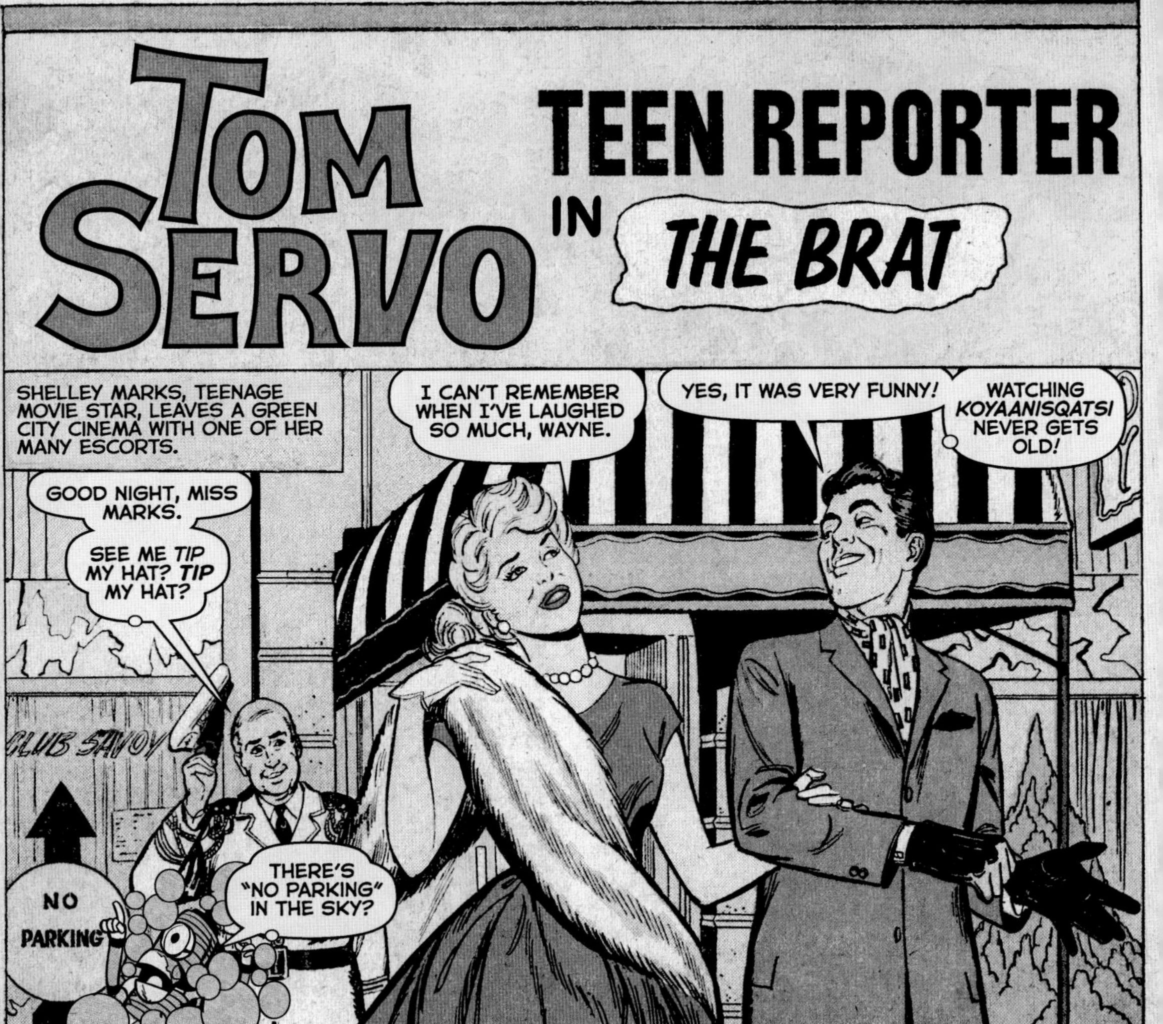
TOM SERVO
TEEN REPORTER
IN
THE BRAT
SHELLEY MARKS, TEENAGE MOVIE STAR, LEAVES A GREEN CITY CINEMA WITH ONE OF HER MANY ESCORTS.
I CAN'T REMEMBER WHEN I'VE LAUGHED SO MUCH, WAYNE.
YES, IT WAS VERY FUNNY!
WATCHING *KOYAANISQATSI* NEVER GETS OLD!
GOOD NIGHT, MISS MARKS.
SEE ME *TIP* MY HAT? *TIP* MY HAT?
CLUB SAVOY
NO PARKING
THERE'S "NO PARKING" IN THE SKY?
YOU'RE GETTING A TERRIBLE UBER RATING!
HELP! POLICE!
C'MON, BABY...WE AIN'T GONNA HURT YA!
I MISS THE DAYS WHEN THUGS WORE DINNER JACKETS.
THEY'VE KIDNAPPED HER!
TIME TO CASH IN THAT "FIRST DATE" LIFE INSURANCE POLICY! HEH, HEH, HEH.
MY WHISTLE IS CLOGGED!

TOM SERVO, TEEN REPORTER, No. 1, September 2018 – Our 30th year! Published by Moon 13 Press, Inc., the Moon. Founder, President, and Queen of All Media: Kinga Forrester, Vice President and Second Banana: ~~TV'S Son of TV's Frank~~ Max, Bubbulat-R Design: Synthia Forrester, Maintenance: Ardy, Taker of Credit: Kinga Forrester. Single copy price $3.99. Printed on the Moon, using state-of-the-art liquid Kingachrome technology, specially ~~stolen~~ designed by Kinga Forrester. It's pretty great and better than any other form of printing there is. Designed, produced, and copyright 2018 Moon 13 Press, Inc. All seats reserved. This thing shall be sold only through retailers cool enough to carry it. Sales of mutilated or leaking copies, or copies with melting covers, and distribution of this periodical for premiums, advertising, giveaways, favors, or bribes are strictly forbidden, and we will find you. So, don't even think about it!

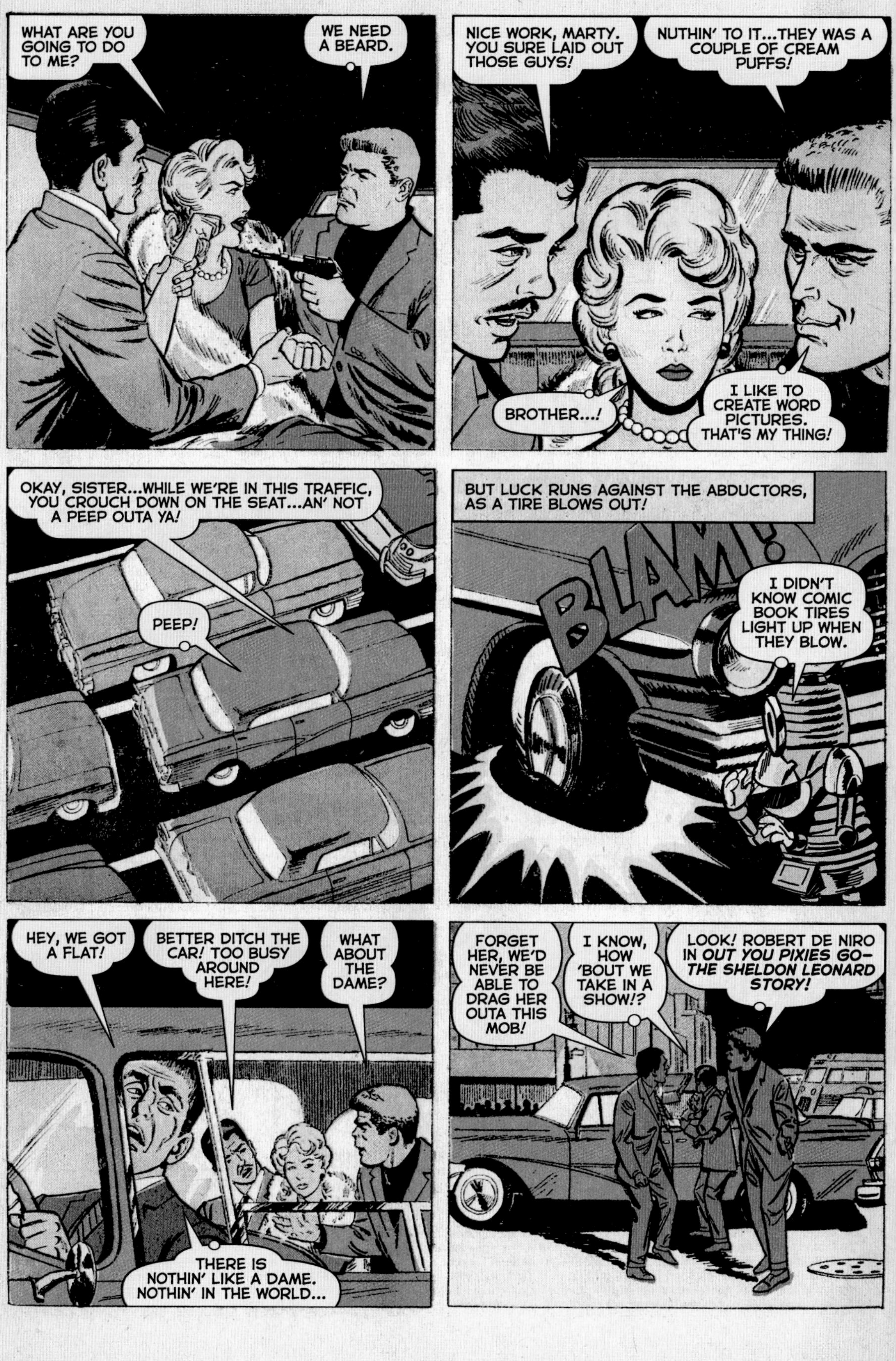
WHAT ARE YOU GOING TO DO TO ME?
WE NEED A BEARD.
NICE WORK, MARTY. YOU SURE LAID OUT THOSE GUYS!
NUTHIN' TO IT...THEY WAS A COUPLE OF CREAM PUFFS!
BROTHER...!
I LIKE TO CREATE WORD PICTURES. THAT'S MY THING!
OKAY, SISTER...WHILE WE'RE IN THIS TRAFFIC, YOU CROUCH DOWN ON THE SEAT...AN' NOT A PEEP OUTA YA!
PEEP!
BUT LUCK RUNS AGAINST THE ABDUCTORS, AS A TIRE BLOWS OUT!
BLAM!
I DIDN'T KNOW COMIC BOOK TIRES LIGHT UP WHEN THEY BLOW.
HEY, WE GOT A FLAT!
BETTER DITCH THE CAR! TOO BUSY AROUND HERE!
WHAT ABOUT THE DAME?
THERE IS NOTHIN' LIKE A DAME. NOTHIN' IN THE WORLD...
FORGET HER, WE'D NEVER BE ABLE TO DRAG HER OUTA THIS MOB!
I KNOW, HOW 'BOUT WE TAKE IN A SHOW!?
LOOK! ROBERT DE NIRO IN *OUT YOU PIXIES GO— THE SHELDON LEONARD STORY!*

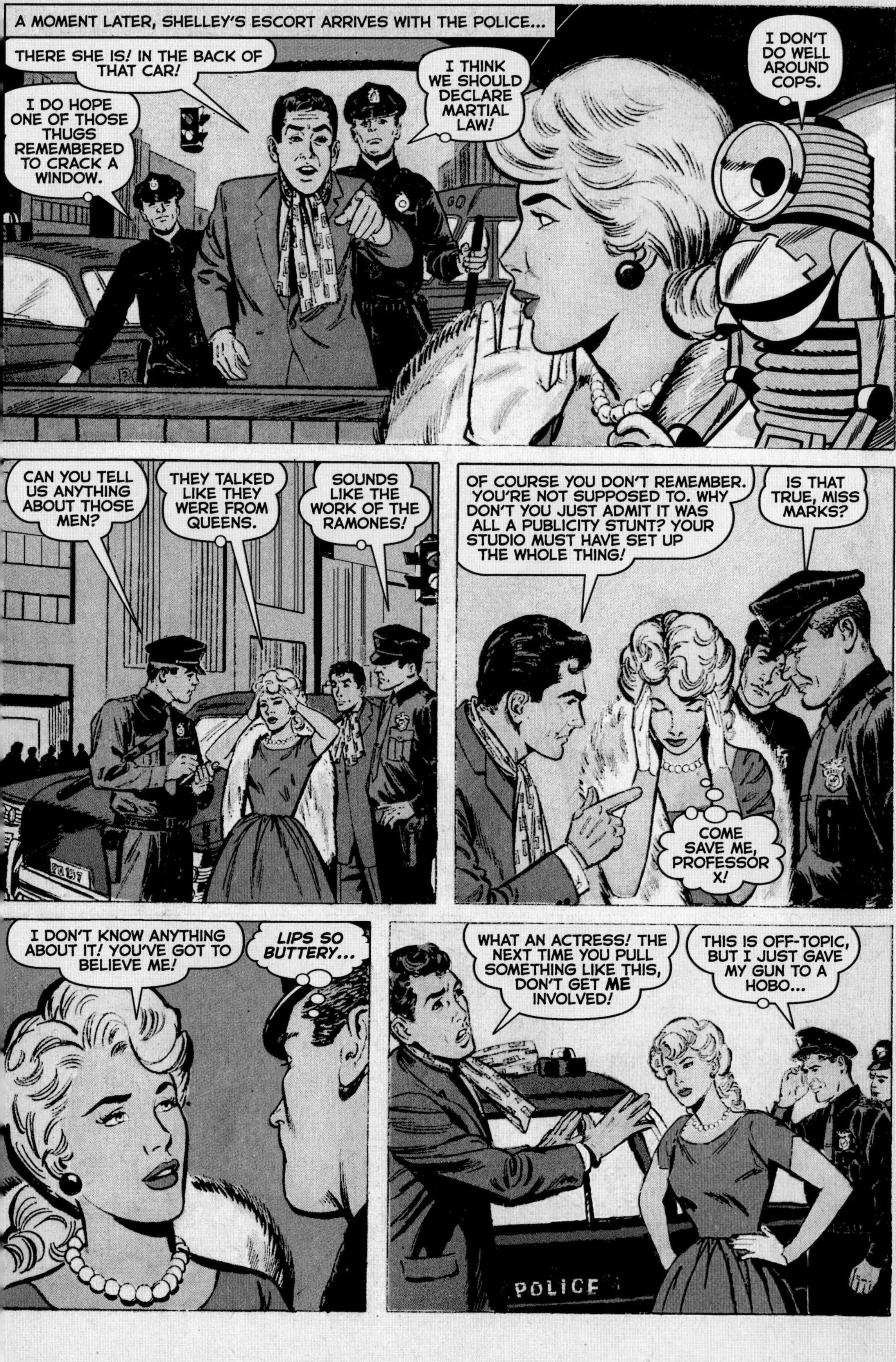
A MOMENT LATER, SHELLEY'S ESCORT ARRIVES WITH THE POLICE...
THERE SHE IS! IN THE BACK OF THAT CAR!
I DO HOPE ONE OF THOSE THUGS REMEMBERED TO CRACK A WINDOW.
I THINK WE SHOULD DECLARE MARTIAL LAW!
I DON'T DO WELL AROUND COPS.
CAN YOU TELL US ANYTHING ABOUT THOSE MEN?
THEY TALKED LIKE THEY WERE FROM QUEENS.
SOUNDS LIKE THE WORK OF THE RAMONES!
OF COURSE YOU DON'T REMEMBER. YOU'RE NOT SUPPOSED TO. WHY DON'T YOU JUST ADMIT IT WAS ALL A PUBLICITY STUNT? YOUR STUDIO MUST HAVE SET UP THE WHOLE THING!
IS THAT TRUE, MISS MARKS?
COME SAVE ME, PROFESSOR X!
I DON'T KNOW ANYTHING ABOUT IT! YOU'VE GOT TO BELIEVE ME!
LIPS SO BUTTERY...
WHAT AN ACTRESS! THE NEXT TIME YOU PULL SOMETHING LIKE THIS, DON'T GET ME INVOLVED!
THIS IS OFF-TOPIC, BUT I JUST GAVE MY GUN TO A HOBO...
POLICE

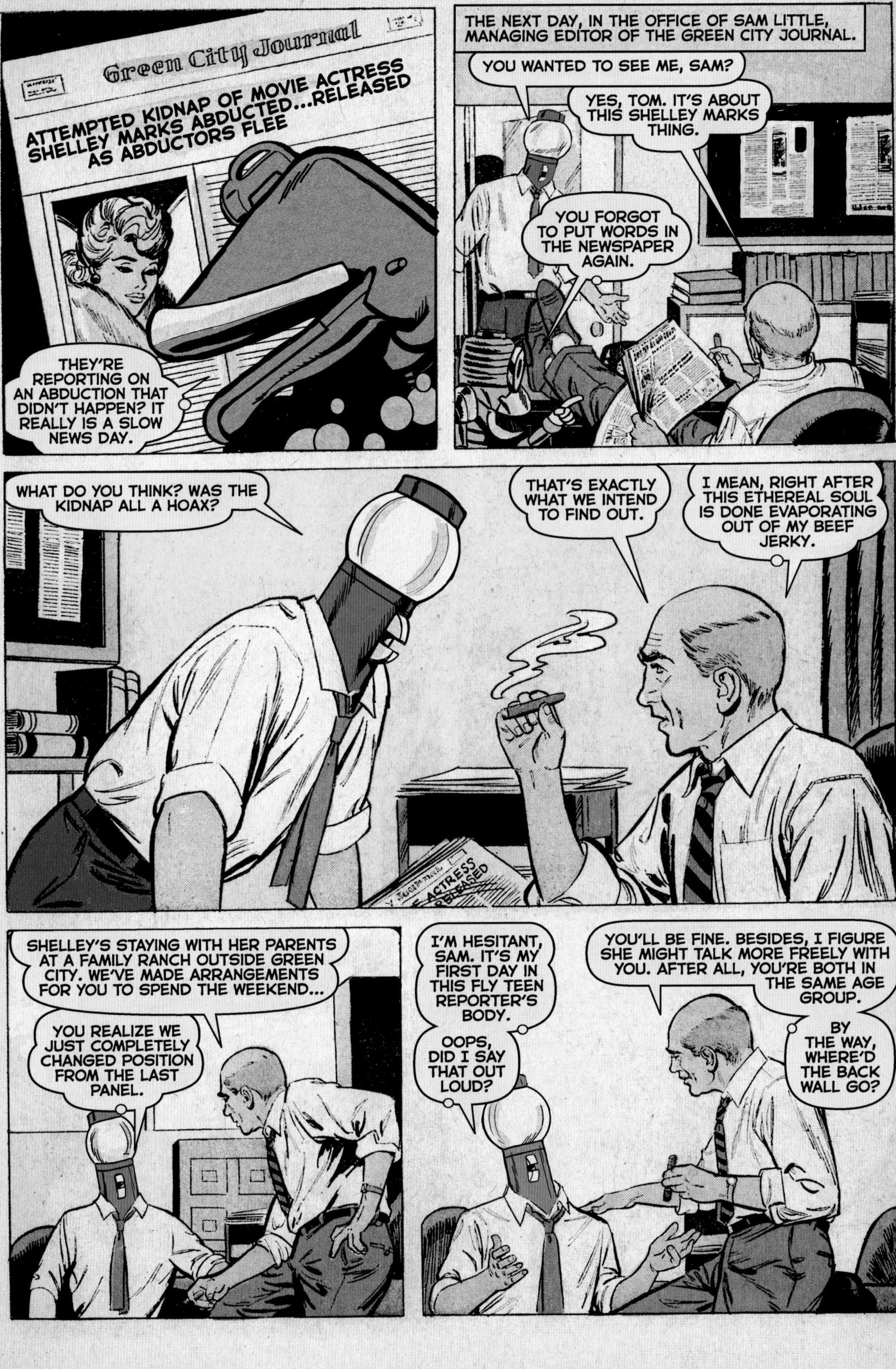
Green City Journal
ATTEMPTED KIDNAP OF MOVIE ACTRESS SHELLEY MARKS ABDUCTED...RELEASED AS ABDUCTORS FLEE
THEY'RE REPORTING ON AN ABDUCTION THAT DIDN'T HAPPEN? IT REALLY IS A SLOW NEWS DAY.
THE NEXT DAY, IN THE OFFICE OF SAM LITTLE, MANAGING EDITOR OF THE GREEN CITY JOURNAL.
YOU WANTED TO SEE ME, SAM?
YES, TOM. IT'S ABOUT THIS SHELLEY MARKS THING.
YOU FORGOT TO PUT WORDS IN THE NEWSPAPER AGAIN.
WHAT DO YOU THINK? WAS THE KIDNAP ALL A HOAX?
THAT'S EXACTLY WHAT WE INTEND TO FIND OUT.
I MEAN, RIGHT AFTER THIS ETHEREAL SOUL IS DONE EVAPORATING OUT OF MY BEEF JERKY.
ACTRESS
RELEASED
SHELLEY'S STAYING WITH HER PARENTS AT A FAMILY RANCH OUTSIDE GREEN CITY. WE'VE MADE ARRANGEMENTS FOR YOU TO SPEND THE WEEKEND...
YOU REALIZE WE JUST COMPLETELY CHANGED POSITION FROM THE LAST PANEL.
I'M HESITANT, SAM. IT'S MY FIRST DAY IN THIS FLY TEEN REPORTER'S BODY.
OOPS, DID I SAY THAT OUT LOUD?
YOU'LL BE FINE. BESIDES, I FIGURE SHE MIGHT TALK MORE FREELY WITH YOU. AFTER ALL, YOU'RE BOTH IN THE SAME AGE GROUP.
BY THE WAY, WHERE'D THE BACK WALL GO?

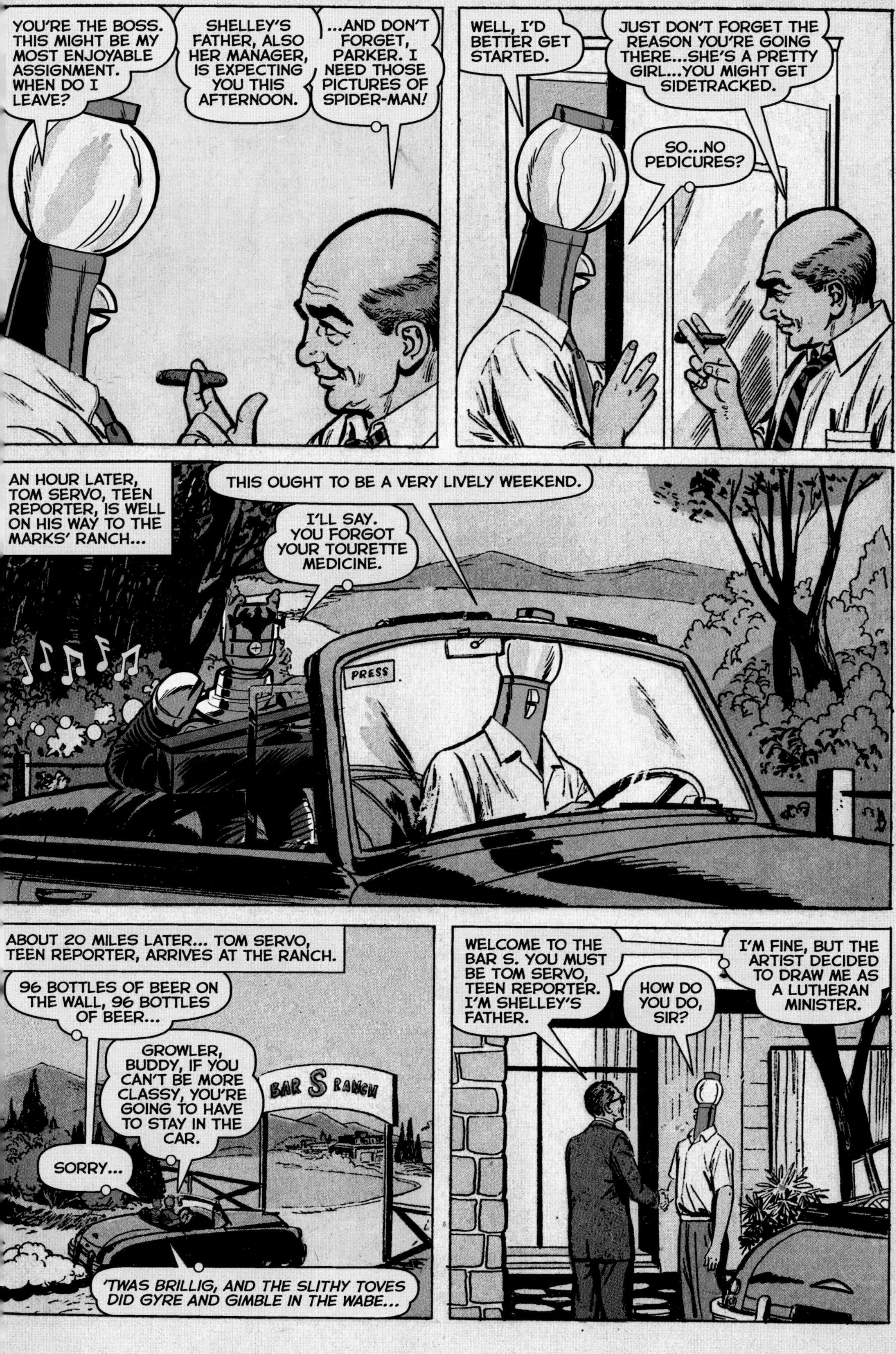
YOU'RE THE BOSS. THIS MIGHT BE MY MOST ENJOYABLE ASSIGNMENT. WHEN DO I LEAVE?
SHELLEY'S FATHER, ALSO HER MANAGER, IS EXPECTING YOU THIS AFTERNOON.
...AND DON'T FORGET, PARKER. I NEED THOSE PICTURES OF SPIDER-MAN!
WELL, I'D BETTER GET STARTED.
JUST DON'T FORGET THE REASON YOU'RE GOING THERE...SHE'S A PRETTY GIRL...YOU MIGHT GET SIDETRACKED.
SO...NO PEDICURES?
AN HOUR LATER, TOM SERVO, TEEN REPORTER, IS WELL ON HIS WAY TO THE MARKS' RANCH...
THIS OUGHT TO BE A VERY LIVELY WEEKEND.
I'LL SAY. YOU FORGOT YOUR TOURETTE MEDICINE.
PRESS
ABOUT 20 MILES LATER... TOM SERVO, TEEN REPORTER, ARRIVES AT THE RANCH.
96 BOTTLES OF BEER ON THE WALL, 96 BOTTLES OF BEER...
GROWLER, BUDDY, IF YOU CAN'T BE MORE CLASSY, YOU'RE GOING TO HAVE TO STAY IN THE CAR.
BAR S RANCH
SORRY...
'TWAS BRILLIG, AND THE SLITHY TOVES DID GYRE AND GIMBLE IN THE WABE...
WELCOME TO THE BAR S. YOU MUST BE TOM SERVO, TEEN REPORTER. I'M SHELLEY'S FATHER.
HOW DO YOU DO, SIR?
I'M FINE, BUT THE ARTIST DECIDED TO DRAW ME AS A LUTHERAN MINISTER.

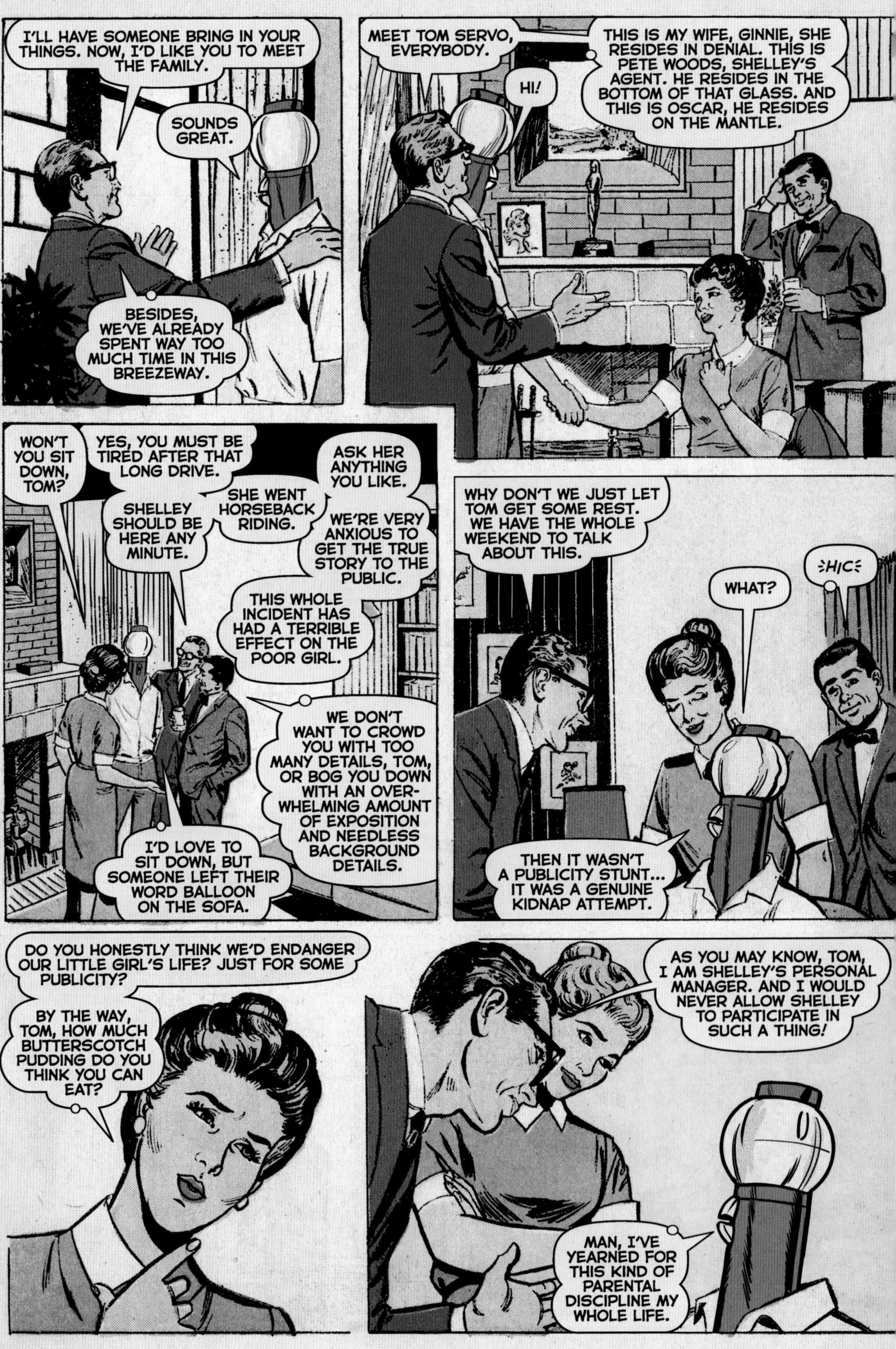
I'LL HAVE SOMEONE BRING IN YOUR THINGS. NOW, I'D LIKE YOU TO MEET THE FAMILY.
SOUNDS GREAT.
BESIDES, WE'VE ALREADY SPENT WAY TOO MUCH TIME IN THIS BREEZEWAY.
MEET TOM SERVO, EVERYBODY.
HI!
THIS IS MY WIFE, GINNIE, SHE RESIDES IN DENIAL. THIS IS PETE WOODS, SHELLEY'S AGENT. HE RESIDES IN THE BOTTOM OF THAT GLASS. AND THIS IS OSCAR, HE RESIDES ON THE MANTLE.
WON'T YOU SIT DOWN, TOM?
YES, YOU MUST BE TIRED AFTER THAT LONG DRIVE.
SHELLEY SHOULD BE HERE ANY MINUTE.
SHE WENT HORSEBACK RIDING.
ASK HER ANYTHING YOU LIKE.
WE'RE VERY ANXIOUS TO GET THE TRUE STORY TO THE PUBLIC.
THIS WHOLE INCIDENT HAS HAD A TERRIBLE EFFECT ON THE POOR GIRL.
WE DON'T WANT TO CROWD YOU WITH TOO MANY DETAILS, TOM, OR BOG YOU DOWN WITH AN OVER-WHELMING AMOUNT OF EXPOSITION AND NEEDLESS BACKGROUND DETAILS.
I'D LOVE TO SIT DOWN, BUT SOMEONE LEFT THEIR WORD BALLOON ON THE SOFA.
WHY DON'T WE JUST LET TOM GET SOME REST. WE HAVE THE WHOLE WEEKEND TO TALK ABOUT THIS.
WHAT?
HIC
THEN IT WASN'T A PUBLICITY STUNT... IT WAS A GENUINE KIDNAP ATTEMPT.
DO YOU HONESTLY THINK WE'D ENDANGER OUR LITTLE GIRL'S LIFE? JUST FOR SOME PUBLICITY?
BY THE WAY, TOM, HOW MUCH BUTTERSCOTCH PUDDING DO YOU THINK YOU CAN EAT?
AS YOU MAY KNOW, TOM, I AM SHELLEY'S PERSONAL MANAGER. AND I WOULD NEVER ALLOW SHELLEY TO PARTICIPATE IN SUCH A THING!
MAN, I'VE YEARNED FOR THIS KIND OF PARENTAL DISCIPLINE MY WHOLE LIFE.

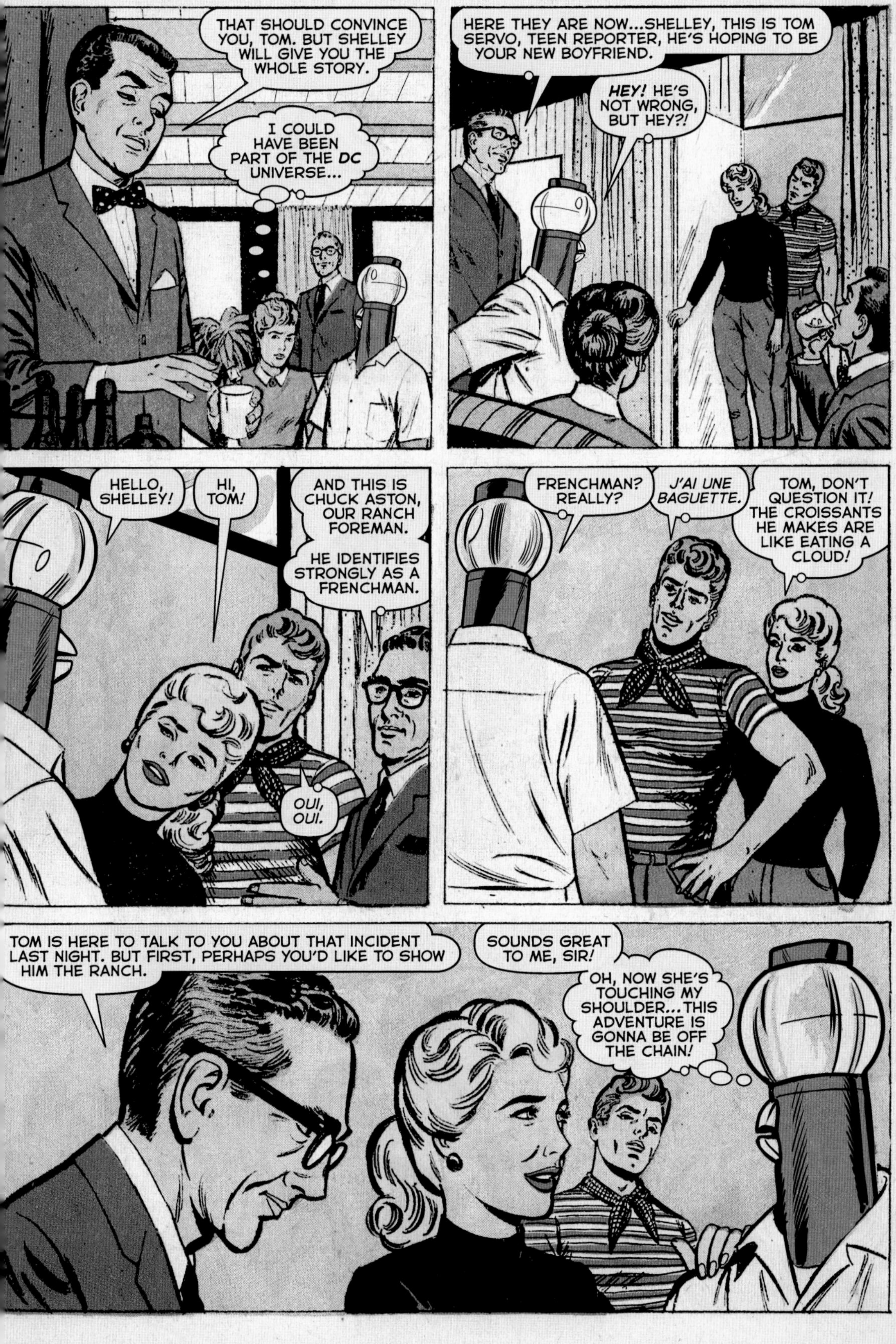
THAT SHOULD CONVINCE YOU, TOM. BUT SHELLEY WILL GIVE YOU THE WHOLE STORY.
I COULD HAVE BEEN PART OF THE *DC* UNIVERSE...
HERE THEY ARE NOW...SHELLEY, THIS IS TOM SERVO, TEEN REPORTER, HE'S HOPING TO BE YOUR NEW BOYFRIEND.
HEY! HE'S NOT WRONG, BUT HEY?!
HELLO, SHELLEY!
HI, TOM!
AND THIS IS CHUCK ASTON, OUR RANCH FOREMAN.
HE IDENTIFIES STRONGLY AS A FRENCHMAN.
OUI, OUI.
FRENCHMAN? REALLY?
J'AI UNE BAGUETTE.
TOM, DON'T QUESTION IT! THE CROISSANTS HE MAKES ARE LIKE EATING A CLOUD!
TOM IS HERE TO TALK TO YOU ABOUT THAT INCIDENT LAST NIGHT. BUT FIRST, PERHAPS YOU'D LIKE TO SHOW HIM THE RANCH.
SOUNDS GREAT TO ME, SIR!
OH, NOW SHE'S TOUCHING MY SHOULDER...THIS ADVENTURE IS GONNA BE OFF THE CHAIN!

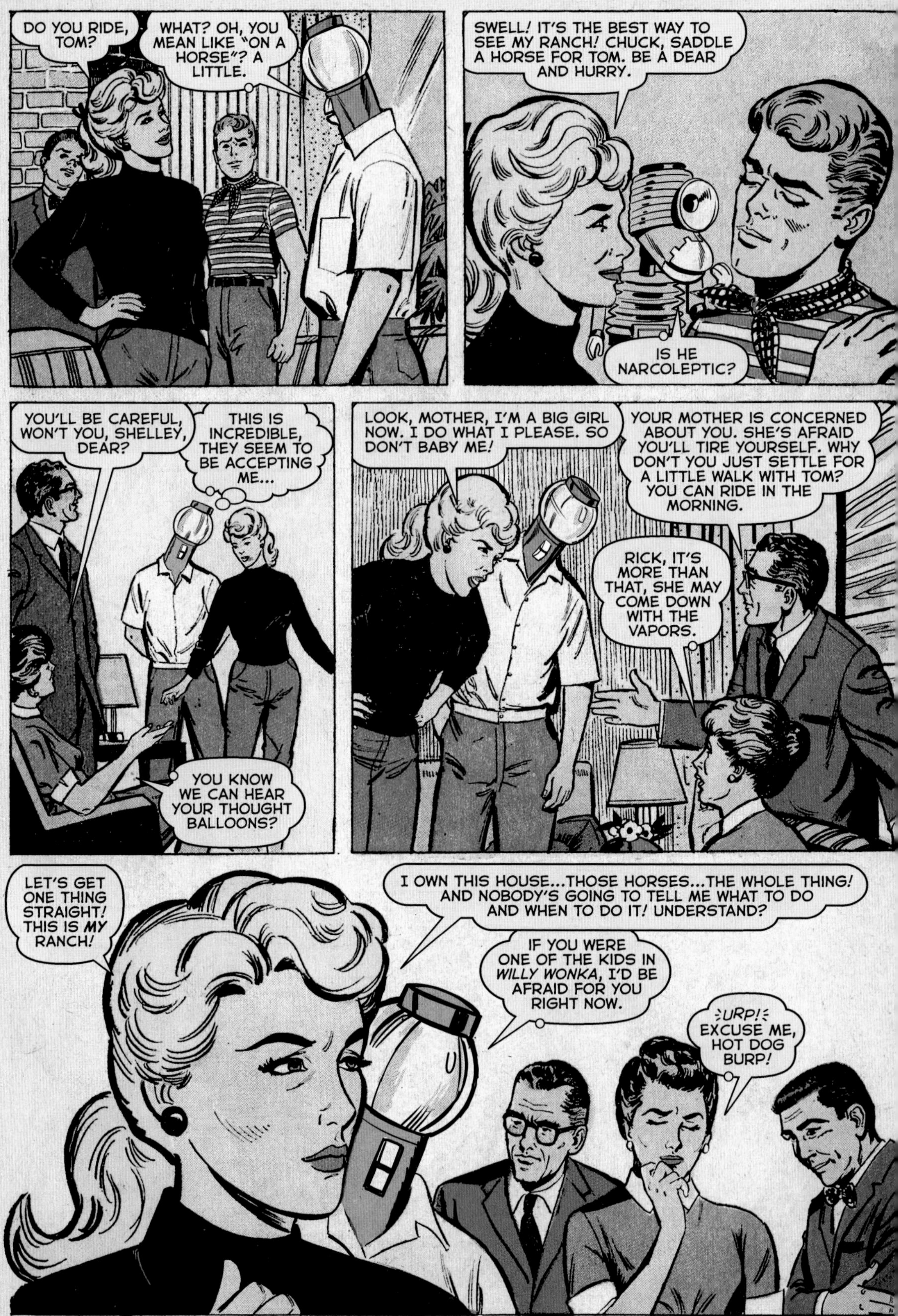
DO YOU RIDE, TOM?
WHAT? OH, YOU MEAN LIKE "ON A HORSE"? A LITTLE.
SWELL! IT'S THE BEST WAY TO SEE MY RANCH! CHUCK, SADDLE A HORSE FOR TOM. BE A DEAR AND HURRY.
IS HE NARCOLEPTIC?
YOU'LL BE CAREFUL, WON'T YOU, SHELLEY, DEAR?
THIS IS INCREDIBLE, THEY SEEM TO BE ACCEPTING ME...
YOU KNOW WE CAN HEAR YOUR THOUGHT BALLOONS?
LOOK, MOTHER, I'M A BIG GIRL NOW. I DO WHAT I PLEASE. SO DON'T BABY ME!
YOUR MOTHER IS CONCERNED ABOUT YOU. SHE'S AFRAID YOU'LL TIRE YOURSELF. WHY DON'T YOU JUST SETTLE FOR A LITTLE WALK WITH TOM? YOU CAN RIDE IN THE MORNING.
RICK, IT'S MORE THAN THAT, SHE MAY COME DOWN WITH THE VAPORS.
LET'S GET ONE THING STRAIGHT! THIS IS *MY* RANCH!
I OWN THIS HOUSE...THOSE HORSES...THE WHOLE THING! AND NOBODY'S GOING TO TELL ME WHAT TO DO AND WHEN TO DO IT! UNDERSTAND?
IF YOU WERE ONE OF THE KIDS IN *WILLY WONKA*, I'D BE AFRAID FOR YOU RIGHT NOW.
URP! EXCUSE ME, HOT DOG BURP!

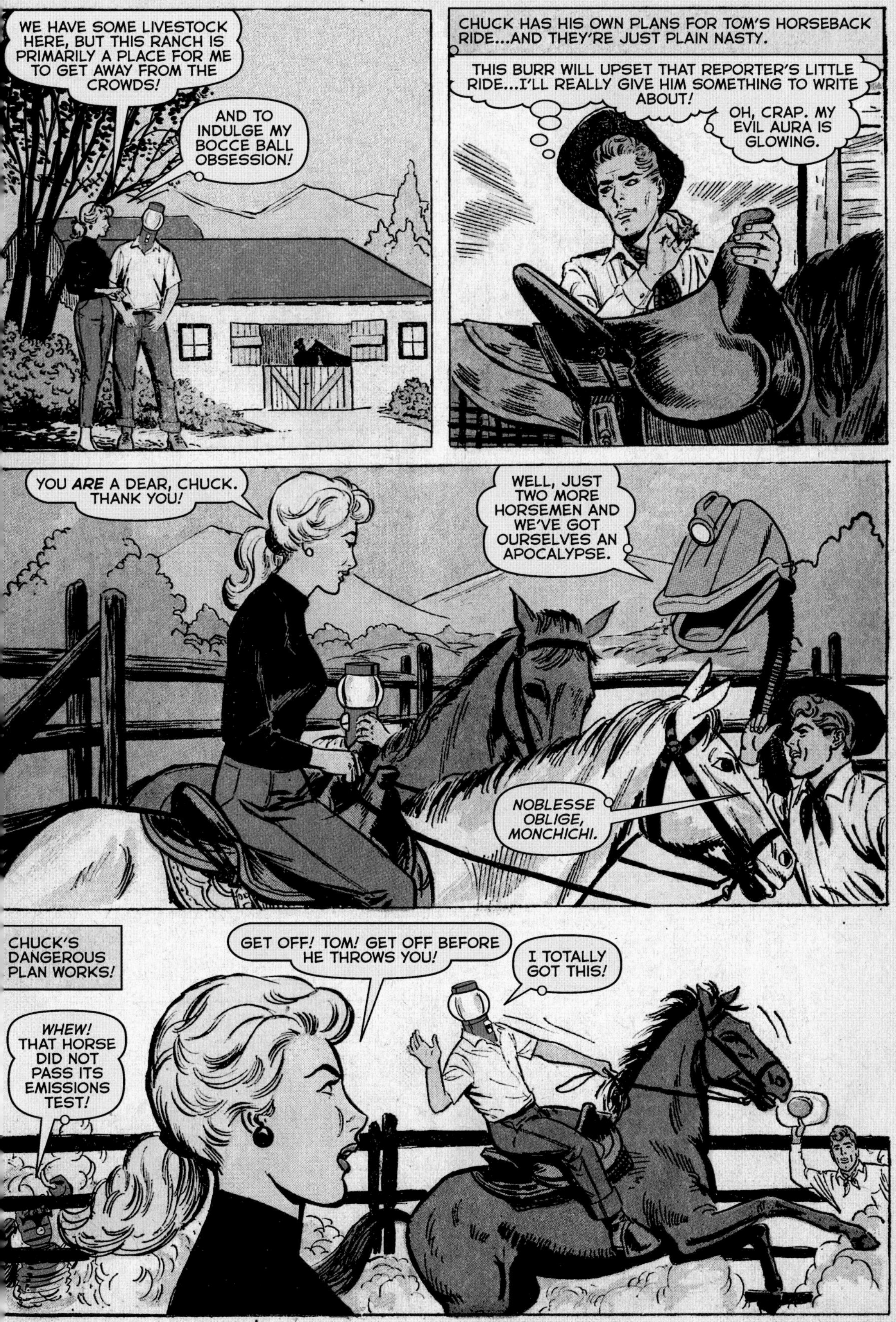
WE HAVE SOME LIVESTOCK HERE, BUT THIS RANCH IS PRIMARILY A PLACE FOR ME TO GET AWAY FROM THE CROWDS!
AND TO INDULGE MY BOCCE BALL OBSESSION!
CHUCK HAS HIS OWN PLANS FOR TOM'S HORSEBACK RIDE...AND THEY'RE JUST PLAIN NASTY.
THIS BURR WILL UPSET THAT REPORTER'S LITTLE RIDE...I'LL REALLY GIVE HIM SOMETHING TO WRITE ABOUT!
OH, CRAP. MY EVIL AURA IS GLOWING.
YOU *ARE* A DEAR, CHUCK. THANK YOU!
WELL, JUST TWO MORE HORSEMEN AND WE'VE GOT OURSELVES AN APOCALYPSE.
NOBLESSE OBLIGE, MONCHICHI.
CHUCK'S DANGEROUS PLAN WORKS!
GET OFF! TOM! GET OFF BEFORE HE THROWS YOU!
I TOTALLY GOT THIS!
WHEW! THAT HORSE DID NOT PASS ITS EMISSIONS TEST!

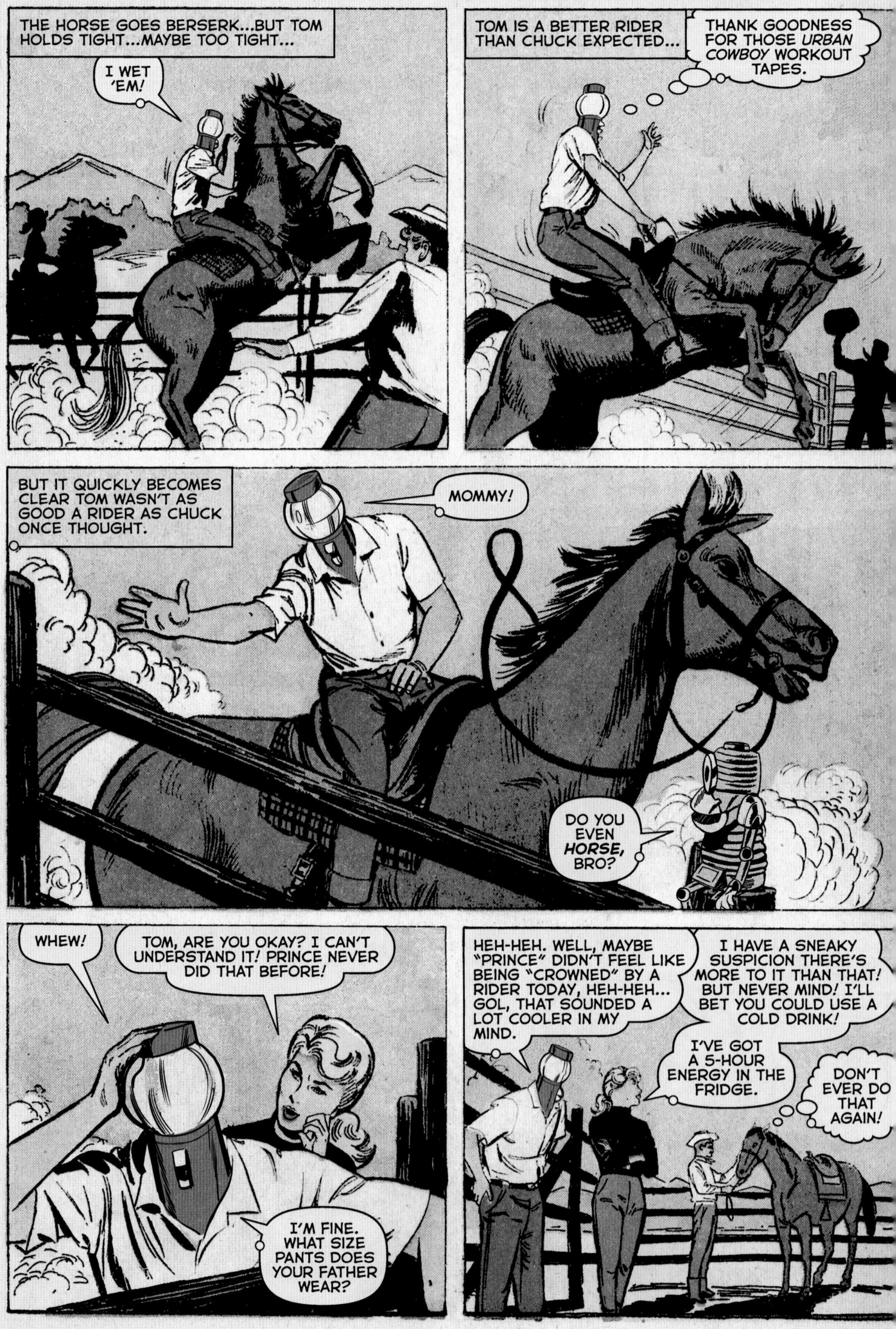
THE HORSE GOES BERSERK...BUT TOM HOLDS TIGHT...MAYBE TOO TIGHT...
I WET 'EM!
TOM IS A BETTER RIDER THAN CHUCK EXPECTED...
THANK GOODNESS FOR THOSE *URBAN COWBOY* WORKOUT TAPES.
BUT IT QUICKLY BECOMES CLEAR TOM WASN'T AS GOOD A RIDER AS CHUCK ONCE THOUGHT.
MOMMY!
DO YOU EVEN ***HORSE,*** BRO?
WHEW!
TOM, ARE YOU OKAY? I CAN'T UNDERSTAND IT! PRINCE NEVER DID THAT BEFORE!
I'M FINE. WHAT SIZE PANTS DOES YOUR FATHER WEAR?
HEH-HEH. WELL, MAYBE "PRINCE" DIDN'T FEEL LIKE BEING "CROWNED" BY A RIDER TODAY, HEH-HEH... GOL, THAT SOUNDED A LOT COOLER IN MY MIND.
I HAVE A SNEAKY SUSPICION THERE'S MORE TO IT THAN THAT! BUT NEVER MIND! I'LL BET YOU COULD USE A COLD DRINK!
I'VE GOT A 5-HOUR ENERGY IN THE FRIDGE.
DON'T EVER DO THAT AGAIN!

IT'S ALMOST TIME FOR DINNER.

IF YOU DON'T MIND, I THINK I'LL SKIP IT. I'D RATHER TAKE A NAP.

HOW DO YOU TAKE A NAP WHEN YOU DON'T HAVE EYES?

I'VE GOT A SLEEP SETTING.

LATER ON THAT EVENING...

WHAT ON EARTH IS THAT NOISE?

TOM, BUDDY. YOU'RE A TEEN AND THAT'S A PARTY. GET OUT THERE!

I CAN'T BELIEVE THIS IS HAPPENING TO ME! I'M A TEENAGER AND I'M ABOUT TO BURST INTO A LAWLESS SIXTIES PARTY! YES!

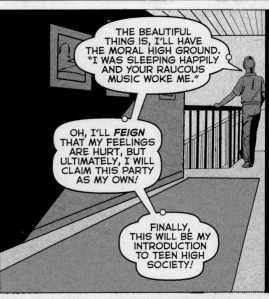

THE BEAUTIFUL THING IS, I'LL HAVE THE MORAL HIGH GROUND. "I WAS SLEEPING HAPPILY AND YOUR RAUCOUS MUSIC WOKE ME."

OH, I'LL *FEIGN* THAT MY FEELINGS ARE HURT, BUT ULTIMATELY, I WILL CLAIM THIS PARTY AS MY OWN!

FINALLY, THIS WILL BE MY INTRODUCTION TO TEEN HIGH SOCIETY!

TOM IS "SURPRISED" TO FIND A CROWDED PARTY IN FULL SWING...

WHY, IF THIS ISN'T THE DEVIL'S DOING, I DON'T KNOW WHAT IS!

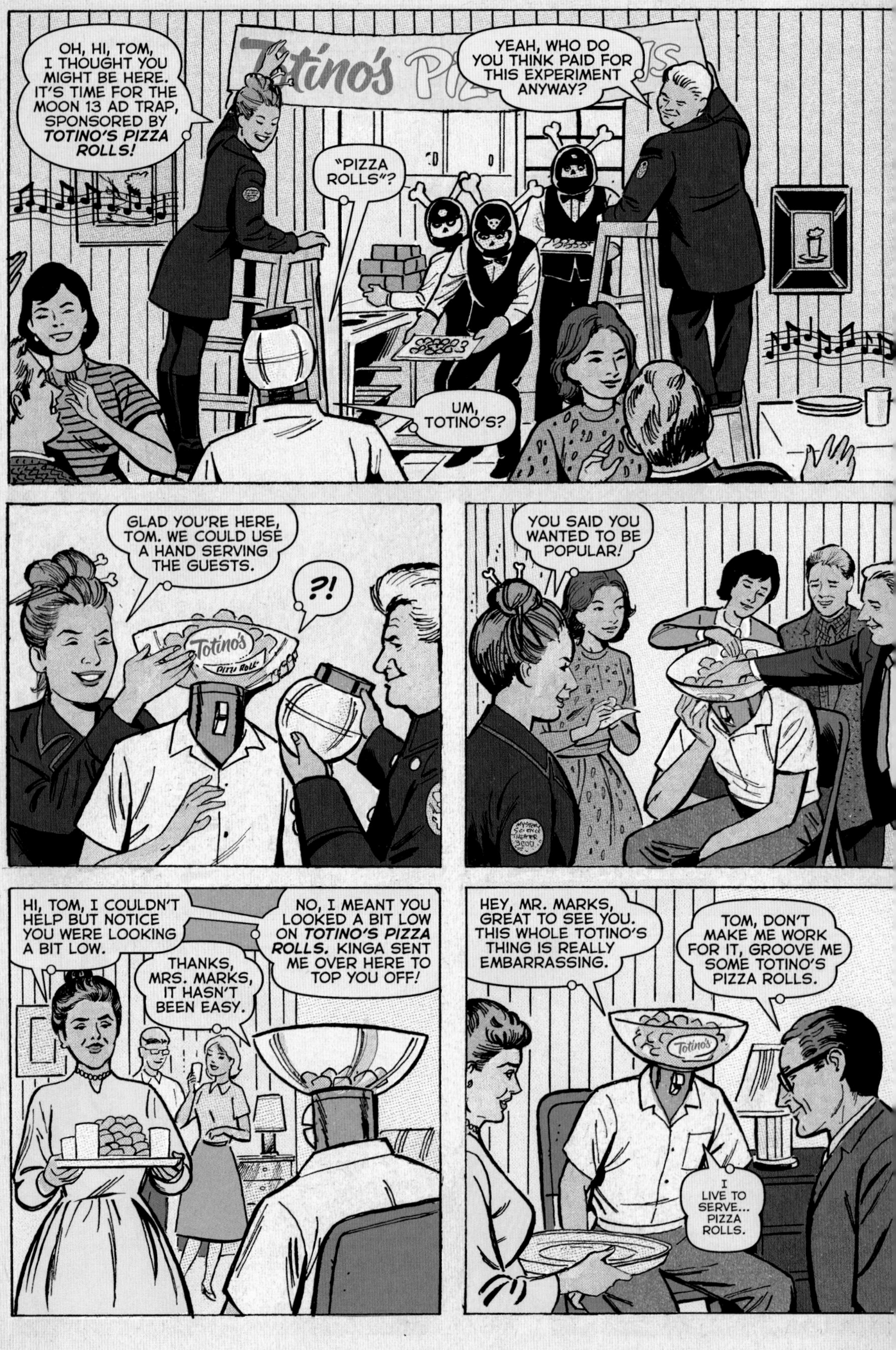
OH, HI, TOM, I THOUGHT YOU MIGHT BE HERE. IT'S TIME FOR THE MOON 13 AD TRAP, SPONSORED BY *TOTINO'S PIZZA ROLLS!*
"PIZZA ROLLS"?
YEAH, WHO DO YOU THINK PAID FOR THIS EXPERIMENT ANYWAY?
UM, TOTINO'S?
GLAD YOU'RE HERE, TOM. WE COULD USE A HAND SERVING THE GUESTS.
?!
YOU SAID YOU WANTED TO BE POPULAR!
HI, TOM, I COULDN'T HELP BUT NOTICE YOU WERE LOOKING A BIT LOW.
THANKS, MRS. MARKS, IT HASN'T BEEN EASY.
NO, I MEANT YOU LOOKED A BIT LOW ON *TOTINO'S PIZZA ROLLS.* KINGA SENT ME OVER HERE TO TOP YOU OFF!
HEY, MR. MARKS, GREAT TO SEE YOU. THIS WHOLE TOTINO'S THING IS REALLY EMBARRASSING.
TOM, DON'T MAKE ME WORK FOR IT, GROOVE ME SOME TOTINO'S PIZZA ROLLS.
I LIVE TO SERVE... PIZZA ROLLS.

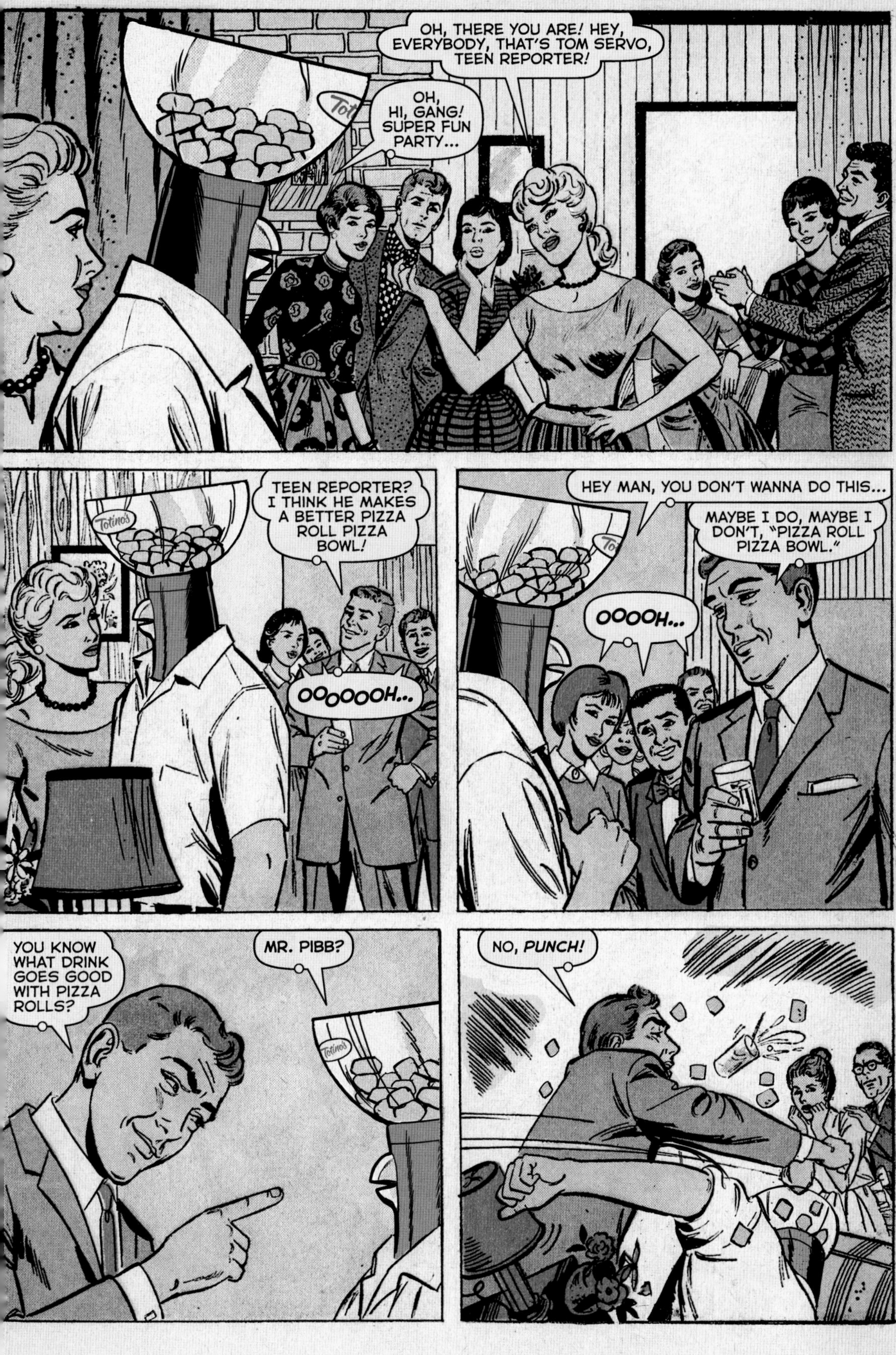
OH, THERE YOU ARE! HEY, EVERYBODY, THAT'S TOM SERVO, TEEN REPORTER!
OH, HI, GANG! SUPER FUN PARTY...
TEEN REPORTER? I THINK HE MAKES A BETTER PIZZA ROLL PIZZA BOWL!
OOOOOOH...
HEY MAN, YOU DON'T WANNA DO THIS...
MAYBE I DO, MAYBE I DON'T, "PIZZA ROLL PIZZA BOWL."
OOOOH...
YOU KNOW WHAT DRINK GOES GOOD WITH PIZZA ROLLS?
MR. PIBB?
NO, *PUNCH!*

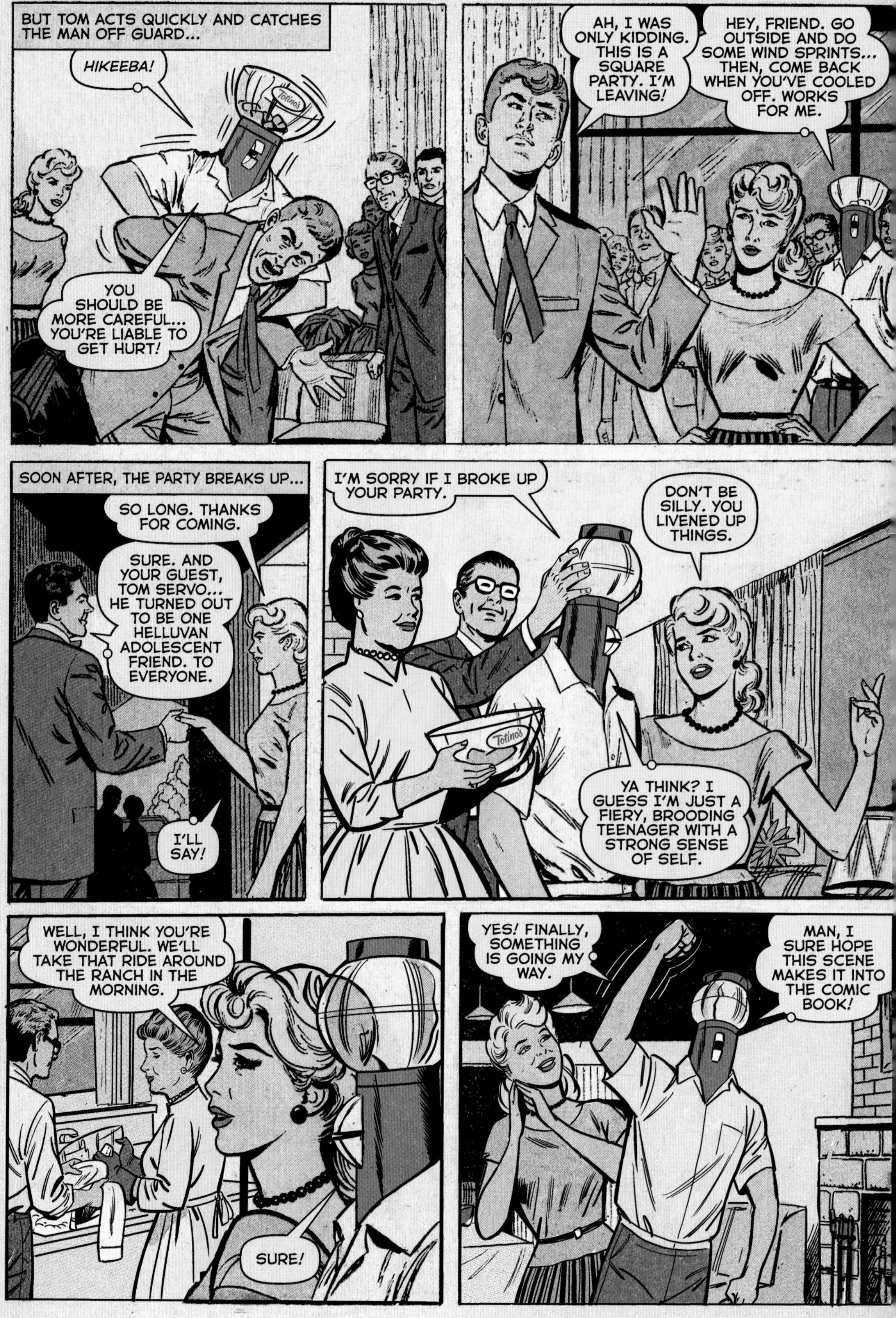

BUT TOM ACTS QUICKLY AND CATCHES THE MAN OFF GUARD...
HIKEEBA!
YOU SHOULD BE MORE CAREFUL... YOU'RE LIABLE TO GET HURT!
AH, I WAS ONLY KIDDING. THIS IS A SQUARE PARTY. I'M LEAVING!
HEY, FRIEND. GO OUTSIDE AND DO SOME WIND SPRINTS... THEN, COME BACK WHEN YOU'VE COOLED OFF. WORKS FOR ME.
SOON AFTER, THE PARTY BREAKS UP...
SO LONG. THANKS FOR COMING.
SURE. AND YOUR GUEST, TOM SERVO... HE TURNED OUT TO BE ONE HELLUVAN ADOLESCENT FRIEND. TO EVERYONE.
I'LL SAY!
I'M SORRY IF I BROKE UP YOUR PARTY.
DON'T BE SILLY. YOU LIVENED UP THINGS.
YA THINK? I GUESS I'M JUST A FIERY, BROODING TEENAGER WITH A STRONG SENSE OF SELF.
WELL, I THINK YOU'RE WONDERFUL. WE'LL TAKE THAT RIDE AROUND THE RANCH IN THE MORNING.
SURE!
YES! FINALLY, SOMETHING IS GOING MY WAY.
MAN, I SURE HOPE THIS SCENE MAKES IT INTO THE COMIC BOOK!

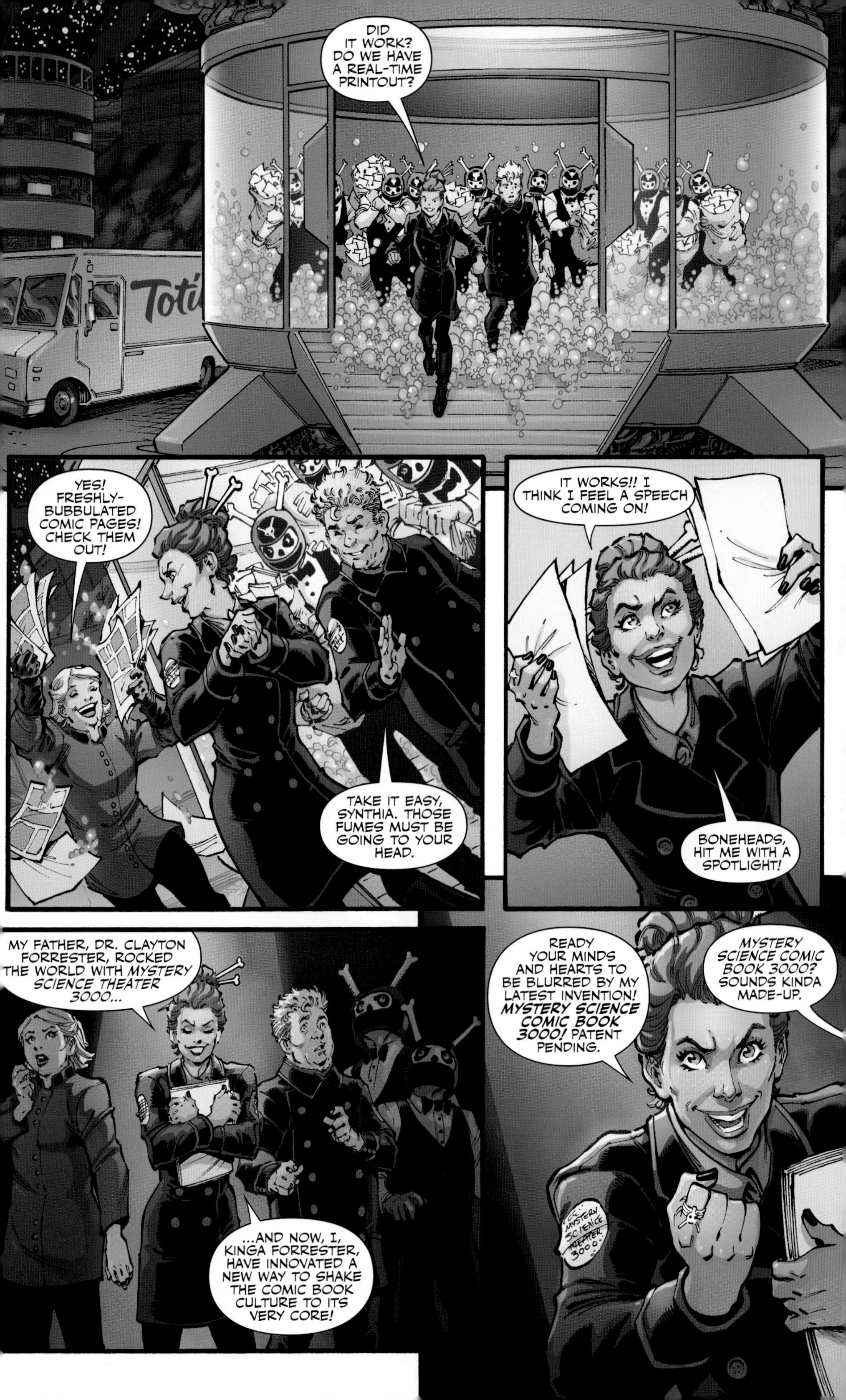
DID IT WORK? DO WE HAVE A REAL-TIME PRINTOUT?
YES! FRESHLY-BUBBULATED COMIC PAGES! CHECK THEM OUT!
TAKE IT EASY, SYNTHIA. THOSE FUMES MUST BE GOING TO YOUR HEAD.
IT WORKS!! I THINK I FEEL A SPEECH COMING ON!
BONEHEADS, HIT ME WITH A SPOTLIGHT!
MY FATHER, DR. CLAYTON FORRESTER, ROCKED THE WORLD WITH *MYSTERY SCIENCE THEATER 3000*...
...AND NOW, I, KINGA FORRESTER, HAVE INNOVATED A NEW WAY TO SHAKE THE COMIC BOOK CULTURE TO ITS VERY CORE!
READY YOUR MINDS AND HEARTS TO BE BLURRED BY MY LATEST INVENTION! ***MYSTERY SCIENCE COMIC BOOK 3000!*** PATENT PENDING.
MYSTERY SCIENCE COMIC BOOK 3000? SOUNDS KINDA MADE-UP.

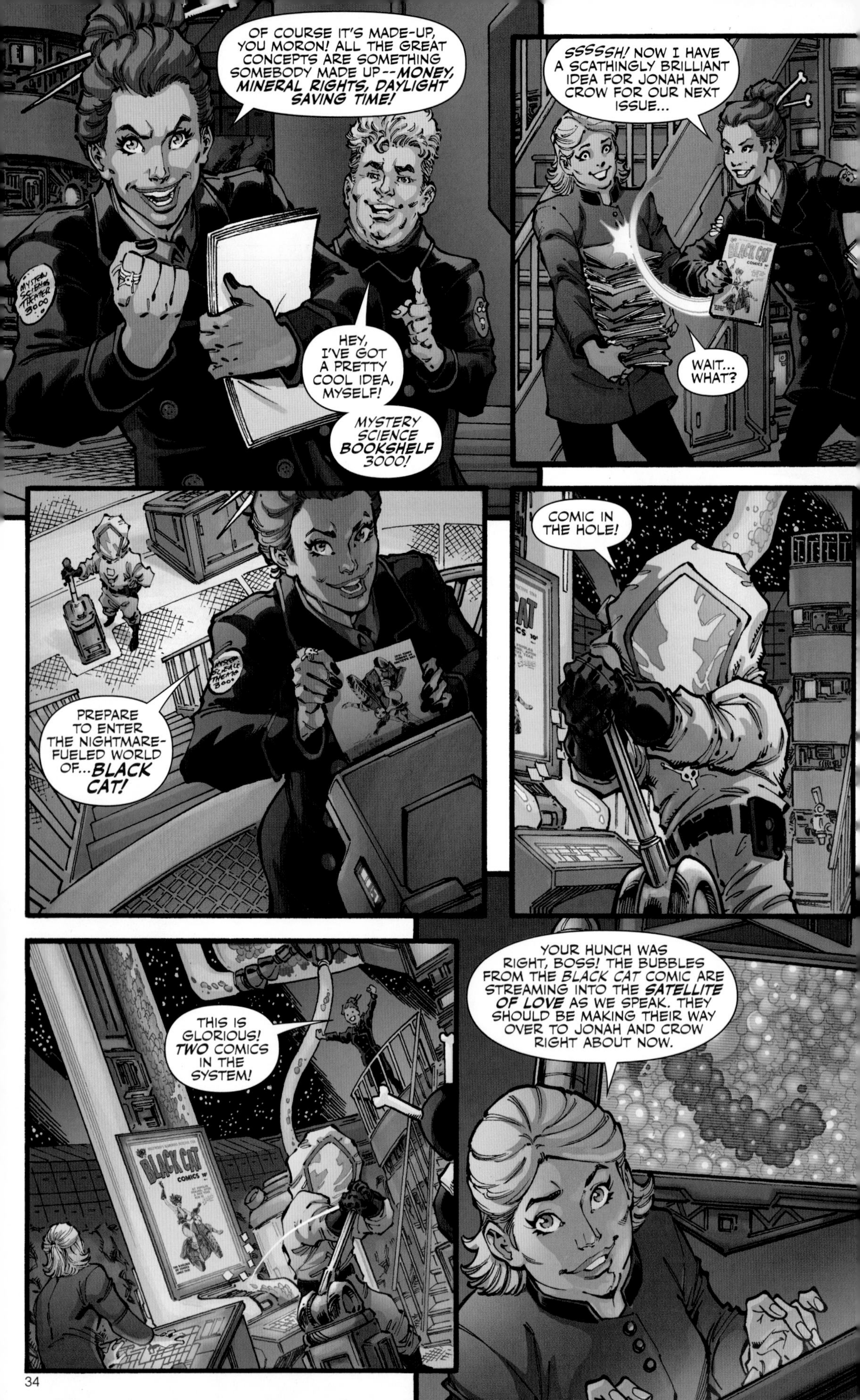
OF COURSE IT'S MADE-UP, YOU MORON! ALL THE GREAT CONCEPTS ARE SOMETHING SOMEBODY MADE UP--MONEY, MINERAL RIGHTS, DAYLIGHT SAVING TIME!
HEY, I'VE GOT A PRETTY COOL IDEA, MYSELF!
MYSTERY SCIENCE BOOKSHELF 3000!
SSSSSH! NOW I HAVE A SCATHINGLY BRILLIANT IDEA FOR JONAH AND CROW FOR OUR NEXT ISSUE...
WAIT... WHAT?
PREPARE TO ENTER THE NIGHTMARE-FUELED WORLD OF...BLACK CAT!
COMIC IN THE HOLE!
THIS IS GLORIOUS! TWO COMICS IN THE SYSTEM!
YOUR HUNCH WAS RIGHT, BOSS! THE BUBBLES FROM THE BLACK CAT COMIC ARE STREAMING INTO THE SATELLITE OF LOVE AS WE SPEAK. THEY SHOULD BE MAKING THEIR WAY OVER TO JONAH AND CROW RIGHT ABOUT NOW.

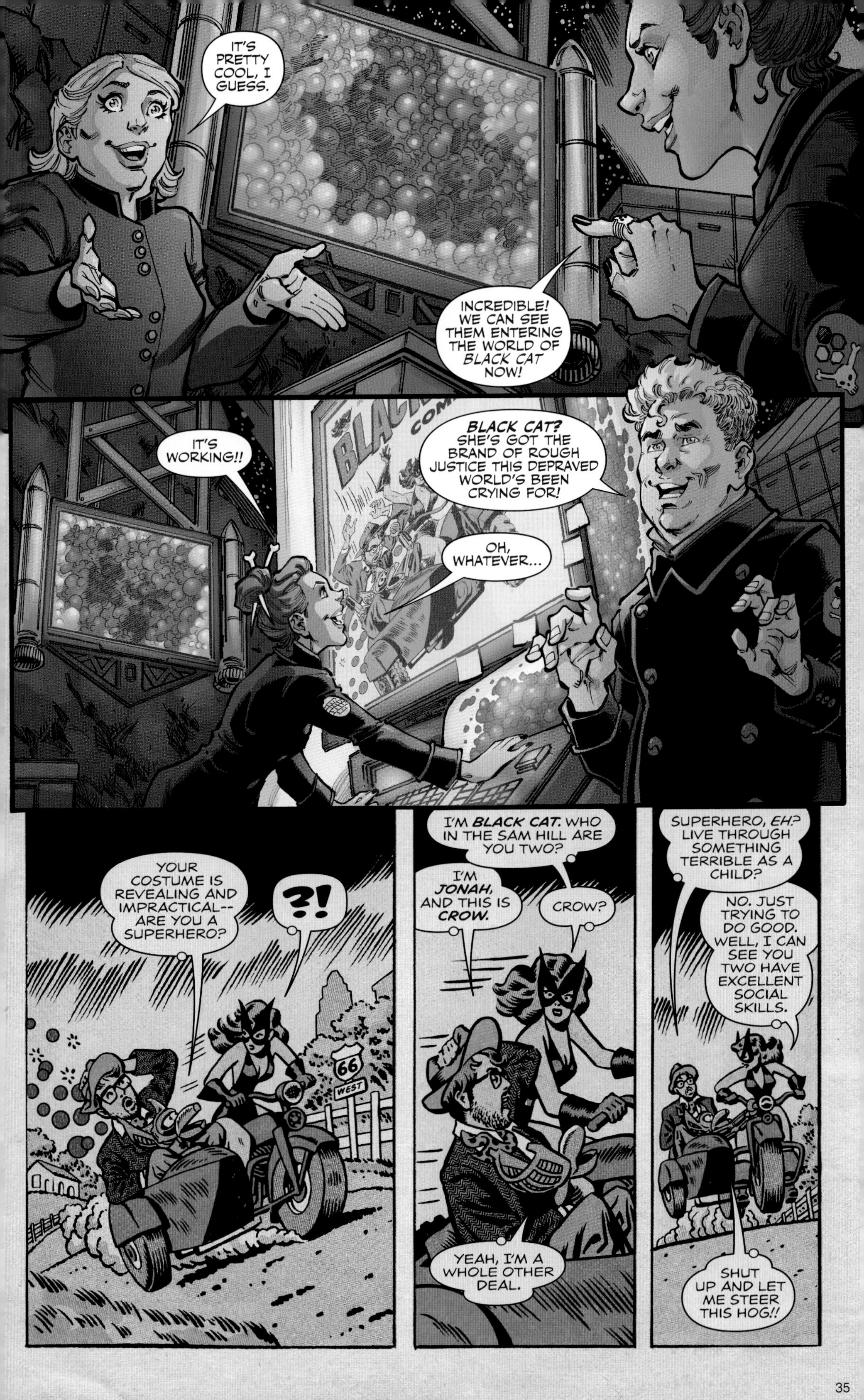
IT'S PRETTY COOL, I GUESS.
INCREDIBLE! WE CAN SEE THEM ENTERING THE WORLD OF BLACK CAT NOW!
IT'S WORKING!!
BLACK CAT? SHE'S GOT THE BRAND OF ROUGH JUSTICE THIS DEPRAVED WORLD'S BEEN CRYING FOR!
OH, WHATEVER...
YOUR COSTUME IS REVEALING AND IMPRACTICAL-- ARE YOU A SUPERHERO?
?!
66
WEST
I'M BLACK CAT. WHO IN THE SAM HILL ARE YOU TWO?
I'M JONAH, AND THIS IS CROW.
CROW?
YEAH, I'M A WHOLE OTHER DEAL.
SUPERHERO, EH? LIVE THROUGH SOMETHING TERRIBLE AS A CHILD?
NO. JUST TRYING TO DO GOOD. WELL, I CAN SEE YOU TWO HAVE EXCELLENT SOCIAL SKILLS.
SHUT UP AND LET ME STEER THIS HOG!!

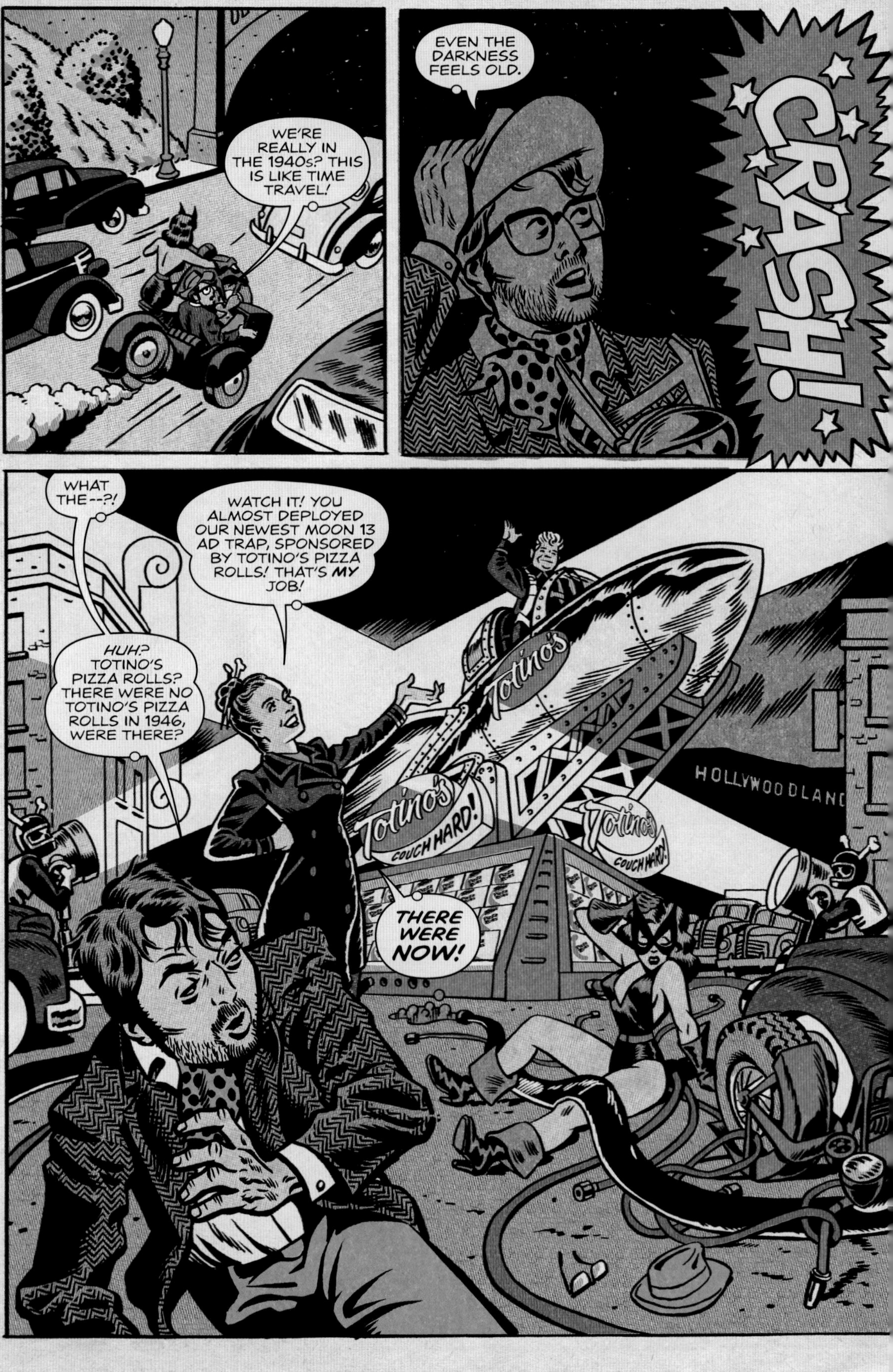
WE'RE REALLY IN THE 1940s? THIS IS LIKE TIME TRAVEL!
EVEN THE DARKNESS FEELS OLD.
CRASH!
WHAT THE--?!
WATCH IT! YOU ALMOST DEPLOYED OUR NEWEST MOON 13 AD TRAP, SPONSORED BY TOTINO'S PIZZA ROLLS! THAT'S MY JOB!
HUH? TOTINO'S PIZZA ROLLS? THERE WERE NO TOTINO'S PIZZA ROLLS IN 1946, WERE THERE?
THERE WERE NOW!
Totino's
Totino's COUCH HARD!
Totino's COUCH HARD!
HOLLYWOODLAND

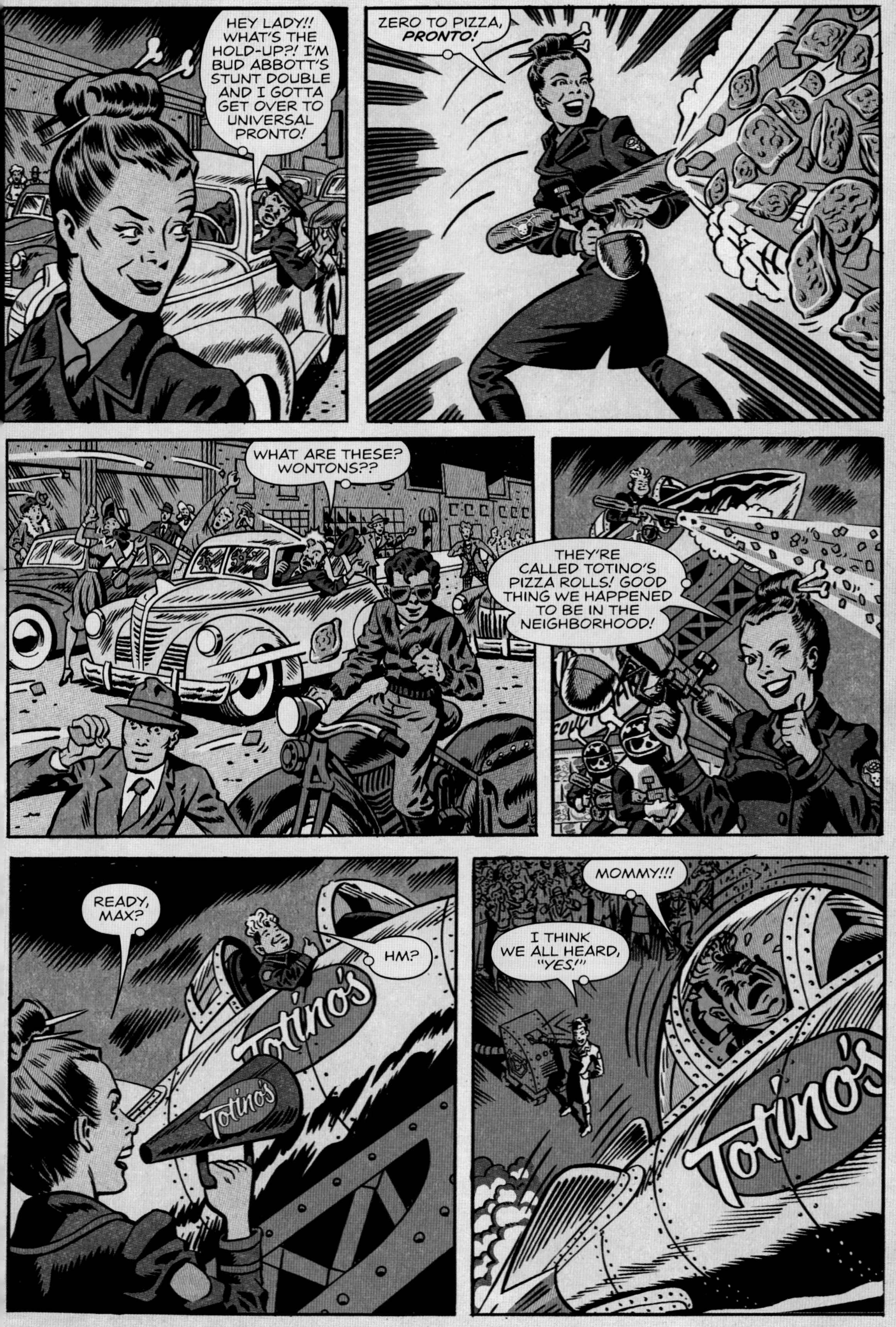
HEY LADY!! WHAT'S THE HOLD-UP?! I'M BUD ABBOTT'S STUNT DOUBLE AND I GOTTA GET OVER TO UNIVERSAL PRONTO!
ZERO TO PIZZA, *PRONTO!*
WHAT ARE THESE? WONTONS??
THEY'RE CALLED TOTINO'S PIZZA ROLLS! GOOD THING WE HAPPENED TO BE IN THE NEIGHBORHOOD!
READY, MAX?
HM?
Totino's
Totino's
MOMMY!!!
I THINK WE ALL HEARD, *"YES!"*
Totino's

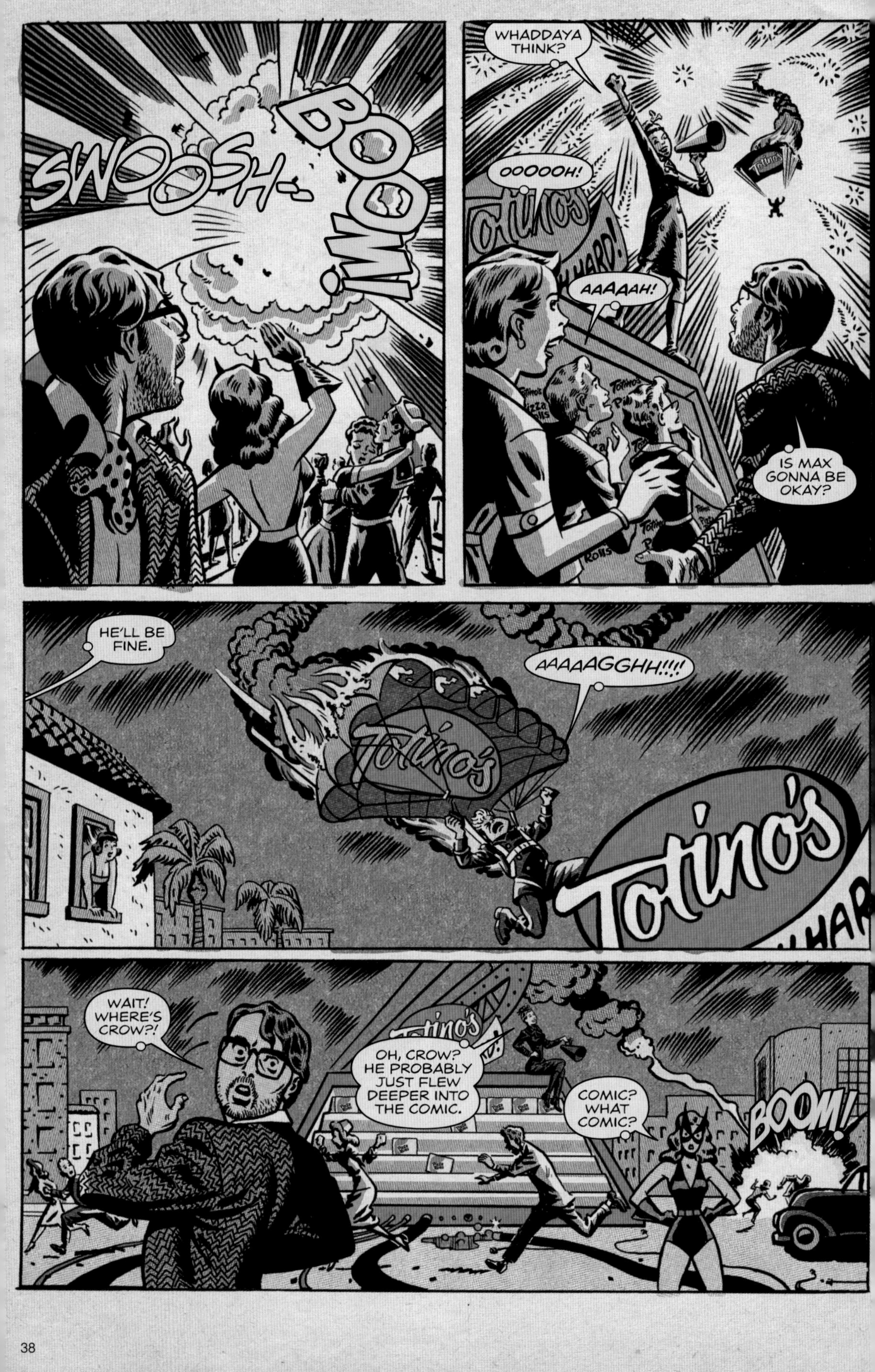
SWOOSH-
BOOM!
WHADDAYA THINK?
OOOOOH!
AAAAAH!
Totino's
IS MAX GONNA BE OKAY?
HE'LL BE FINE.
AAAAAGGHH!!!!
Totino's
Totino's
WAIT! WHERE'S CROW?!
Totino's
OH, CROW? HE PROBABLY JUST FLEW DEEPER INTO THE COMIC.
COMIC? WHAT COMIC?
BOOM!

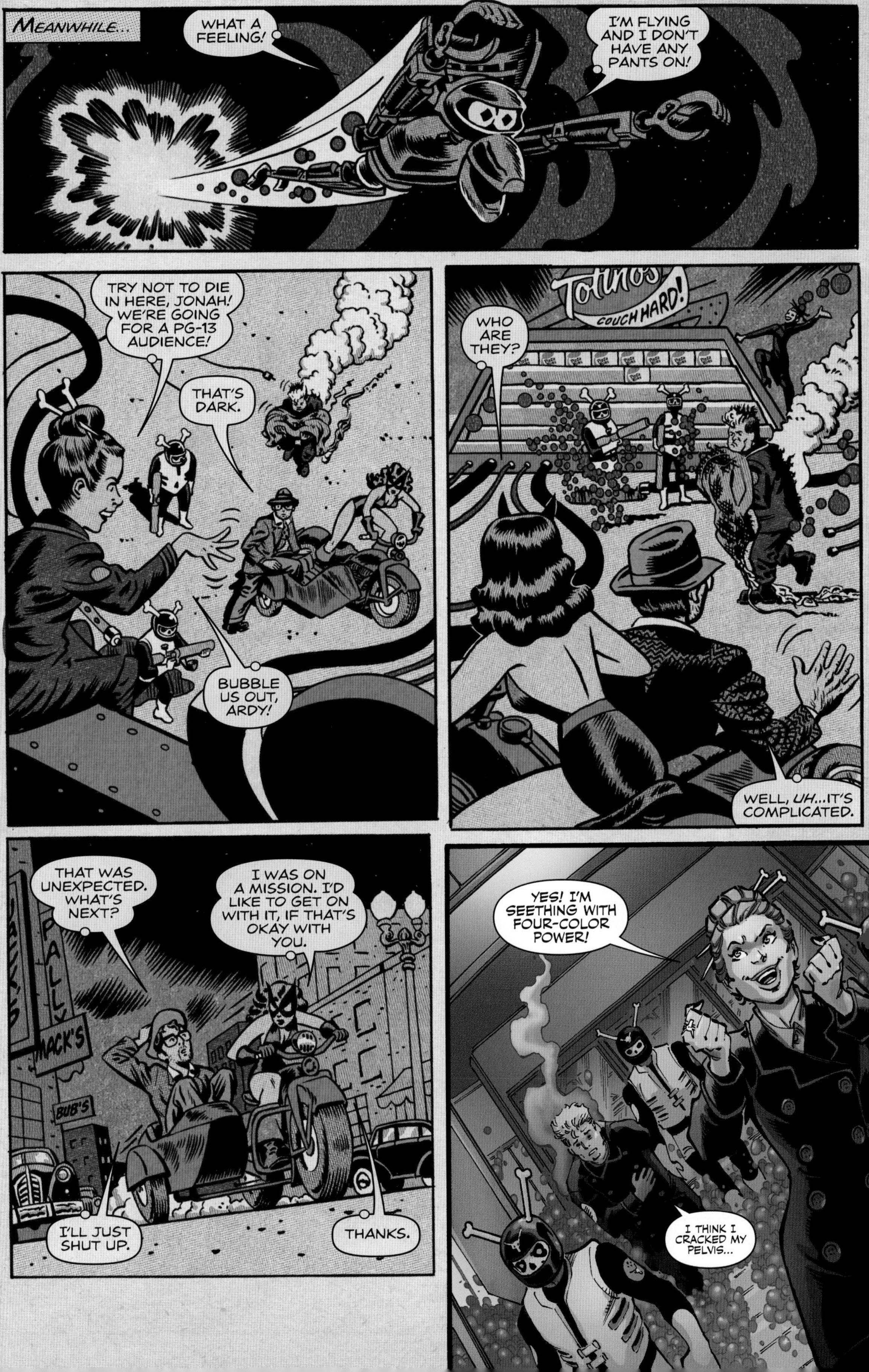
MEANWHILE...
WHAT A FEELING!
I'M FLYING AND I DON'T HAVE ANY PANTS ON!
TRY NOT TO DIE IN HERE, JONAH! WE'RE GOING FOR A PG-13 AUDIENCE!
THAT'S DARK.
BUBBLE US OUT, ARDY!
TOTINO'S
COUCH HARD!
WHO ARE THEY?
WELL, UH...IT'S COMPLICATED.
THAT WAS UNEXPECTED. WHAT'S NEXT?
I WAS ON A MISSION. I'D LIKE TO GET ON WITH IT, IF THAT'S OKAY WITH YOU.
MACK'S
BUB'S
I'LL JUST SHUT UP.
THANKS.
YES! I'M SEETHING WITH FOUR-COLOR POWER!
I THINK I CRACKED MY PELVIS...

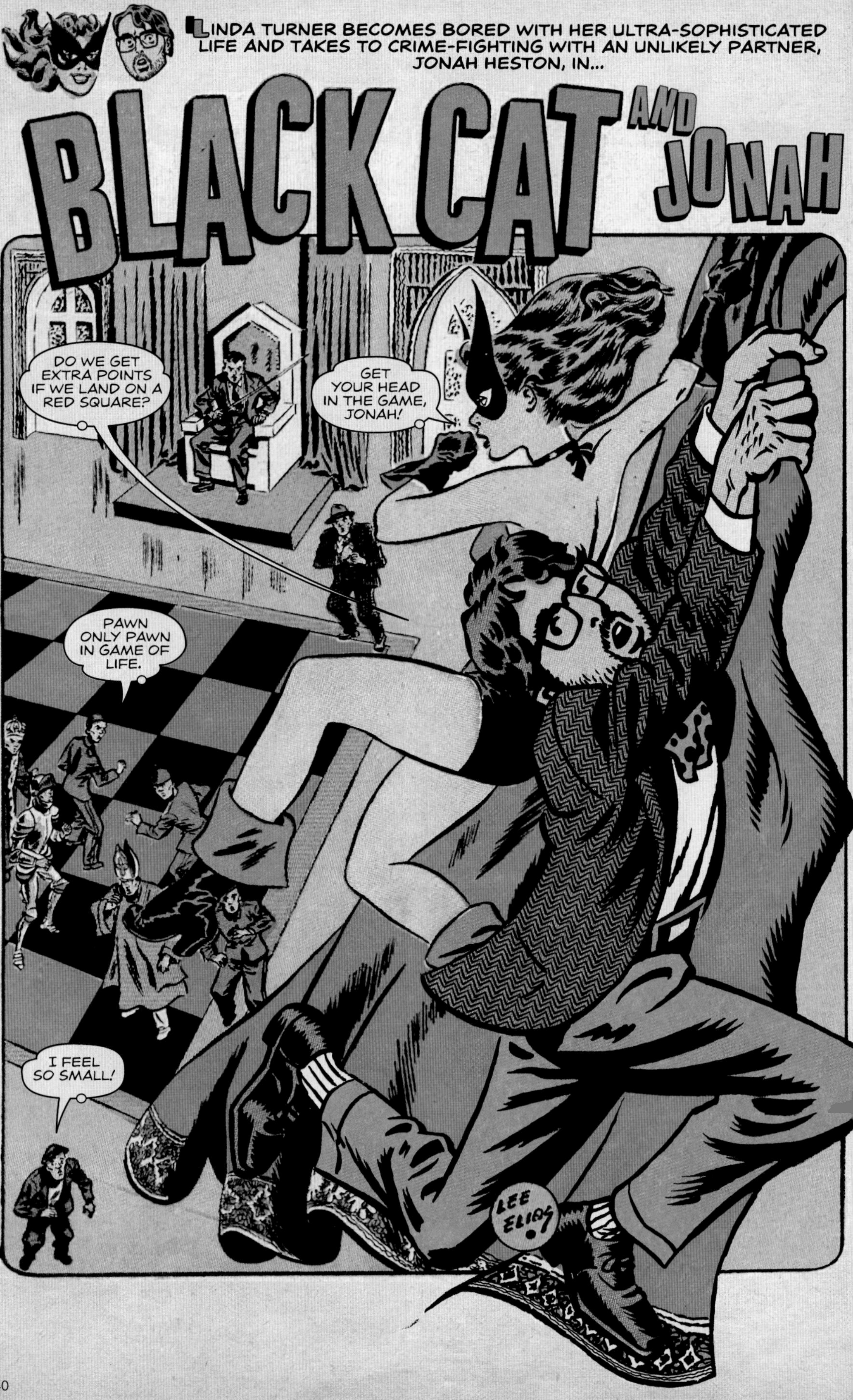
LINDA TURNER BECOMES BORED WITH HER ULTRA-SOPHISTICATED LIFE AND TAKES TO CRIME-FIGHTING WITH AN UNLIKELY PARTNER, JONAH HESTON, IN...
BLACK CAT AND JONAH
DO WE GET EXTRA POINTS IF WE LAND ON A RED SQUARE?
GET YOUR HEAD IN THE GAME, JONAH!
PAWN ONLY PAWN IN GAME OF LIFE.
I FEEL SO SMALL!
LEE ELIAS

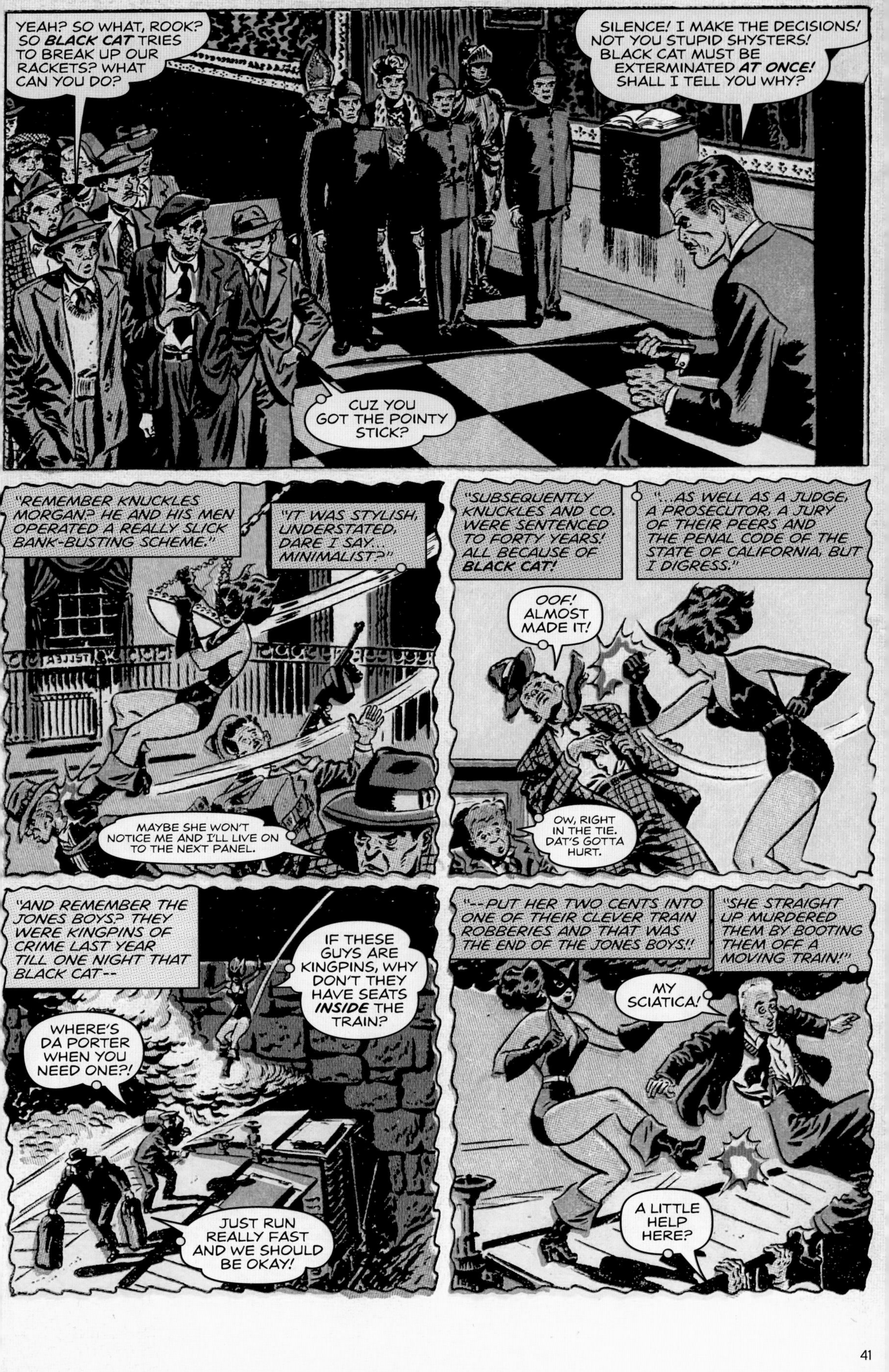
YEAH? SO WHAT, ROOK? SO BLACK CAT TRIES TO BREAK UP OUR RACKETS? WHAT CAN YOU DO?
SILENCE! I MAKE THE DECISIONS! NOT YOU STUPID SHYSTERS! BLACK CAT MUST BE EXTERMINATED AT ONCE! SHALL I TELL YOU WHY?
CUZ YOU GOT THE POINTY STICK?
"REMEMBER KNUCKLES MORGAN? HE AND HIS MEN OPERATED A REALLY SLICK BANK-BUSTING SCHEME."
"IT WAS STYLISH, UNDERSTATED, DARE I SAY... MINIMALIST?"
MAYBE SHE WON'T NOTICE ME AND I'LL LIVE ON TO THE NEXT PANEL.
"SUBSEQUENTLY KNUCKLES AND CO. WERE SENTENCED TO FORTY YEARS! ALL BECAUSE OF BLACK CAT!
"...AS WELL AS A JUDGE, A PROSECUTOR, A JURY OF THEIR PEERS AND THE PENAL CODE OF THE STATE OF CALIFORNIA, BUT I DIGRESS."
OOF! ALMOST MADE IT!
OW, RIGHT IN THE TIE. DAT'S GOTTA HURT.
"AND REMEMBER THE JONES BOYS? THEY WERE KINGPINS OF CRIME LAST YEAR TILL ONE NIGHT THAT BLACK CAT--
IF THESE GUYS ARE KINGPINS, WHY DON'T THEY HAVE SEATS INSIDE THE TRAIN?
WHERE'S DA PORTER WHEN YOU NEED ONE?!
JUST RUN REALLY FAST AND WE SHOULD BE OKAY!
"--PUT HER TWO CENTS INTO ONE OF THEIR CLEVER TRAIN ROBBERIES AND THAT WAS THE END OF THE JONES BOYS!!
"SHE STRAIGHT UP MURDERED THEM BY BOOTING THEM OFF A MOVING TRAIN!"
MY SCIATICA!
A LITTLE HELP HERE?

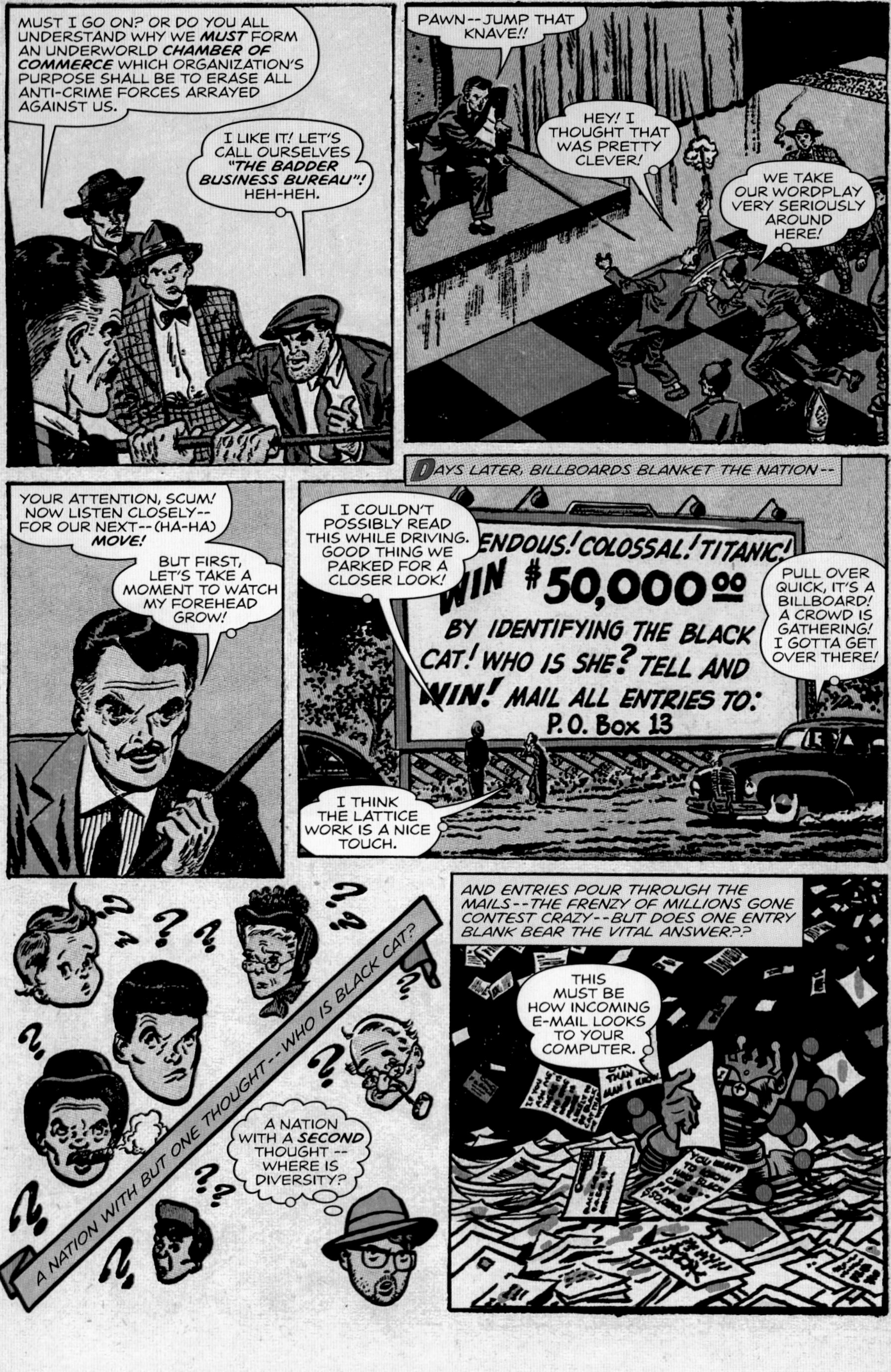
MUST I GO ON? OR DO YOU ALL UNDERSTAND WHY WE MUST FORM AN UNDERWORLD CHAMBER OF COMMERCE WHICH ORGANIZATION'S PURPOSE SHALL BE TO ERASE ALL ANTI-CRIME FORCES ARRAYED AGAINST US.
I LIKE IT! LET'S CALL OURSELVES "THE BADDER BUSINESS BUREAU"! HEH-HEH.
PAWN--JUMP THAT KNAVE!!
HEY! I THOUGHT THAT WAS PRETTY CLEVER!
WE TAKE OUR WORDPLAY VERY SERIOUSLY AROUND HERE!
YOUR ATTENTION, SCUM! NOW LISTEN CLOSELY--FOR OUR NEXT--(HA-HA) MOVE!
BUT FIRST, LET'S TAKE A MOMENT TO WATCH MY FOREHEAD GROW!
DAYS LATER, BILLBOARDS BLANKET THE NATION--
I COULDN'T POSSIBLY READ THIS WHILE DRIVING. GOOD THING WE PARKED FOR A CLOSER LOOK!
ENDOUS! COLOSSAL! TITANIC! WIN $50,000.00 BY IDENTIFYING THE BLACK CAT! WHO IS SHE? TELL AND WIN! MAIL ALL ENTRIES TO: P.O. Box 13
PULL OVER QUICK, IT'S A BILLBOARD! A CROWD IS GATHERING! I GOTTA GET OVER THERE!
I THINK THE LATTICE WORK IS A NICE TOUCH.
A NATION WITH BUT ONE THOUGHT--WHO IS BLACK CAT?
A NATION WITH A SECOND THOUGHT--WHERE IS DIVERSITY?
AND ENTRIES POUR THROUGH THE MAILS--THE FRENZY OF MILLIONS GONE CONTEST CRAZY--BUT DOES ONE ENTRY BLANK BEAR THE VITAL ANSWER??
THIS MUST BE HOW INCOMING E-MAIL LOOKS TO YOUR COMPUTER.

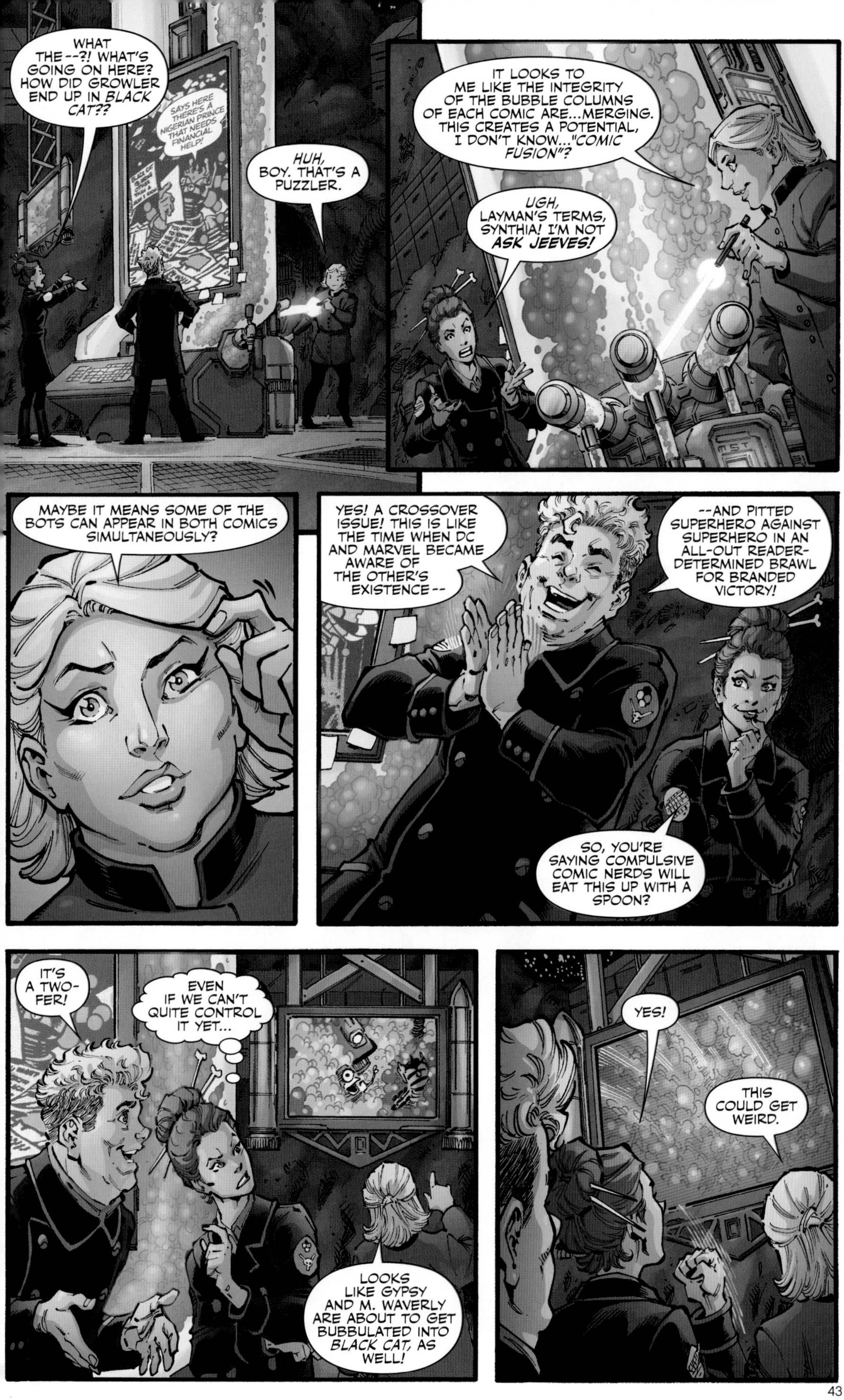
WHAT THE--?! WHAT'S GOING ON HERE? HOW DID GROWLER END UP IN *BLACK CAT*??
SAYS HERE THERE'S A NIGERIAN PRINCE THAT NEEDS FINANCIAL HELP!
HUH, BOY. THAT'S A PUZZLER.
IT LOOKS TO ME LIKE THE INTEGRITY OF THE BUBBLE COLUMNS OF EACH COMIC ARE...MERGING. THIS CREATES A POTENTIAL, I DON'T KNOW..."*COMIC FUSION*"?
UGH, LAYMAN'S TERMS, SYNTHIA! I'M NOT ***ASK JEEVES!***
MAYBE IT MEANS SOME OF THE BOTS CAN APPEAR IN BOTH COMICS SIMULTANEOUSLY?
YES! A CROSSOVER ISSUE! THIS IS LIKE THE TIME WHEN DC AND MARVEL BECAME AWARE OF THE OTHER'S EXISTENCE--
--AND PITTED SUPERHERO AGAINST SUPERHERO IN AN ALL-OUT READER-DETERMINED BRAWL FOR BRANDED VICTORY!
SO, YOU'RE SAYING COMPULSIVE COMIC NERDS WILL EAT THIS UP WITH A SPOON?
IT'S A TWO-FER!
EVEN IF WE CAN'T QUITE CONTROL IT YET...
LOOKS LIKE GYPSY AND M. WAVERLY ARE ABOUT TO GET BUBBULATED INTO *BLACK CAT*, AS WELL!
YES!
THIS COULD GET WEIRD.

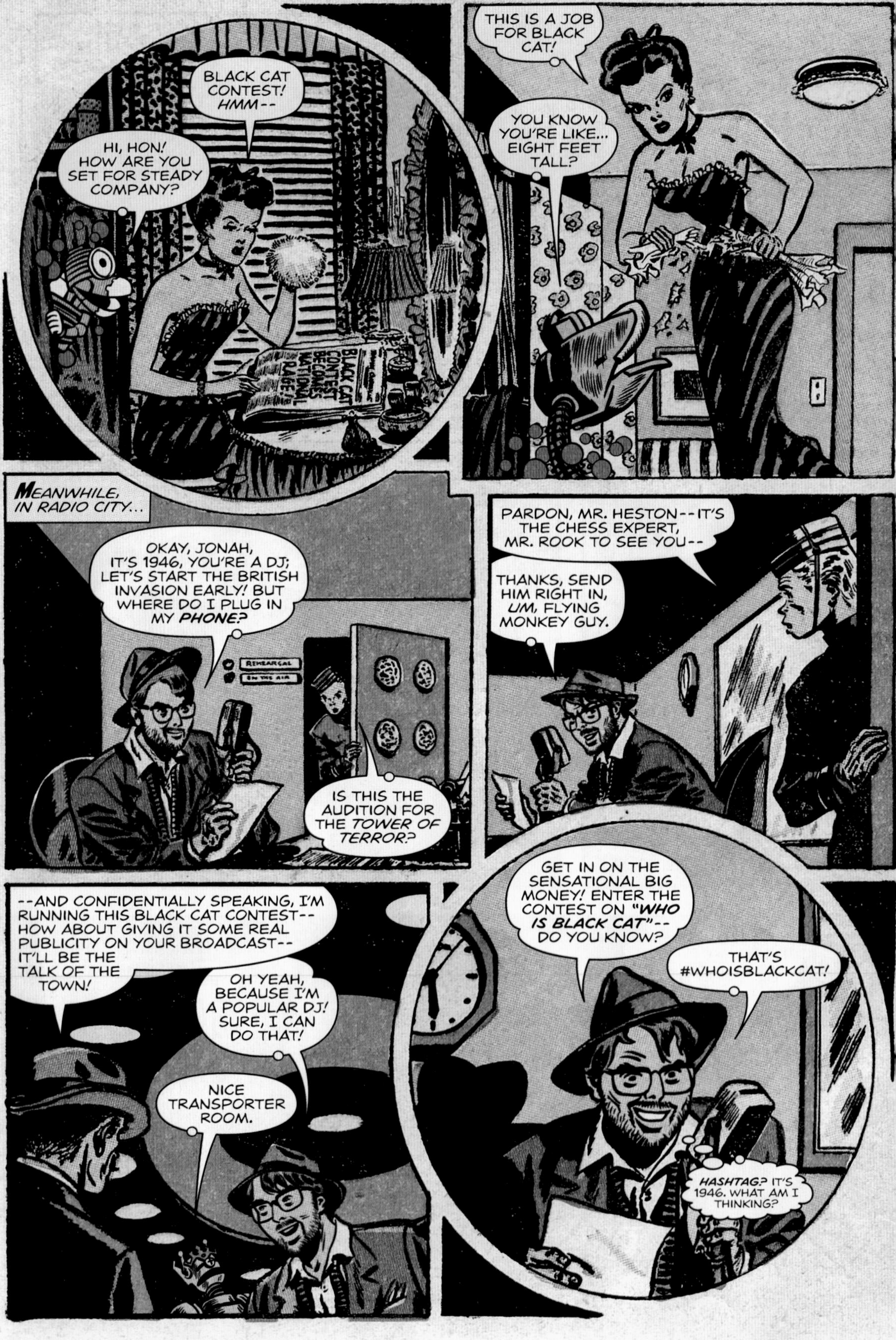
HI, HON! HOW ARE YOU SET FOR STEADY COMPANY?
BLACK CAT CONTEST! HMM--
BLACK CAT CONTEST BECOMES NATIONAL RAGE!
THIS IS A JOB FOR BLACK CAT!
YOU KNOW YOU'RE LIKE... EIGHT FEET TALL?
MEANWHILE, IN RADIO CITY...
OKAY, JONAH, IT'S 1946, YOU'RE A DJ; LET'S START THE BRITISH INVASION EARLY! BUT WHERE DO I PLUG IN MY PHONE?
REHEARSAL
ON THE AIR
IS THIS THE AUDITION FOR THE TOWER OF TERROR?
PARDON, MR. HESTON--IT'S THE CHESS EXPERT, MR. ROOK TO SEE YOU--
THANKS, SEND HIM RIGHT IN, UM, FLYING MONKEY GUY.
--AND CONFIDENTIALLY SPEAKING, I'M RUNNING THIS BLACK CAT CONTEST--HOW ABOUT GIVING IT SOME REAL PUBLICITY ON YOUR BROADCAST--IT'LL BE THE TALK OF THE TOWN!
OH YEAH, BECAUSE I'M A POPULAR DJ! SURE, I CAN DO THAT!
NICE TRANSPORTER ROOM.
GET IN ON THE SENSATIONAL BIG MONEY! ENTER THE CONTEST ON "WHO IS BLACK CAT"--DO YOU KNOW?
THAT'S #WHOISBLACKCAT!
HASHTAG? IT'S 1946. WHAT AM I THINKING?

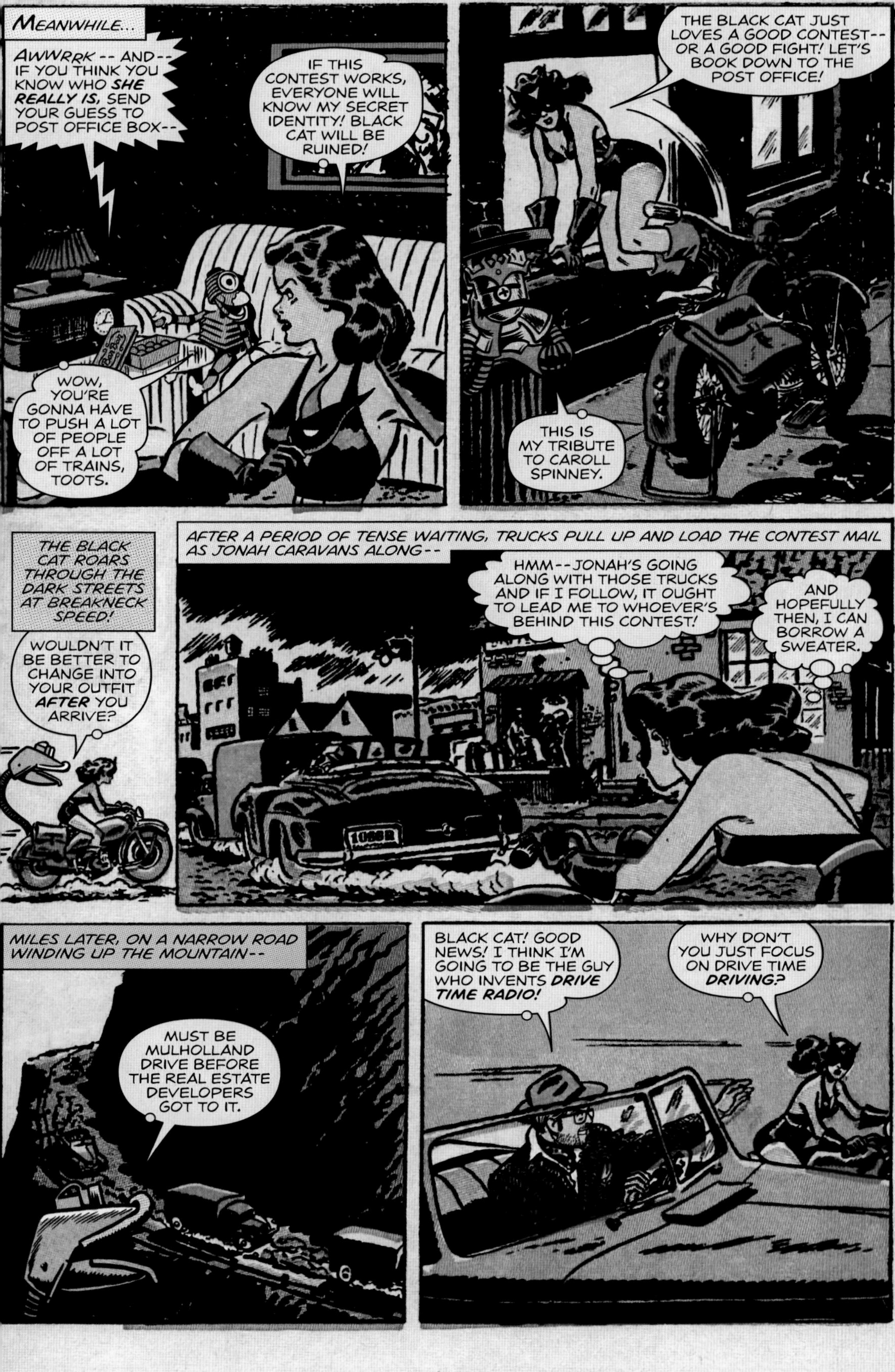
MEANWHILE...
AWWRRK -- AND-- IF YOU THINK YOU KNOW WHO SHE REALLY IS, SEND YOUR GUESS TO POST OFFICE BOX--
IF THIS CONTEST WORKS, EVERYONE WILL KNOW MY SECRET IDENTITY! BLACK CAT WILL BE RUINED!
WOW, YOU'RE GONNA HAVE TO PUSH A LOT OF PEOPLE OFF A LOT OF TRAINS, TOOTS.
THE BLACK CAT JUST LOVES A GOOD CONTEST-- OR A GOOD FIGHT! LET'S BOOK DOWN TO THE POST OFFICE!
THIS IS MY TRIBUTE TO CAROLL SPINNEY.
THE BLACK CAT ROARS THROUGH THE DARK STREETS AT BREAKNECK SPEED!
WOULDN'T IT BE BETTER TO CHANGE INTO YOUR OUTFIT AFTER YOU ARRIVE?
AFTER A PERIOD OF TENSE WAITING, TRUCKS PULL UP AND LOAD THE CONTEST MAIL AS JONAH CARAVANS ALONG--
HMM--JONAH'S GOING ALONG WITH THOSE TRUCKS AND IF I FOLLOW, IT OUGHT TO LEAD ME TO WHOEVER'S BEHIND THIS CONTEST!
AND HOPEFULLY THEN, I CAN BORROW A SWEATER.
MILES LATER, ON A NARROW ROAD WINDING UP THE MOUNTAIN--
MUST BE MULHOLLAND DRIVE BEFORE THE REAL ESTATE DEVELOPERS GOT TO IT.
BLACK CAT! GOOD NEWS! I THINK I'M GOING TO BE THE GUY WHO INVENTS DRIVE TIME RADIO!
WHY DON'T YOU JUST FOCUS ON DRIVE TIME DRIVING?

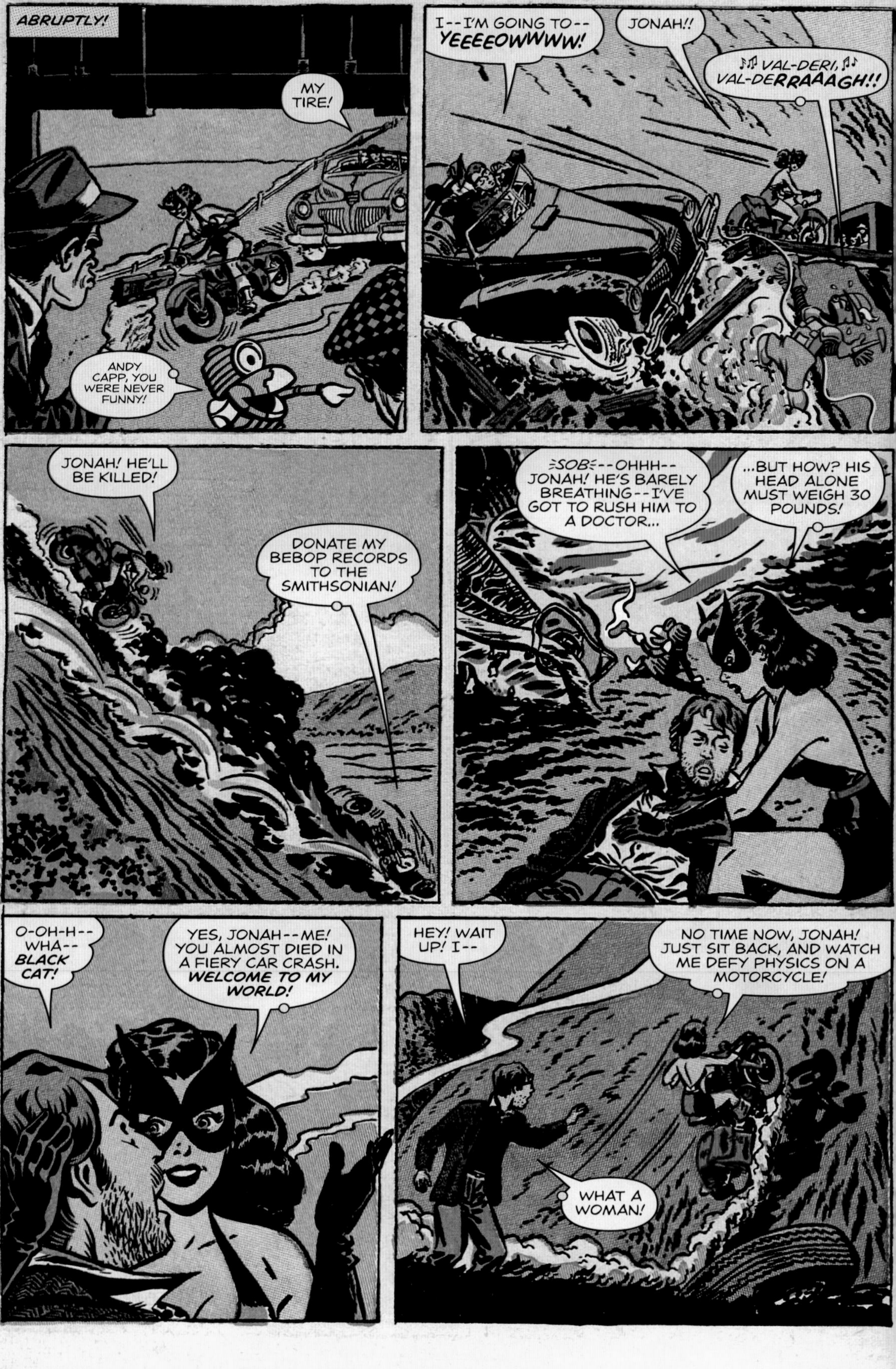
ABRUPTLY!
MY TIRE!
ANDY CAPP, YOU WERE NEVER FUNNY!
I--I'M GOING TO-- YEEEEOWWWW!
JONAH!!
♫ VAL-DERI, ♫ VAL-DERRAAAGH!!
JONAH! HE'LL BE KILLED!
DONATE MY BEBOP RECORDS TO THE SMITHSONIAN!
SOB--OHHH-- JONAH! HE'S BARELY BREATHING--I'VE GOT TO RUSH HIM TO A DOCTOR...
...BUT HOW? HIS HEAD ALONE MUST WEIGH 30 POUNDS!
O-OH-H-- WHA-- BLACK CAT!
YES, JONAH--ME! YOU ALMOST DIED IN A FIERY CAR CRASH. WELCOME TO MY WORLD!
HEY! WAIT UP! I--
NO TIME NOW, JONAH! JUST SIT BACK, AND WATCH ME DEFY PHYSICS ON A MOTORCYCLE!
WHAT A WOMAN!

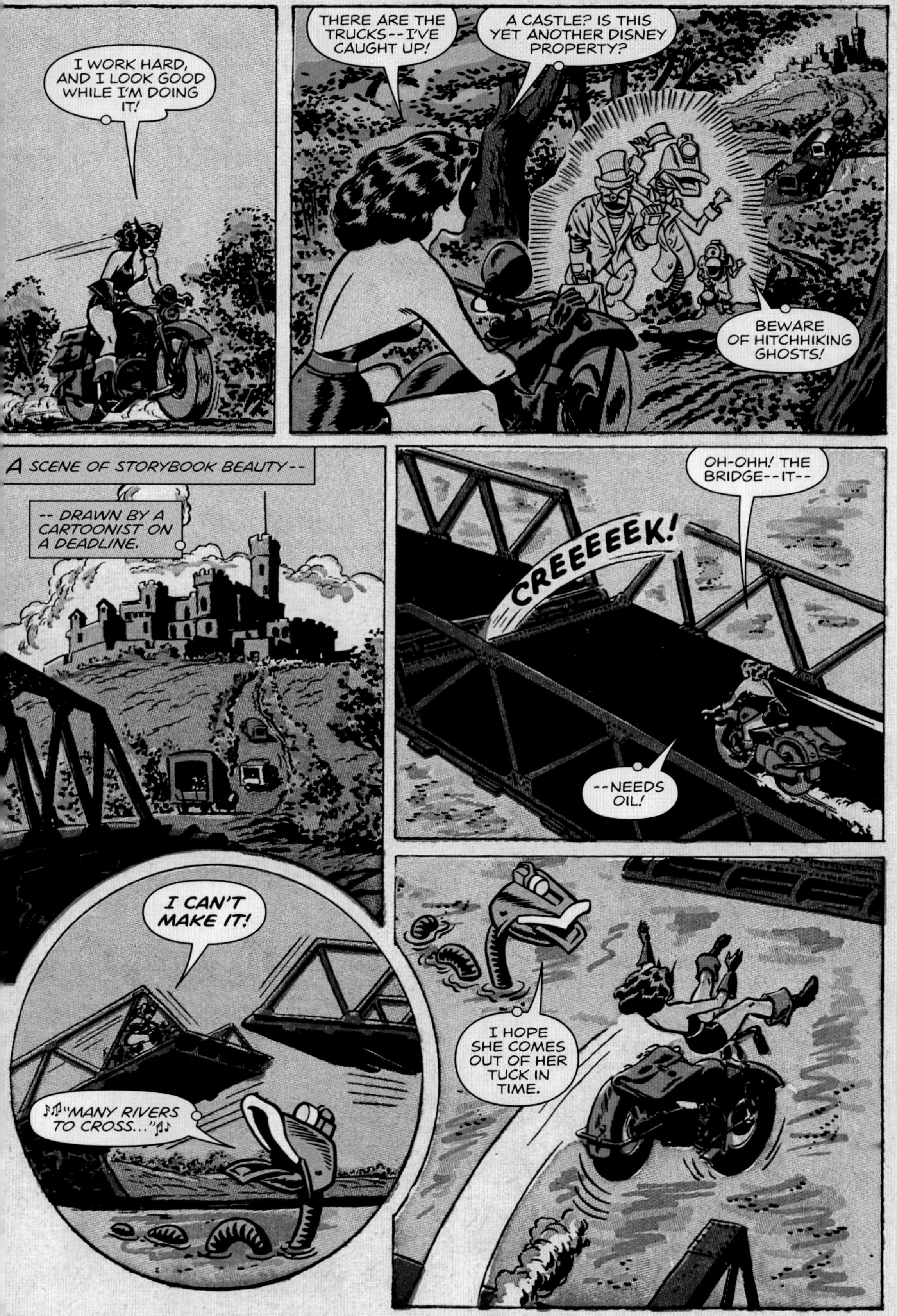
I WORK HARD, AND I LOOK GOOD WHILE I'M DOING IT!
THERE ARE THE TRUCKS--I'VE CAUGHT UP!
A CASTLE? IS THIS YET ANOTHER DISNEY PROPERTY?
BEWARE OF HITCHHIKING GHOSTS!
A SCENE OF STORYBOOK BEAUTY--
--DRAWN BY A CARTOONIST ON A DEADLINE.
OH-OHH! THE BRIDGE--IT--
CREEEEEK!
--NEEDS OIL!
I CAN'T MAKE IT!
♪♫"MANY RIVERS TO CROSS..."♫♪
I HOPE SHE COMES OUT OF HER TUCK IN TIME.

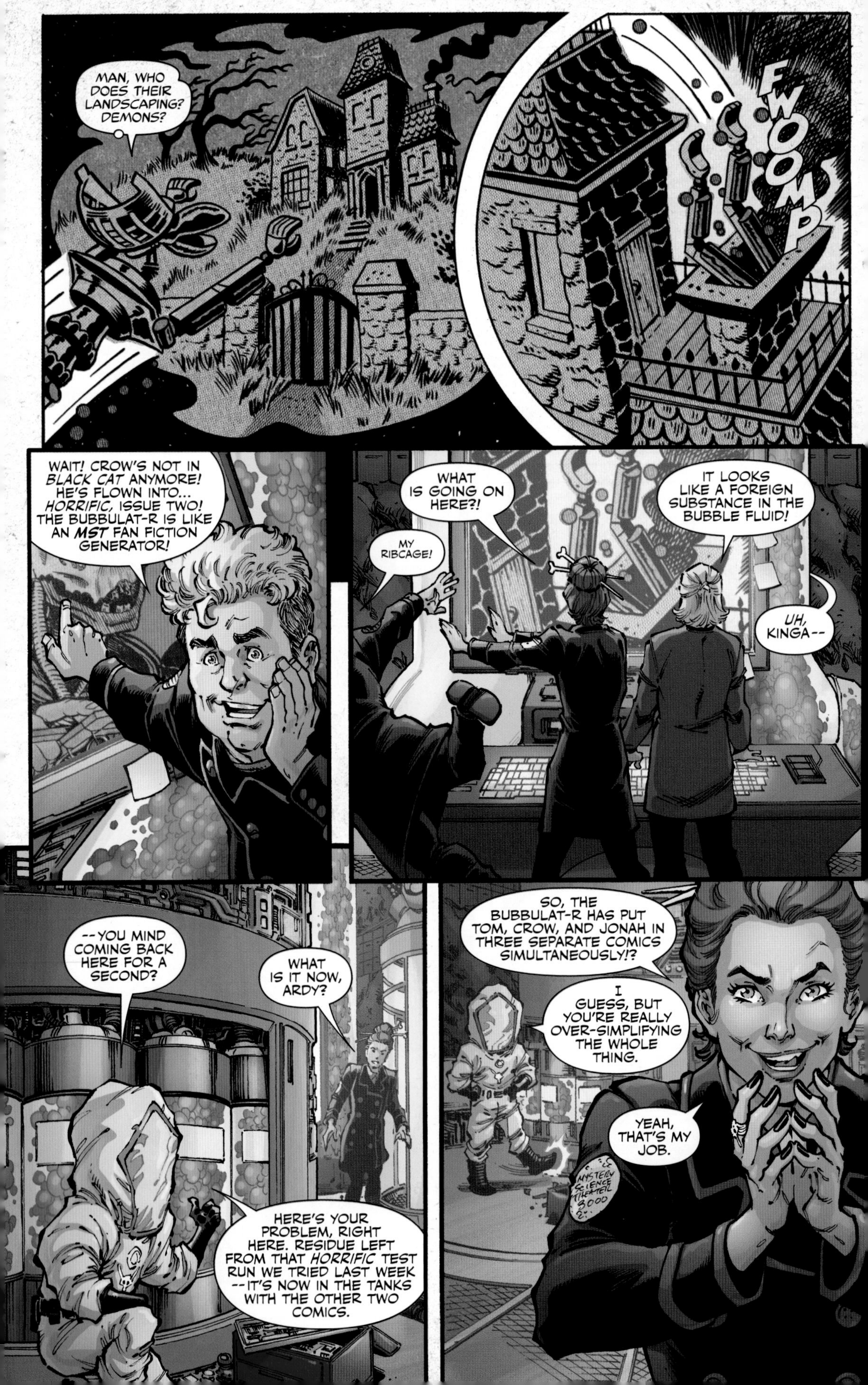
MAN, WHO DOES THEIR LANDSCAPING? DEMONS?
FWOOMP
WAIT! CROW'S NOT IN *BLACK CAT* ANYMORE! HE'S FLOWN INTO... *HORRIFIC*, ISSUE TWO! THE BUBBULAT-R IS LIKE AN ***MST*** FAN FICTION GENERATOR!
WHAT IS GOING ON HERE?!
MY RIBCAGE!
IT LOOKS LIKE A FOREIGN SUBSTANCE IN THE BUBBLE FLUID!
UH, KINGA--
--YOU MIND COMING BACK HERE FOR A SECOND?
WHAT IS IT NOW, ARDY?
HERE'S YOUR PROBLEM, RIGHT HERE. RESIDUE LEFT FROM THAT *HORRIFIC* TEST RUN WE TRIED LAST WEEK --IT'S NOW IN THE TANKS WITH THE OTHER TWO COMICS.
SO, THE BUBBULAT-R HAS PUT TOM, CROW, AND JONAH IN THREE SEPARATE COMICS SIMULTANEOUSLY!?
I GUESS, BUT YOU'RE REALLY OVER-SIMPLIFYING THE WHOLE THING.
YEAH, THAT'S MY JOB.
MYSTERY SCIENCE THEATER 3000

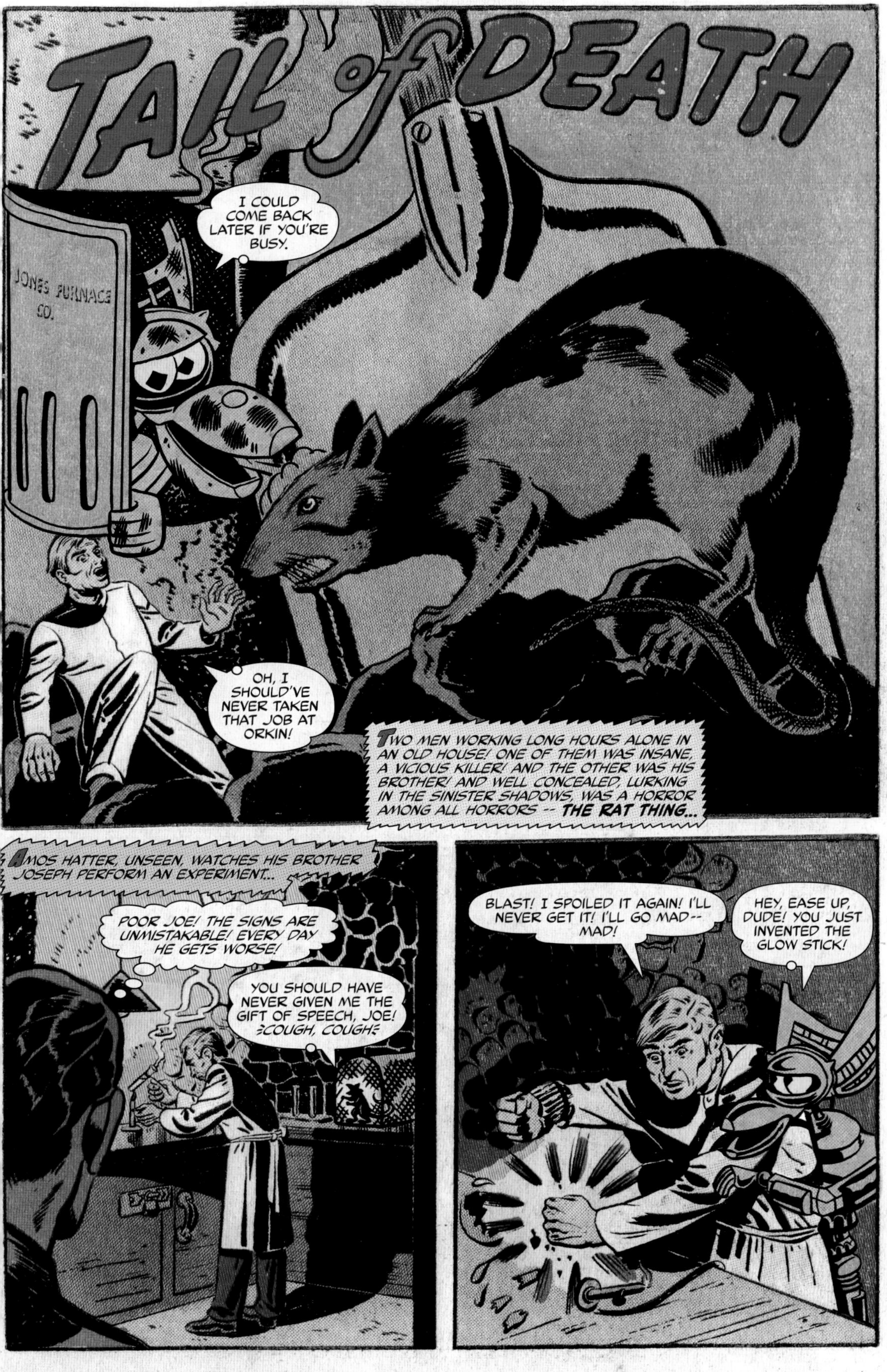
TAIL of DEATH
I COULD COME BACK LATER IF YOU'RE BUSY.
JONES FURNACE CO.
OH, I SHOULD'VE NEVER TAKEN THAT JOB AT ORKIN!
TWO MEN WORKING LONG HOURS ALONE IN AN OLD HOUSE! ONE OF THEM WAS INSANE, A VICIOUS KILLER! AND THE OTHER WAS HIS BROTHER! AND WELL CONCEALED, LURKING IN THE SINISTER SHADOWS, WAS A HORROR AMONG ALL HORRORS -- THE RAT THING...
AMOS HATTER, UNSEEN, WATCHES HIS BROTHER JOSEPH PERFORM AN EXPERIMENT...
POOR JOE! THE SIGNS ARE UNMISTAKABLE! EVERY DAY HE GETS WORSE!
YOU SHOULD HAVE NEVER GIVEN ME THE GIFT OF SPEECH, JOE! ≈COUGH, COUGH≈
BLAST! I SPOILED IT AGAIN! I'LL NEVER GET IT! I'LL GO MAD-- MAD!
HEY, EASE UP, DUDE! YOU JUST INVENTED THE GLOW STICK!

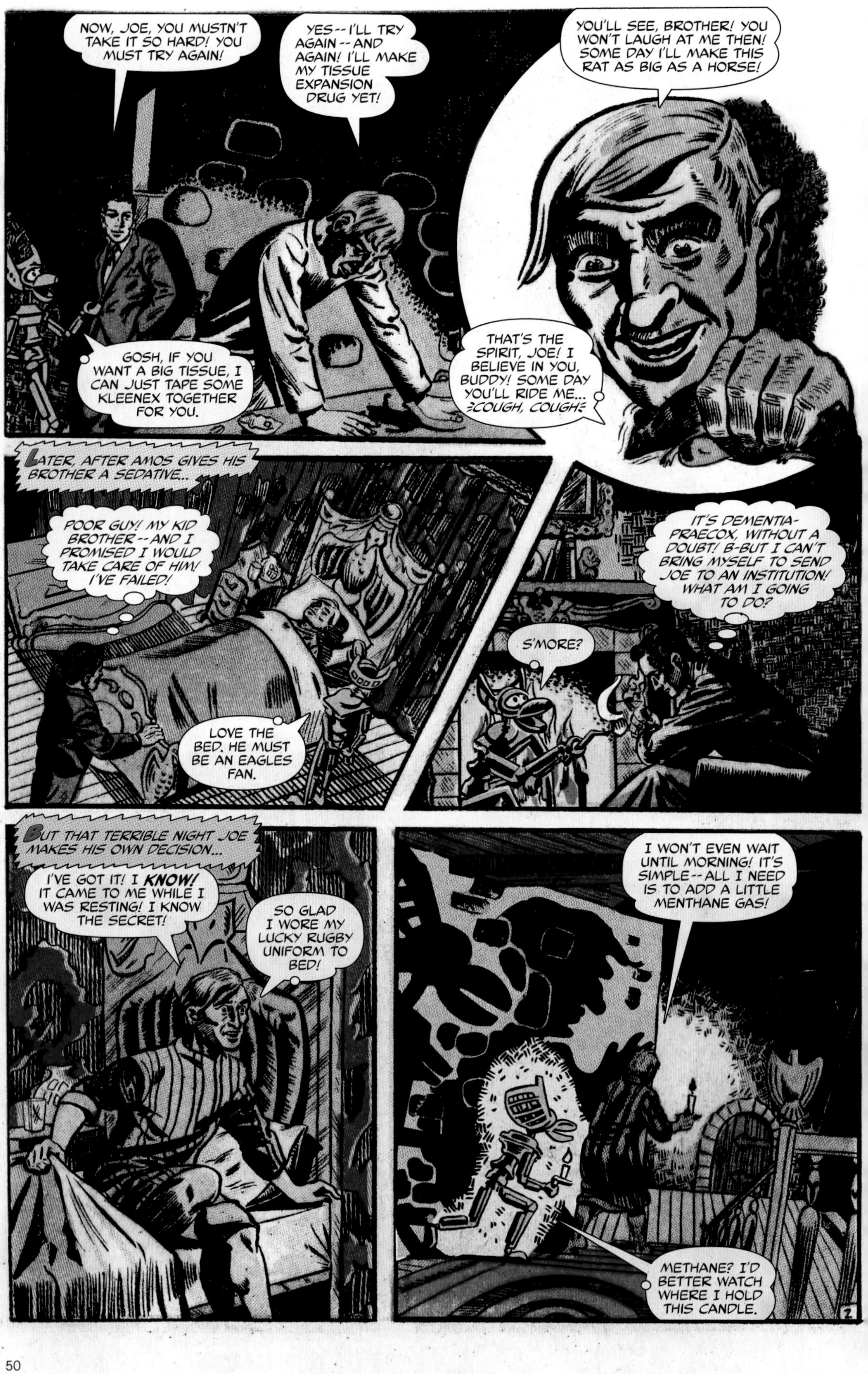
NOW, JOE, YOU MUSTN'T TAKE IT SO HARD! YOU MUST TRY AGAIN!
YES--I'LL TRY AGAIN--AND AGAIN! I'LL MAKE MY TISSUE EXPANSION DRUG YET!
YOU'LL SEE, BROTHER! YOU WON'T LAUGH AT ME THEN! SOME DAY I'LL MAKE THIS RAT AS BIG AS A HORSE!
GOSH, IF YOU WANT A BIG TISSUE, I CAN JUST TAPE SOME KLEENEX TOGETHER FOR YOU.
THAT'S THE SPIRIT, JOE! I BELIEVE IN YOU, BUDDY! SOME DAY YOU'LL RIDE ME... COUGH, COUGH
LATER, AFTER AMOS GIVES HIS BROTHER A SEDATIVE...
POOR GUY! MY KID BROTHER--AND I PROMISED I WOULD TAKE CARE OF HIM! I'VE FAILED!
LOVE THE BED. HE MUST BE AN EAGLES FAN.
IT'S DEMENTIA-PRAECOX, WITHOUT A DOUBT! B-BUT I CAN'T BRING MYSELF TO SEND JOE TO AN INSTITUTION! WHAT AM I GOING TO DO?
S'MORE?
BUT THAT TERRIBLE NIGHT JOE MAKES HIS OWN DECISION...
I'VE GOT IT! I KNOW! IT CAME TO ME WHILE I WAS RESTING! I KNOW THE SECRET!
SO GLAD I WORE MY LUCKY RUGBY UNIFORM TO BED!
I WON'T EVEN WAIT UNTIL MORNING! IT'S SIMPLE--ALL I NEED IS TO ADD A LITTLE MENTHANE GAS!
METHANE? I'D BETTER WATCH WHERE I HOLD THIS CANDLE.
2

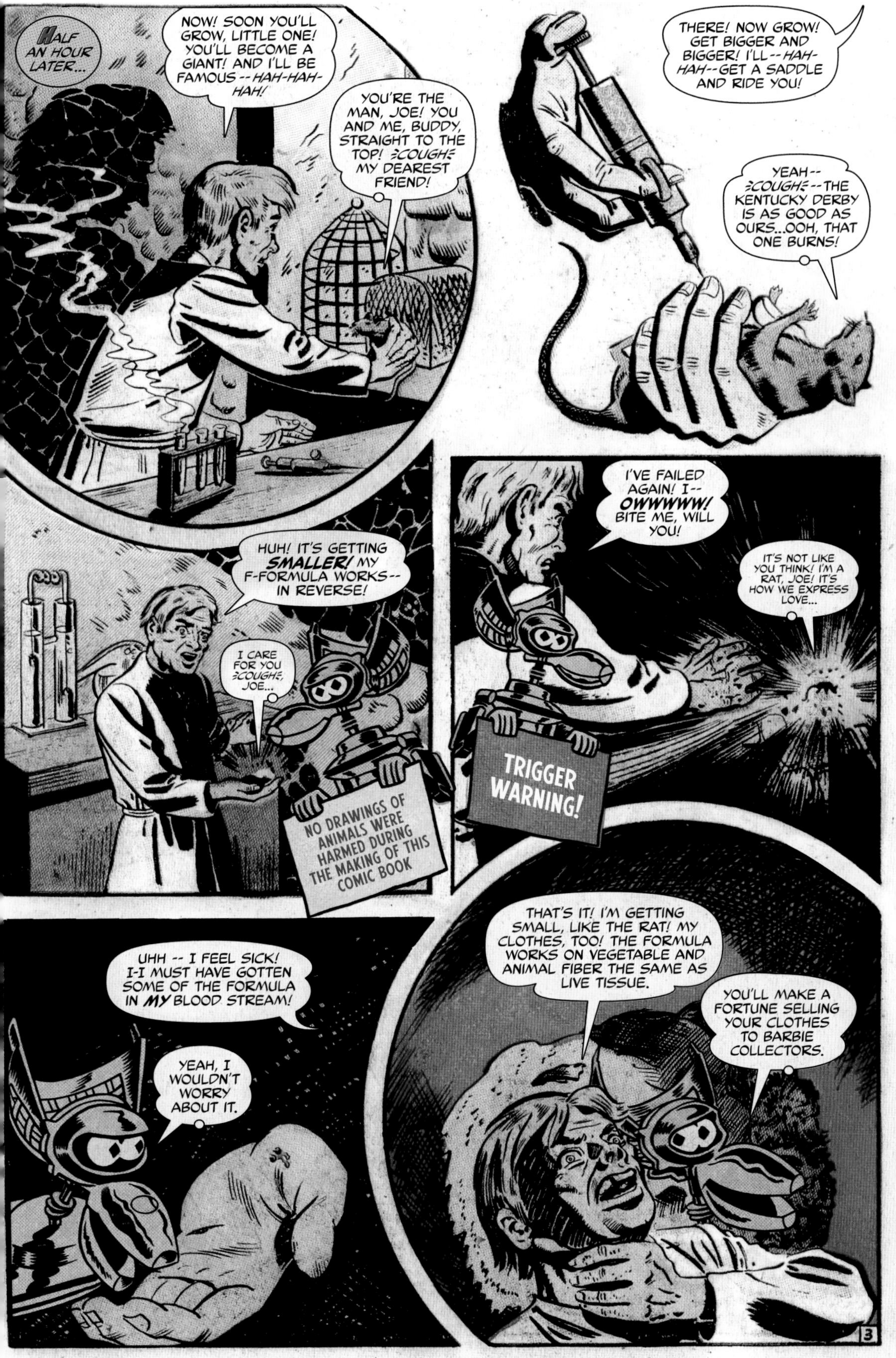
HALF AN HOUR LATER...
NOW! SOON YOU'LL GROW, LITTLE ONE! YOU'LL BECOME A GIANT! AND I'LL BE FAMOUS -- HAH-HAH-HAH!
YOU'RE THE MAN, JOE! YOU AND ME, BUDDY, STRAIGHT TO THE TOP! ≋COUGH≋ MY DEAREST FRIEND!
THERE! NOW GROW! GET BIGGER AND BIGGER! I'LL -- HAH-HAH -- GET A SADDLE AND RIDE YOU!
YEAH -- ≋COUGH≋ -- THE KENTUCKY DERBY IS AS GOOD AS OURS...OOH, THAT ONE BURNS!
HUH! IT'S GETTING SMALLER! MY F-FORMULA WORKS -- IN REVERSE!
I CARE FOR YOU ≋COUGH≋, JOE...
NO DRAWINGS OF ANIMALS WERE HARMED DURING THE MAKING OF THIS COMIC BOOK
I'VE FAILED AGAIN! I-- OWWWWW! BITE ME, WILL YOU!
IT'S NOT LIKE YOU THINK! I'M A RAT, JOE! IT'S HOW WE EXPRESS LOVE...
TRIGGER WARNING!
UHH -- I FEEL SICK! I-I MUST HAVE GOTTEN SOME OF THE FORMULA IN MY BLOOD STREAM!
YEAH, I WOULDN'T WORRY ABOUT IT.
THAT'S IT! I'M GETTING SMALL, LIKE THE RAT! MY CLOTHES, TOO! THE FORMULA WORKS ON VEGETABLE AND ANIMAL FIBER THE SAME AS LIVE TISSUE.
YOU'LL MAKE A FORTUNE SELLING YOUR CLOTHES TO BARBIE COLLECTORS.
3

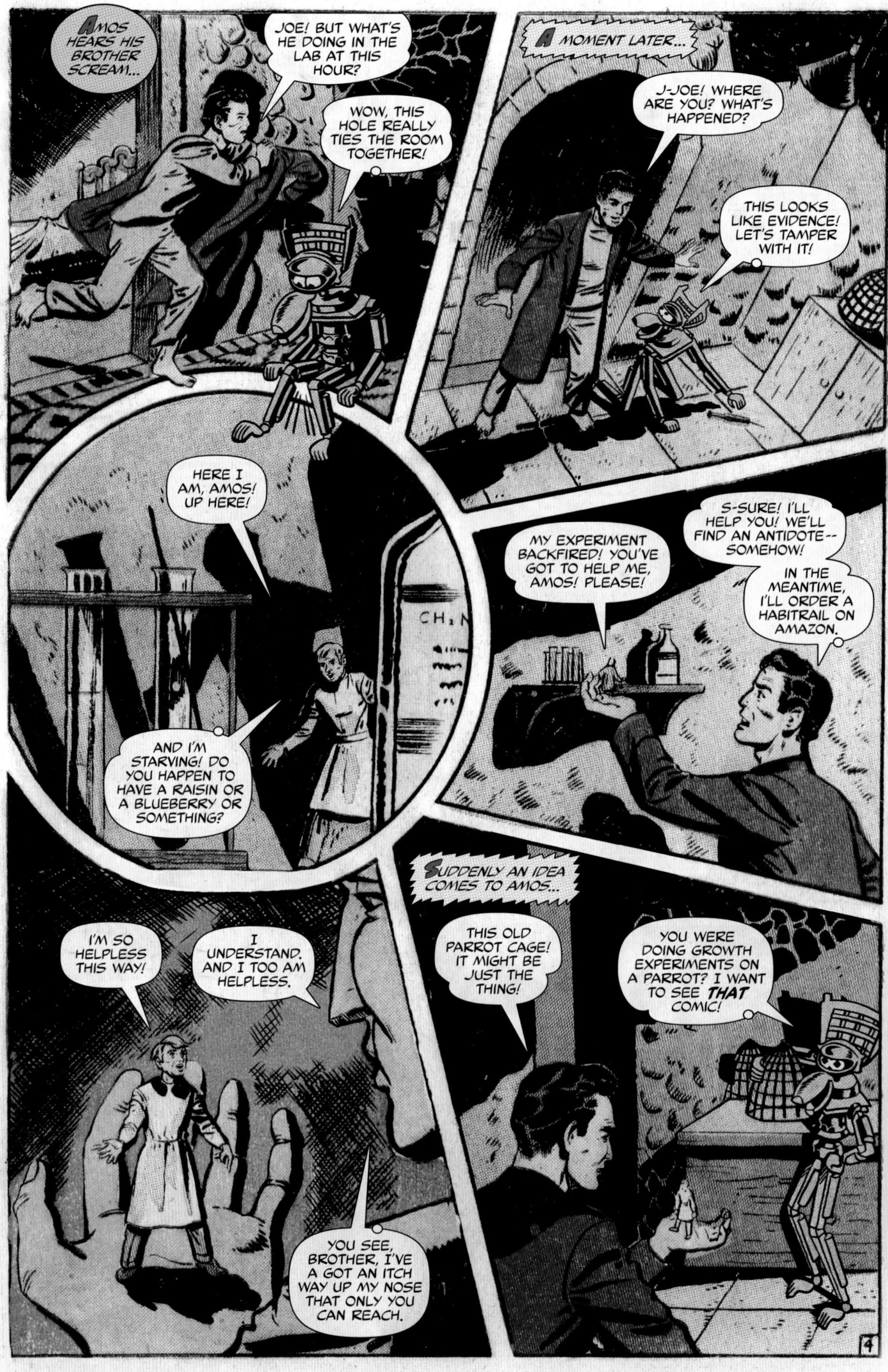
AMOS HEARS HIS BROTHER SCREAM...
JOE! BUT WHAT'S HE DOING IN THE LAB AT THIS HOUR?
WOW, THIS HOLE REALLY TIES THE ROOM TOGETHER!
A MOMENT LATER...
J-JOE! WHERE ARE YOU? WHAT'S HAPPENED?
THIS LOOKS LIKE EVIDENCE! LET'S TAMPER WITH IT!
HERE I AM, AMOS! UP HERE!
AND I'M STARVING! DO YOU HAPPEN TO HAVE A RAISIN OR A BLUEBERRY OR SOMETHING?
MY EXPERIMENT BACKFIRED! YOU'VE GOT TO HELP ME, AMOS! PLEASE!
S-SURE! I'LL HELP YOU! WE'LL FIND AN ANTIDOTE-- SOMEHOW!
IN THE MEANTIME, I'LL ORDER A HABITRAIL ON AMAZON.
I'M SO HELPLESS THIS WAY!
I UNDERSTAND. AND I TOO AM HELPLESS.
YOU SEE, BROTHER, I'VE A GOT AN ITCH WAY UP MY NOSE THAT ONLY YOU CAN REACH.
SUDDENLY AN IDEA COMES TO AMOS...
THIS OLD PARROT CAGE! IT MIGHT BE JUST THE THING!
YOU WERE DOING GROWTH EXPERIMENTS ON A PARROT? I WANT TO SEE THAT COMIC!
4

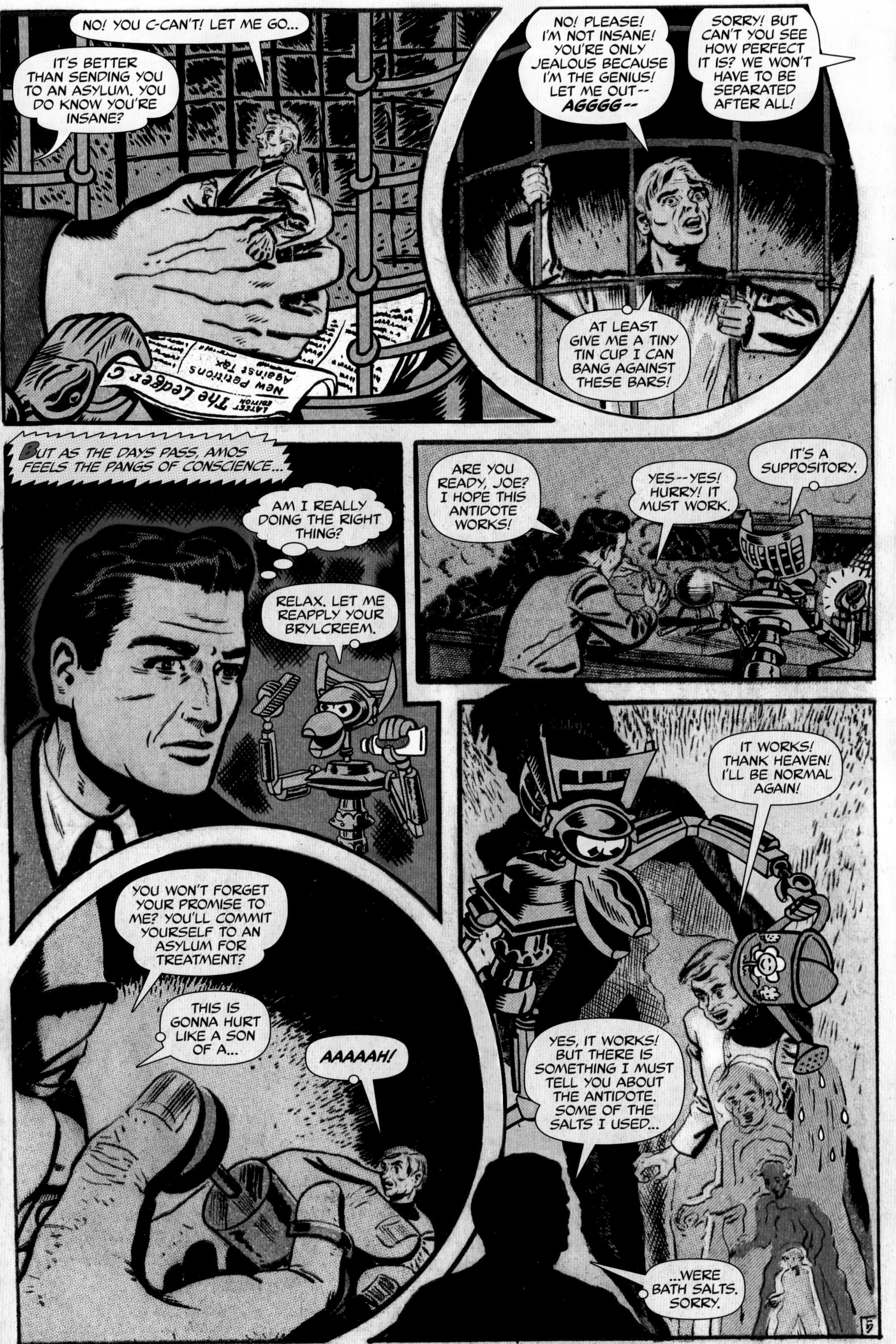
NO! YOU C-CAN'T! LET ME GO...
IT'S BETTER THAN SENDING YOU TO AN ASYLUM. YOU DO KNOW YOU'RE INSANE?
LATEST EDITION The Ledger
New Petitions Against Tax
NO! PLEASE! I'M NOT INSANE! YOU'RE ONLY JEALOUS BECAUSE I'M THE GENIUS! LET ME OUT-- AGGGG--
SORRY! BUT CAN'T YOU SEE HOW PERFECT IT IS? WE WON'T HAVE TO BE SEPARATED AFTER ALL!
AT LEAST GIVE ME A TINY TIN CUP I CAN BANG AGAINST THESE BARS!
BUT AS THE DAYS PASS, AMOS FEELS THE PANGS OF CONSCIENCE...
AM I REALLY DOING THE RIGHT THING?
RELAX. LET ME REAPPLY YOUR BRYLCREEM.
ARE YOU READY, JOE? I HOPE THIS ANTIDOTE WORKS!
YES--YES! HURRY! IT MUST WORK.
IT'S A SUPPOSITORY.
IT WORKS! THANK HEAVEN! I'LL BE NORMAL AGAIN!
YOU WON'T FORGET YOUR PROMISE TO ME? YOU'LL COMMIT YOURSELF TO AN ASYLUM FOR TREATMENT?
THIS IS GONNA HURT LIKE A SON OF A...
AAAAAH!
YES, IT WORKS! BUT THERE IS SOMETHING I MUST TELL YOU ABOUT THE ANTIDOTE. SOME OF THE SALTS I USED...
...WERE BATH SALTS. SORRY.

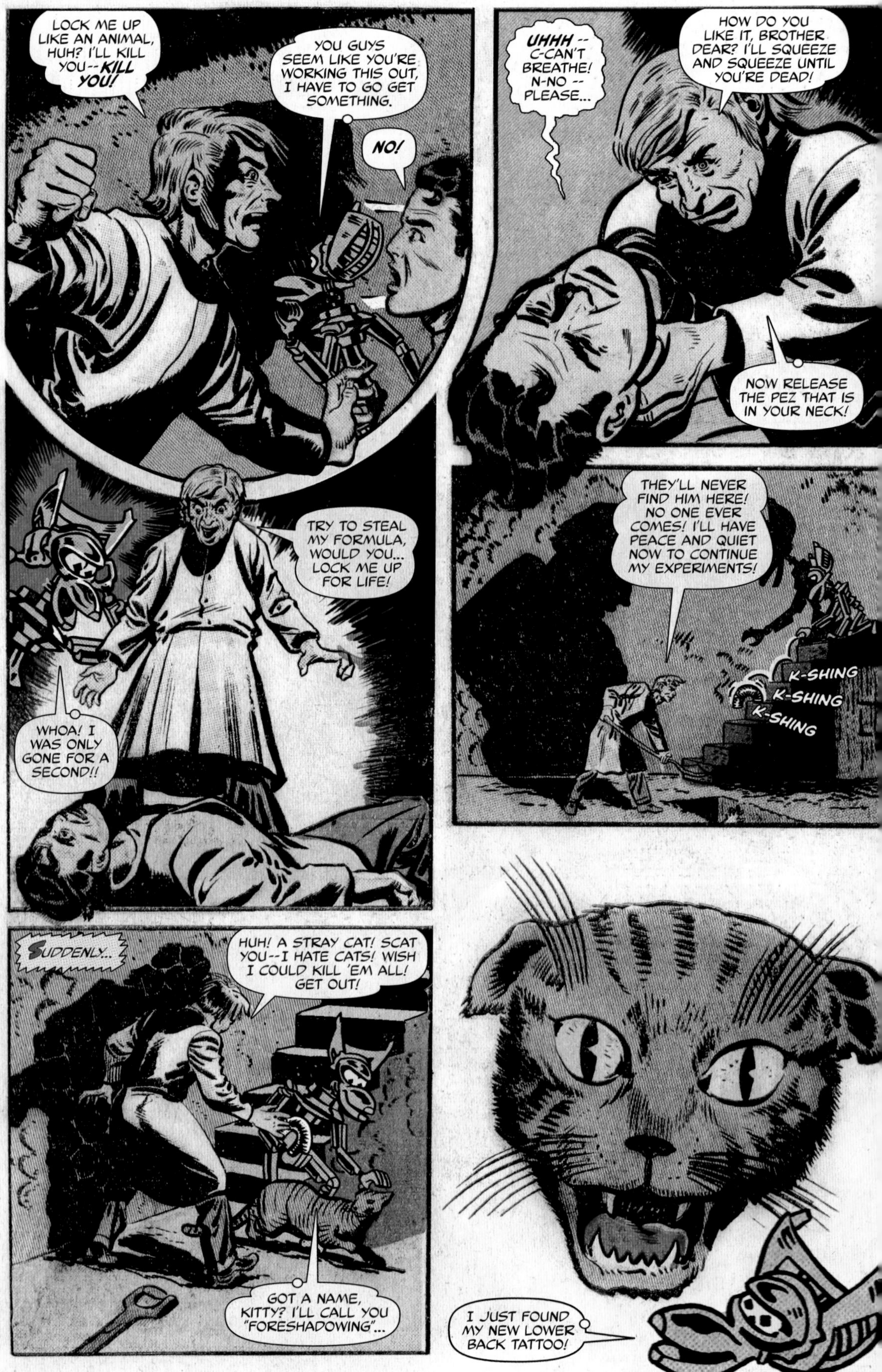

LOCK ME UP LIKE AN ANIMAL, HUH? I'LL KILL YOU--KILL YOU!
YOU GUYS SEEM LIKE YOU'RE WORKING THIS OUT, I HAVE TO GO GET SOMETHING.
NO!
UHHH -- C-CAN'T BREATHE! N-NO -- PLEASE...
HOW DO YOU LIKE IT, BROTHER DEAR? I'LL SQUEEZE AND SQUEEZE UNTIL YOU'RE DEAD!
NOW RELEASE THE PEZ THAT IS IN YOUR NECK!
TRY TO STEAL MY FORMULA, WOULD YOU... LOCK ME UP FOR LIFE!
WHOA! I WAS ONLY GONE FOR A SECOND!!
THEY'LL NEVER FIND HIM HERE! NO ONE EVER COMES! I'LL HAVE PEACE AND QUIET NOW TO CONTINUE MY EXPERIMENTS!
K-SHING
K-SHING
K-SHING
SUDDENLY...
HUH! A STRAY CAT! SCAT YOU--I HATE CATS! WISH I COULD KILL 'EM ALL! GET OUT!
GOT A NAME, KITTY? I'LL CALL YOU "FORESHADOWING"...
I JUST FOUND MY NEW LOWER BACK TATTOO!

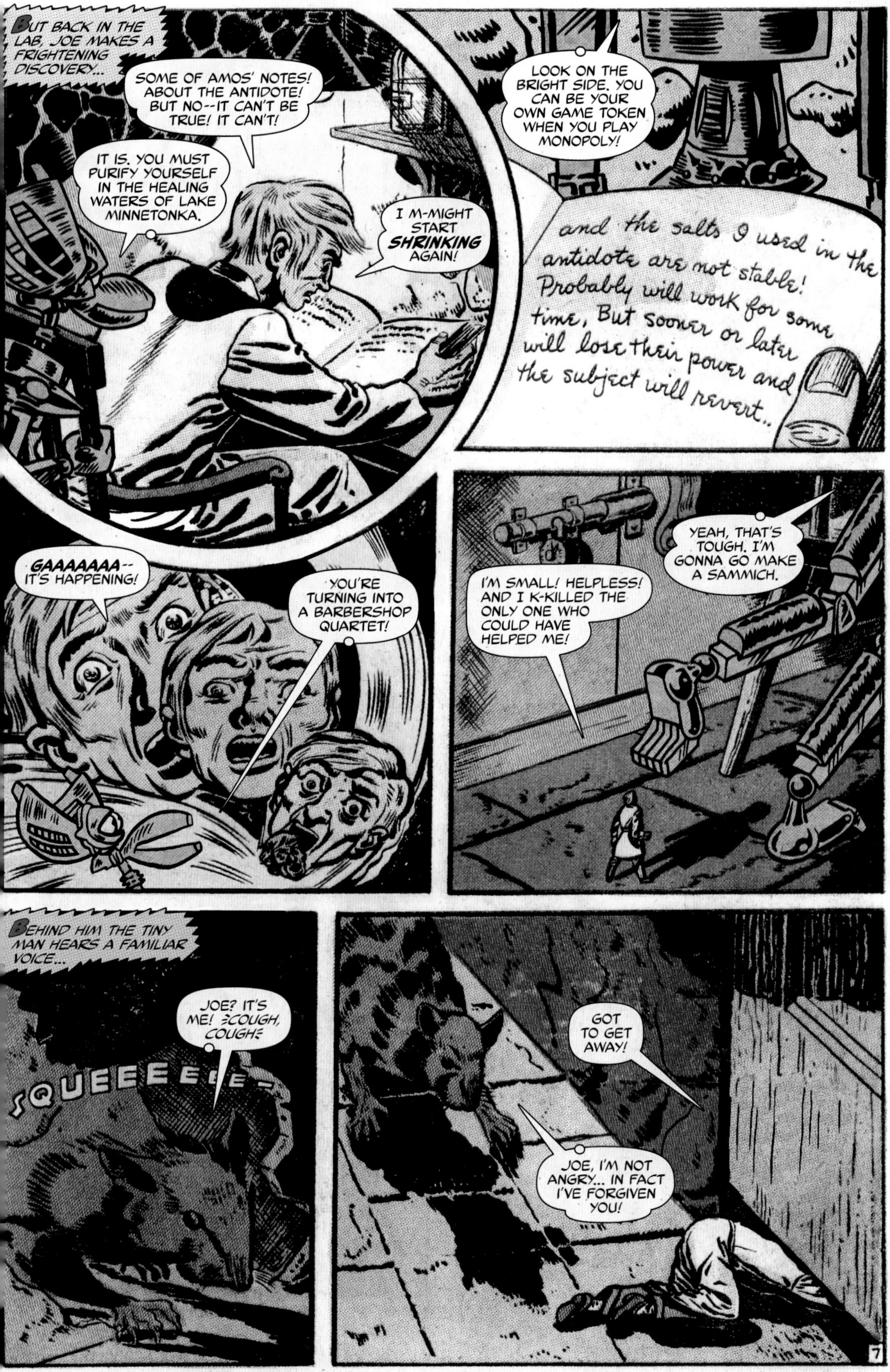
BUT BACK IN THE LAB, JOE MAKES A FRIGHTENING DISCOVERY...
SOME OF AMOS' NOTES! ABOUT THE ANTIDOTE! BUT NO--IT CAN'T BE TRUE! IT CAN'T!
IT IS. YOU MUST PURIFY YOURSELF IN THE HEALING WATERS OF LAKE MINNETONKA.
I M-MIGHT START SHRINKING AGAIN!
LOOK ON THE BRIGHT SIDE. YOU CAN BE YOUR OWN GAME TOKEN WHEN YOU PLAY MONOPOLY!
and the salts I used in the antidote are not stable! Probably will work for some time, But sooner or later will lose their power and the subject will revert..
GAAAAAAA-- IT'S HAPPENING!
YOU'RE TURNING INTO A BARBERSHOP QUARTET!
I'M SMALL! HELPLESS! AND I K-KILLED THE ONLY ONE WHO COULD HAVE HELPED ME!
YEAH, THAT'S TOUGH. I'M GONNA GO MAKE A SAMMICH.
BEHIND HIM THE TINY MAN HEARS A FAMILIAR VOICE...
JOE? IT'S ME! COUGH, COUGH
SQUEEEEEEE-
GOT TO GET AWAY!
JOE, I'M NOT ANGRY... IN FACT I'VE FORGIVEN YOU!
7

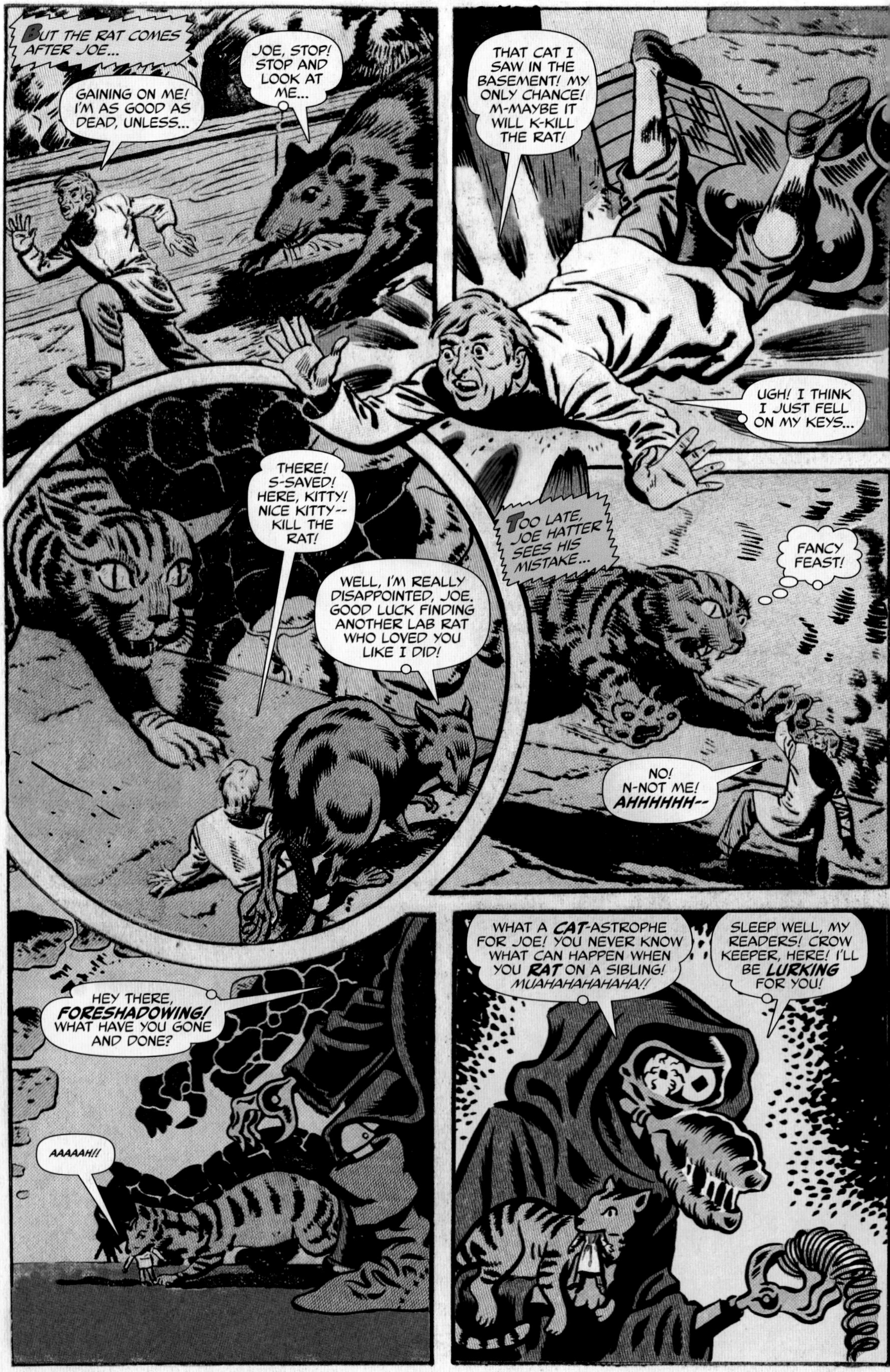

BUT THE RAT COMES AFTER JOE...
GAINING ON ME! I'M AS GOOD AS DEAD, UNLESS...
JOE, STOP! STOP AND LOOK AT ME...
THAT CAT I SAW IN THE BASEMENT! MY ONLY CHANCE! M-MAYBE IT WILL K-KILL THE RAT!
UGH! I THINK I JUST FELL ON MY KEYS...
THERE! S-SAVED! HERE, KITTY! NICE KITTY-- KILL THE RAT!
WELL, I'M REALLY DISAPPOINTED, JOE. GOOD LUCK FINDING ANOTHER LAB RAT WHO LOVED YOU LIKE I DID!
TOO LATE, JOE HATTER SEES HIS MISTAKE...
FANCY FEAST!
NO! N-NOT ME! AHHHHHH--
HEY THERE, FORESHADOWING! WHAT HAVE YOU GONE AND DONE?
AAAAAH!!
WHAT A CAT-ASTROPHE FOR JOE! YOU NEVER KNOW WHAT CAN HAPPEN WHEN YOU RAT ON A SIBLING! MUAHAHAHAHAHA!!
SLEEP WELL, MY READERS! CROW KEEPER, HERE! I'LL BE LURKING FOR YOU!

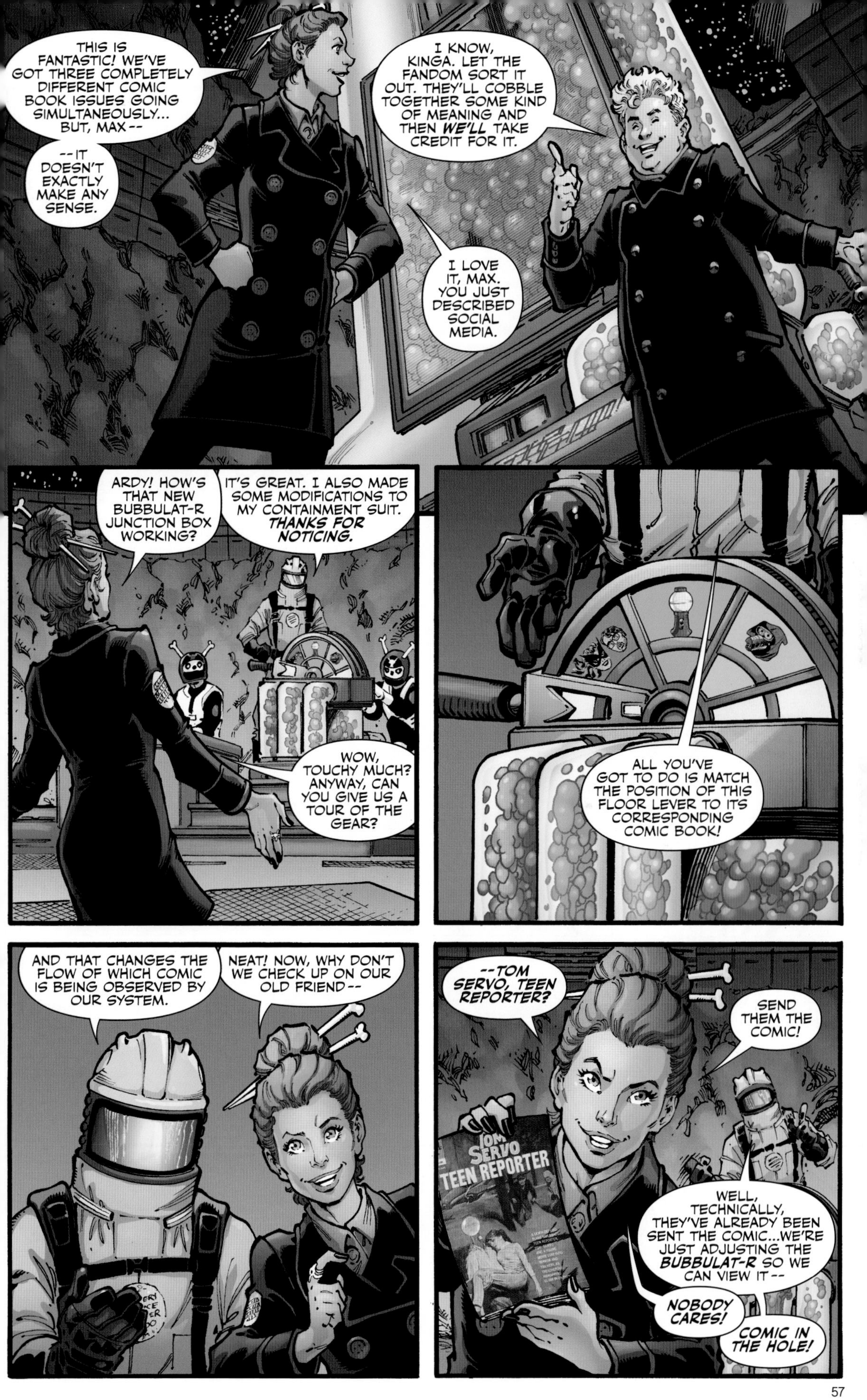
THIS IS FANTASTIC! WE'VE GOT THREE COMPLETELY DIFFERENT COMIC BOOK ISSUES GOING SIMULTANEOUSLY... BUT, MAX--
--IT DOESN'T EXACTLY MAKE ANY SENSE.
I KNOW, KINGA. LET THE FANDOM SORT IT OUT. THEY'LL COBBLE TOGETHER SOME KIND OF MEANING AND THEN WE'LL TAKE CREDIT FOR IT.
I LOVE IT, MAX. YOU JUST DESCRIBED SOCIAL MEDIA.
ARDY! HOW'S THAT NEW BUBBULAT-R JUNCTION BOX WORKING?
IT'S GREAT. I ALSO MADE SOME MODIFICATIONS TO MY CONTAINMENT SUIT. THANKS FOR NOTICING.
WOW, TOUCHY MUCH? ANYWAY, CAN YOU GIVE US A TOUR OF THE GEAR?
ALL YOU'VE GOT TO DO IS MATCH THE POSITION OF THIS FLOOR LEVER TO ITS CORRESPONDING COMIC BOOK!
AND THAT CHANGES THE FLOW OF WHICH COMIC IS BEING OBSERVED BY OUR SYSTEM.
NEAT! NOW, WHY DON'T WE CHECK UP ON OUR OLD FRIEND--
--TOM SERVO, TEEN REPORTER?
TOM SERVO TEEN REPORTER
SEND THEM THE COMIC!
WELL, TECHNICALLY, THEY'VE ALREADY BEEN SENT THE COMIC...WE'RE JUST ADJUSTING THE BUBBULAT-R SO WE CAN VIEW IT--
NOBODY CARES!
COMIC IN THE HOLE!

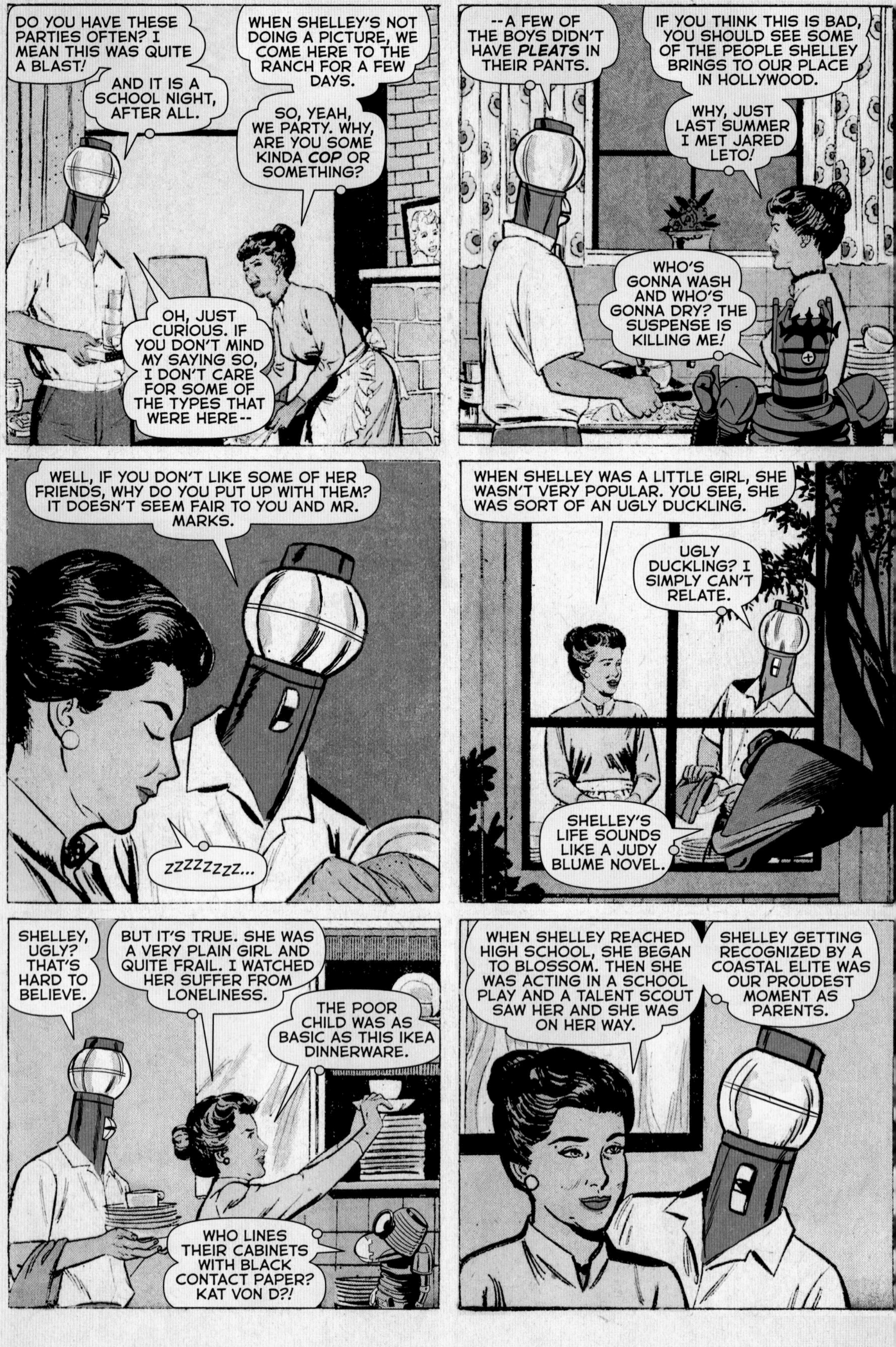
DO YOU HAVE THESE PARTIES OFTEN? I MEAN THIS WAS QUITE A BLAST!
AND IT IS A SCHOOL NIGHT, AFTER ALL.
WHEN SHELLEY'S NOT DOING A PICTURE, WE COME HERE TO THE RANCH FOR A FEW DAYS.
SO, YEAH, WE PARTY. WHY, ARE YOU SOME KINDA *COP* OR SOMETHING?
OH, JUST CURIOUS. IF YOU DON'T MIND MY SAYING SO, I DON'T CARE FOR SOME OF THE TYPES THAT WERE HERE--
--A FEW OF THE BOYS DIDN'T HAVE *PLEATS* IN THEIR PANTS.
IF YOU THINK THIS IS BAD, YOU SHOULD SEE SOME OF THE PEOPLE SHELLEY BRINGS TO OUR PLACE IN HOLLYWOOD.
WHY, JUST LAST SUMMER I MET JARED LETO!
WHO'S GONNA WASH AND WHO'S GONNA DRY? THE SUSPENSE IS KILLING ME!
WELL, IF YOU DON'T LIKE SOME OF HER FRIENDS, WHY DO YOU PUT UP WITH THEM? IT DOESN'T SEEM FAIR TO YOU AND MR. MARKS.
ZZZZZZZZ...
WHEN SHELLEY WAS A LITTLE GIRL, SHE WASN'T VERY POPULAR. YOU SEE, SHE WAS SORT OF AN UGLY DUCKLING.
UGLY DUCKLING? I SIMPLY CAN'T RELATE.
SHELLEY'S LIFE SOUNDS LIKE A JUDY BLUME NOVEL.
SHELLEY, UGLY? THAT'S HARD TO BELIEVE.
BUT IT'S TRUE. SHE WAS A VERY PLAIN GIRL AND QUITE FRAIL. I WATCHED HER SUFFER FROM LONELINESS.
THE POOR CHILD WAS AS BASIC AS THIS IKEA DINNERWARE.
WHO LINES THEIR CABINETS WITH BLACK CONTACT PAPER? KAT VON D?!
WHEN SHELLEY REACHED HIGH SCHOOL, SHE BEGAN TO BLOSSOM. THEN SHE WAS ACTING IN A SCHOOL PLAY AND A TALENT SCOUT SAW HER AND SHE WAS ON HER WAY.
SHELLEY GETTING RECOGNIZED BY A COASTAL ELITE WAS OUR PROUDEST MOMENT AS PARENTS.

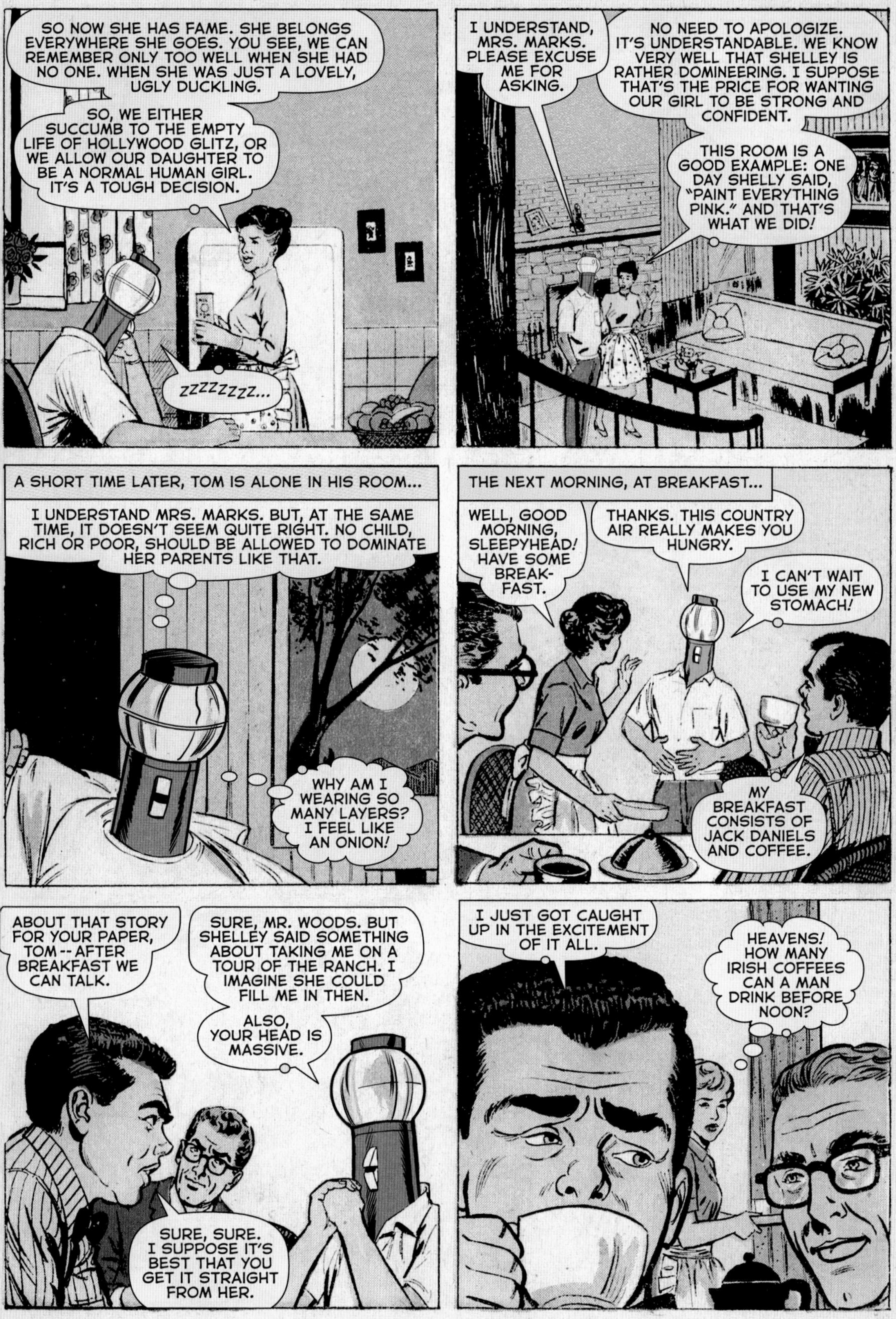

SO NOW SHE HAS FAME. SHE BELONGS EVERYWHERE SHE GOES. YOU SEE, WE CAN REMEMBER ONLY TOO WELL WHEN SHE HAD NO ONE. WHEN SHE WAS JUST A LOVELY, UGLY DUCKLING.
SO, WE EITHER SUCCUMB TO THE EMPTY LIFE OF HOLLYWOOD GLITZ, OR WE ALLOW OUR DAUGHTER TO BE A NORMAL HUMAN GIRL. IT'S A TOUGH DECISION.
ZZZZZZZZ...
I UNDERSTAND, MRS. MARKS. PLEASE EXCUSE ME FOR ASKING.
NO NEED TO APOLOGIZE. IT'S UNDERSTANDABLE. WE KNOW VERY WELL THAT SHELLEY IS RATHER DOMINEERING. I SUPPOSE THAT'S THE PRICE FOR WANTING OUR GIRL TO BE STRONG AND CONFIDENT.
THIS ROOM IS A GOOD EXAMPLE: ONE DAY SHELLY SAID, "PAINT EVERYTHING PINK." AND THAT'S WHAT WE DID!
A SHORT TIME LATER, TOM IS ALONE IN HIS ROOM...
I UNDERSTAND MRS. MARKS. BUT, AT THE SAME TIME, IT DOESN'T SEEM QUITE RIGHT. NO CHILD, RICH OR POOR, SHOULD BE ALLOWED TO DOMINATE HER PARENTS LIKE THAT.
WHY AM I WEARING SO MANY LAYERS? I FEEL LIKE AN ONION!
THE NEXT MORNING, AT BREAKFAST...
WELL, GOOD MORNING, SLEEPYHEAD! HAVE SOME BREAK-FAST.
THANKS. THIS COUNTRY AIR REALLY MAKES YOU HUNGRY.
I CAN'T WAIT TO USE MY NEW STOMACH!
MY BREAKFAST CONSISTS OF JACK DANIELS AND COFFEE.
ABOUT THAT STORY FOR YOUR PAPER, TOM -- AFTER BREAKFAST WE CAN TALK.
SURE, MR. WOODS. BUT SHELLEY SAID SOMETHING ABOUT TAKING ME ON A TOUR OF THE RANCH. I IMAGINE SHE COULD FILL ME IN THEN.
ALSO, YOUR HEAD IS MASSIVE.
SURE, SURE. I SUPPOSE IT'S BEST THAT YOU GET IT STRAIGHT FROM HER.
I JUST GOT CAUGHT UP IN THE EXCITEMENT OF IT ALL.
HEAVENS! HOW MANY IRISH COFFEES CAN A MAN DRINK BEFORE NOON?

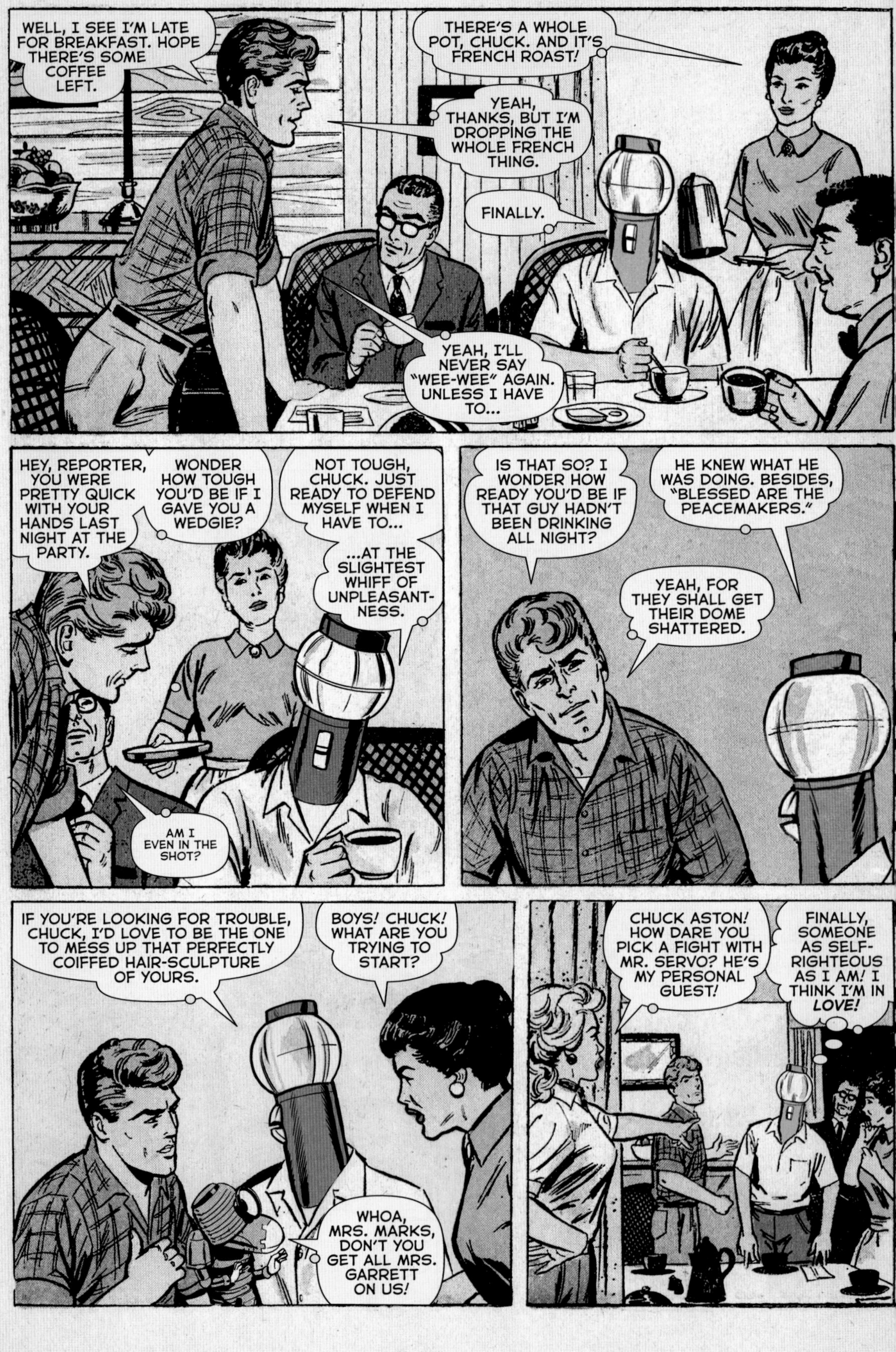
WELL, I SEE I'M LATE FOR BREAKFAST. HOPE THERE'S SOME COFFEE LEFT.
THERE'S A WHOLE POT, CHUCK. AND IT'S FRENCH ROAST!
YEAH, THANKS, BUT I'M DROPPING THE WHOLE FRENCH THING.
FINALLY.
YEAH, I'LL NEVER SAY "WEE-WEE" AGAIN. UNLESS I HAVE TO...
HEY, REPORTER, YOU WERE PRETTY QUICK WITH YOUR HANDS LAST NIGHT AT THE PARTY.
WONDER HOW TOUGH YOU'D BE IF I GAVE YOU A WEDGIE?
NOT TOUGH, CHUCK. JUST READY TO DEFEND MYSELF WHEN I HAVE TO...
...AT THE SLIGHTEST WHIFF OF UNPLEASANT-NESS.
AM I EVEN IN THE SHOT?
IS THAT SO? I WONDER HOW READY YOU'D BE IF THAT GUY HADN'T BEEN DRINKING ALL NIGHT?
HE KNEW WHAT HE WAS DOING. BESIDES, "BLESSED ARE THE PEACEMAKERS."
YEAH, FOR THEY SHALL GET THEIR DOME SHATTERED.
IF YOU'RE LOOKING FOR TROUBLE, CHUCK, I'D LOVE TO BE THE ONE TO MESS UP THAT PERFECTLY COIFFED HAIR-SCULPTURE OF YOURS.
BOYS! CHUCK! WHAT ARE YOU TRYING TO START?
WHOA, MRS. MARKS, DON'T YOU GET ALL MRS. GARRETT ON US!
CHUCK ASTON! HOW DARE YOU PICK A FIGHT WITH MR. SERVO? HE'S MY PERSONAL GUEST!
FINALLY, SOMEONE AS SELF-RIGHTEOUS AS I AM! I THINK I'M IN LOVE!

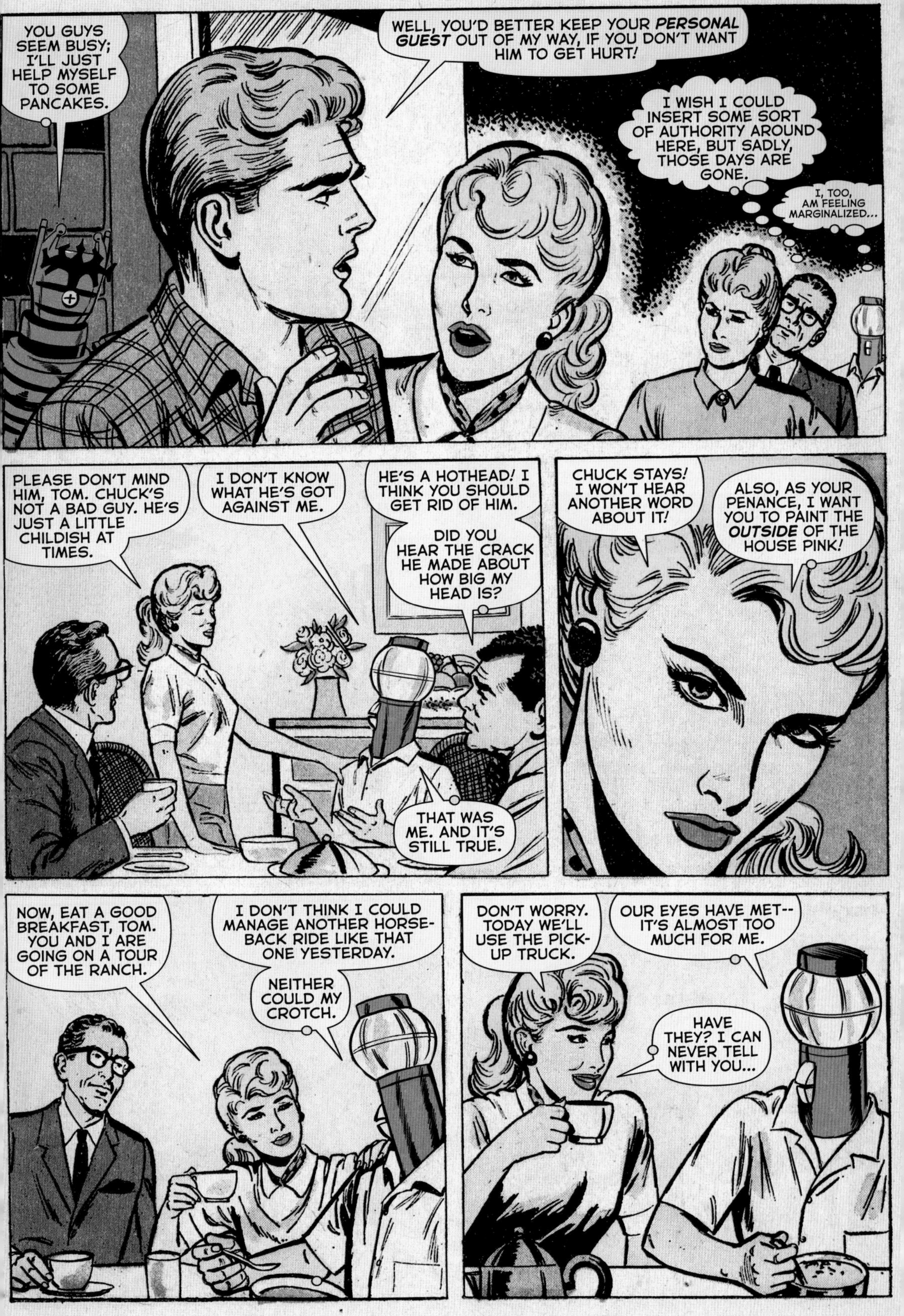

YOU GUYS SEEM BUSY; I'LL JUST HELP MYSELF TO SOME PANCAKES.
WELL, YOU'D BETTER KEEP YOUR PERSONAL GUEST OUT OF MY WAY, IF YOU DON'T WANT HIM TO GET HURT!
I WISH I COULD INSERT SOME SORT OF AUTHORITY AROUND HERE, BUT SADLY, THOSE DAYS ARE GONE.
I, TOO, AM FEELING MARGINALIZED...
PLEASE DON'T MIND HIM, TOM. CHUCK'S NOT A BAD GUY. HE'S JUST A LITTLE CHILDISH AT TIMES.
I DON'T KNOW WHAT HE'S GOT AGAINST ME.
HE'S A HOTHEAD! I THINK YOU SHOULD GET RID OF HIM.
DID YOU HEAR THE CRACK HE MADE ABOUT HOW BIG MY HEAD IS?
THAT WAS ME. AND IT'S STILL TRUE.
CHUCK STAYS! I WON'T HEAR ANOTHER WORD ABOUT IT!
ALSO, AS YOUR PENANCE, I WANT YOU TO PAINT THE OUTSIDE OF THE HOUSE PINK!
NOW, EAT A GOOD BREAKFAST, TOM. YOU AND I ARE GOING ON A TOUR OF THE RANCH.
I DON'T THINK I COULD MANAGE ANOTHER HORSE-BACK RIDE LIKE THAT ONE YESTERDAY.
NEITHER COULD MY CROTCH.
DON'T WORRY. TODAY WE'LL USE THE PICK-UP TRUCK.
OUR EYES HAVE MET-- IT'S ALMOST TOO MUCH FOR ME.
HAVE THEY? I CAN NEVER TELL WITH YOU...

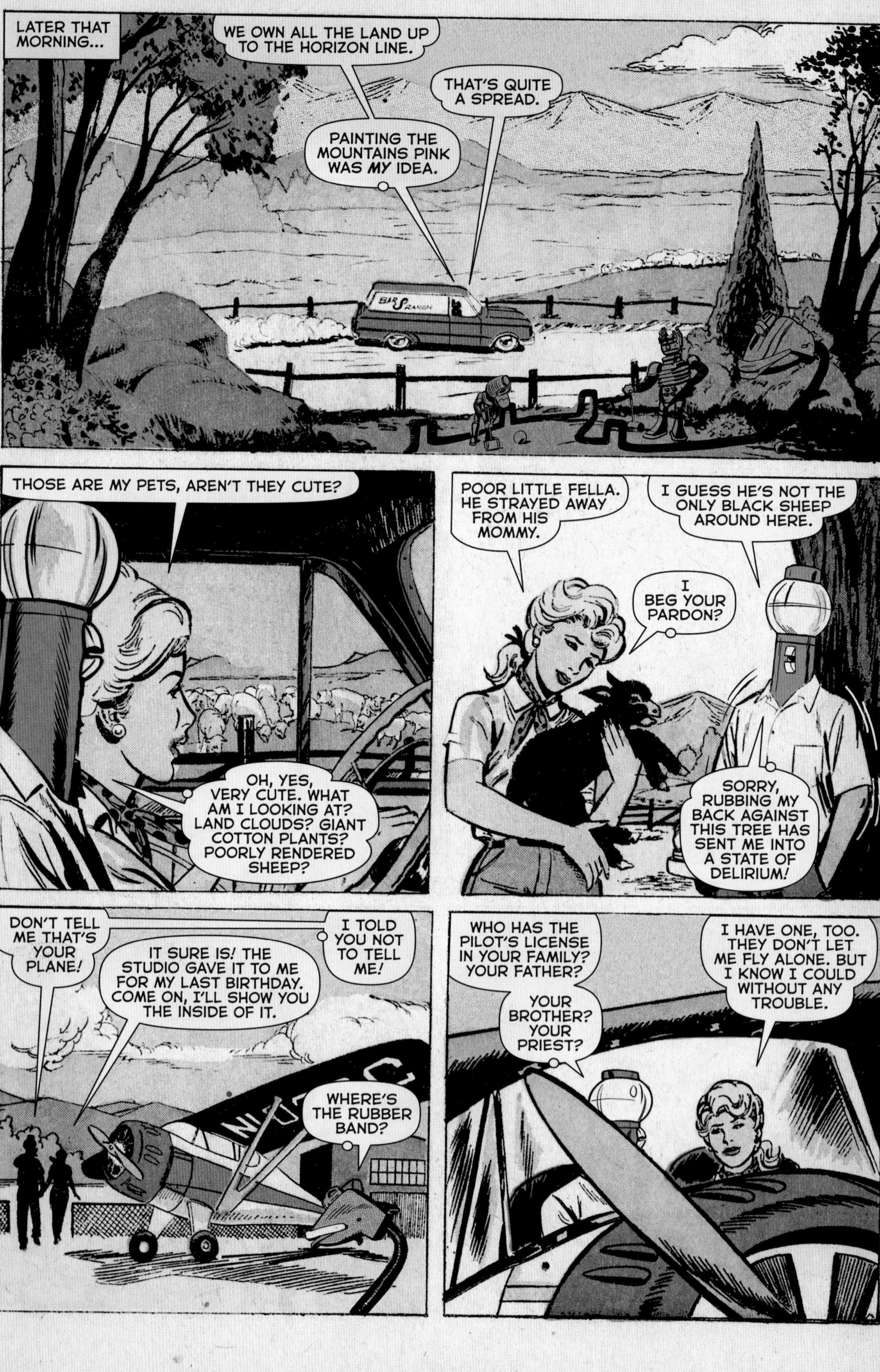

LATER THAT MORNING...
WE OWN ALL THE LAND UP TO THE HORIZON LINE.
THAT'S QUITE A SPREAD.
PAINTING THE MOUNTAINS PINK WAS *MY* IDEA.
BAR S RANCH
THOSE ARE MY PETS, AREN'T THEY CUTE?
OH, YES, VERY CUTE. WHAT AM I LOOKING AT? LAND CLOUDS? GIANT COTTON PLANTS? POORLY RENDERED SHEEP?
POOR LITTLE FELLA. HE STRAYED AWAY FROM HIS MOMMY.
I GUESS HE'S NOT THE ONLY BLACK SHEEP AROUND HERE.
I BEG YOUR PARDON?
SORRY, RUBBING MY BACK AGAINST THIS TREE HAS SENT ME INTO A STATE OF DELIRIUM!
DON'T TELL ME THAT'S YOUR PLANE!
I TOLD YOU NOT TO TELL ME!
IT SURE IS! THE STUDIO GAVE IT TO ME FOR MY LAST BIRTHDAY. COME ON, I'LL SHOW YOU THE INSIDE OF IT.
WHERE'S THE RUBBER BAND?
WHO HAS THE PILOT'S LICENSE IN YOUR FAMILY? YOUR FATHER?
YOUR BROTHER? YOUR PRIEST?
I HAVE ONE, TOO. THEY DON'T LET ME FLY ALONE. BUT I KNOW I COULD WITHOUT ANY TROUBLE.

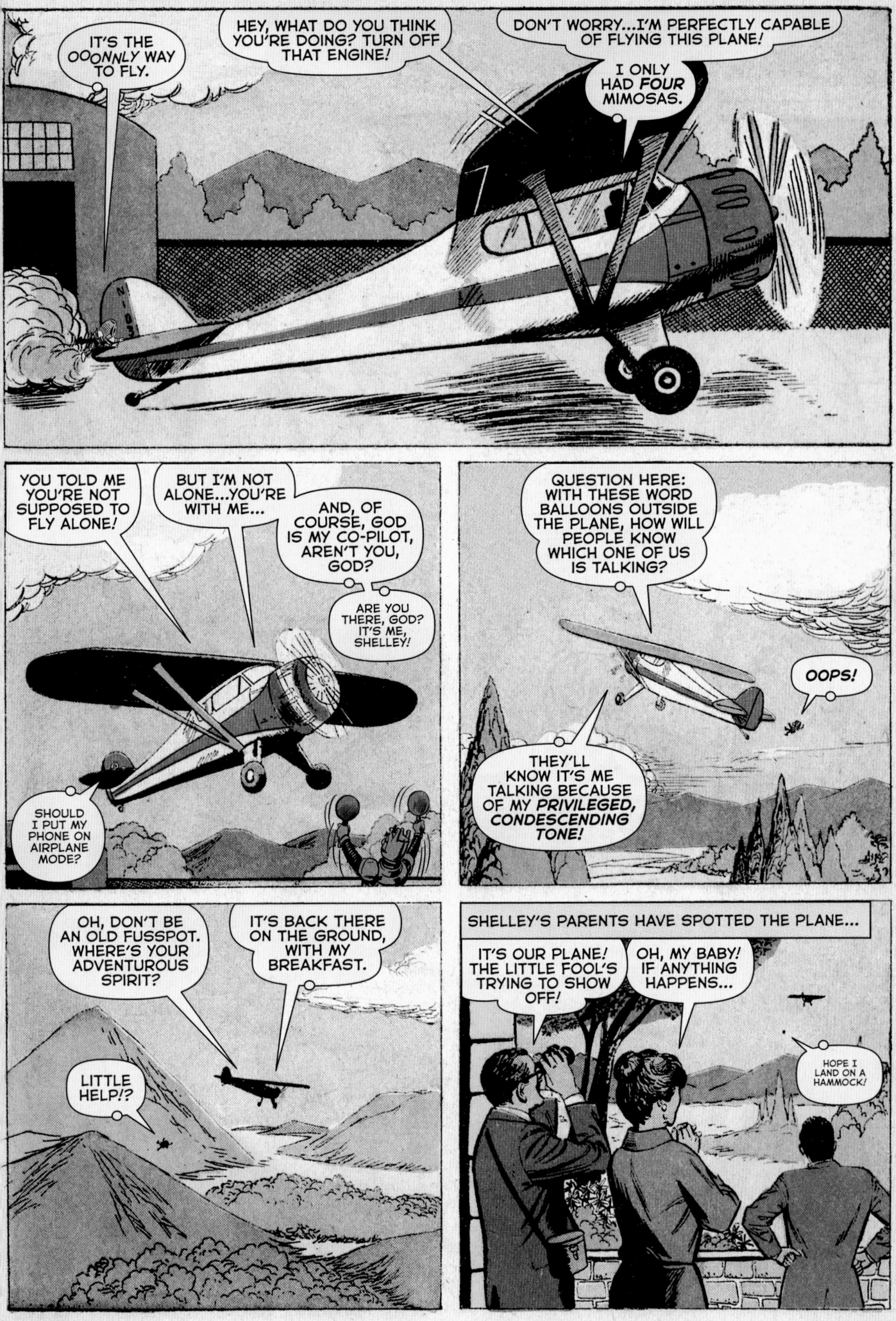

IT'S THE OOONNLY WAY TO FLY.
HEY, WHAT DO YOU THINK YOU'RE DOING? TURN OFF THAT ENGINE!
DON'T WORRY...I'M PERFECTLY CAPABLE OF FLYING THIS PLANE!
I ONLY HAD FOUR MIMOSAS.
YOU TOLD ME YOU'RE NOT SUPPOSED TO FLY ALONE!
BUT I'M NOT ALONE...YOU'RE WITH ME...
AND, OF COURSE, GOD IS MY CO-PILOT, AREN'T YOU, GOD?
ARE YOU THERE, GOD? IT'S ME, SHELLEY!
SHOULD I PUT MY PHONE ON AIRPLANE MODE?
QUESTION HERE: WITH THESE WORD BALLOONS OUTSIDE THE PLANE, HOW WILL PEOPLE KNOW WHICH ONE OF US IS TALKING?
OOPS!
THEY'LL KNOW IT'S ME TALKING BECAUSE OF MY PRIVILEGED, CONDESCENDING TONE!
OH, DON'T BE AN OLD FUSSPOT. WHERE'S YOUR ADVENTUROUS SPIRIT?
IT'S BACK THERE ON THE GROUND, WITH MY BREAKFAST.
LITTLE HELP!?
SHELLEY'S PARENTS HAVE SPOTTED THE PLANE...
IT'S OUR PLANE! THE LITTLE FOOL'S TRYING TO SHOW OFF!
OH, MY BABY! IF ANYTHING HAPPENS...
HOPE I LAND ON A HAMMOCK!

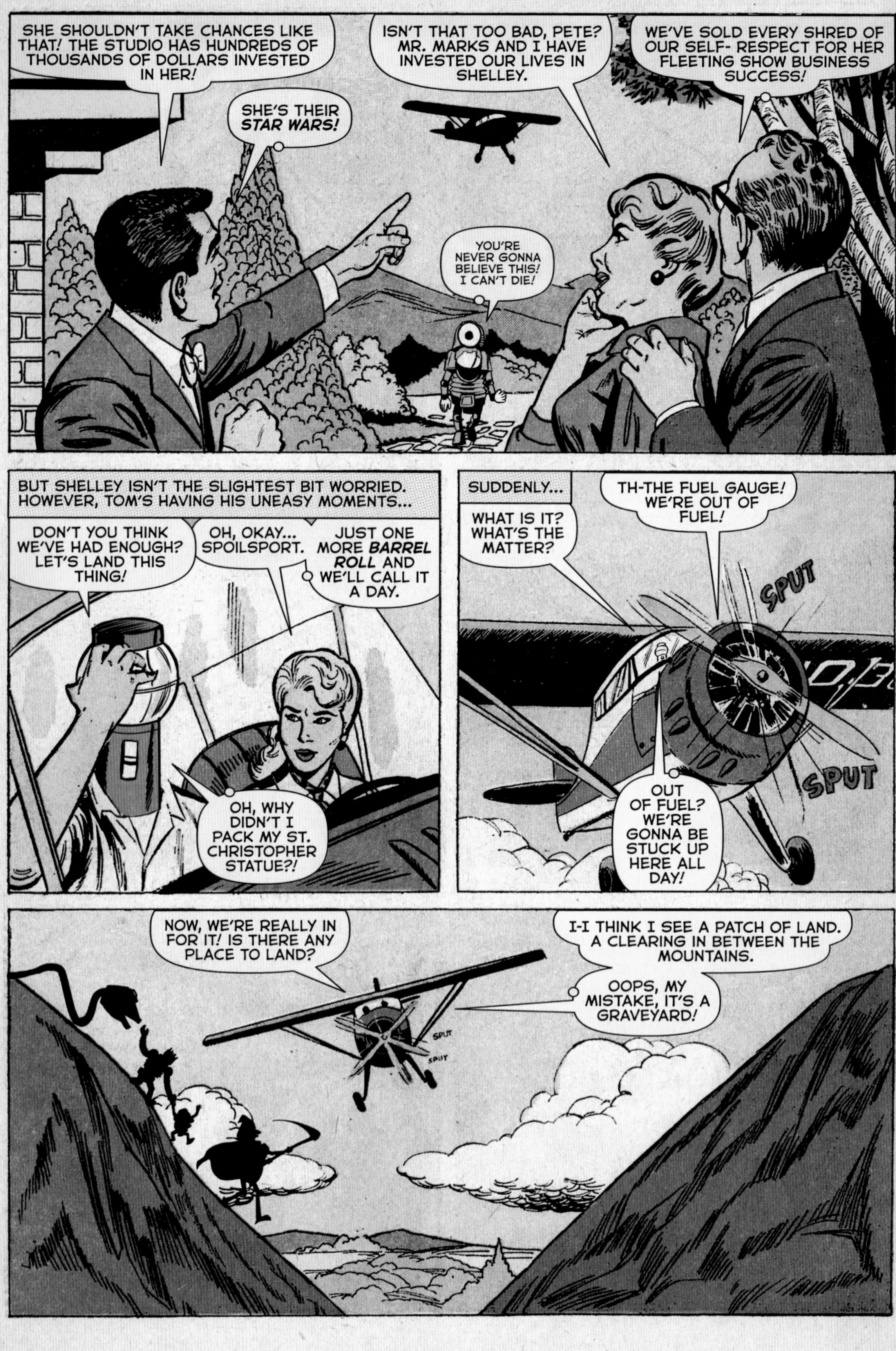
SHE SHOULDN'T TAKE CHANCES LIKE THAT! THE STUDIO HAS HUNDREDS OF THOUSANDS OF DOLLARS INVESTED IN HER!
SHE'S THEIR STAR WARS!
ISN'T THAT TOO BAD, PETE? MR. MARKS AND I HAVE INVESTED OUR LIVES IN SHELLEY.
WE'VE SOLD EVERY SHRED OF OUR SELF- RESPECT FOR HER FLEETING SHOW BUSINESS SUCCESS!
YOU'RE NEVER GONNA BELIEVE THIS! I CAN'T DIE!
BUT SHELLEY ISN'T THE SLIGHTEST BIT WORRIED. HOWEVER, TOM'S HAVING HIS UNEASY MOMENTS...
DON'T YOU THINK WE'VE HAD ENOUGH? LET'S LAND THIS THING!
OH, OKAY... SPOILSPORT.
JUST ONE MORE BARREL ROLL AND WE'LL CALL IT A DAY.
OH, WHY DIDN'T I PACK MY ST. CHRISTOPHER STATUE?!
SUDDENLY...
WHAT IS IT? WHAT'S THE MATTER?
TH-THE FUEL GAUGE! WE'RE OUT OF FUEL!
SPUT
SPUT
OUT OF FUEL? WE'RE GONNA BE STUCK UP HERE ALL DAY!
NOW, WE'RE REALLY IN FOR IT! IS THERE ANY PLACE TO LAND?
I-I THINK I SEE A PATCH OF LAND. A CLEARING IN BETWEEN THE MOUNTAINS.
OOPS, MY MISTAKE, IT'S A GRAVEYARD!
SPUT
SPUT

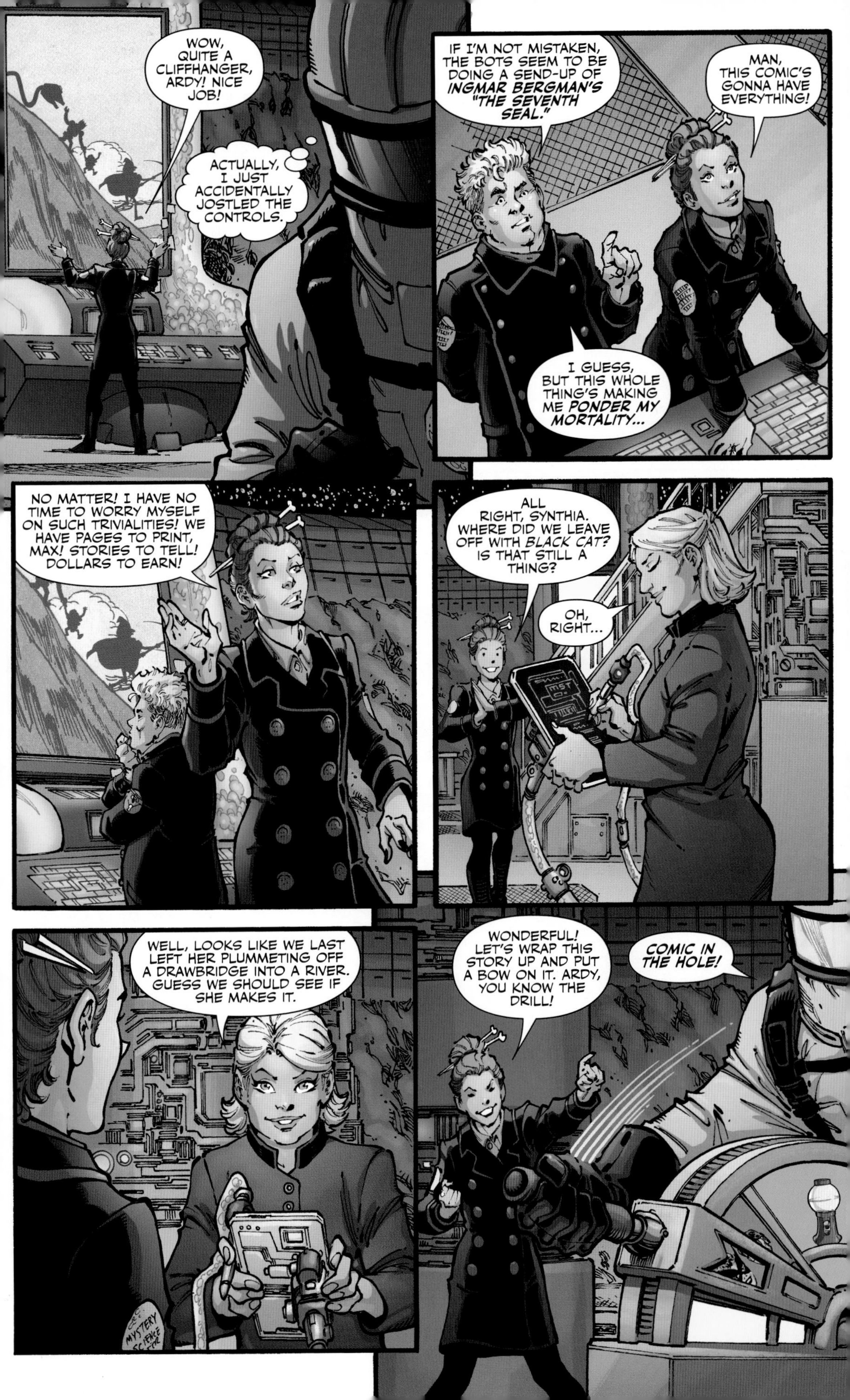
WOW, QUITE A CLIFFHANGER, ARDY! NICE JOB!
ACTUALLY, I JUST ACCIDENTALLY JOSTLED THE CONTROLS.
IF I'M NOT MISTAKEN, THE BOTS SEEM TO BE DOING A SEND-UP OF *INGMAR BERGMAN'S "THE SEVENTH SEAL."*
MAN, THIS COMIC'S GONNA HAVE EVERYTHING!
I GUESS, BUT THIS WHOLE THING'S MAKING ME *PONDER MY MORTALITY...*
NO MATTER! I HAVE NO TIME TO WORRY MYSELF ON SUCH TRIVIALITIES! WE HAVE PAGES TO PRINT, MAX! STORIES TO TELL! DOLLARS TO EARN!
ALL RIGHT, SYNTHIA. WHERE DID WE LEAVE OFF WITH *BLACK CAT?* IS THAT STILL A THING?
OH, RIGHT...
WELL, LOOKS LIKE WE LAST LEFT HER PLUMMETING OFF A DRAWBRIDGE INTO A RIVER. GUESS WE SHOULD SEE IF SHE MAKES IT.
WONDERFUL! LET'S WRAP THIS STORY UP AND PUT A BOW ON IT. ARDY, YOU KNOW THE DRILL!
COMIC IN THE HOLE!

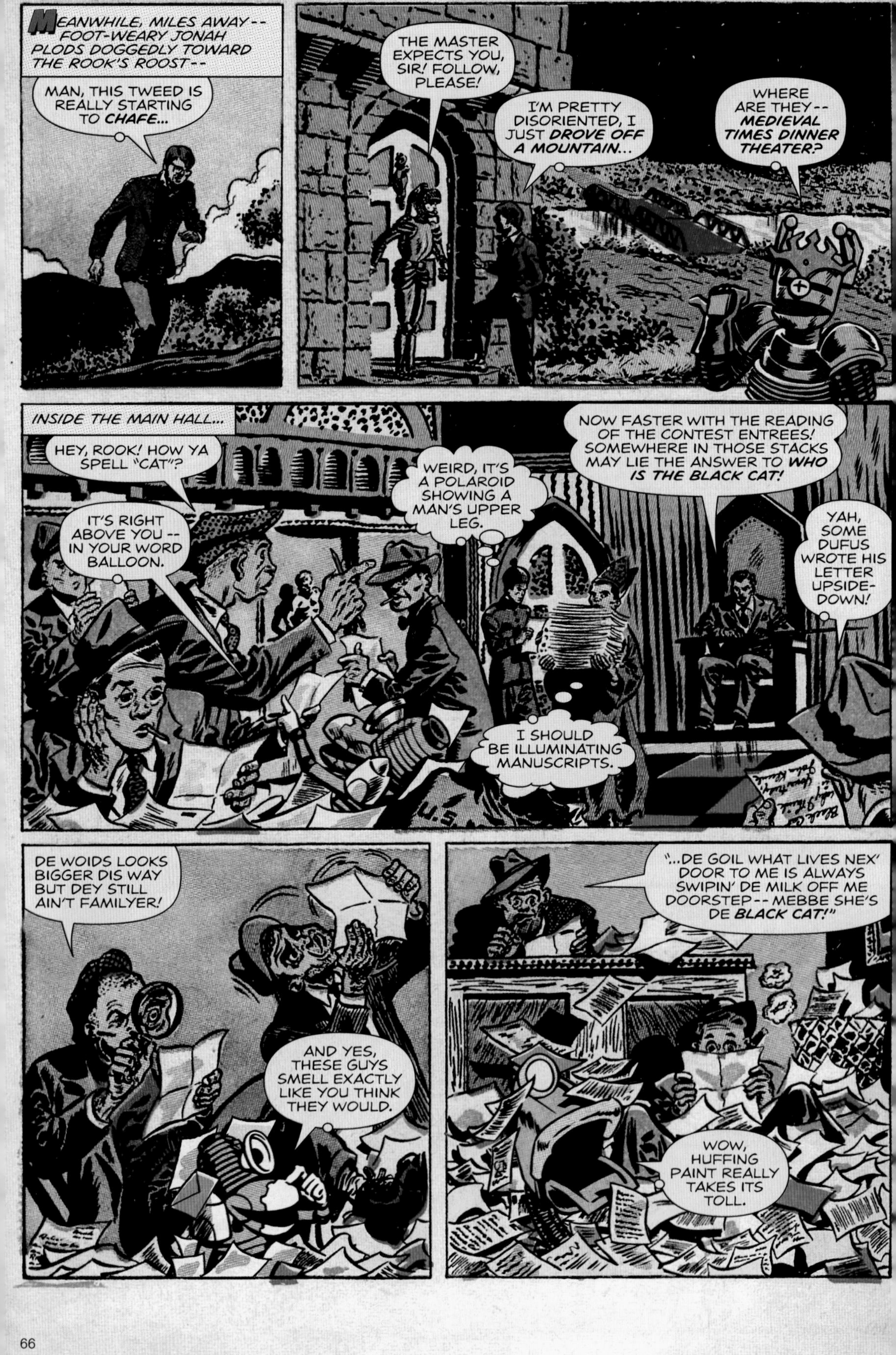
MEANWHILE, MILES AWAY-- FOOT-WEARY JONAH PLODS DOGGEDLY TOWARD THE ROOK'S ROOST--
MAN, THIS TWEED IS REALLY STARTING TO CHAFE...
THE MASTER EXPECTS YOU, SIR! FOLLOW, PLEASE!
I'M PRETTY DISORIENTED, I JUST DROVE OFF A MOUNTAIN...
WHERE ARE THEY-- MEDIEVAL TIMES DINNER THEATER?
INSIDE THE MAIN HALL...
HEY, ROOK! HOW YA SPELL "CAT"?
IT'S RIGHT ABOVE YOU-- IN YOUR WORD BALLOON.
WEIRD, IT'S A POLAROID SHOWING A MAN'S UPPER LEG.
NOW FASTER WITH THE READING OF THE CONTEST ENTREES! SOMEWHERE IN THOSE STACKS MAY LIE THE ANSWER TO WHO IS THE BLACK CAT!
YAH, SOME DUFUS WROTE HIS LETTER UPSIDE-DOWN!
I SHOULD BE ILLUMINATING MANUSCRIPTS.
DE WOIDS LOOKS BIGGER DIS WAY BUT DEY STILL AIN'T FAMILYER!
AND YES, THESE GUYS SMELL EXACTLY LIKE YOU THINK THEY WOULD.
"...DE GOIL WHAT LIVES NEX' DOOR TO ME IS ALWAYS SWIPIN' DE MILK OFF ME DOORSTEP--MEBBE SHE'S DE BLACK CAT!"
WOW, HUFFING PAINT REALLY TAKES ITS TOLL.

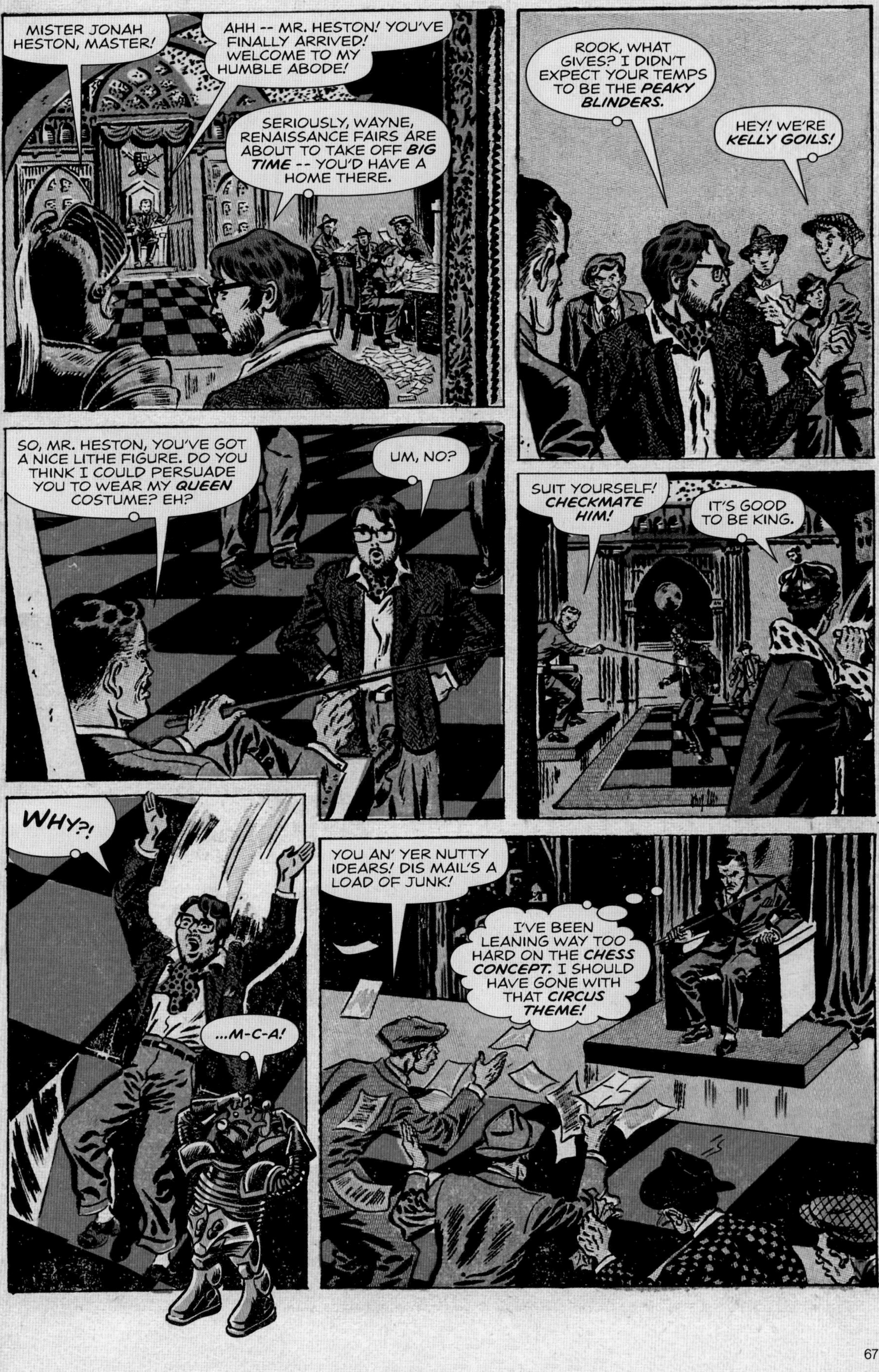
MISTER JONAH HESTON, MASTER!
AHH -- MR. HESTON! YOU'VE FINALLY ARRIVED! WELCOME TO MY HUMBLE ABODE!
SERIOUSLY, WAYNE, RENAISSANCE FAIRS ARE ABOUT TO TAKE OFF BIG TIME -- YOU'D HAVE A HOME THERE.
ROOK, WHAT GIVES? I DIDN'T EXPECT YOUR TEMPS TO BE THE PEAKY BLINDERS.
HEY! WE'RE KELLY GOILS!
SO, MR. HESTON, YOU'VE GOT A NICE LITHE FIGURE. DO YOU THINK I COULD PERSUADE YOU TO WEAR MY QUEEN COSTUME? EH?
UM, NO?
SUIT YOURSELF! CHECKMATE HIM!
IT'S GOOD TO BE KING.
WHY?!
...M-C-A!
YOU AN' YER NUTTY IDEARS! DIS MAIL'S A LOAD OF JUNK!
I'VE BEEN LEANING WAY TOO HARD ON THE CHESS CONCEPT. I SHOULD HAVE GONE WITH THAT CIRCUS THEME!

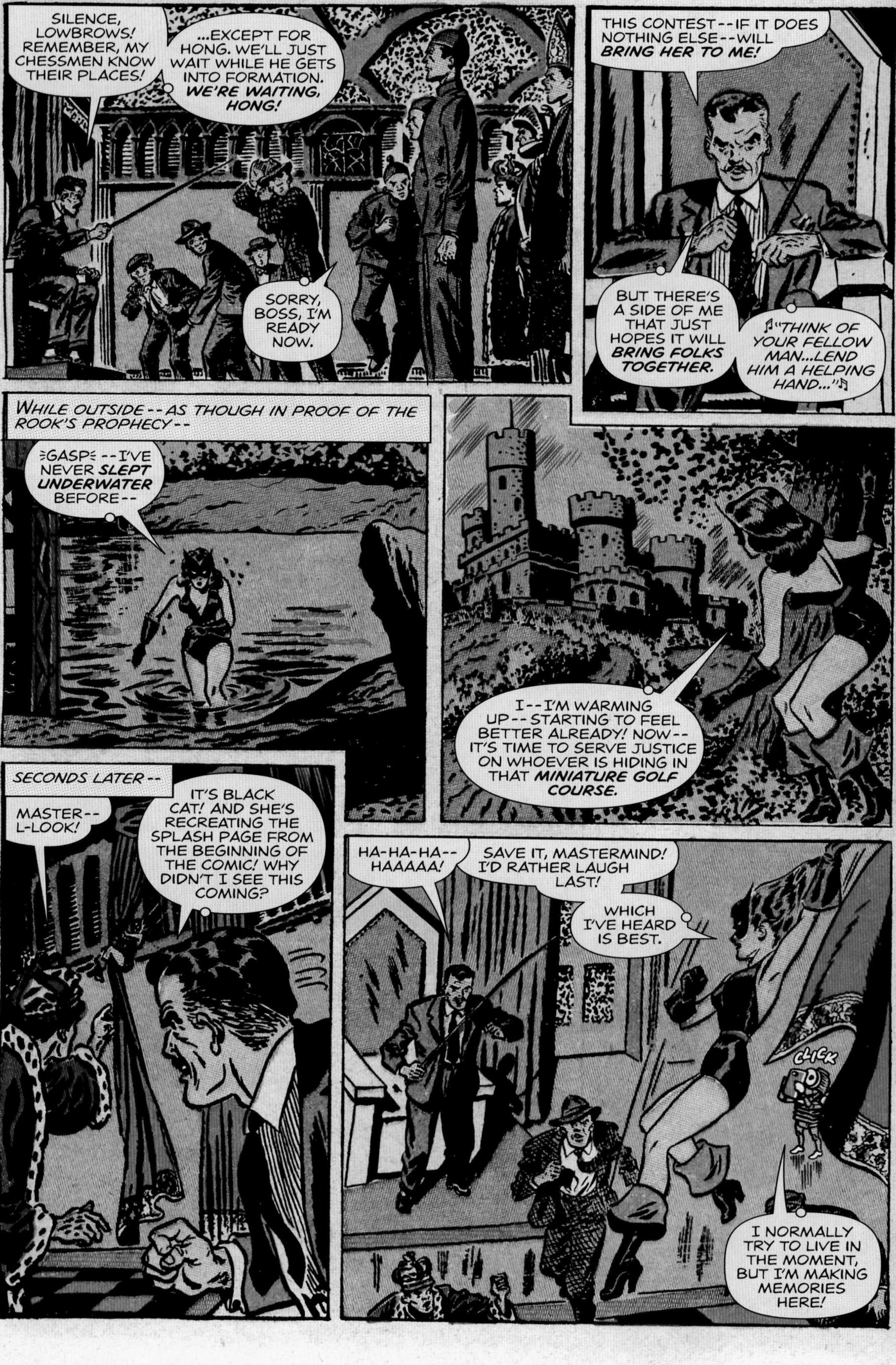
SILENCE, LOWBROWS! REMEMBER, MY CHESSMEN KNOW THEIR PLACES!
...EXCEPT FOR HONG. WE'LL JUST WAIT WHILE HE GETS INTO FORMATION. WE'RE WAITING, HONG!
SORRY, BOSS, I'M READY NOW.
THIS CONTEST--IF IT DOES NOTHING ELSE--WILL BRING HER TO ME!
BUT THERE'S A SIDE OF ME THAT JUST HOPES IT WILL BRING FOLKS TOGETHER.
♪"THINK OF YOUR FELLOW MAN...LEND HIM A HELPING HAND..."♪
WHILE OUTSIDE--AS THOUGH IN PROOF OF THE ROOK'S PROPHECY--
GASP --I'VE NEVER SLEPT UNDERWATER BEFORE--
I--I'M WARMING UP--STARTING TO FEEL BETTER ALREADY! NOW--IT'S TIME TO SERVE JUSTICE ON WHOEVER IS HIDING IN THAT MINIATURE GOLF COURSE.
SECONDS LATER--
MASTER--L-LOOK!
IT'S BLACK CAT! AND SHE'S RECREATING THE SPLASH PAGE FROM THE BEGINNING OF THE COMIC! WHY DIDN'T I SEE THIS COMING?
HA-HA-HA--HAAAAA!
SAVE IT, MASTERMIND! I'D RATHER LAUGH LAST!
WHICH I'VE HEARD IS BEST.
CLICK
I NORMALLY TRY TO LIVE IN THE MOMENT, BUT I'M MAKING MEMORIES HERE!

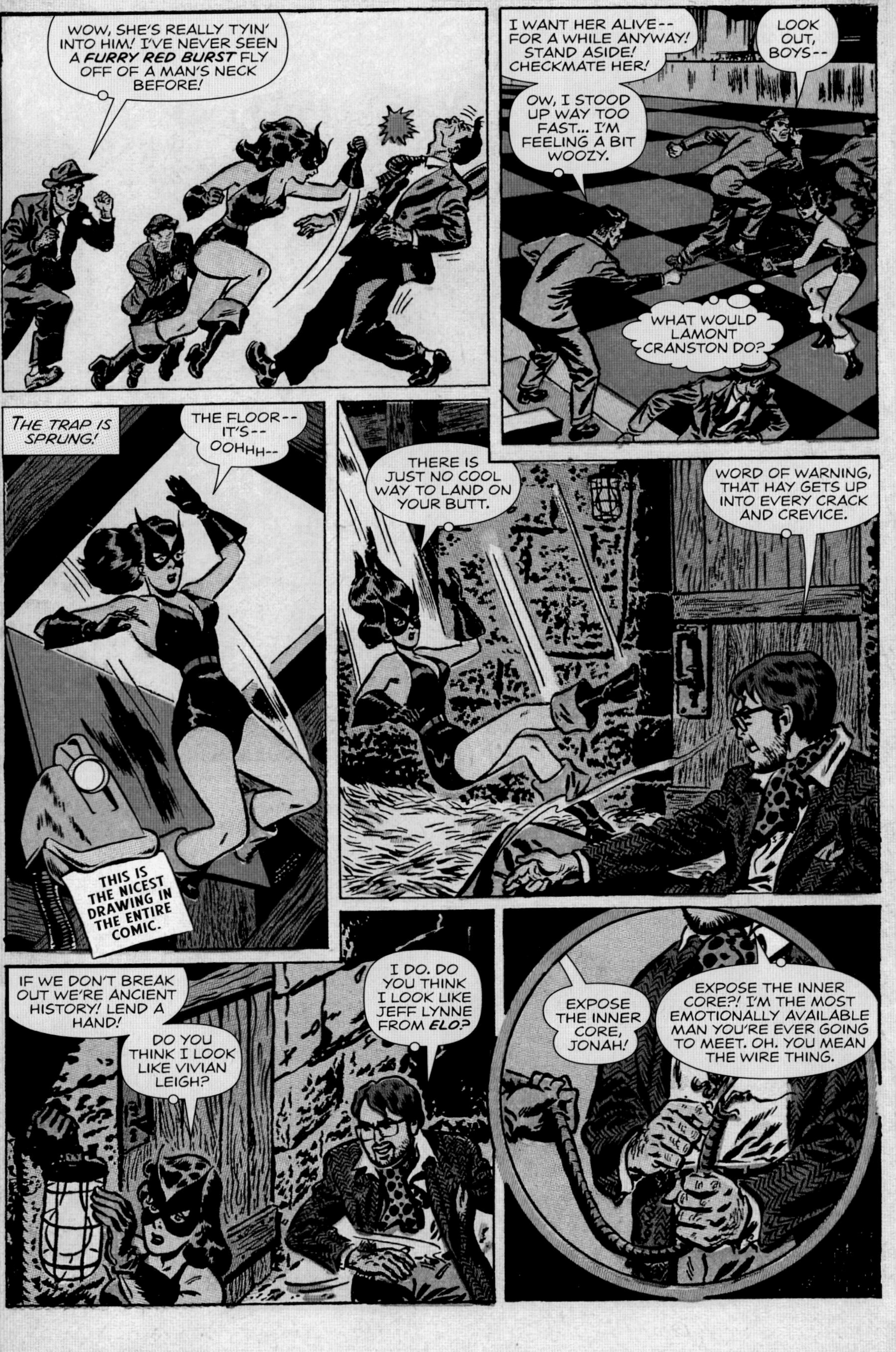

WOW, SHE'S REALLY TYIN' INTO HIM! I'VE NEVER SEEN A **FURRY RED BURST** FLY OFF OF A MAN'S NECK BEFORE!
I WANT HER ALIVE-- FOR A WHILE ANYWAY! STAND ASIDE! CHECKMATE HER!
LOOK OUT, BOYS--
OW, I STOOD UP WAY TOO FAST... I'M FEELING A BIT WOOZY.
WHAT WOULD LAMONT CRANSTON DO?
THE TRAP IS SPRUNG!
THE FLOOR-- IT'S-- OOHHH--
THIS IS THE NICEST DRAWING IN THE ENTIRE COMIC.
THERE IS JUST NO COOL WAY TO LAND ON YOUR BUTT.
WORD OF WARNING, THAT HAY GETS UP INTO EVERY CRACK AND CREVICE.
IF WE DON'T BREAK OUT WE'RE ANCIENT HISTORY! LEND A HAND!
DO YOU THINK I LOOK LIKE VIVIAN LEIGH?
I DO. DO YOU THINK I LOOK LIKE JEFF LYNNE FROM **ELO?**
EXPOSE THE INNER CORE, JONAH!
EXPOSE THE INNER CORE?! I'M THE MOST EMOTIONALLY AVAILABLE MAN YOU'RE EVER GOING TO MEET. OH. YOU MEAN THE WIRE THING.

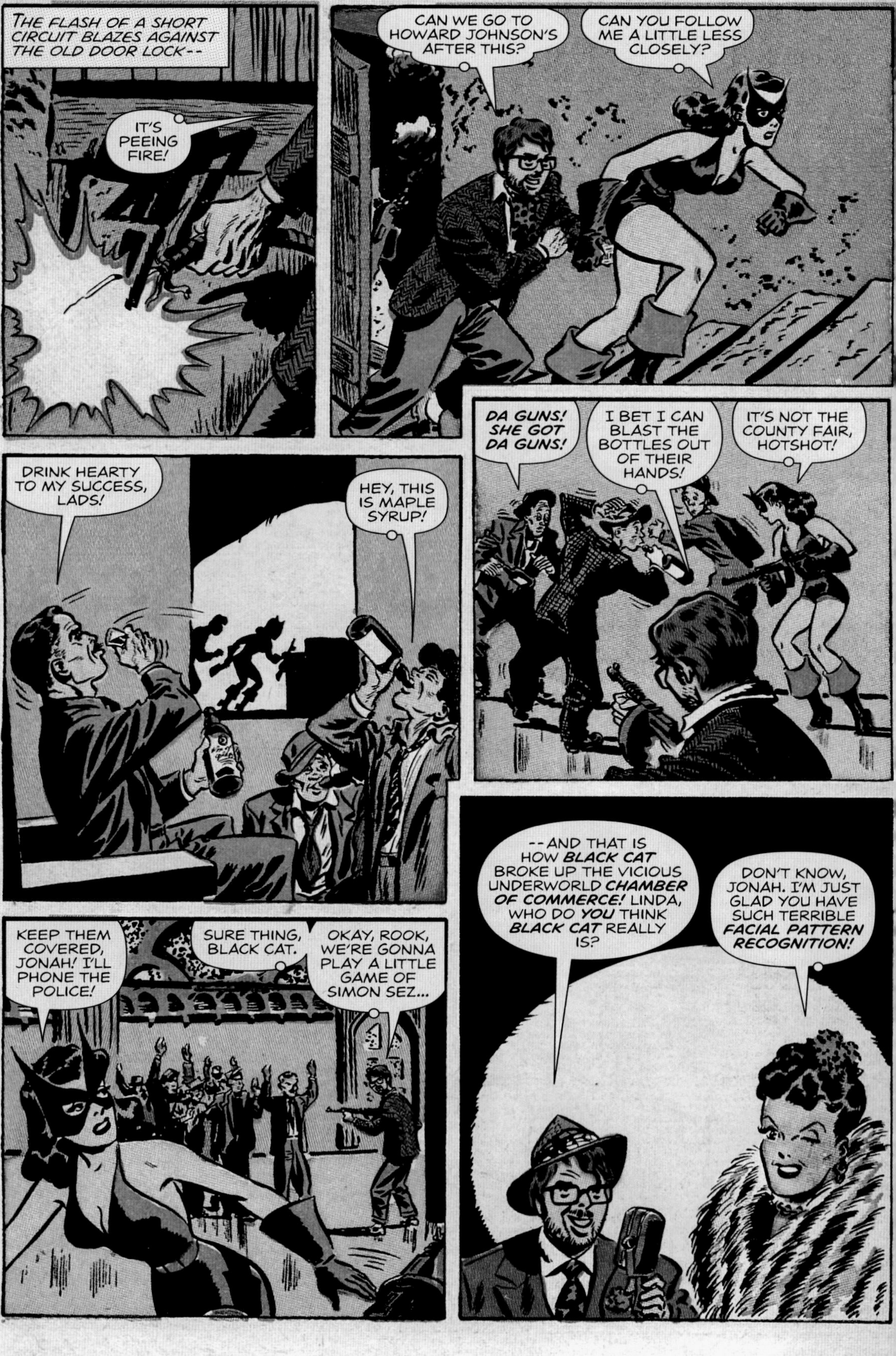
THE FLASH OF A SHORT CIRCUIT BLAZES AGAINST THE OLD DOOR LOCK--
IT'S PEEING FIRE!
CAN WE GO TO HOWARD JOHNSON'S AFTER THIS?
CAN YOU FOLLOW ME A LITTLE LESS CLOSELY?
DRINK HEARTY TO MY SUCCESS, LADS!
HEY, THIS IS MAPLE SYRUP!
DA GUNS! SHE GOT DA GUNS!
I BET I CAN BLAST THE BOTTLES OUT OF THEIR HANDS!
IT'S NOT THE COUNTY FAIR, HOTSHOT!
KEEP THEM COVERED, JONAH! I'LL PHONE THE POLICE!
SURE THING, BLACK CAT.
OKAY, ROOK, WE'RE GONNA PLAY A LITTLE GAME OF SIMON SEZ...
--AND THAT IS HOW BLACK CAT BROKE UP THE VICIOUS UNDERWORLD CHAMBER OF COMMERCE! LINDA, WHO DO YOU THINK BLACK CAT REALLY IS?
DON'T KNOW, JONAH. I'M JUST GLAD YOU HAVE SUCH TERRIBLE FACIAL PATTERN RECOGNITION!

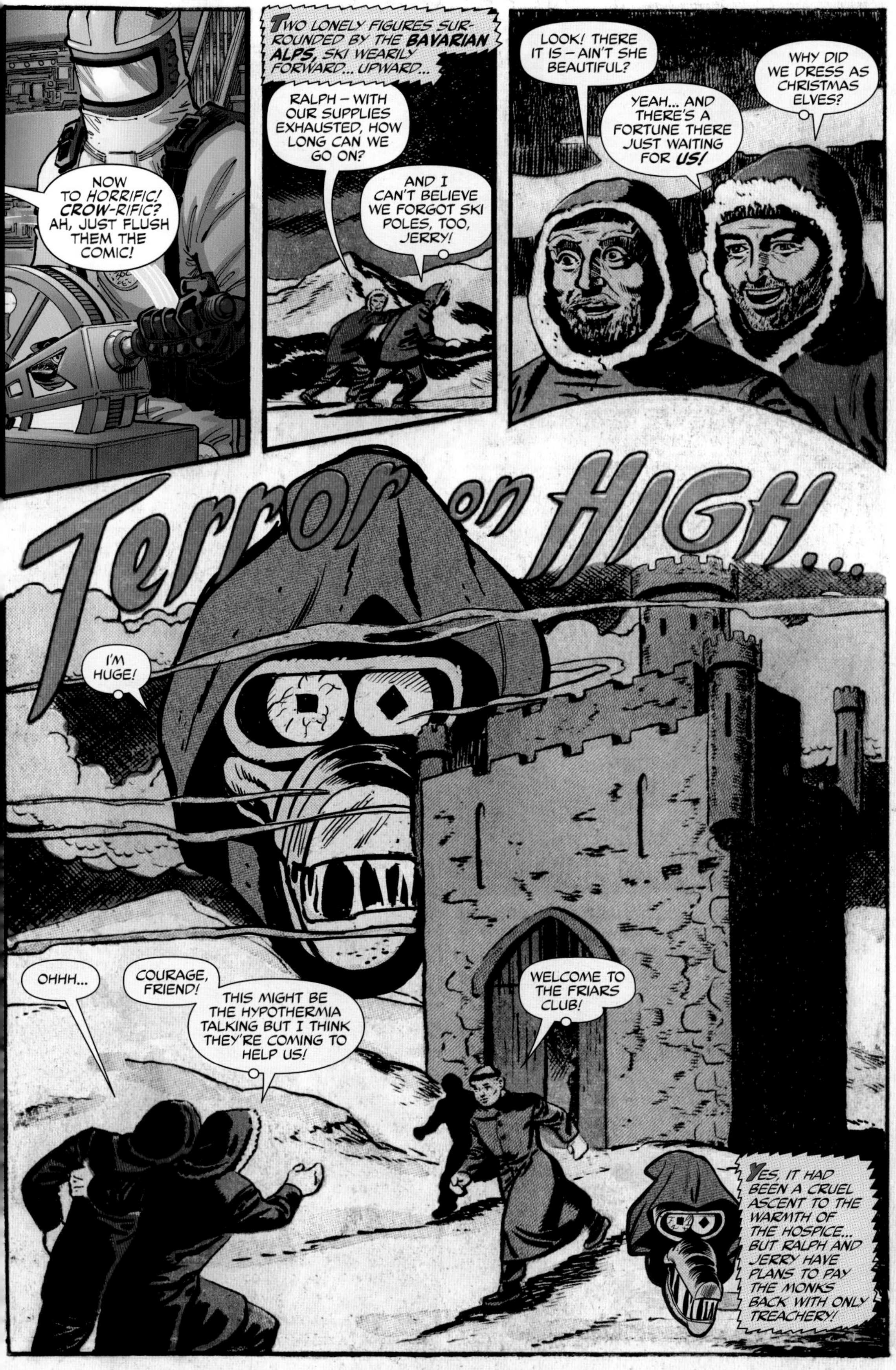
NOW TO HORRIFIC! CROW-RIFIC? AH, JUST FLUSH THEM THE COMIC!
TWO LONELY FIGURES SURROUNDED BY THE BAVARIAN ALPS, SKI WEARILY FORWARD... UPWARD...
RALPH – WITH OUR SUPPLIES EXHAUSTED, HOW LONG CAN WE GO ON?
AND I CAN'T BELIEVE WE FORGOT SKI POLES, TOO, JERRY!
LOOK! THERE IT IS – AIN'T SHE BEAUTIFUL?
YEAH... AND THERE'S A FORTUNE THERE JUST WAITING FOR US!
WHY DID WE DRESS AS CHRISTMAS ELVES?
TERROR ON HIGH...
I'M HUGE!
OHHH...
COURAGE, FRIEND!
THIS MIGHT BE THE HYPOTHERMIA TALKING BUT I THINK THEY'RE COMING TO HELP US!
WELCOME TO THE FRIARS CLUB!
YES, IT HAD BEEN A CRUEL ASCENT TO THE WARMTH OF THE HOSPICE... BUT RALPH AND JERRY HAVE PLANS TO PAY THE MONKS BACK WITH ONLY TREACHERY!

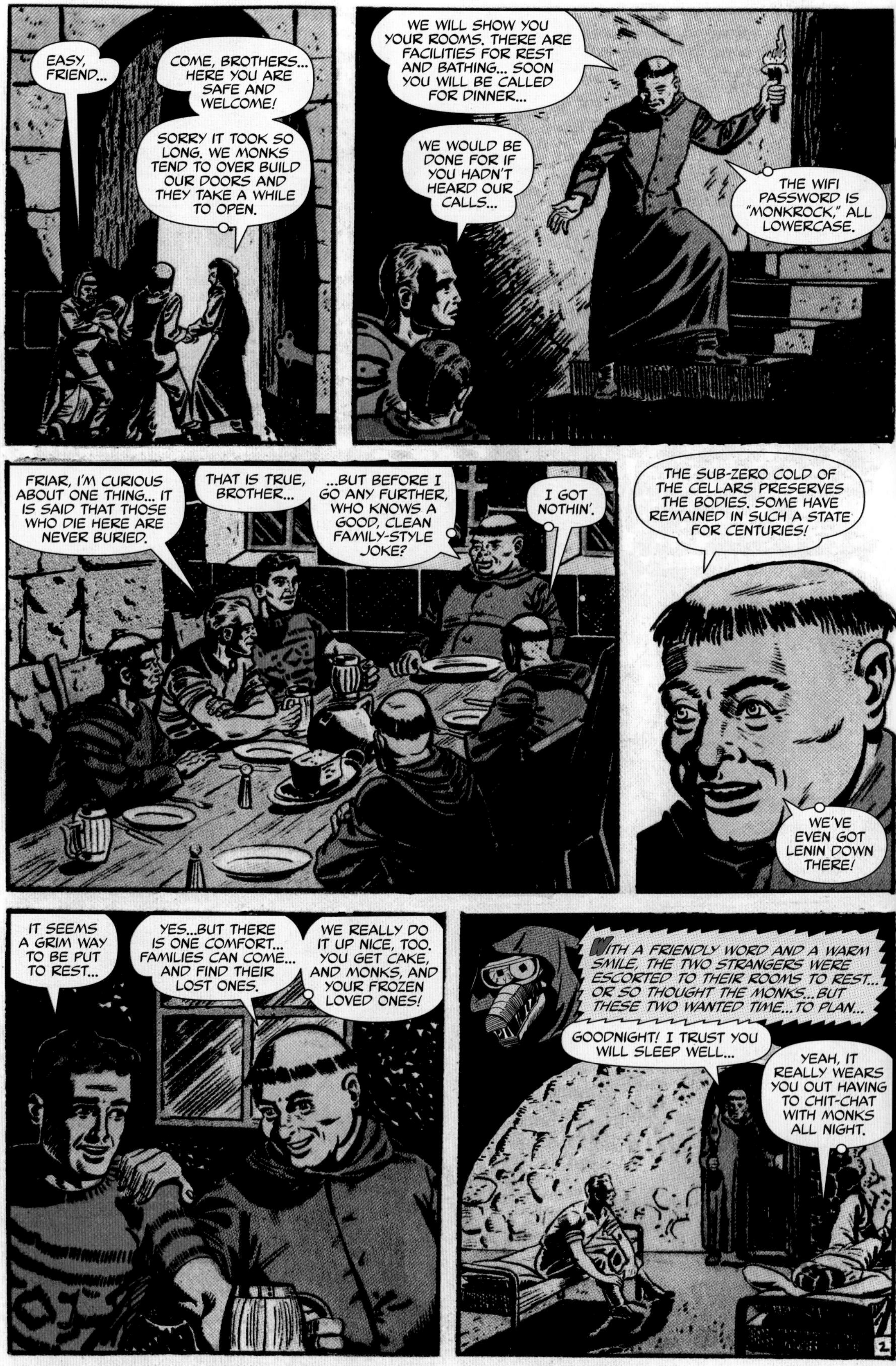

EASY, FRIEND...
COME, BROTHERS... HERE YOU ARE SAFE AND WELCOME!
SORRY IT TOOK SO LONG. WE MONKS TEND TO OVER BUILD OUR DOORS AND THEY TAKE A WHILE TO OPEN.
WE WILL SHOW YOU YOUR ROOMS. THERE ARE FACILITIES FOR REST AND BATHING... SOON YOU WILL BE CALLED FOR DINNER...
WE WOULD BE DONE FOR IF YOU HADN'T HEARD OUR CALLS...
THE WIFI PASSWORD IS "MONKROCK," ALL LOWERCASE.
FRIAR, I'M CURIOUS ABOUT ONE THING... IT IS SAID THAT THOSE WHO DIE HERE ARE NEVER BURIED.
THAT IS TRUE, BROTHER...
...BUT BEFORE I GO ANY FURTHER, WHO KNOWS A GOOD, CLEAN FAMILY-STYLE JOKE?
I GOT NOTHIN'.
THE SUB-ZERO COLD OF THE CELLARS PRESERVES THE BODIES. SOME HAVE REMAINED IN SUCH A STATE FOR CENTURIES!
WE'VE EVEN GOT LENIN DOWN THERE!
IT SEEMS A GRIM WAY TO BE PUT TO REST...
YES...BUT THERE IS ONE COMFORT... FAMILIES CAN COME... AND FIND THEIR LOST ONES.
WE REALLY DO IT UP NICE, TOO. YOU GET CAKE, AND MONKS, AND YOUR FROZEN LOVED ONES!
WITH A FRIENDLY WORD AND A WARM SMILE, THE TWO STRANGERS WERE ESCORTED TO THEIR ROOMS TO REST... OR SO THOUGHT THE MONKS...BUT THESE TWO WANTED TIME...TO PLAN...
GOODNIGHT! I TRUST YOU WILL SLEEP WELL...
YEAH, IT REALLY WEARS YOU OUT HAVING TO CHIT-CHAT WITH MONKS ALL NIGHT.
2

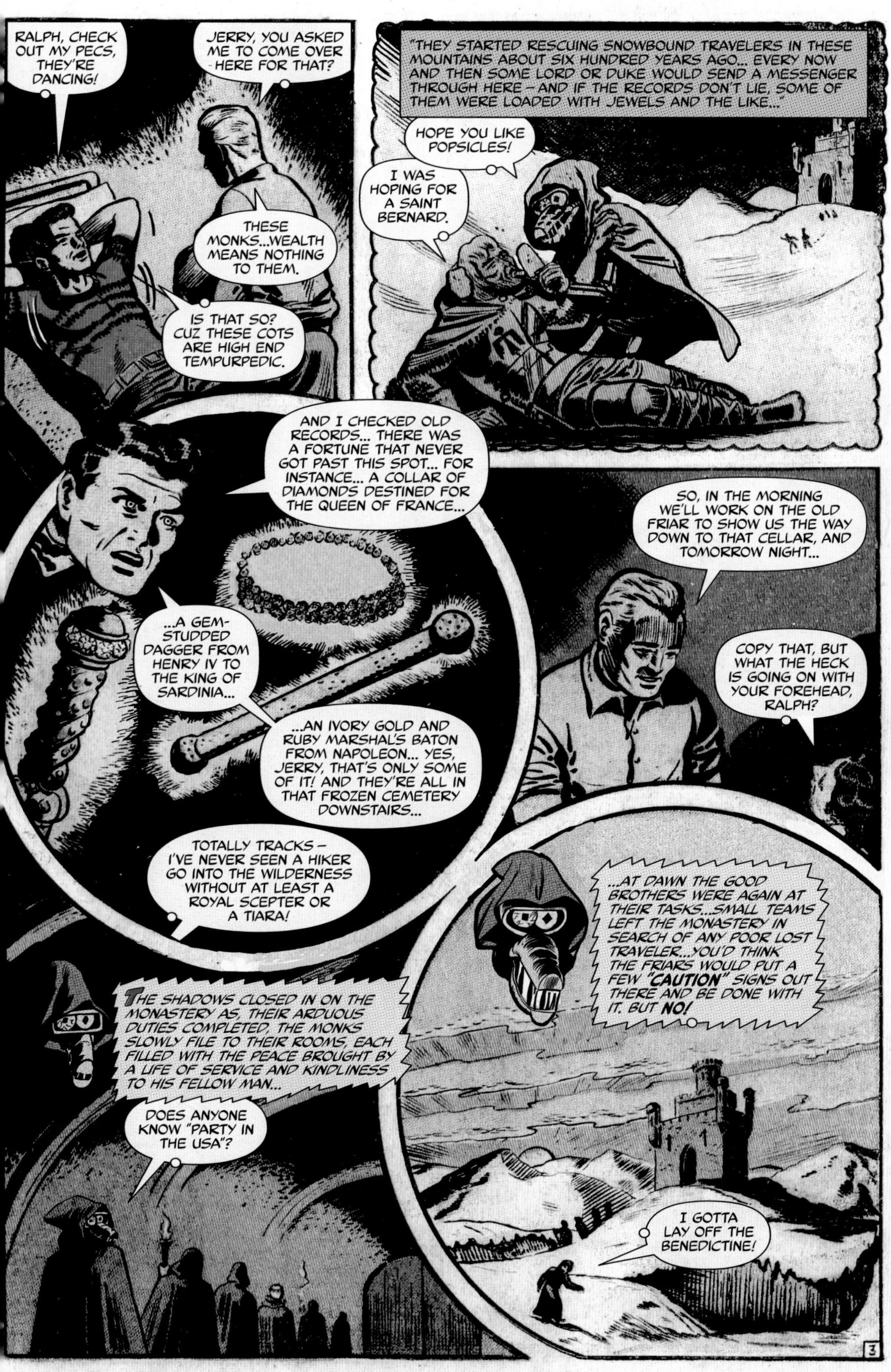
RALPH, CHECK OUT MY PECS, THEY'RE DANCING!
JERRY, YOU ASKED ME TO COME OVER HERE FOR THAT?
THESE MONKS...WEALTH MEANS NOTHING TO THEM.
IS THAT SO? CUZ THESE COTS ARE HIGH END TEMPURPEDIC.
"THEY STARTED RESCUING SNOWBOUND TRAVELERS IN THESE MOUNTAINS ABOUT SIX HUNDRED YEARS AGO... EVERY NOW AND THEN SOME LORD OR DUKE WOULD SEND A MESSENGER THROUGH HERE – AND IF THE RECORDS DON'T LIE, SOME OF THEM WERE LOADED WITH JEWELS AND THE LIKE..."
HOPE YOU LIKE POPSICLES!
I WAS HOPING FOR A SAINT BERNARD.
AND I CHECKED OLD RECORDS... THERE WAS A FORTUNE THAT NEVER GOT PAST THIS SPOT... FOR INSTANCE... A COLLAR OF DIAMONDS DESTINED FOR THE QUEEN OF FRANCE...
...A GEM-STUDDED DAGGER FROM HENRY IV TO THE KING OF SARDINIA...
...AN IVORY GOLD AND RUBY MARSHAL'S BATON FROM NAPOLEON... YES, JERRY, THAT'S ONLY SOME OF IT! AND THEY'RE ALL IN THAT FROZEN CEMETERY DOWNSTAIRS...
TOTALLY TRACKS – I'VE NEVER SEEN A HIKER GO INTO THE WILDERNESS WITHOUT AT LEAST A ROYAL SCEPTER OR A TIARA!
SO, IN THE MORNING WE'LL WORK ON THE OLD FRIAR TO SHOW US THE WAY DOWN TO THAT CELLAR, AND TOMORROW NIGHT...
COPY THAT, BUT WHAT THE HECK IS GOING ON WITH YOUR FOREHEAD, RALPH?
THE SHADOWS CLOSED IN ON THE MONASTERY AS, THEIR ARDUOUS DUTIES COMPLETED, THE MONKS SLOWLY FILE TO THEIR ROOMS, EACH FILLED WITH THE PEACE BROUGHT BY A LIFE OF SERVICE AND KINDLINESS TO HIS FELLOW MAN...
DOES ANYONE KNOW "PARTY IN THE USA"?
...AT DAWN THE GOOD BROTHERS WERE AGAIN AT THEIR TASKS...SMALL TEAMS LEFT THE MONASTERY IN SEARCH OF ANY POOR LOST TRAVELER...YOU'D THINK THE FRIARS WOULD PUT A FEW "CAUTION" SIGNS OUT THERE AND BE DONE WITH IT. BUT NO!
I GOTTA LAY OFF THE BENEDICTINE!
3

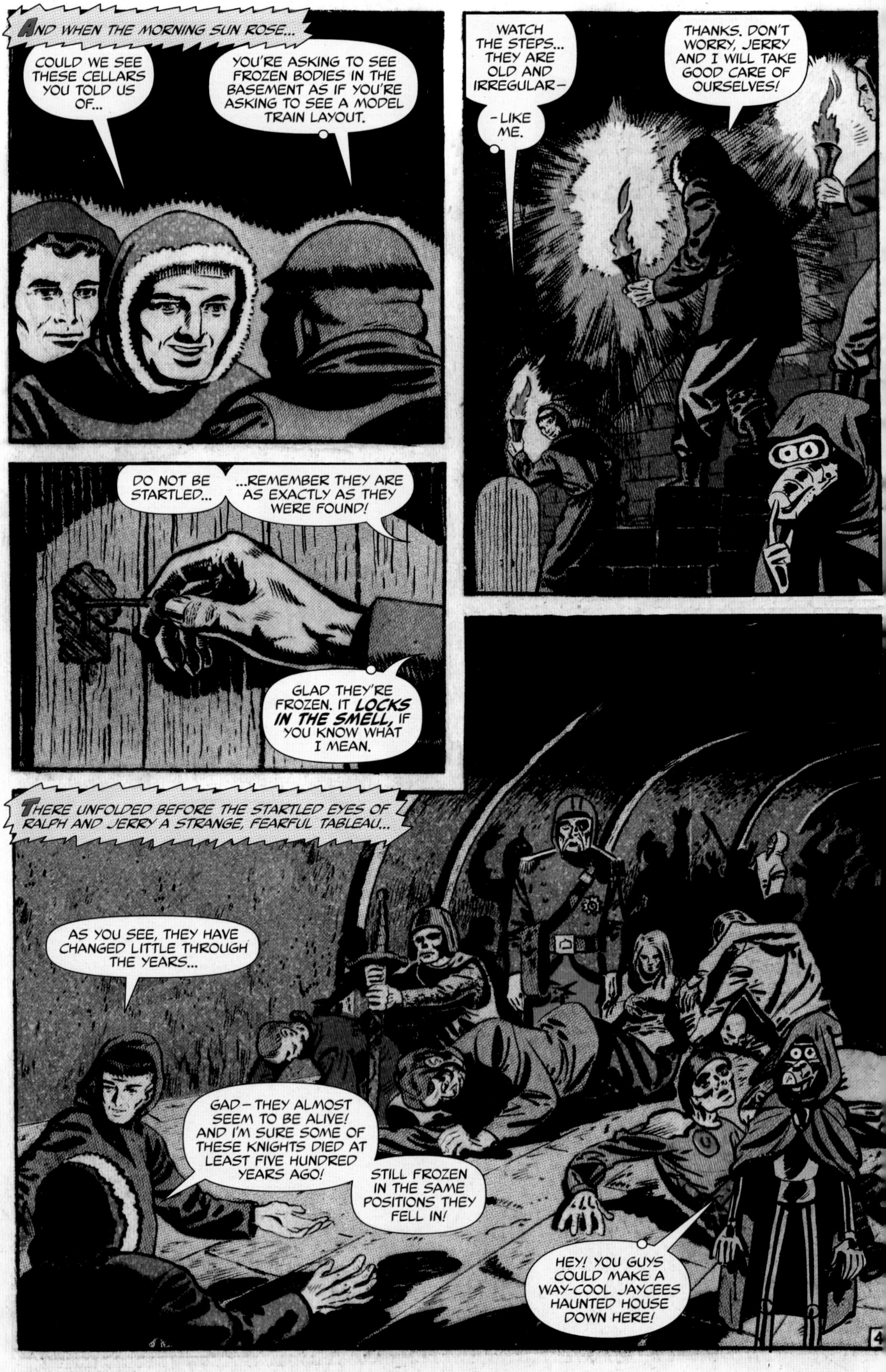
AND WHEN THE MORNING SUN ROSE...
COULD WE SEE THESE CELLARS YOU TOLD US OF...
YOU'RE ASKING TO SEE FROZEN BODIES IN THE BASEMENT AS IF YOU'RE ASKING TO SEE A MODEL TRAIN LAYOUT.
WATCH THE STEPS... THEY ARE OLD AND IRREGULAR–
–LIKE ME.
THANKS. DON'T WORRY, JERRY AND I WILL TAKE GOOD CARE OF OURSELVES!
DO NOT BE STARTLED...
...REMEMBER THEY ARE AS EXACTLY AS THEY WERE FOUND!
GLAD THEY'RE FROZEN. IT LOCKS IN THE SMELL, IF YOU KNOW WHAT I MEAN.
THERE UNFOLDED BEFORE THE STARTLED EYES OF RALPH AND JERRY A STRANGE, FEARFUL TABLEAU...
AS YOU SEE, THEY HAVE CHANGED LITTLE THROUGH THE YEARS...
GAD–THEY ALMOST SEEM TO BE ALIVE! AND I'M SURE SOME OF THESE KNIGHTS DIED AT LEAST FIVE HUNDRED YEARS AGO!
STILL FROZEN IN THE SAME POSITIONS THEY FELL IN!
HEY! YOU GUYS COULD MAKE A WAY-COOL JAYCEES HAUNTED HOUSE DOWN HERE!
4

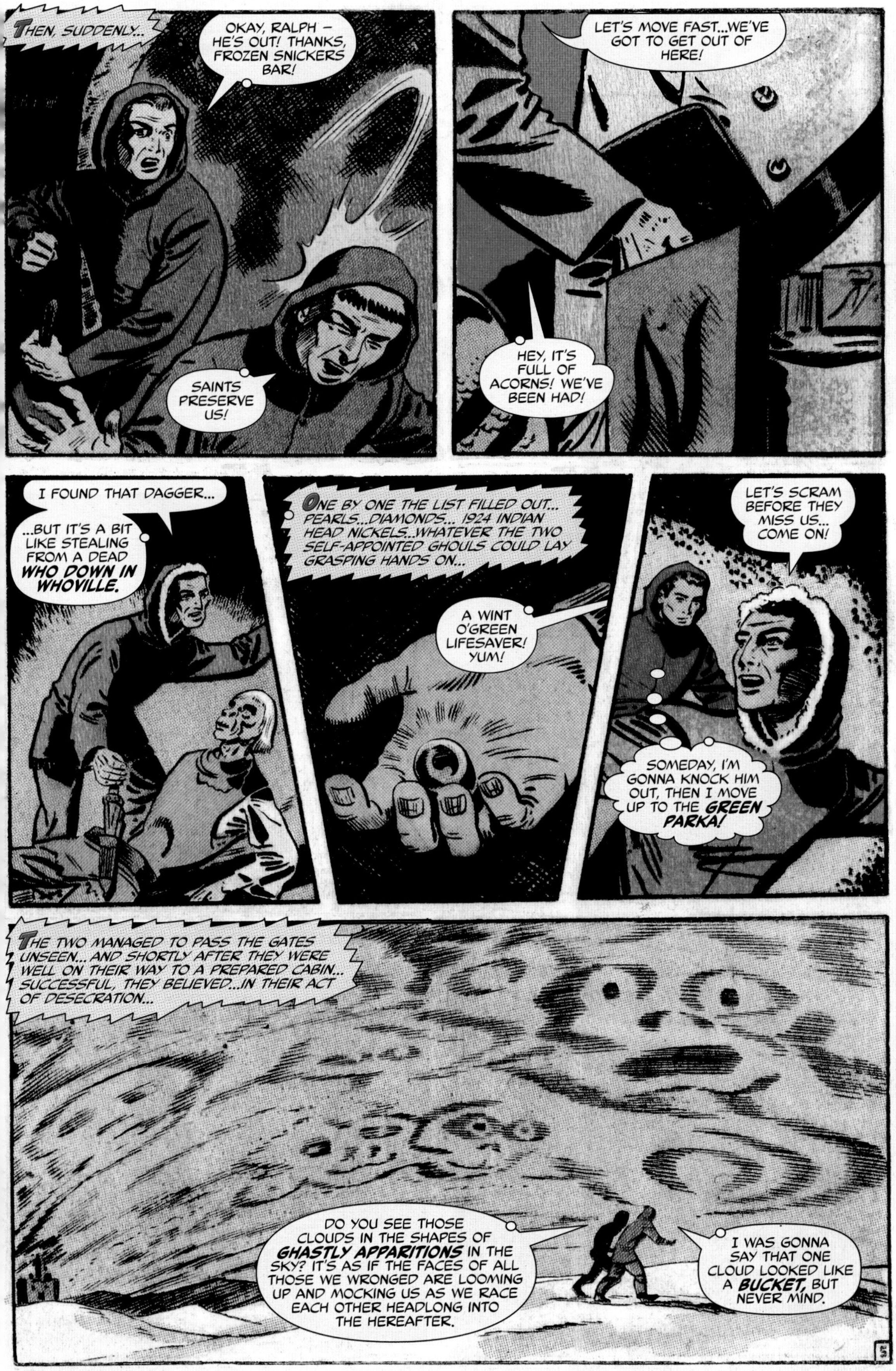

THEN, SUDDENLY...
OKAY, RALPH — HE'S OUT! THANKS, FROZEN SNICKERS BAR!
SAINTS PRESERVE US!
LET'S MOVE FAST...WE'VE GOT TO GET OUT OF HERE!
HEY, IT'S FULL OF ACORNS! WE'VE BEEN HAD!
I FOUND THAT DAGGER...
...BUT IT'S A BIT LIKE STEALING FROM A DEAD WHO DOWN IN WHOVILLE.
ONE BY ONE THE LIST FILLED OUT... PEARLS...DIAMONDS... 1924 INDIAN HEAD NICKELS..WHATEVER THE TWO SELF-APPOINTED GHOULS COULD LAY GRASPING HANDS ON...
A WINT O'GREEN LIFESAVER! YUM!
LET'S SCRAM BEFORE THEY MISS US... COME ON!
SOMEDAY, I'M GONNA KNOCK HIM OUT, THEN I MOVE UP TO THE GREEN PARKA!
THE TWO MANAGED TO PASS THE GATES UNSEEN... AND SHORTLY AFTER THEY WERE WELL ON THEIR WAY TO A PREPARED CABIN... SUCCESSFUL, THEY BELIEVED...IN THEIR ACT OF DESECRATION...
DO YOU SEE THOSE CLOUDS IN THE SHAPES OF GHASTLY APPARITIONS IN THE SKY? IT'S AS IF THE FACES OF ALL THOSE WE WRONGED ARE LOOMING UP AND MOCKING US AS WE RACE EACH OTHER HEADLONG INTO THE HEREAFTER.
I WAS GONNA SAY THAT ONE CLOUD LOOKED LIKE A BUCKET, BUT NEVER MIND.
5

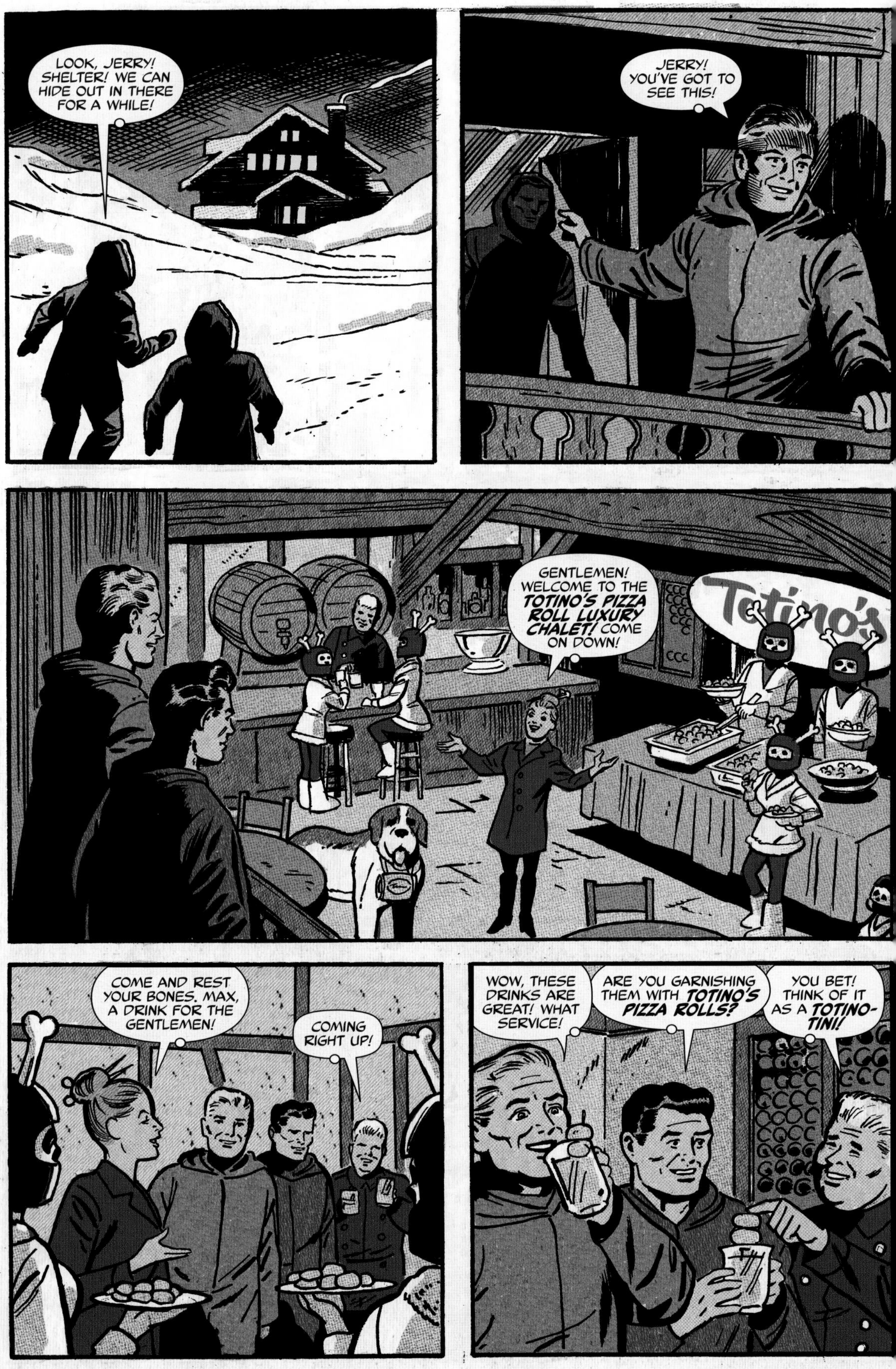
LOOK, JERRY! SHELTER! WE CAN HIDE OUT IN THERE FOR A WHILE!
JERRY! YOU'VE GOT TO SEE THIS!
GENTLEMEN! WELCOME TO THE TOTINO'S PIZZA ROLL LUXURY CHALET! COME ON DOWN!
Totino's
COME AND REST YOUR BONES. MAX, A DRINK FOR THE GENTLEMEN!
COMING RIGHT UP!
WOW, THESE DRINKS ARE GREAT! WHAT SERVICE!
ARE YOU GARNISHING THEM WITH TOTINO'S PIZZA ROLLS?
YOU BET! THINK OF IT AS A TOTINO-TINI!

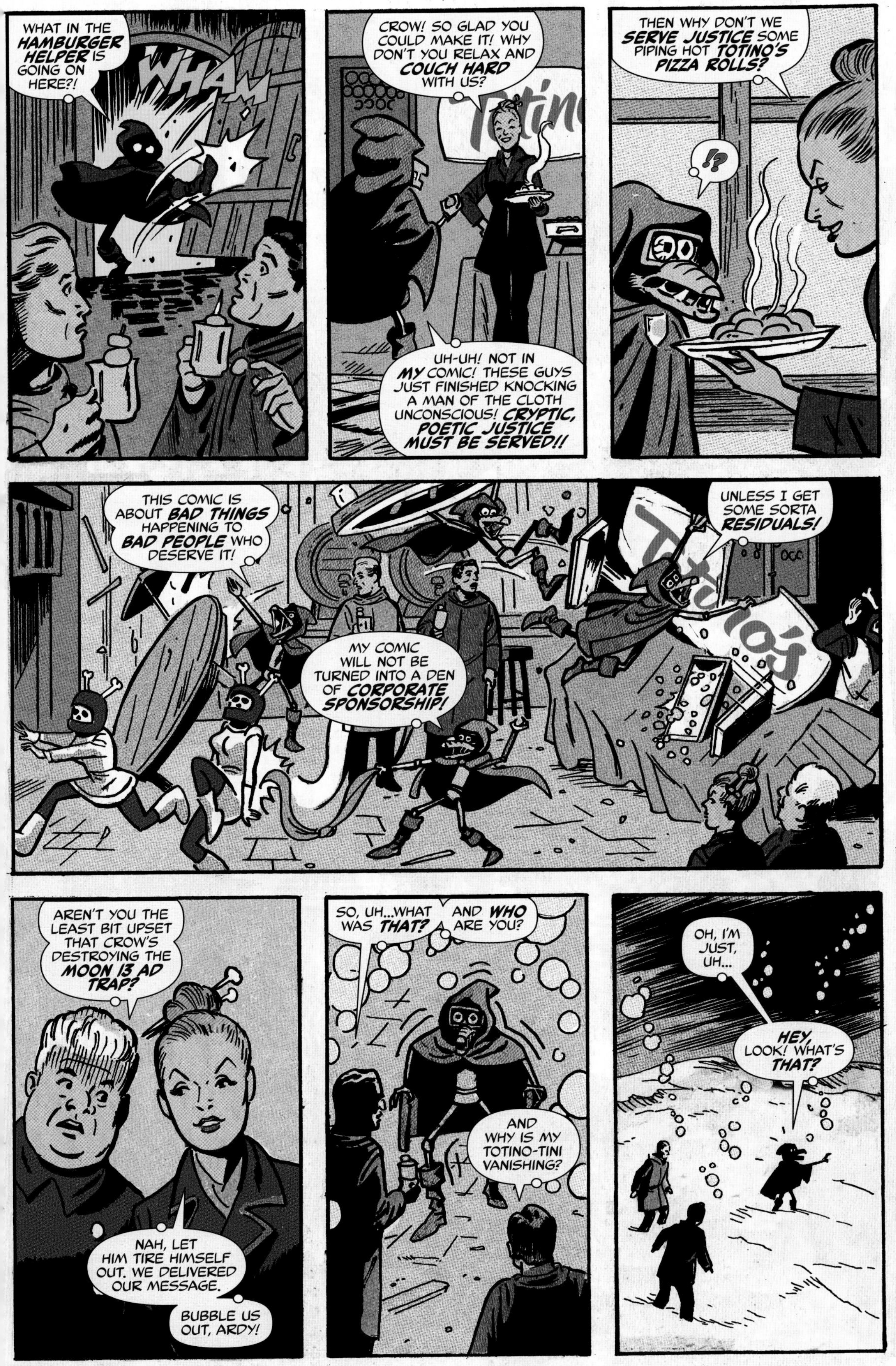

WHAT IN THE HAMBURGER HELPER IS GOING ON HERE?!
WHAM
CROW! SO GLAD YOU COULD MAKE IT! WHY DON'T YOU RELAX AND COUCH HARD WITH US?
UH-UH! NOT IN MY COMIC! THESE GUYS JUST FINISHED KNOCKING A MAN OF THE CLOTH UNCONSCIOUS! CRYPTIC, POETIC JUSTICE MUST BE SERVED!!
THEN WHY DON'T WE SERVE JUSTICE SOME PIPING HOT TOTINO'S PIZZA ROLLS?
!?
THIS COMIC IS ABOUT BAD THINGS HAPPENING TO BAD PEOPLE WHO DESERVE IT!
MY COMIC WILL NOT BE TURNED INTO A DEN OF CORPORATE SPONSORSHIP!
UNLESS I GET SOME SORTA RESIDUALS!
Totino's
AREN'T YOU THE LEAST BIT UPSET THAT CROW'S DESTROYING THE MOON 13 AD TRAP?
NAH, LET HIM TIRE HIMSELF OUT. WE DELIVERED OUR MESSAGE.
BUBBLE US OUT, ARDY!
SO, UH...WHAT WAS THAT?
AND WHO ARE YOU?
AND WHY IS MY TOTINO-TINI VANISHING?
OH, I'M JUST, UH...
HEY, LOOK! WHAT'S THAT?

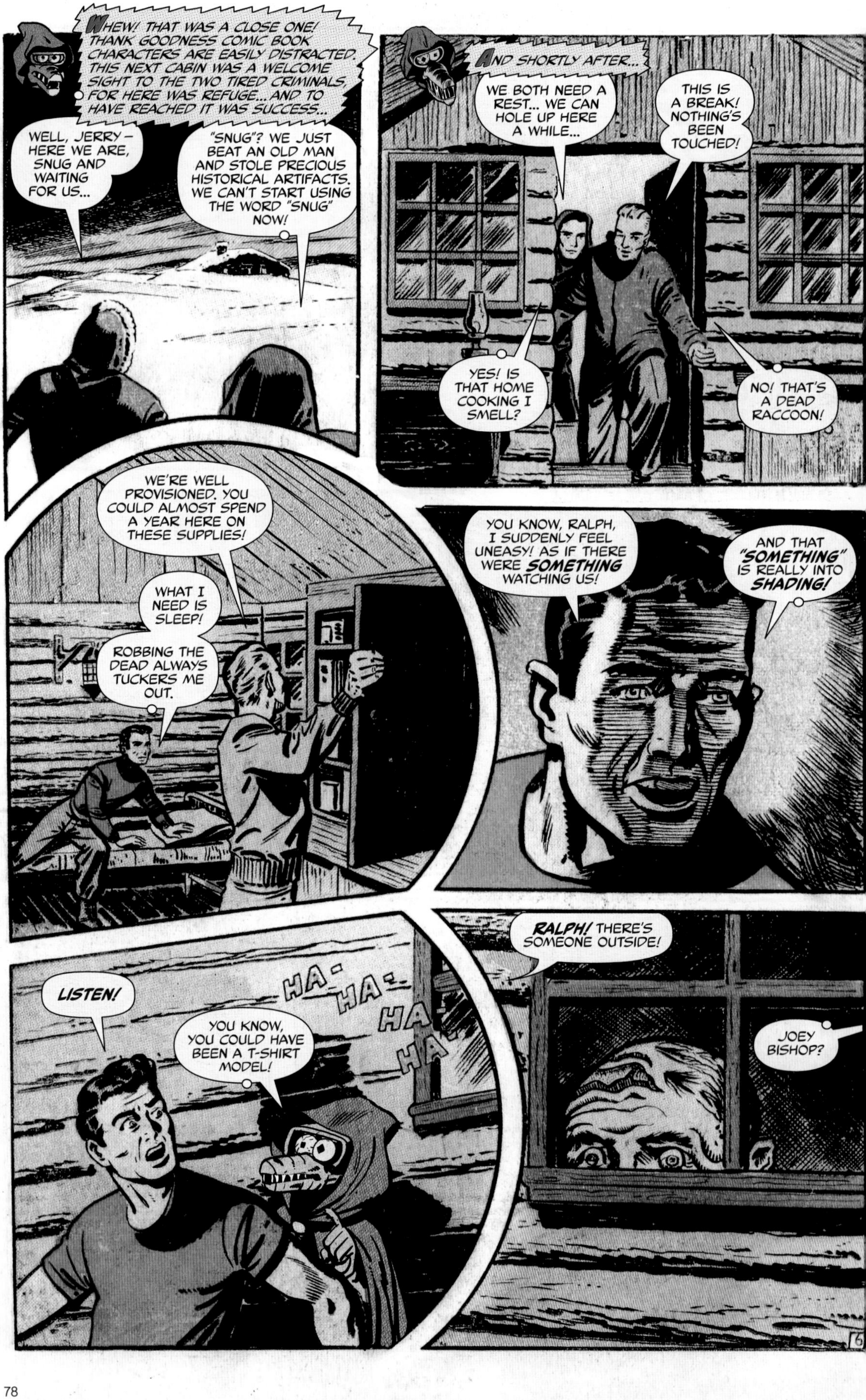
WHEW! THAT WAS A CLOSE ONE! THANK GOODNESS COMIC BOOK CHARACTERS ARE EASILY DISTRACTED. THIS NEXT CABIN WAS A WELCOME SIGHT TO THE TWO TIRED CRIMINALS, FOR HERE WAS REFUGE... AND TO HAVE REACHED IT WAS SUCCESS...
WELL, JERRY— HERE WE ARE, SNUG AND WAITING FOR US...
"SNUG"? WE JUST BEAT AN OLD MAN AND STOLE PRECIOUS HISTORICAL ARTIFACTS. WE CAN'T START USING THE WORD "SNUG" NOW!
AND SHORTLY AFTER...
WE BOTH NEED A REST... WE CAN HOLE UP HERE A WHILE...
THIS IS A BREAK! NOTHING'S BEEN TOUCHED!
YES! IS THAT HOME COOKING I SMELL?
NO! THAT'S A DEAD RACCOON!
WE'RE WELL PROVISIONED. YOU COULD ALMOST SPEND A YEAR HERE ON THESE SUPPLIES!
WHAT I NEED IS SLEEP!
ROBBING THE DEAD ALWAYS TUCKERS ME OUT.
YOU KNOW, RALPH, I SUDDENLY FEEL UNEASY! AS IF THERE WERE SOMETHING WATCHING US!
AND THAT "SOMETHING" IS REALLY INTO SHADING!
LISTEN!
HA-HA-HA-HA
YOU KNOW, YOU COULD HAVE BEEN A T-SHIRT MODEL!
RALPH! THERE'S SOMEONE OUTSIDE!
JOEY BISHOP?
6

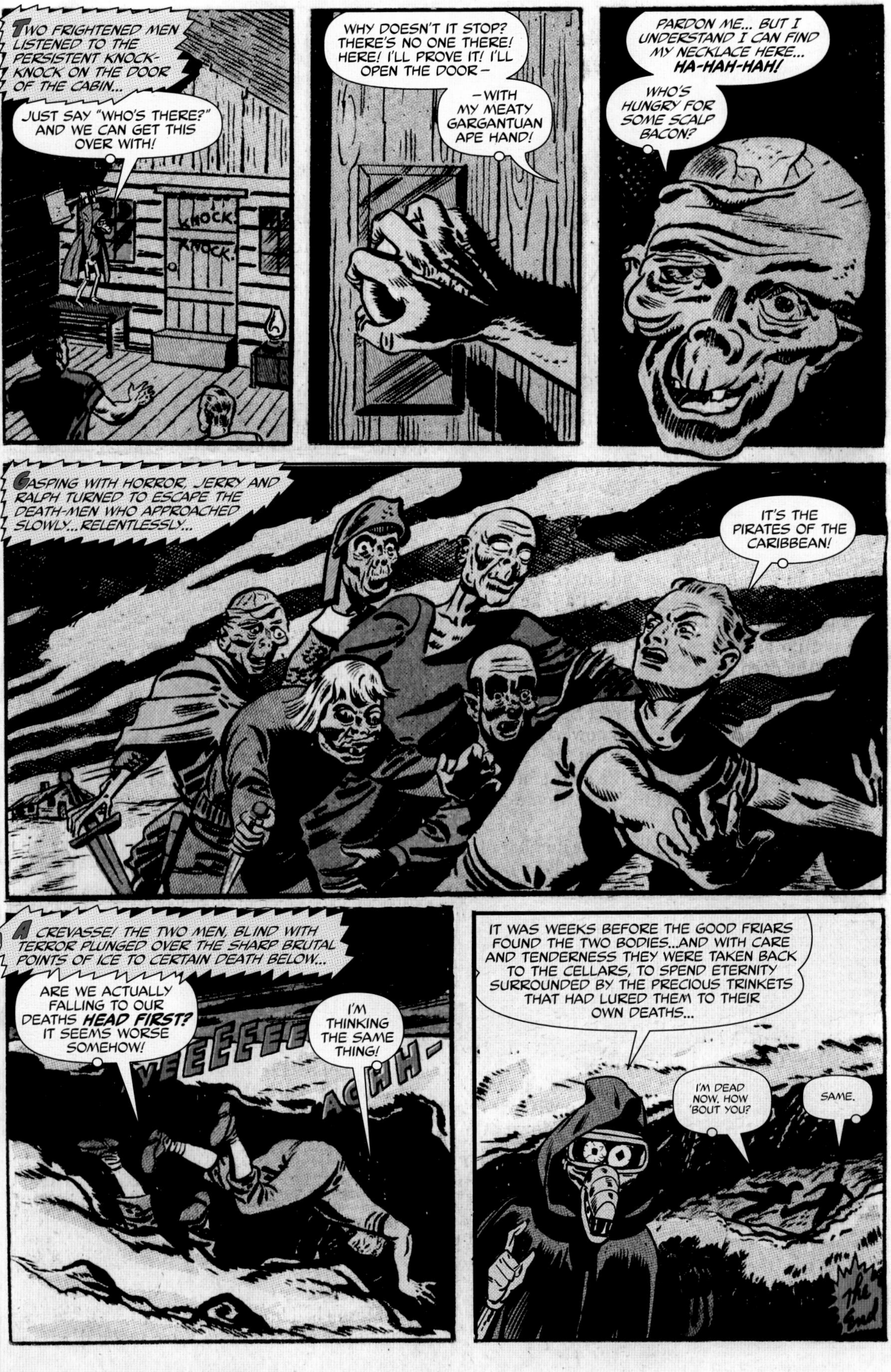
TWO FRIGHTENED MEN LISTENED TO THE PERSISTENT KNOCK-KNOCK ON THE DOOR OF THE CABIN...
JUST SAY "WHO'S THERE?" AND WE CAN GET THIS OVER WITH!
KNOCK KNOCK
WHY DOESN'T IT STOP? THERE'S NO ONE THERE! HERE! I'LL PROVE IT! I'LL OPEN THE DOOR—
—WITH MY MEATY GARGANTUAN APE HAND!
PARDON ME... BUT I UNDERSTAND I CAN FIND MY NECKLACE HERE... HA-HAH-HAH!
WHO'S HUNGRY FOR SOME SCALP BACON?
GASPING WITH HORROR, JERRY AND RALPH TURNED TO ESCAPE THE DEATH-MEN WHO APPROACHED SLOWLY...RELENTLESSLY...
IT'S THE PIRATES OF THE CARIBBEAN!
A CREVASSE! THE TWO MEN, BLIND WITH TERROR PLUNGED OVER THE SHARP BRUTAL POINTS OF ICE TO CERTAIN DEATH BELOW...
ARE WE ACTUALLY FALLING TO OUR DEATHS HEAD FIRST? IT SEEMS WORSE SOMEHOW!
I'M THINKING THE SAME THING!
EEEEEE
AGHH-
IT WAS WEEKS BEFORE THE GOOD FRIARS FOUND THE TWO BODIES...AND WITH CARE AND TENDERNESS THEY WERE TAKEN BACK TO THE CELLARS, TO SPEND ETERNITY SURROUNDED BY THE PRECIOUS TRINKETS THAT HAD LURED THEM TO THEIR OWN DEATHS...
I'M DEAD NOW. HOW 'BOUT YOU?
SAME.
the End

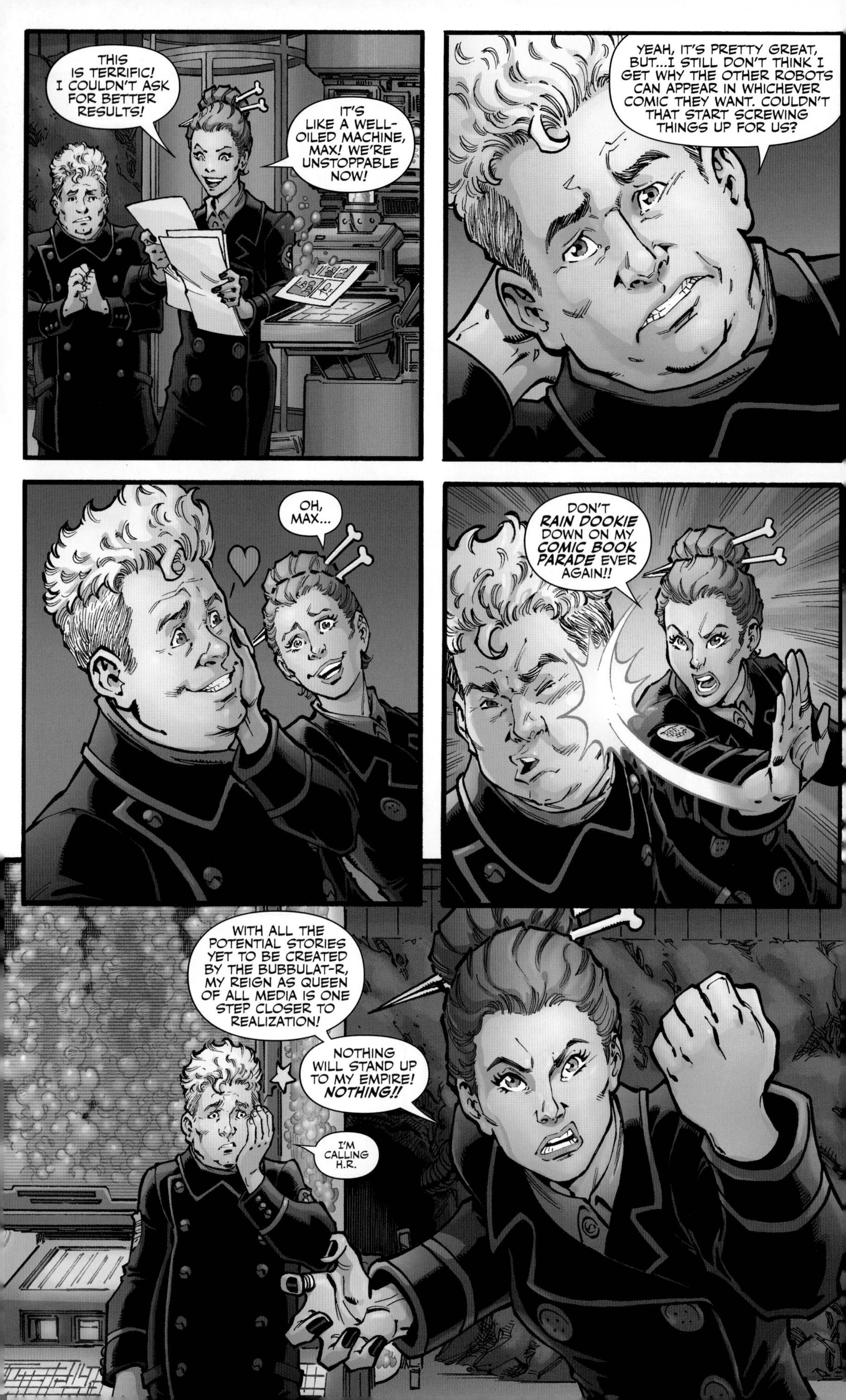
THIS IS TERRIFIC! I COULDN'T ASK FOR BETTER RESULTS!
IT'S LIKE A WELL-OILED MACHINE, MAX! WE'RE UNSTOPPABLE NOW!
YEAH, IT'S PRETTY GREAT, BUT...I STILL DON'T THINK I GET WHY THE OTHER ROBOTS CAN APPEAR IN WHICHEVER COMIC THEY WANT. COULDN'T THAT START SCREWING THINGS UP FOR US?
OH, MAX...
DON'T *RAIN DOOKIE* DOWN ON MY *COMIC BOOK PARADE* EVER AGAIN!!
WITH ALL THE POTENTIAL STORIES YET TO BE CREATED BY THE BUBBULAT-R, MY REIGN AS QUEEN OF ALL MEDIA IS ONE STEP CLOSER TO REALIZATION!
NOTHING WILL STAND UP TO MY EMPIRE! *NOTHING!!*
I'M CALLING H.R.

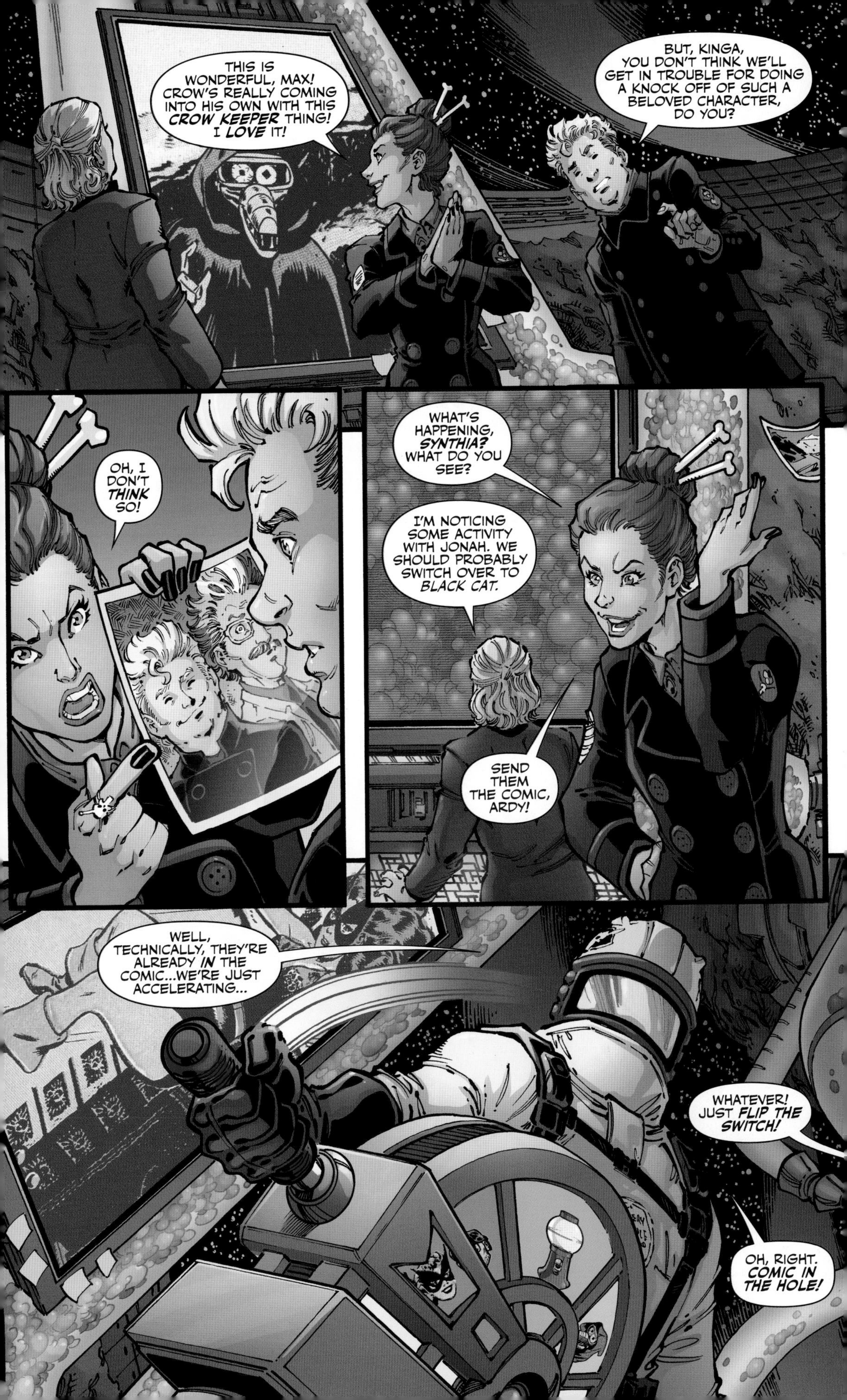
THIS IS WONDERFUL, MAX! CROW'S REALLY COMING INTO HIS OWN WITH THIS **CROW KEEPER** THING! I **LOVE** IT!
BUT, KINGA, YOU DON'T THINK WE'LL GET IN TROUBLE FOR DOING A KNOCK OFF OF SUCH A BELOVED CHARACTER, DO YOU?
OH, I DON'T **THINK** SO!
WHAT'S HAPPENING, **SYNTHIA?** WHAT DO YOU SEE?
I'M NOTICING SOME ACTIVITY WITH JONAH. WE SHOULD PROBABLY SWITCH OVER TO *BLACK CAT.*
SEND THEM THE COMIC, ARDY!
WELL, TECHNICALLY, THEY'RE ALREADY **IN** THE COMIC...WE'RE JUST ACCELERATING...
WHATEVER! JUST **FLIP THE SWITCH!**
OH, RIGHT. **COMIC IN THE HOLE!**

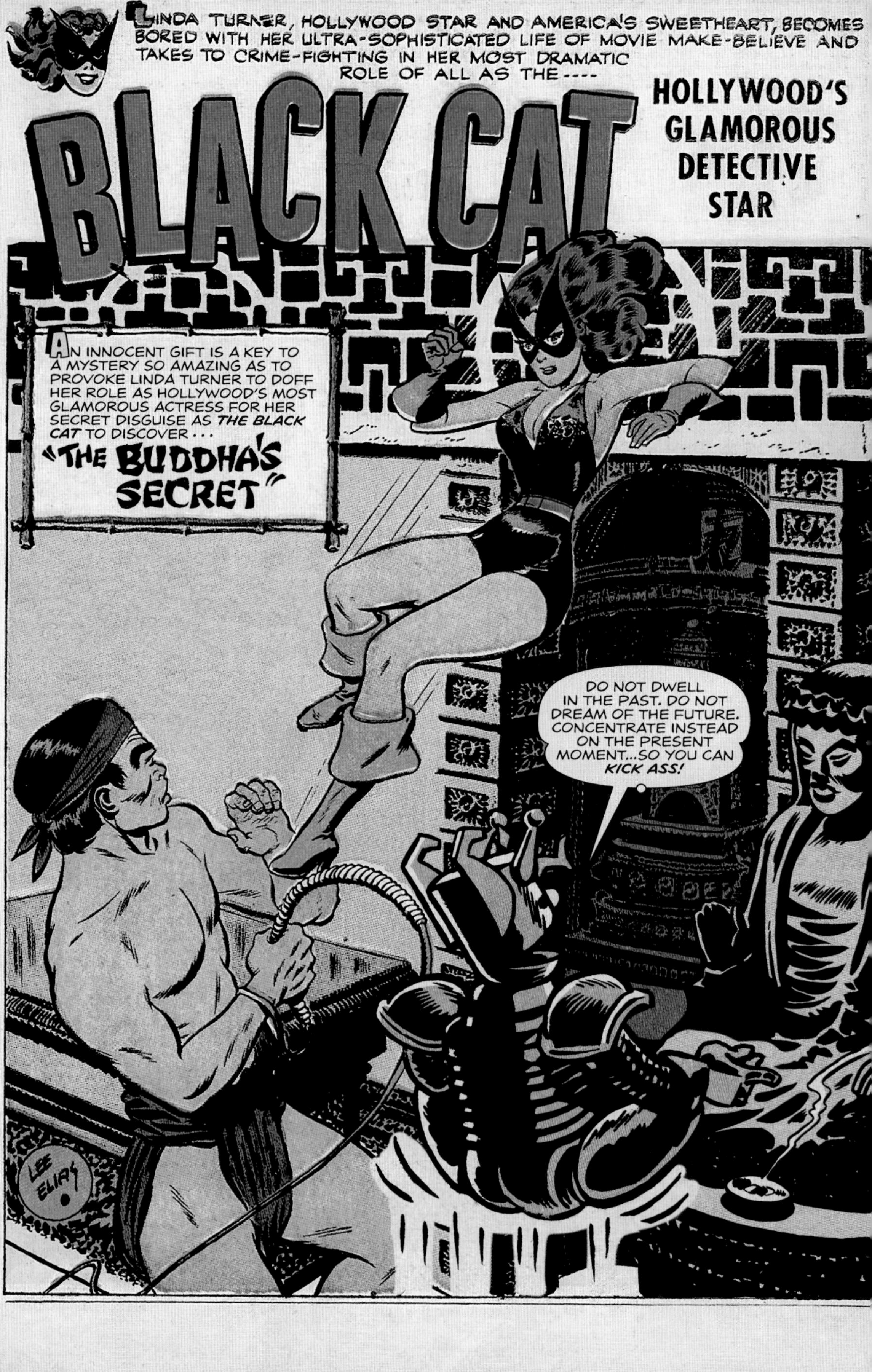
LINDA TURNER, HOLLYWOOD STAR AND AMERICA'S SWEETHEART, BECOMES BORED WITH HER ULTRA-SOPHISTICATED LIFE OF MOVIE MAKE-BELIEVE AND TAKES TO CRIME-FIGHTING IN HER MOST DRAMATIC ROLE OF ALL AS THE----
BLACK CAT
HOLLYWOOD'S GLAMOROUS DETECTIVE STAR
AN INNOCENT GIFT IS A KEY TO A MYSTERY SO AMAZING AS TO PROVOKE LINDA TURNER TO DOFF HER ROLE AS HOLLYWOOD'S MOST GLAMOROUS ACTRESS FOR HER SECRET DISGUISE AS THE BLACK CAT TO DISCOVER . . .
"THE BUDDHA'S SECRET"
DO NOT DWELL IN THE PAST. DO NOT DREAM OF THE FUTURE. CONCENTRATE INSTEAD ON THE PRESENT MOMENT...SO YOU CAN KICK ASS!
LEE ELIAS

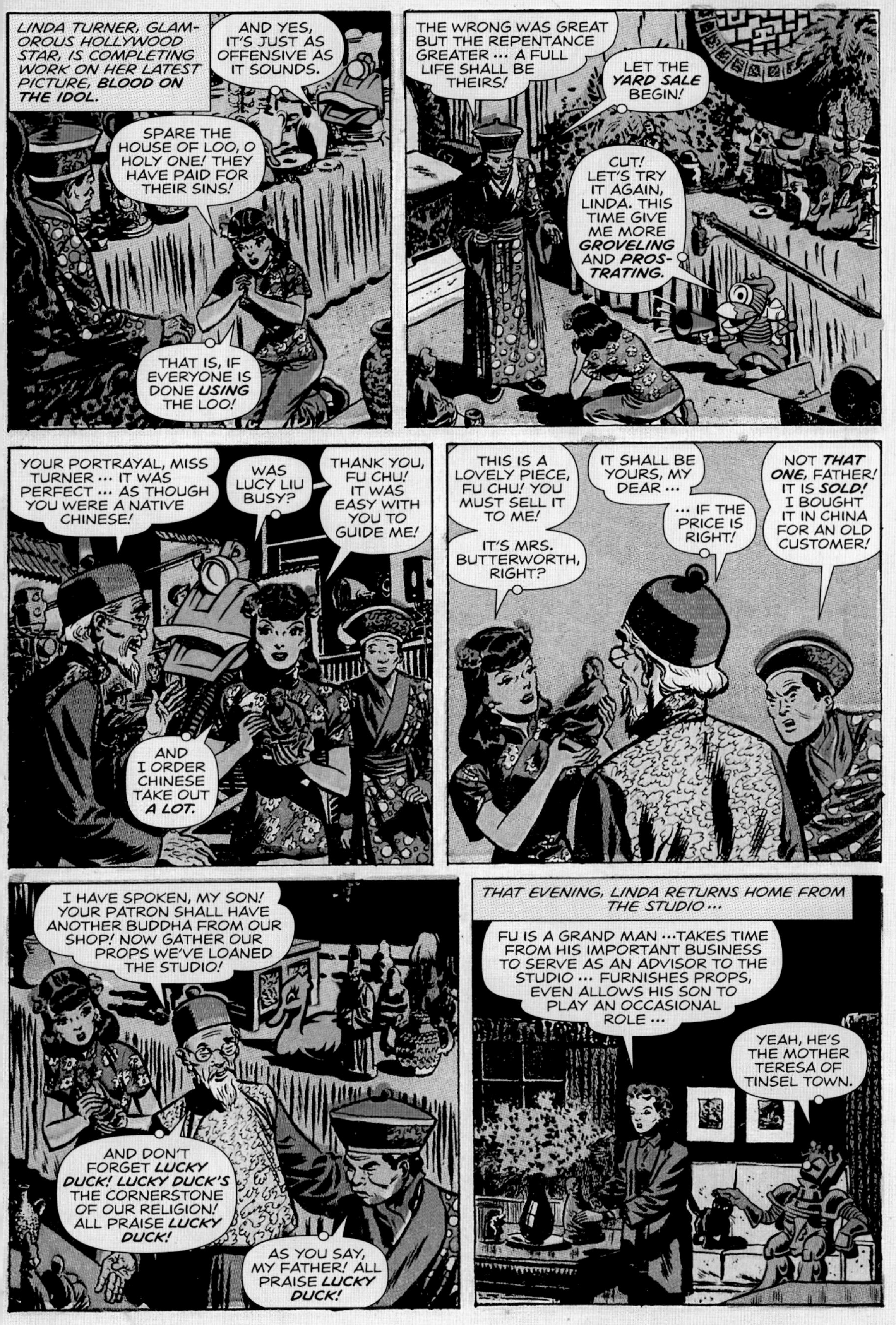
LINDA TURNER, GLAMOROUS HOLLYWOOD STAR, IS COMPLETING WORK ON HER LATEST PICTURE, BLOOD ON THE IDOL.
AND YES, IT'S JUST AS OFFENSIVE AS IT SOUNDS.
SPARE THE HOUSE OF LOO, O HOLY ONE! THEY HAVE PAID FOR THEIR SINS!
THAT IS, IF EVERYONE IS DONE USING THE LOO!
THE WRONG WAS GREAT BUT THE REPENTANCE GREATER ... A FULL LIFE SHALL BE THEIRS!
LET THE YARD SALE BEGIN!
CUT! LET'S TRY IT AGAIN, LINDA. THIS TIME GIVE ME MORE GROVELING AND PROSTRATING.
YOUR PORTRAYAL, MISS TURNER ... IT WAS PERFECT ... AS THOUGH YOU WERE A NATIVE CHINESE!
WAS LUCY LIU BUSY?
THANK YOU, FU CHU! IT WAS EASY WITH YOU TO GUIDE ME!
AND I ORDER CHINESE TAKE OUT A LOT.
THIS IS A LOVELY PIECE, FU CHU! YOU MUST SELL IT TO ME!
IT'S MRS. BUTTERWORTH, RIGHT?
IT SHALL BE YOURS, MY DEAR ...
... IF THE PRICE IS RIGHT!
NOT THAT ONE, FATHER! IT IS SOLD! I BOUGHT IT IN CHINA FOR AN OLD CUSTOMER!
I HAVE SPOKEN, MY SON! YOUR PATRON SHALL HAVE ANOTHER BUDDHA FROM OUR SHOP! NOW GATHER OUR PROPS WE'VE LOANED THE STUDIO!
AND DON'T FORGET LUCKY DUCK! LUCKY DUCK'S THE CORNERSTONE OF OUR RELIGION! ALL PRAISE LUCKY DUCK!
AS YOU SAY, MY FATHER! ALL PRAISE LUCKY DUCK!
THAT EVENING, LINDA RETURNS HOME FROM THE STUDIO ...
FU IS A GRAND MAN ... TAKES TIME FROM HIS IMPORTANT BUSINESS TO SERVE AS AN ADVISOR TO THE STUDIO ... FURNISHES PROPS, EVEN ALLOWS HIS SON TO PLAY AN OCCASIONAL ROLE ...
YEAH, HE'S THE MOTHER TERESA OF TINSEL TOWN.

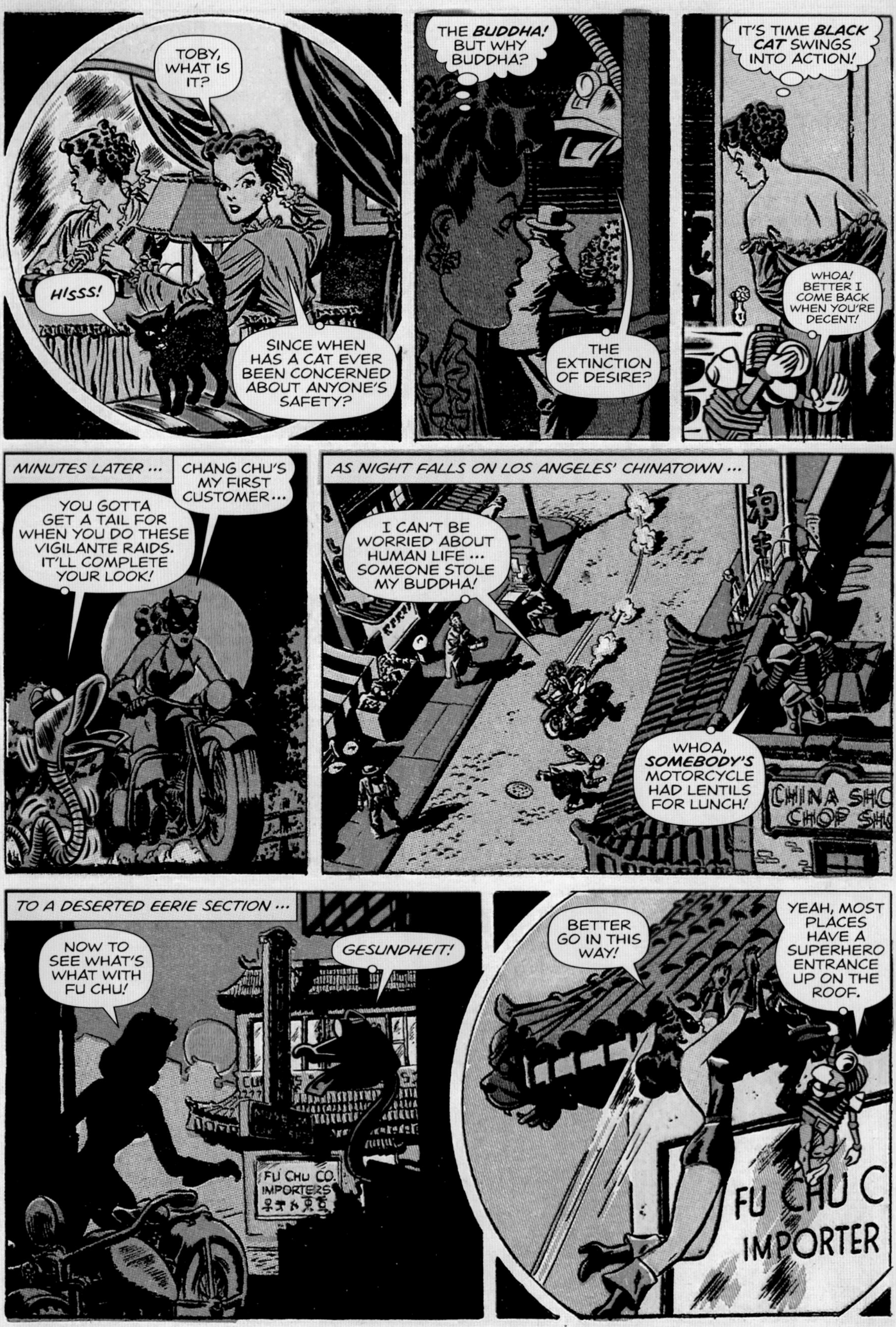

TOBY, WHAT IS IT?
HISSS!
SINCE WHEN HAS A CAT EVER BEEN CONCERNED ABOUT ANYONE'S SAFETY?
THE BUDDHA! BUT WHY BUDDHA?
THE EXTINCTION OF DESIRE?
IT'S TIME BLACK CAT SWINGS INTO ACTION!
WHOA! BETTER I COME BACK WHEN YOU'RE DECENT!
MINUTES LATER ...
CHANG CHU'S MY FIRST CUSTOMER ...
YOU GOTTA GET A TAIL FOR WHEN YOU DO THESE VIGILANTE RAIDS. IT'LL COMPLETE YOUR LOOK!
AS NIGHT FALLS ON LOS ANGELES' CHINATOWN ...
I CAN'T BE WORRIED ABOUT HUMAN LIFE ... SOMEONE STOLE MY BUDDHA!
WHOA, SOMEBODY'S MOTORCYCLE HAD LENTILS FOR LUNCH!
CHINA SHO
CHOP SH
TO A DESERTED EERIE SECTION ...
NOW TO SEE WHAT'S WHAT WITH FU CHU!
GESUNDHEIT!
FU CHU CO.
IMPORTERS
BETTER GO IN THIS WAY!
YEAH, MOST PLACES HAVE A SUPERHERO ENTRANCE UP ON THE ROOF.
FU CHU C
IMPORTER

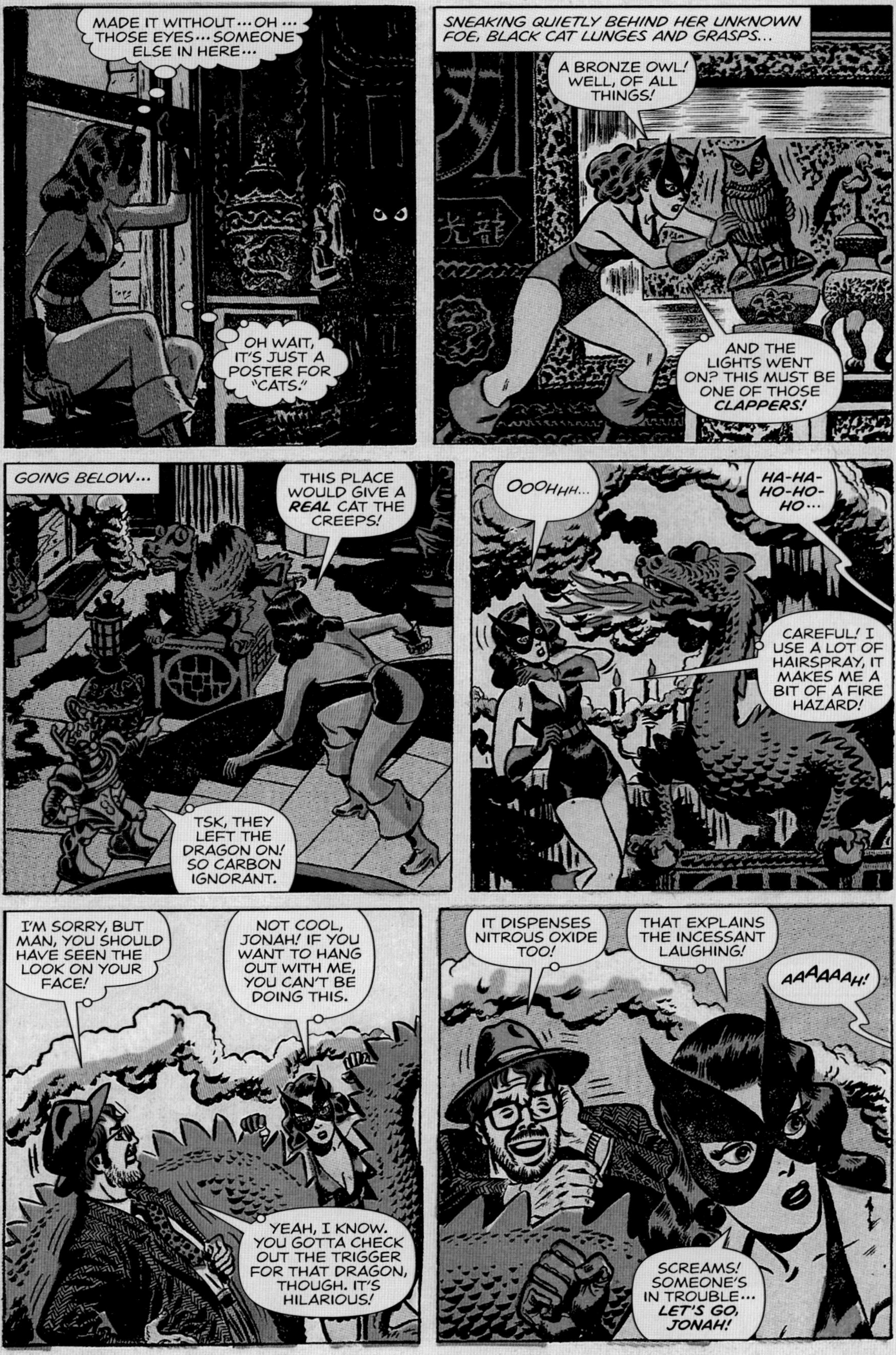

MADE IT WITHOUT... OH ... THOSE EYES... SOMEONE ELSE IN HERE...
OH WAIT, IT'S JUST A POSTER FOR "CATS."
SNEAKING QUIETLY BEHIND HER UNKNOWN FOE, BLACK CAT LUNGES AND GRASPS...
A BRONZE OWL! WELL, OF ALL THINGS!
AND THE LIGHTS WENT ON? THIS MUST BE ONE OF THOSE CLAPPERS!
GOING BELOW...
THIS PLACE WOULD GIVE A REAL CAT THE CREEPS!
TSK, THEY LEFT THE DRAGON ON! SO CARBON IGNORANT.
OOOHHH...
HA-HA-HO-HO-HO...
CAREFUL! I USE A LOT OF HAIRSPRAY, IT MAKES ME A BIT OF A FIRE HAZARD!
I'M SORRY, BUT MAN, YOU SHOULD HAVE SEEN THE LOOK ON YOUR FACE!
NOT COOL, JONAH! IF YOU WANT TO HANG OUT WITH ME, YOU CAN'T BE DOING THIS.
YEAH, I KNOW. YOU GOTTA CHECK OUT THE TRIGGER FOR THAT DRAGON, THOUGH. IT'S HILARIOUS!
IT DISPENSES NITROUS OXIDE TOO!
THAT EXPLAINS THE INCESSANT LAUGHING!
AAAAAAH!
SCREAMS! SOMEONE'S IN TROUBLE... LET'S GO, JONAH!

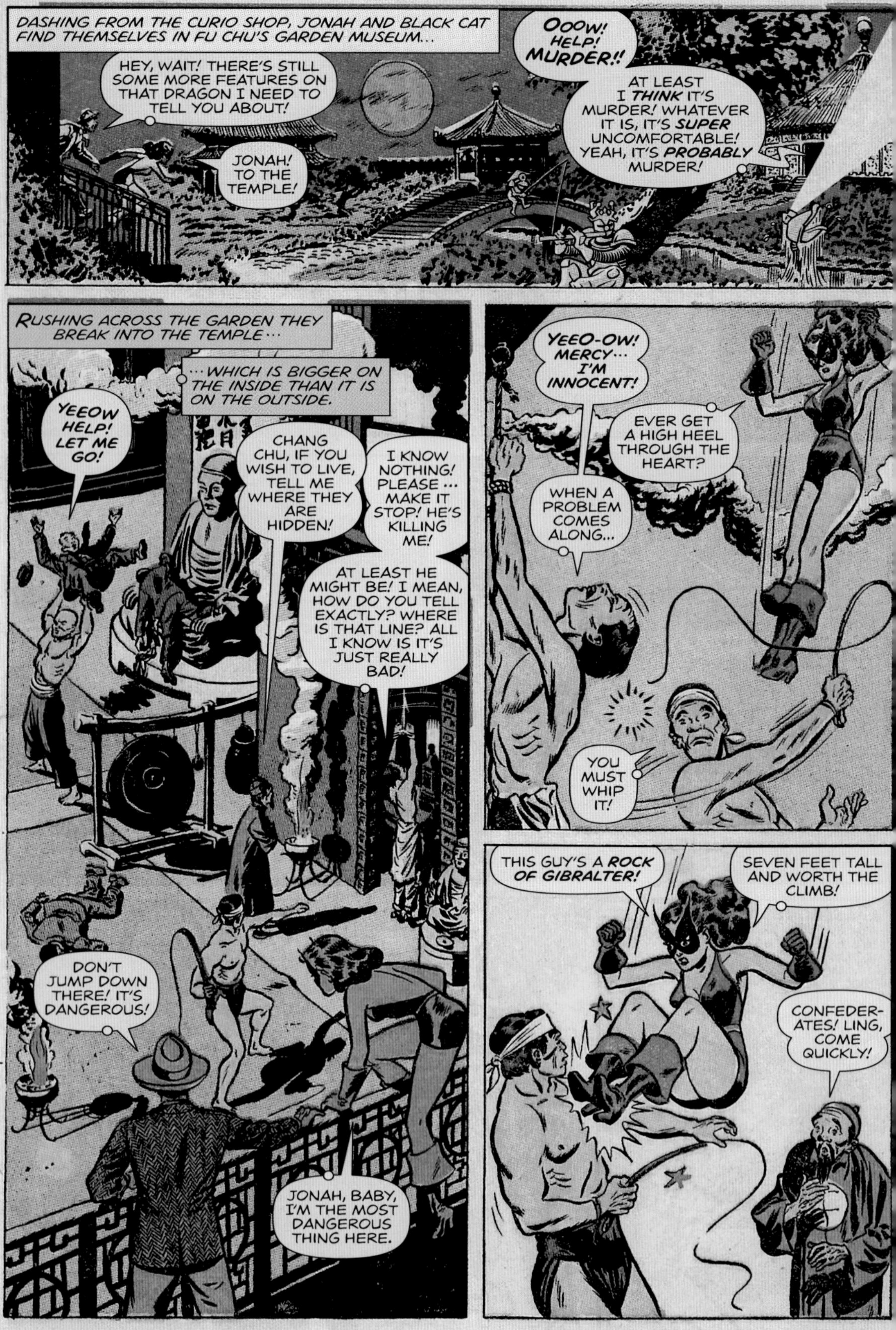
DASHING FROM THE CURIO SHOP, JONAH AND BLACK CAT FIND THEMSELVES IN FU CHU'S GARDEN MUSEUM...
HEY, WAIT! THERE'S STILL SOME MORE FEATURES ON THAT DRAGON I NEED TO TELL YOU ABOUT!
JONAH! TO THE TEMPLE!
OOOW! HELP! MURDER!!
AT LEAST I THINK IT'S MURDER! WHATEVER IT IS, IT'S SUPER UNCOMFORTABLE! YEAH, IT'S PROBABLY MURDER!
RUSHING ACROSS THE GARDEN THEY BREAK INTO THE TEMPLE...
...WHICH IS BIGGER ON THE INSIDE THAN IT IS ON THE OUTSIDE.
YEEOW HELP! LET ME GO!
CHANG CHU, IF YOU WISH TO LIVE, TELL ME WHERE THEY ARE HIDDEN!
I KNOW NOTHING! PLEASE... MAKE IT STOP! HE'S KILLING ME!
AT LEAST HE MIGHT BE! I MEAN, HOW DO YOU TELL EXACTLY? WHERE IS THAT LINE? ALL I KNOW IS IT'S JUST REALLY BAD!
DON'T JUMP DOWN THERE! IT'S DANGEROUS!
JONAH, BABY, I'M THE MOST DANGEROUS THING HERE.
YEEO-OW! MERCY... I'M INNOCENT!
EVER GET A HIGH HEEL THROUGH THE HEART?
WHEN A PROBLEM COMES ALONG...
YOU MUST WHIP IT!
THIS GUY'S A ROCK OF GIBRALTER!
SEVEN FEET TALL AND WORTH THE CLIMB!
CONFEDER-ATES! LING, COME QUICKLY!

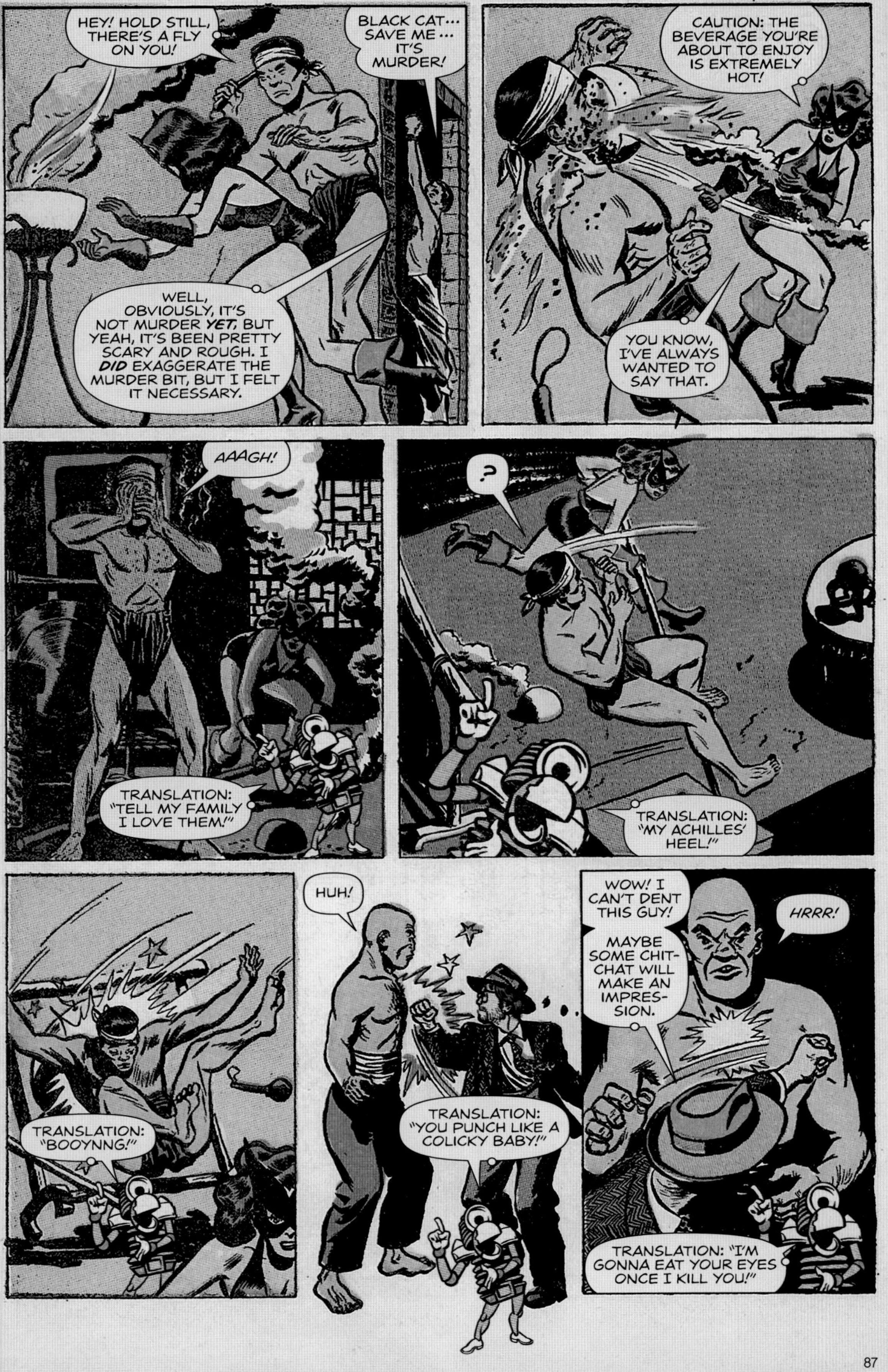
HEY! HOLD STILL, THERE'S A FLY ON YOU!
BLACK CAT... SAVE ME... IT'S MURDER!
WELL, OBVIOUSLY, IT'S NOT MURDER *YET,* BUT YEAH, IT'S BEEN PRETTY SCARY AND ROUGH. I *DID* EXAGGERATE THE MURDER BIT, BUT I FELT IT NECESSARY.
CAUTION: THE BEVERAGE YOU'RE ABOUT TO ENJOY IS EXTREMELY HOT!
YOU KNOW, I'VE ALWAYS WANTED TO SAY THAT.
AAAGH!
TRANSLATION: "TELL MY FAMILY I LOVE THEM!"
?
TRANSLATION: "MY ACHILLES' HEEL!"
TRANSLATION: "BOOYNNG!"
HUH!
TRANSLATION: "YOU PUNCH LIKE A COLICKY BABY!"
WOW! I CAN'T DENT THIS GUY!
MAYBE SOME CHIT-CHAT WILL MAKE AN IMPRES-SION.
HRRR!
TRANSLATION: "I'M GONNA EAT YOUR EYES ONCE I KILL YOU!"

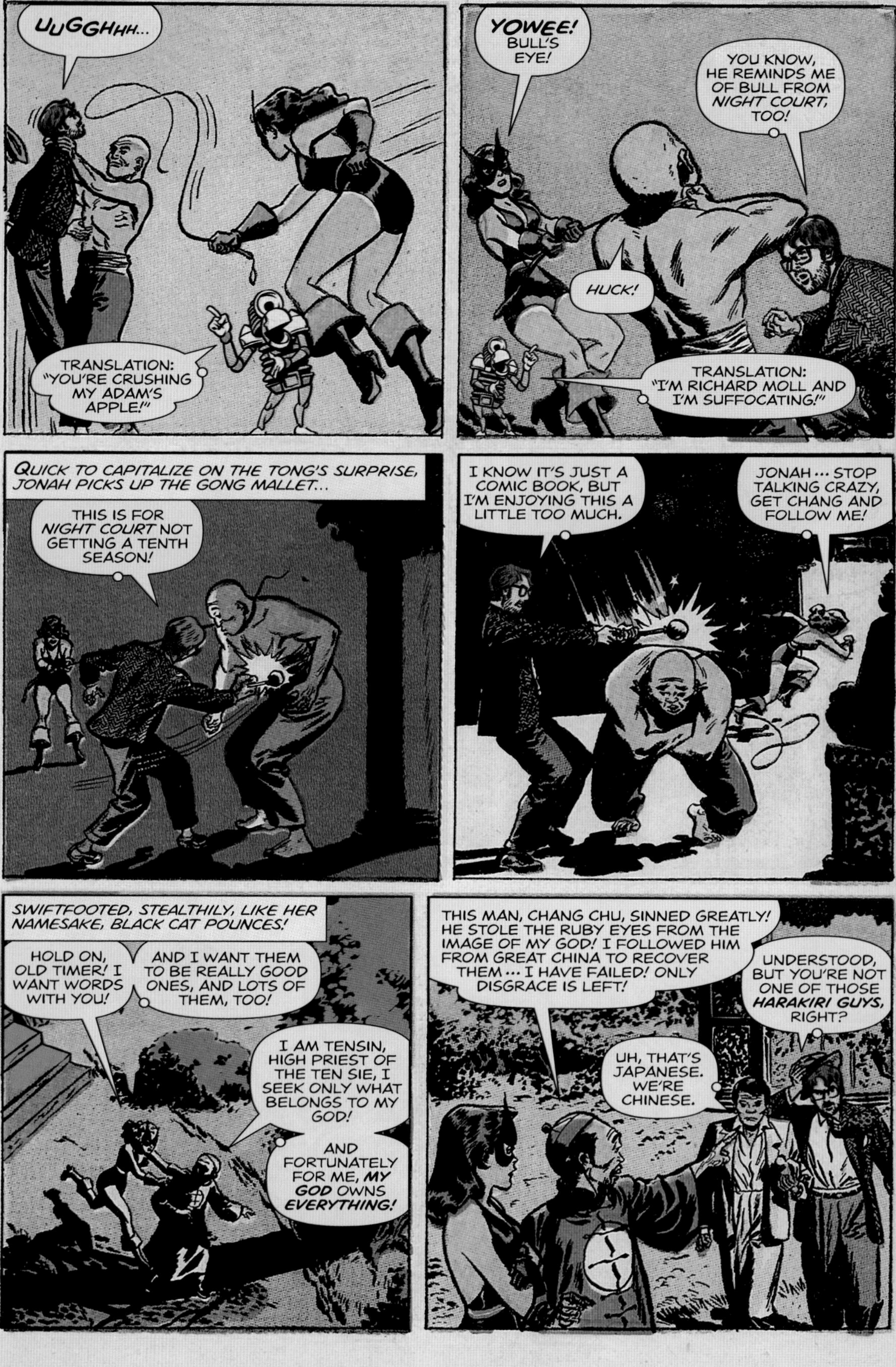
UUGGHHH...
TRANSLATION: "YOU'RE CRUSHING MY ADAM'S APPLE!"
YOWEE! BULL'S EYE!
YOU KNOW, HE REMINDS ME OF BULL FROM NIGHT COURT, TOO!
HUCK!
TRANSLATION: "I'M RICHARD MOLL AND I'M SUFFOCATING!"
QUICK TO CAPITALIZE ON THE TONG'S SURPRISE, JONAH PICKS UP THE GONG MALLET...
THIS IS FOR NIGHT COURT NOT GETTING A TENTH SEASON!
I KNOW IT'S JUST A COMIC BOOK, BUT I'M ENJOYING THIS A LITTLE TOO MUCH.
JONAH ... STOP TALKING CRAZY, GET CHANG AND FOLLOW ME!
SWIFTFOOTED, STEALTHILY, LIKE HER NAMESAKE, BLACK CAT POUNCES!
HOLD ON, OLD TIMER! I WANT WORDS WITH YOU!
AND I WANT THEM TO BE REALLY GOOD ONES, AND LOTS OF THEM, TOO!
I AM TENSIN, HIGH PRIEST OF THE TEN SIE, I SEEK ONLY WHAT BELONGS TO MY GOD!
AND FORTUNATELY FOR ME, MY GOD OWNS EVERYTHING!
THIS MAN, CHANG CHU, SINNED GREATLY! HE STOLE THE RUBY EYES FROM THE IMAGE OF MY GOD! I FOLLOWED HIM FROM GREAT CHINA TO RECOVER THEM ... I HAVE FAILED! ONLY DISGRACE IS LEFT!
UNDERSTOOD, BUT YOU'RE NOT ONE OF THOSE HARAKIRI GUYS, RIGHT?
UH, THAT'S JAPANESE. WE'RE CHINESE.

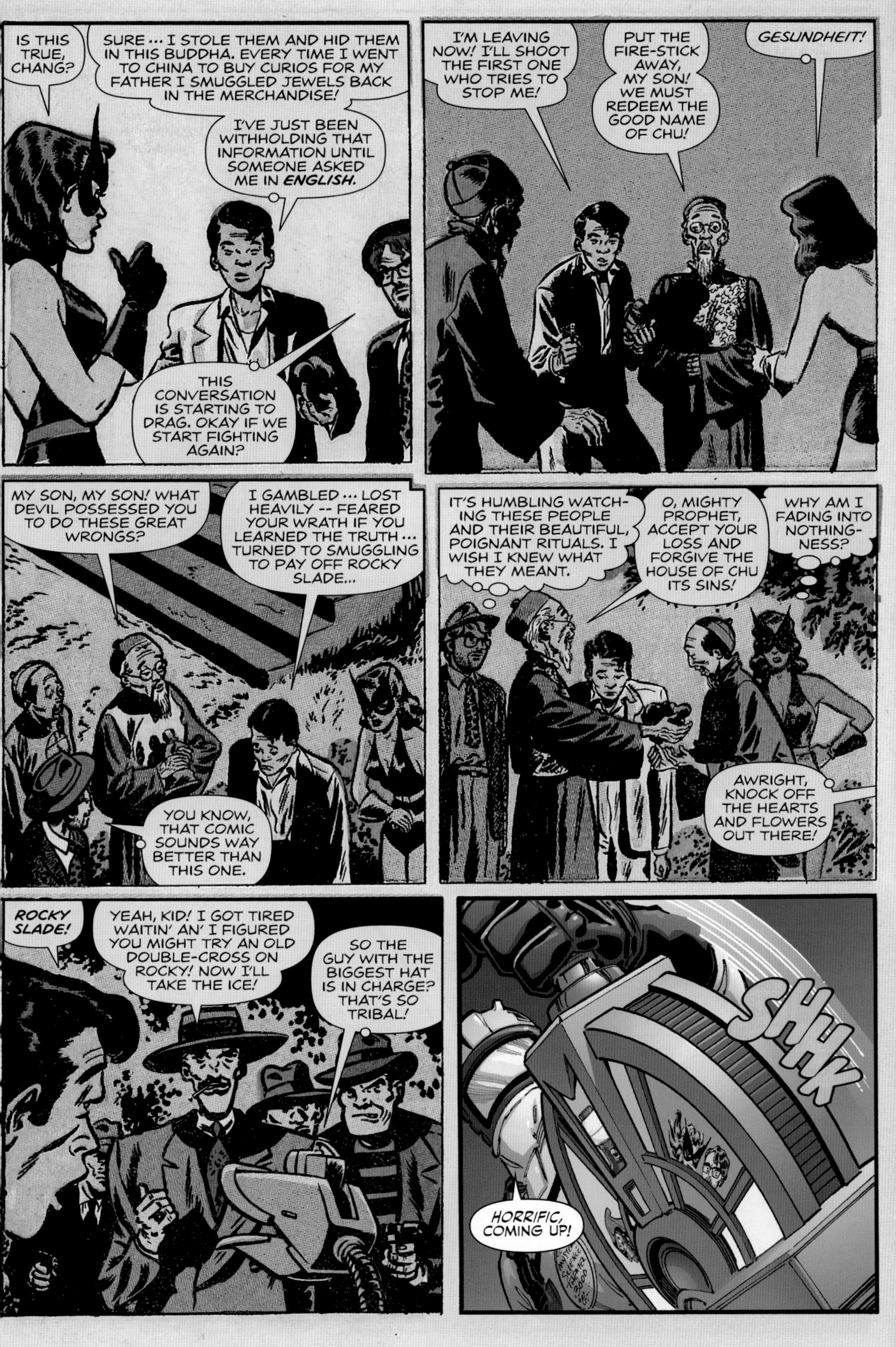
IS THIS TRUE, CHANG?
SURE ... I STOLE THEM AND HID THEM IN THIS BUDDHA. EVERY TIME I WENT TO CHINA TO BUY CURIOS FOR MY FATHER I SMUGGLED JEWELS BACK IN THE MERCHANDISE!
I'VE JUST BEEN WITHHOLDING THAT INFORMATION UNTIL SOMEONE ASKED ME IN *ENGLISH.*
THIS CONVERSATION IS STARTING TO DRAG. OKAY IF WE START FIGHTING AGAIN?
I'M LEAVING NOW! I'LL SHOOT THE FIRST ONE WHO TRIES TO STOP ME!
PUT THE FIRE-STICK AWAY, MY SON! WE MUST REDEEM THE GOOD NAME OF CHU!
GESUNDHEIT!
MY SON, MY SON! WHAT DEVIL POSSESSED YOU TO DO THESE GREAT WRONGS?
I GAMBLED ... LOST HEAVILY -- FEARED YOUR WRATH IF YOU LEARNED THE TRUTH ... TURNED TO SMUGGLING TO PAY OFF ROCKY SLADE...
YOU KNOW, THAT COMIC SOUNDS WAY BETTER THAN THIS ONE.
IT'S HUMBLING WATCHING THESE PEOPLE AND THEIR BEAUTIFUL, POIGNANT RITUALS. I WISH I KNEW WHAT THEY MEANT.
O, MIGHTY PROPHET, ACCEPT YOUR LOSS AND FORGIVE THE HOUSE OF CHU ITS SINS!
WHY AM I FADING INTO NOTHING-NESS?
AWRIGHT, KNOCK OFF THE HEARTS AND FLOWERS OUT THERE!
ROCKY SLADE!
YEAH, KID! I GOT TIRED WAITIN' AN' I FIGURED YOU MIGHT TRY AN OLD DOUBLE-CROSS ON ROCKY! NOW I'LL TAKE THE ICE!
SO THE GUY WITH THE BIGGEST HAT IS IN CHARGE? THAT'S SO TRIBAL!
SHHK
HORRIFIC, COMING UP!

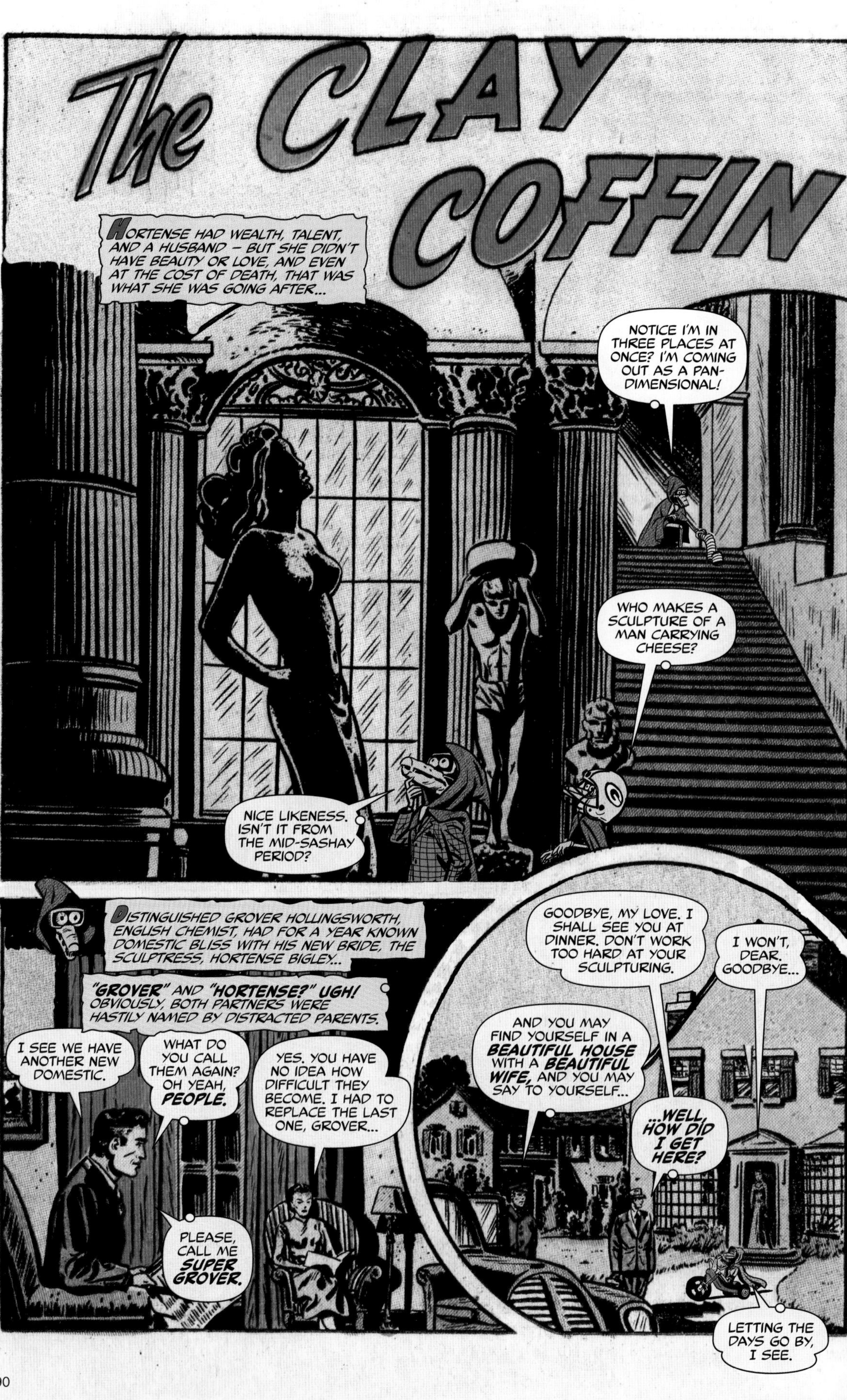
The CLAY COFFIN
HORTENSE HAD WEALTH, TALENT, AND A HUSBAND – BUT SHE DIDN'T HAVE BEAUTY OR LOVE, AND EVEN AT THE COST OF DEATH, THAT WAS WHAT SHE WAS GOING AFTER...
NOTICE I'M IN THREE PLACES AT ONCE? I'M COMING OUT AS A PAN-DIMENSIONAL!
WHO MAKES A SCULPTURE OF A MAN CARRYING CHEESE?
NICE LIKENESS. ISN'T IT FROM THE MID-SASHAY PERIOD?
DISTINGUISHED GROVER HOLLINGSWORTH, ENGLISH CHEMIST, HAD FOR A YEAR KNOWN DOMESTIC BLISS WITH HIS NEW BRIDE, THE SCULPTRESS, HORTENSE BIGLEY...
"GROVER" AND "HORTENSE?" UGH! OBVIOUSLY, BOTH PARTNERS WERE HASTILY NAMED BY DISTRACTED PARENTS.
I SEE WE HAVE ANOTHER NEW DOMESTIC.
WHAT DO YOU CALL THEM AGAIN? OH YEAH, PEOPLE.
YES. YOU HAVE NO IDEA HOW DIFFICULT THEY BECOME. I HAD TO REPLACE THE LAST ONE, GROVER...
PLEASE, CALL ME SUPER GROVER.
GOODBYE, MY LOVE. I SHALL SEE YOU AT DINNER. DON'T WORK TOO HARD AT YOUR SCULPTURING.
I WON'T, DEAR. GOODBYE...
AND YOU MAY FIND YOURSELF IN A BEAUTIFUL HOUSE WITH A BEAUTIFUL WIFE, AND YOU MAY SAY TO YOURSELF...
...WELL, HOW DID I GET HERE?
LETTING THE DAYS GO BY, I SEE.

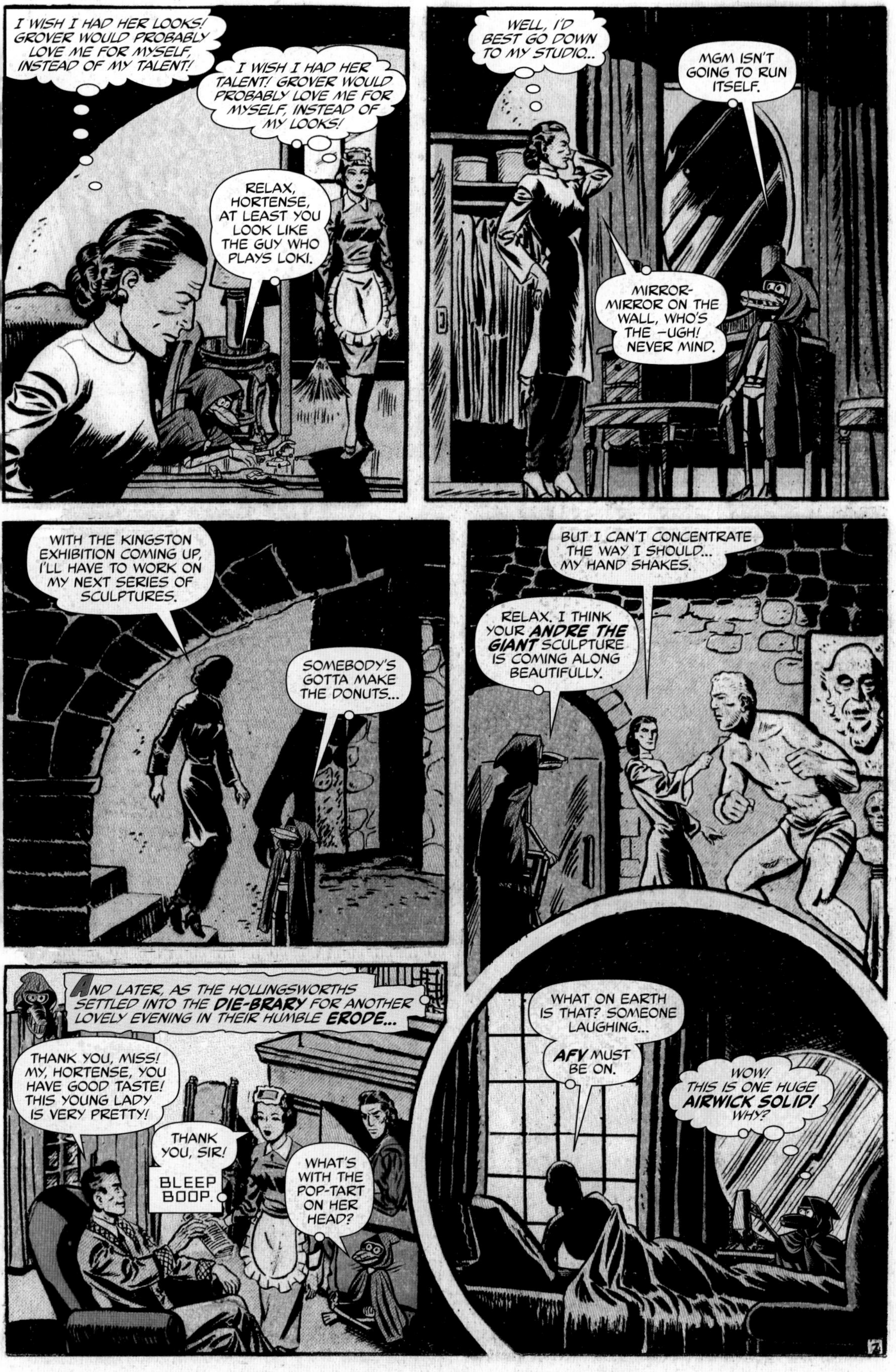
I WISH I HAD HER LOOKS! GROVER WOULD PROBABLY LOVE ME FOR MYSELF, INSTEAD OF MY TALENT!
I WISH I HAD HER TALENT! GROVER WOULD PROBABLY LOVE ME FOR MYSELF, INSTEAD OF MY LOOKS!
RELAX, HORTENSE, AT LEAST YOU LOOK LIKE THE GUY WHO PLAYS LOKI.
WELL, I'D BEST GO DOWN TO MY STUDIO...
MGM ISN'T GOING TO RUN ITSELF.
MIRROR-MIRROR ON THE WALL, WHO'S THE —UGH! NEVER MIND.
WITH THE KINGSTON EXHIBITION COMING UP, I'LL HAVE TO WORK ON MY NEXT SERIES OF SCULPTURES.
SOMEBODY'S GOTTA MAKE THE DONUTS...
BUT I CAN'T CONCENTRATE THE WAY I SHOULD... MY HAND SHAKES.
RELAX. I THINK YOUR ANDRE THE GIANT SCULPTURE IS COMING ALONG BEAUTIFULLY.
AND LATER, AS THE HOLLINGSWORTHS SETTLED INTO THE DIE-BRARY FOR ANOTHER LOVELY EVENING IN THEIR HUMBLE ERODE...
THANK YOU, MISS! MY, HORTENSE, YOU HAVE GOOD TASTE! THIS YOUNG LADY IS VERY PRETTY!
THANK YOU, SIR!
BLEEP BOOP.
WHAT'S WITH THE POP-TART ON HER HEAD?
WHAT ON EARTH IS THAT? SOMEONE LAUGHING...
AFV MUST BE ON.
WOW! THIS IS ONE HUGE AIRWICK SOLID! WHY?
7

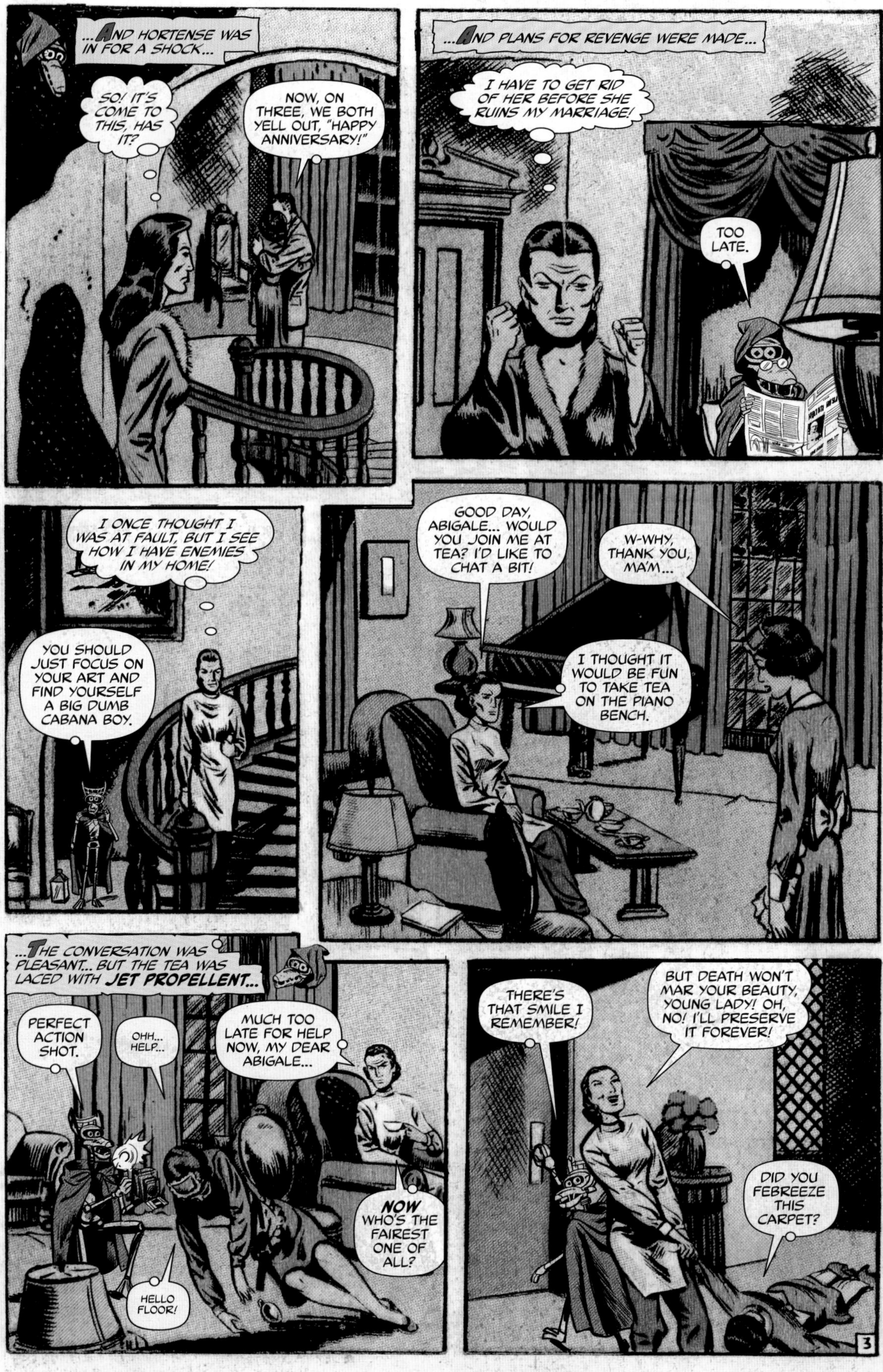
...AND HORTENSE WAS IN FOR A SHOCK...
SO! IT'S COME TO THIS, HAS IT?
NOW, ON THREE, WE BOTH YELL OUT, "HAPPY ANNIVERSARY!"
...AND PLANS FOR REVENGE WERE MADE...
I HAVE TO GET RID OF HER BEFORE SHE RUINS MY MARRIAGE!
TOO LATE.
I ONCE THOUGHT I WAS AT FAULT, BUT I SEE HOW I HAVE ENEMIES IN MY HOME!
YOU SHOULD JUST FOCUS ON YOUR ART AND FIND YOURSELF A BIG DUMB CABANA BOY.
GOOD DAY, ABIGALE... WOULD YOU JOIN ME AT TEA? I'D LIKE TO CHAT A BIT!
W-WHY, THANK YOU, MA'M...
I THOUGHT IT WOULD BE FUN TO TAKE TEA ON THE PIANO BENCH.
...THE CONVERSATION WAS PLEASANT... BUT THE TEA WAS LACED WITH JET PROPELLENT...
PERFECT ACTION SHOT.
OHH... HELP...
MUCH TOO LATE FOR HELP NOW, MY DEAR ABIGALE...
NOW WHO'S THE FAIREST ONE OF ALL?
HELLO FLOOR!
THERE'S THAT SMILE I REMEMBER!
BUT DEATH WON'T MAR YOUR BEAUTY, YOUNG LADY! OH, NO! I'LL PRESERVE IT FOREVER!
DID YOU FEBREEZE THIS CARPET?
3

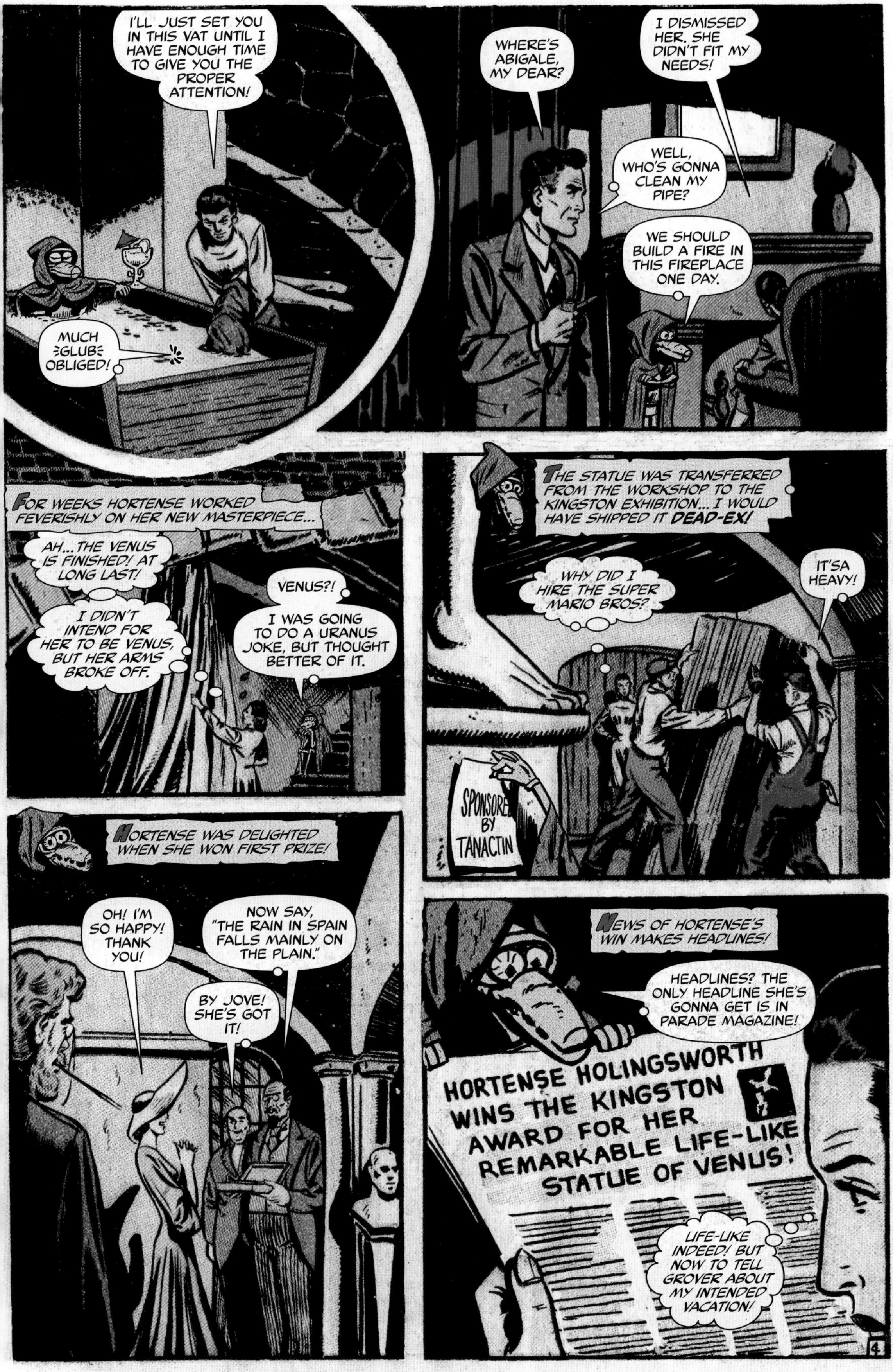
I'LL JUST SET YOU IN THIS VAT UNTIL I HAVE ENOUGH TIME TO GIVE YOU THE PROPER ATTENTION!
MUCH GLUB OBLIGED!
WHERE'S ABIGALE, MY DEAR?
I DISMISSED HER. SHE DIDN'T FIT MY NEEDS!
WELL, WHO'S GONNA CLEAN MY PIPE?
WE SHOULD BUILD A FIRE IN THIS FIREPLACE ONE DAY.
FOR WEEKS HORTENSE WORKED FEVERISHLY ON HER NEW MASTERPIECE...
AH... THE VENUS IS FINISHED! AT LONG LAST!
I DIDN'T INTEND FOR HER TO BE VENUS, BUT HER ARMS BROKE OFF.
VENUS?!
I WAS GOING TO DO A URANUS JOKE, BUT THOUGHT BETTER OF IT.
THE STATUE WAS TRANSFERRED FROM THE WORKSHOP TO THE KINGSTON EXHIBITION... I WOULD HAVE SHIPPED IT DEAD-EX!
WHY DID I HIRE THE SUPER MARIO BROS?
IT'SA HEAVY!
SPONSORE
BY
TANACTIN
HORTENSE WAS DELIGHTED WHEN SHE WON FIRST PRIZE!
OH! I'M SO HAPPY! THANK YOU!
NOW SAY, "THE RAIN IN SPAIN FALLS MAINLY ON THE PLAIN."
BY JOVE! SHE'S GOT IT!
NEWS OF HORTENSE'S WIN MAKES HEADLINES!
HEADLINES? THE ONLY HEADLINE SHE'S GONNA GET IS IN PARADE MAGAZINE!
HORTENSE HOLINGSWORTH WINS THE KINGSTON AWARD FOR HER REMARKABLE LIFE-LIKE STATUE OF VENUS!
LIFE-LIKE INDEED! BUT NOW TO TELL GROVER ABOUT MY INTENDED VACATION!
4

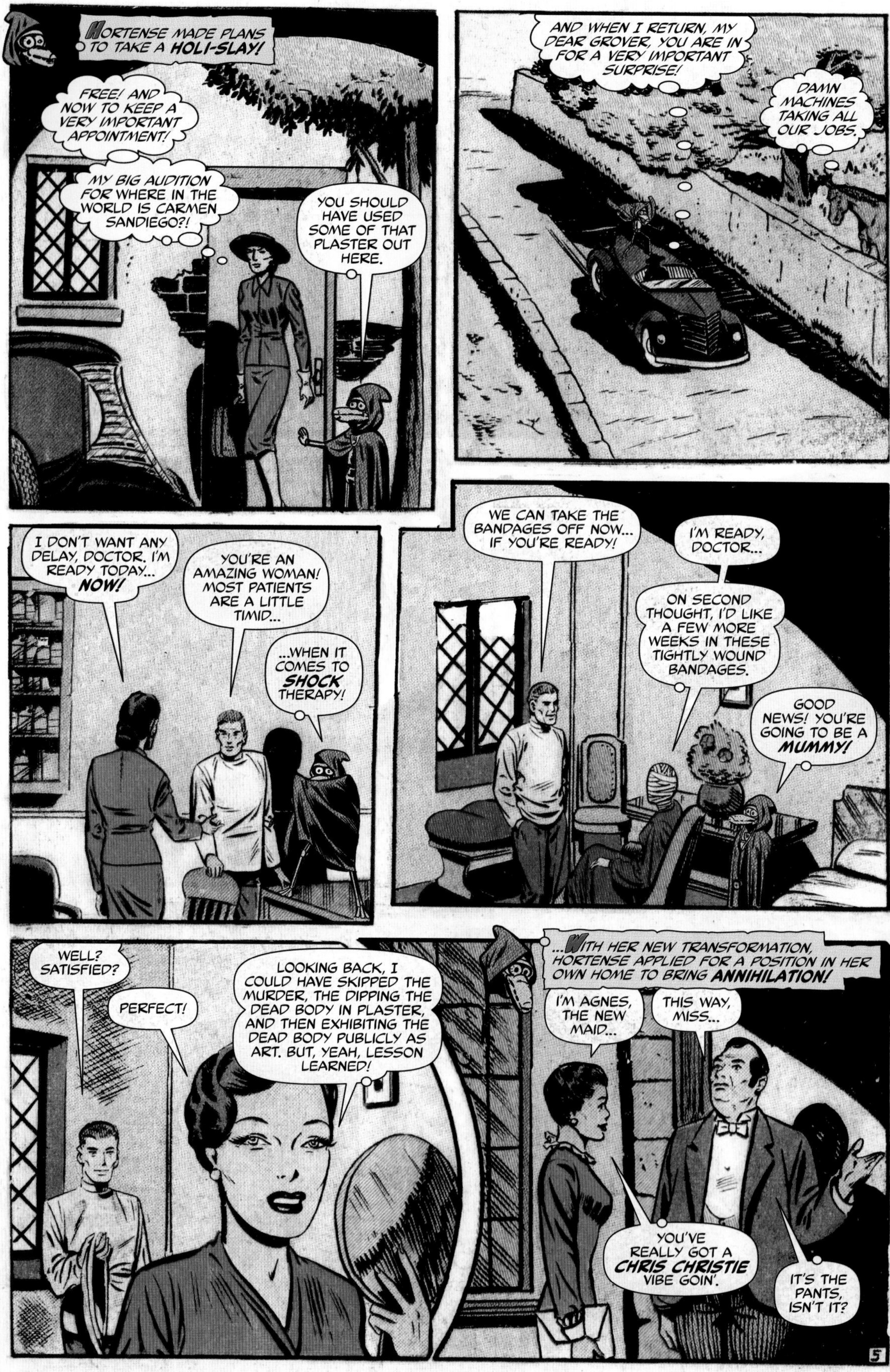
HORTENSE MADE PLANS TO TAKE A HOLI-SLAY!
FREE! AND NOW TO KEEP A VERY IMPORTANT APPOINTMENT!
MY BIG AUDITION FOR WHERE IN THE WORLD IS CARMEN SANDIEGO?!
YOU SHOULD HAVE USED SOME OF THAT PLASTER OUT HERE.
AND WHEN I RETURN, MY DEAR GROVER, YOU ARE IN FOR A VERY IMPORTANT SURPRISE!
DAMN MACHINES TAKING ALL OUR JOBS.
I DON'T WANT ANY DELAY, DOCTOR. I'M READY TODAY... NOW!
YOU'RE AN AMAZING WOMAN! MOST PATIENTS ARE A LITTLE TIMID...
...WHEN IT COMES TO SHOCK THERAPY!
WE CAN TAKE THE BANDAGES OFF NOW... IF YOU'RE READY!
I'M READY, DOCTOR...
ON SECOND THOUGHT, I'D LIKE A FEW MORE WEEKS IN THESE TIGHTLY WOUND BANDAGES.
GOOD NEWS! YOU'RE GOING TO BE A MUMMY!
WELL? SATISFIED?
PERFECT!
LOOKING BACK, I COULD HAVE SKIPPED THE MURDER, THE DIPPING THE DEAD BODY IN PLASTER, AND THEN EXHIBITING THE DEAD BODY PUBLICLY AS ART. BUT, YEAH, LESSON LEARNED!
...WITH HER NEW TRANSFORMATION, HORTENSE APPLIED FOR A POSITION IN HER OWN HOME TO BRING ANNIHILATION!
I'M AGNES, THE NEW MAID...
THIS WAY, MISS...
YOU'VE REALLY GOT A CHRIS CHRISTIE VIBE GOIN'.
IT'S THE PANTS, ISN'T IT?
5

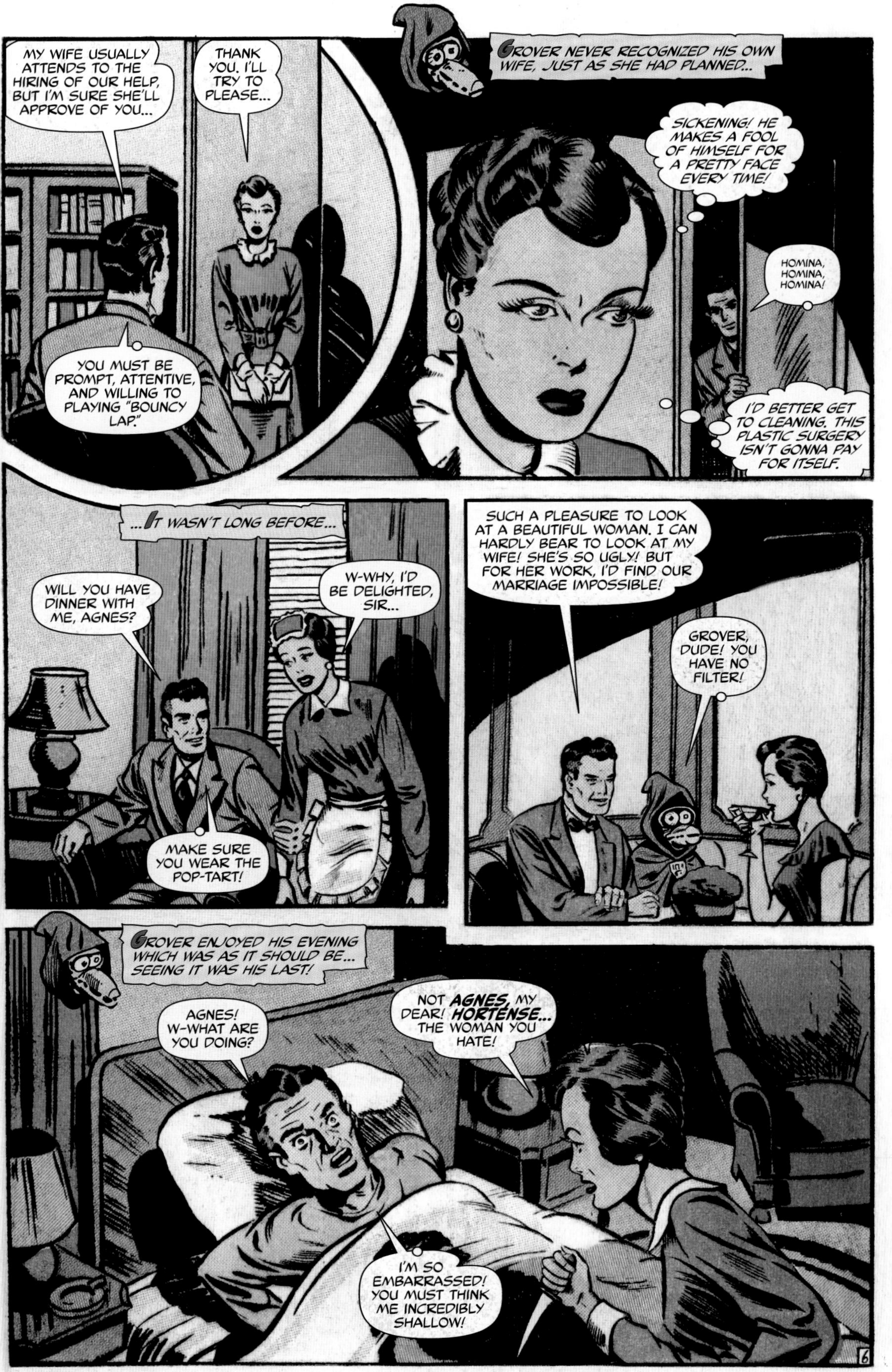

MY WIFE USUALLY ATTENDS TO THE HIRING OF OUR HELP, BUT I'M SURE SHE'LL APPROVE OF YOU...
THANK YOU. I'LL TRY TO PLEASE...
YOU MUST BE PROMPT, ATTENTIVE, AND WILLING TO PLAYING "BOUNCY LAP."
GROVER NEVER RECOGNIZED HIS OWN WIFE, JUST AS SHE HAD PLANNED...
SICKENING! HE MAKES A FOOL OF HIMSELF FOR A PRETTY FACE EVERY TIME!
HOMINA, HOMINA, HOMINA!
I'D BETTER GET TO CLEANING. THIS PLASTIC SURGERY ISN'T GONNA PAY FOR ITSELF.
...IT WASN'T LONG BEFORE...
WILL YOU HAVE DINNER WITH ME, AGNES?
W-WHY, I'D BE DELIGHTED, SIR...
MAKE SURE YOU WEAR THE POP-TART!
SUCH A PLEASURE TO LOOK AT A BEAUTIFUL WOMAN. I CAN HARDLY BEAR TO LOOK AT MY WIFE! SHE'S SO UGLY! BUT FOR HER WORK, I'D FIND OUR MARRIAGE IMPOSSIBLE!
GROVER, DUDE! YOU HAVE NO FILTER!
GROVER ENJOYED HIS EVENING WHICH WAS AS IT SHOULD BE... SEEING IT WAS HIS LAST!
AGNES! W-WHAT ARE YOU DOING?
NOT AGNES, MY DEAR! HORTENSE... THE WOMAN YOU HATE!
I'M SO EMBARRASSED! YOU MUST THINK ME INCREDIBLY SHALLOW!
6

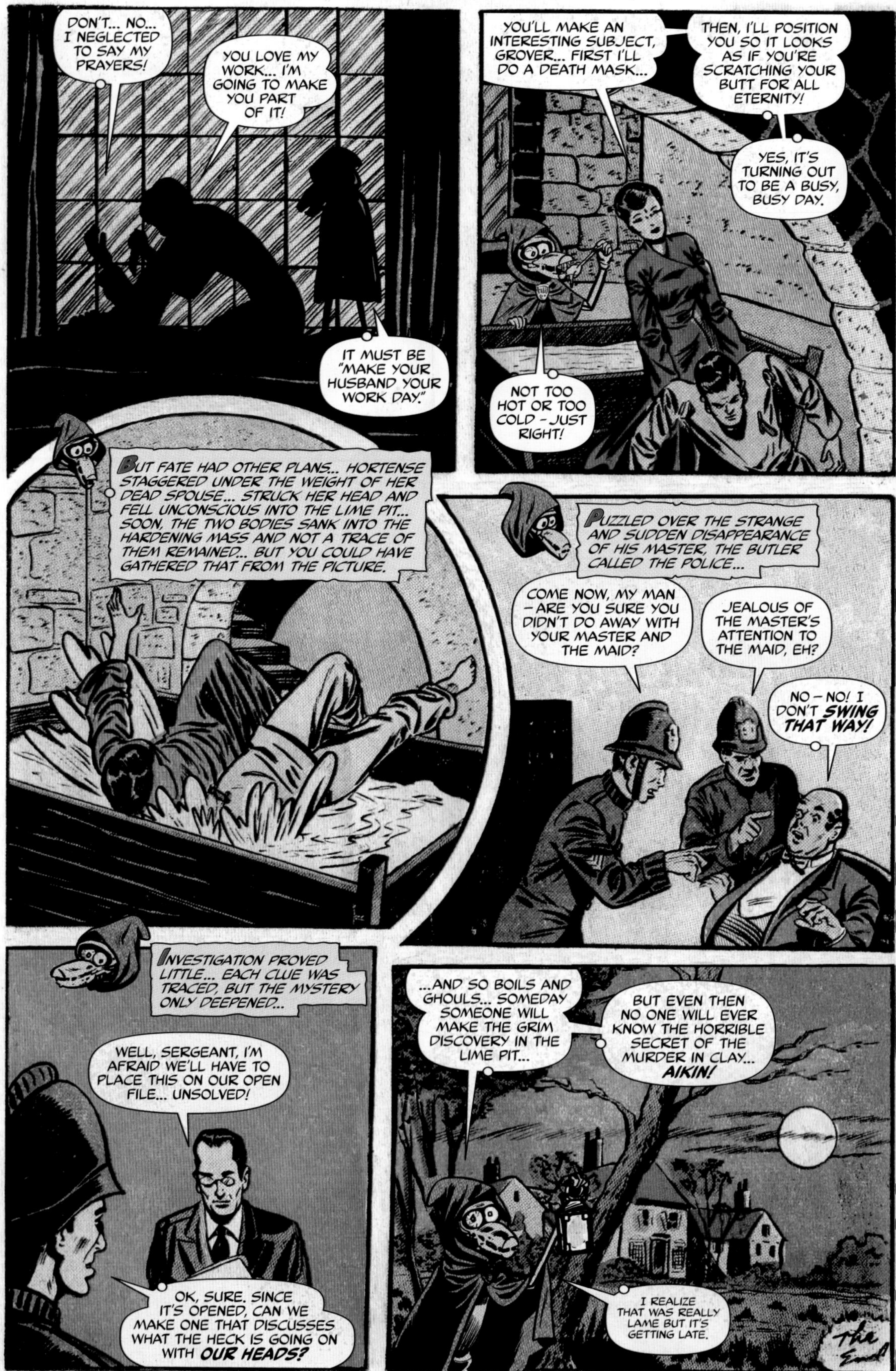
DON'T... NO... I NEGLECTED TO SAY MY PRAYERS!
YOU LOVE MY WORK... I'M GOING TO MAKE YOU PART OF IT!
IT MUST BE "MAKE YOUR HUSBAND YOUR WORK DAY."
YOU'LL MAKE AN INTERESTING SUBJECT, GROVER... FIRST I'LL DO A DEATH MASK...
THEN, I'LL POSITION YOU SO IT LOOKS AS IF YOU'RE SCRATCHING YOUR BUTT FOR ALL ETERNITY!
YES, IT'S TURNING OUT TO BE A BUSY, BUSY DAY.
NOT TOO HOT OR TOO COLD - JUST RIGHT!
BUT FATE HAD OTHER PLANS... HORTENSE STAGGERED UNDER THE WEIGHT OF HER DEAD SPOUSE... STRUCK HER HEAD AND FELL UNCONSCIOUS INTO THE LIME PIT... SOON, THE TWO BODIES SANK INTO THE HARDENING MASS AND NOT A TRACE OF THEM REMAINED... BUT YOU COULD HAVE GATHERED THAT FROM THE PICTURE.
PUZZLED OVER THE STRANGE AND SUDDEN DISAPPEARANCE OF HIS MASTER, THE BUTLER CALLED THE POLICE...
COME NOW, MY MAN - ARE YOU SURE YOU DIDN'T DO AWAY WITH YOUR MASTER AND THE MAID?
JEALOUS OF THE MASTER'S ATTENTION TO THE MAID, EH?
NO - NO! I DON'T SWING THAT WAY!
INVESTIGATION PROVED LITTLE... EACH CLUE WAS TRACED, BUT THE MYSTERY ONLY DEEPENED...
WELL, SERGEANT, I'M AFRAID WE'LL HAVE TO PLACE THIS ON OUR OPEN FILE... UNSOLVED!
OK, SURE. SINCE IT'S OPENED, CAN WE MAKE ONE THAT DISCUSSES WHAT THE HECK IS GOING ON WITH OUR HEADS?
...AND SO BOILS AND GHOULS... SOMEDAY SOMEONE WILL MAKE THE GRIM DISCOVERY IN THE LIME PIT...
BUT EVEN THEN NO ONE WILL EVER KNOW THE HORRIBLE SECRET OF THE MURDER IN CLAY... AIKIN!
I REALIZE THAT WAS REALLY LAME BUT IT'S GETTING LATE.
The End

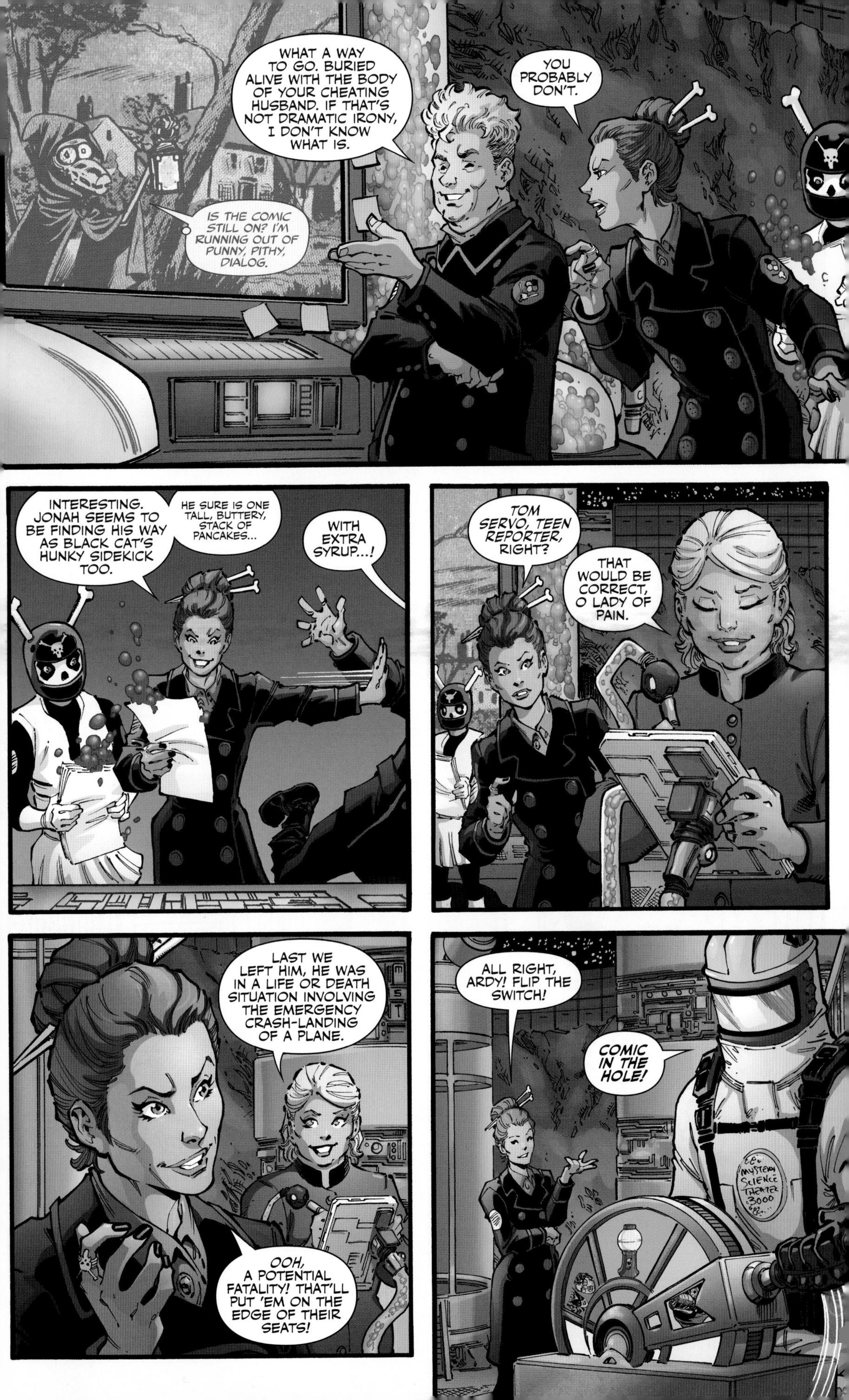
WHAT A WAY TO GO. BURIED ALIVE WITH THE BODY OF YOUR CHEATING HUSBAND. IF THAT'S NOT DRAMATIC IRONY, I DON'T KNOW WHAT IS.
YOU PROBABLY DON'T.
IS THE COMIC STILL ON? I'M RUNNING OUT OF PUNNY, PITHY, DIALOG.
INTERESTING. JONAH SEEMS TO BE FINDING HIS WAY AS BLACK CAT'S HUNKY SIDEKICK TOO.
HE SURE IS ONE TALL, BUTTERY, STACK OF PANCAKES...
WITH EXTRA SYRUP...!
TOM SERVO, TEEN REPORTER, RIGHT?
THAT WOULD BE CORRECT, O LADY OF PAIN.
LAST WE LEFT HIM, HE WAS IN A LIFE OR DEATH SITUATION INVOLVING THE EMERGENCY CRASH-LANDING OF A PLANE.
OOH, A POTENTIAL FATALITY! THAT'LL PUT 'EM ON THE EDGE OF THEIR SEATS!
ALL RIGHT, ARDY! FLIP THE SWITCH!
COMIC IN THE HOLE!

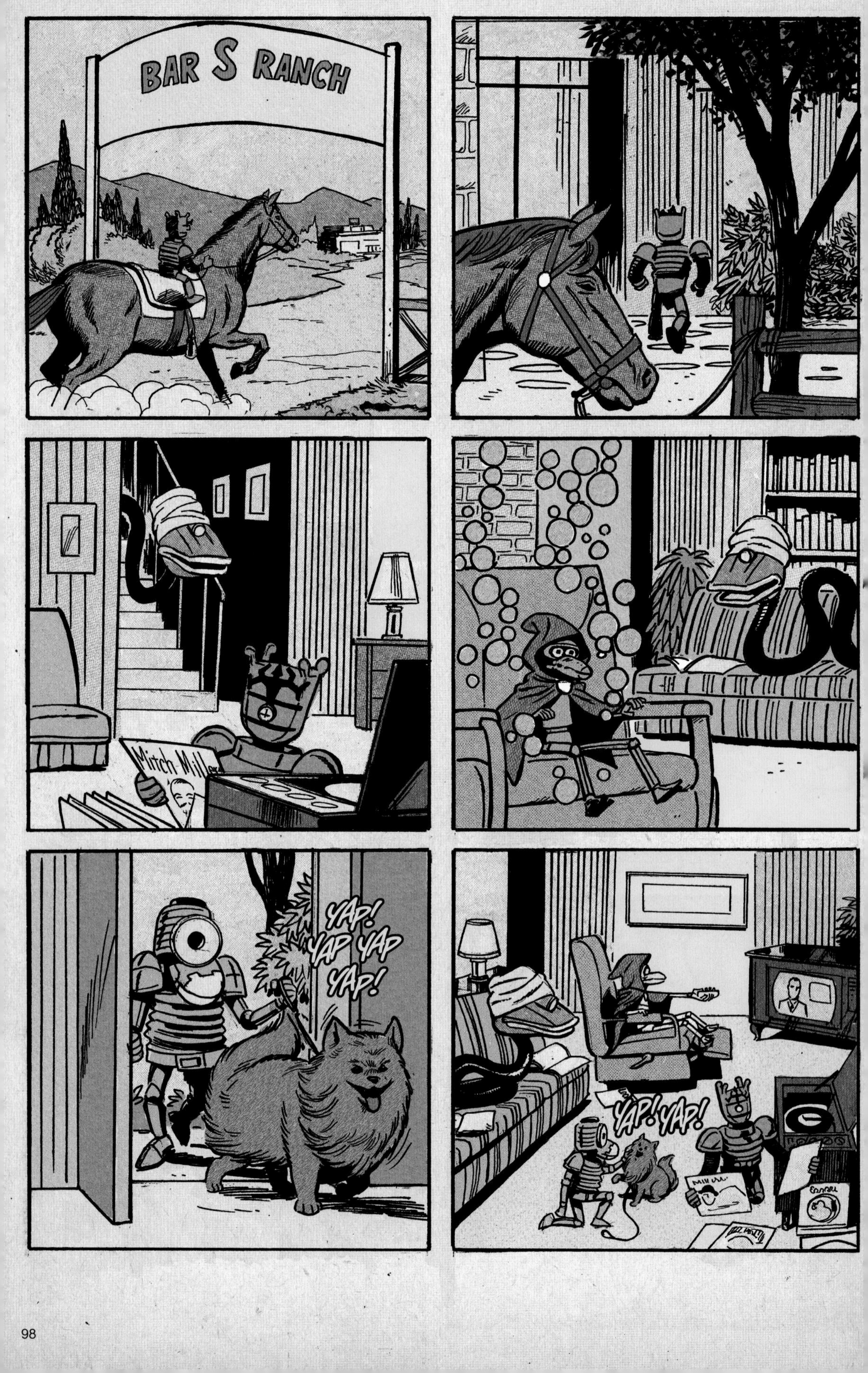
BAR S RANCH
YAP! YAP YAP YAP!
YAP! YAP!

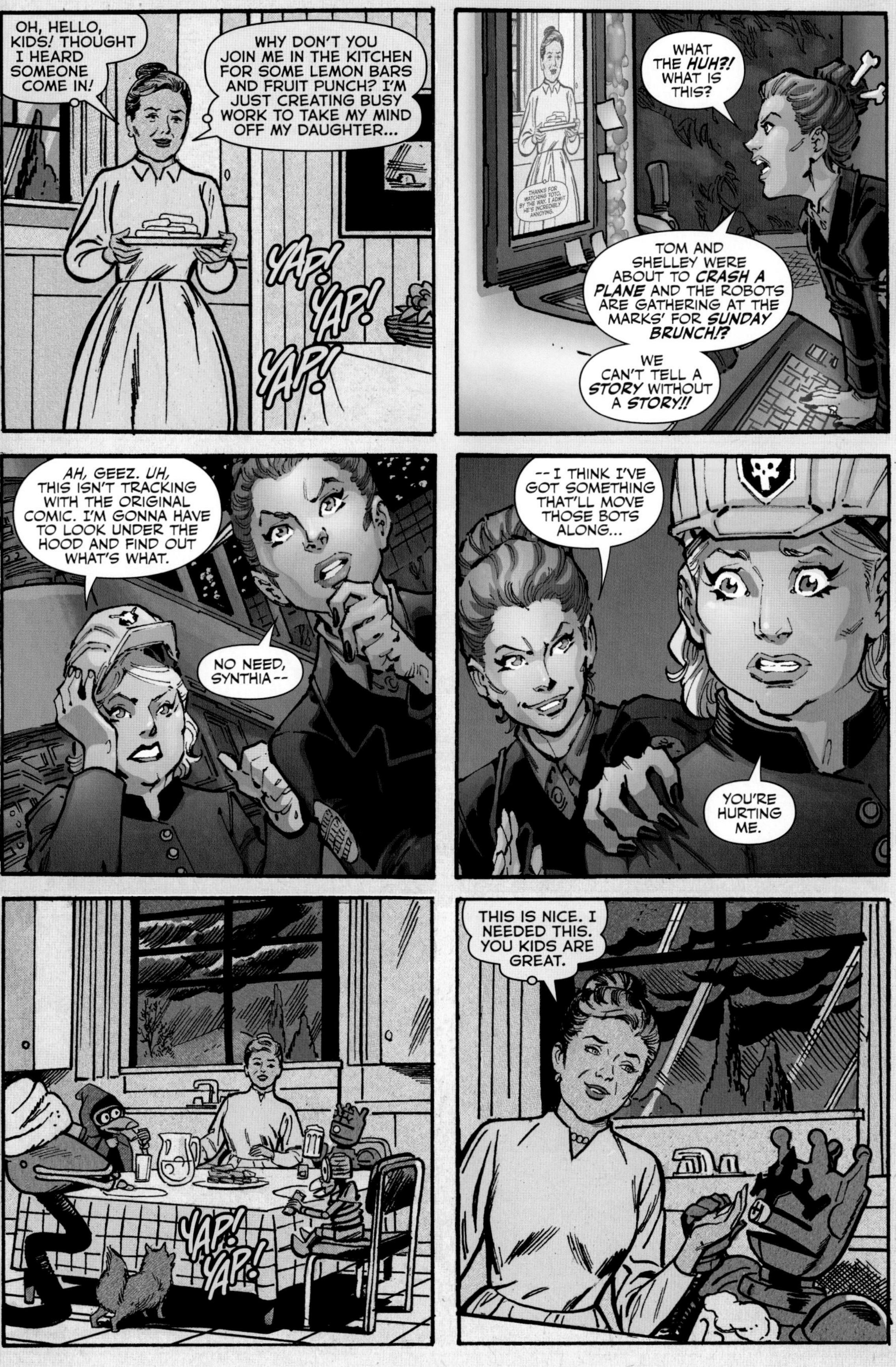
OH, HELLO, KIDS! THOUGHT I HEARD SOMEONE COME IN!
WHY DON'T YOU JOIN ME IN THE KITCHEN FOR SOME LEMON BARS AND FRUIT PUNCH? I'M JUST CREATING BUSY WORK TO TAKE MY MIND OFF MY DAUGHTER...
YAP! YAP! YAP!
THANKS FOR WATCHING TOTO, BY THE WAY. I ADMIT HE'S INCREDIBLY ANNOYING.
WHAT THE HUH?! WHAT IS THIS?
TOM AND SHELLEY WERE ABOUT TO CRASH A PLANE AND THE ROBOTS ARE GATHERING AT THE MARKS' FOR SUNDAY BRUNCH!?
WE CAN'T TELL A STORY WITHOUT A STORY!!
AH, GEEZ. UH, THIS ISN'T TRACKING WITH THE ORIGINAL COMIC. I'M GONNA HAVE TO LOOK UNDER THE HOOD AND FIND OUT WHAT'S WHAT.
NO NEED, SYNTHIA--
--I THINK I'VE GOT SOMETHING THAT'LL MOVE THOSE BOTS ALONG...
YOU'RE HURTING ME.
YAP! YAP!
THIS IS NICE. I NEEDED THIS. YOU KIDS ARE GREAT.

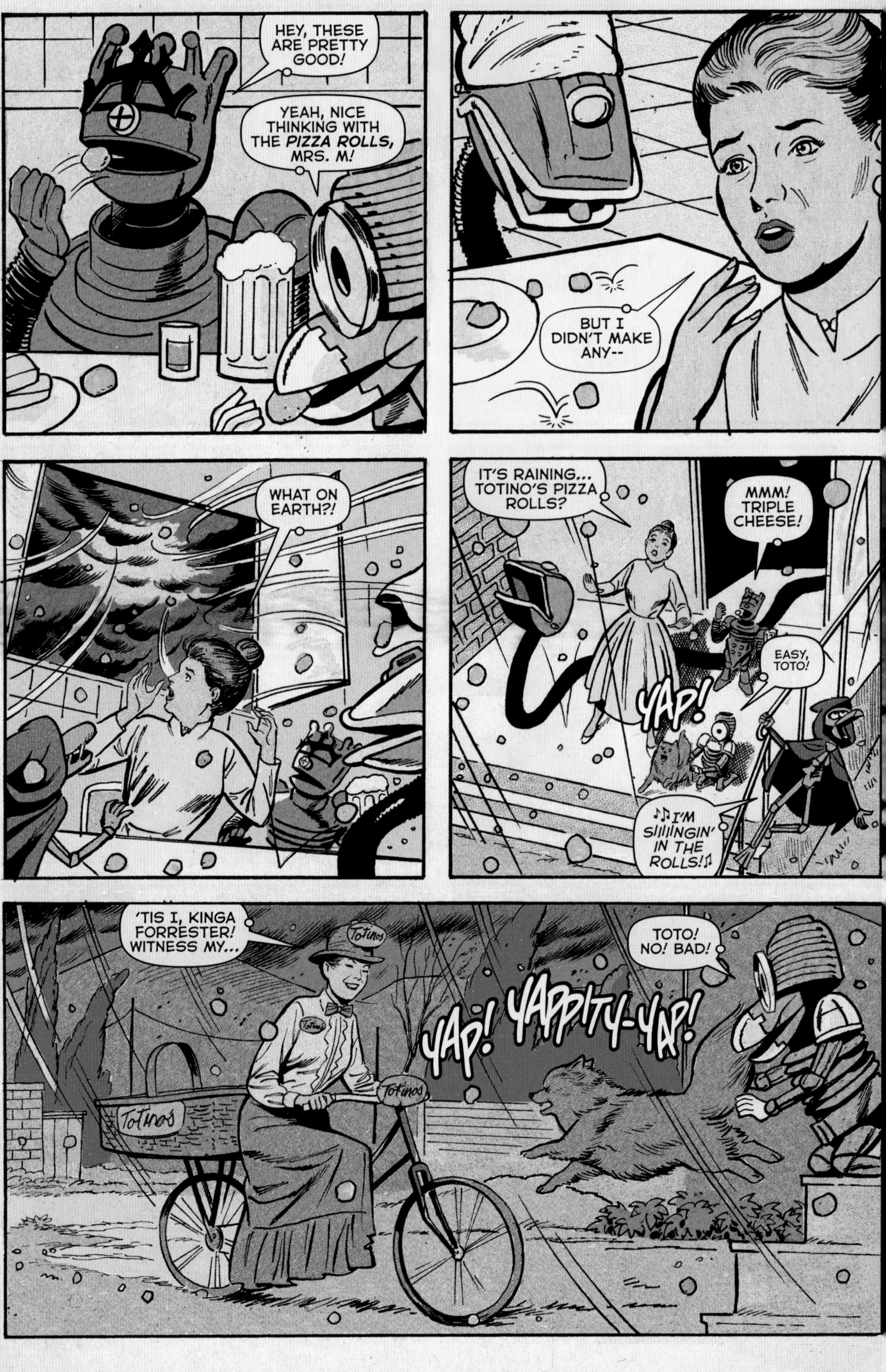
HEY, THESE ARE PRETTY GOOD!
YEAH, NICE THINKING WITH THE PIZZA ROLLS, MRS. M!
BUT I DIDN'T MAKE ANY--
WHAT ON EARTH?!
IT'S RAINING... TOTINO'S PIZZA ROLLS?
MMM! TRIPLE CHEESE!
EASY, TOTO!
YAP!
♪♫I'M SIIIIINGIN' IN THE ROLLS!♫
'TIS I, KINGA FORRESTER! WITNESS MY...
TOTO! NO! BAD!
YAP! YAPPITY-YAP!
Totino's

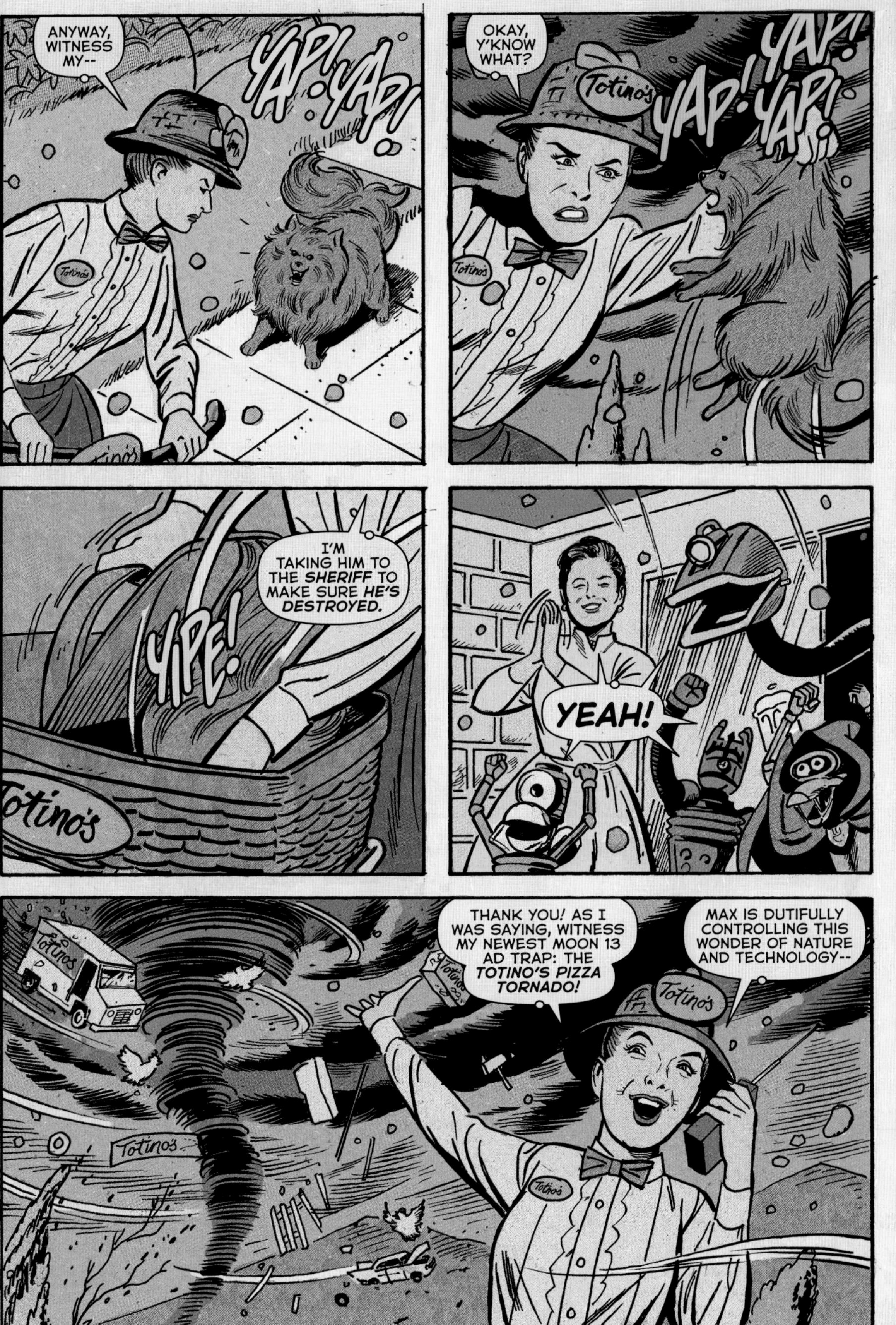
ANYWAY, WITNESS MY--
YAP! YAP!
OKAY, Y'KNOW WHAT?
YAP! YAP! YAP! YAP!
I'M TAKING HIM TO THE *SHERIFF* TO MAKE SURE *HE'S DESTROYED.*
YIPE!
Totino's
YEAH!
THANK YOU! AS I WAS SAYING, WITNESS MY NEWEST MOON 13 AD TRAP: THE *TOTINO'S PIZZA TORNADO!*
MAX IS DUTIFULLY CONTROLLING THIS WONDER OF NATURE AND TECHNOLOGY--
Totino's

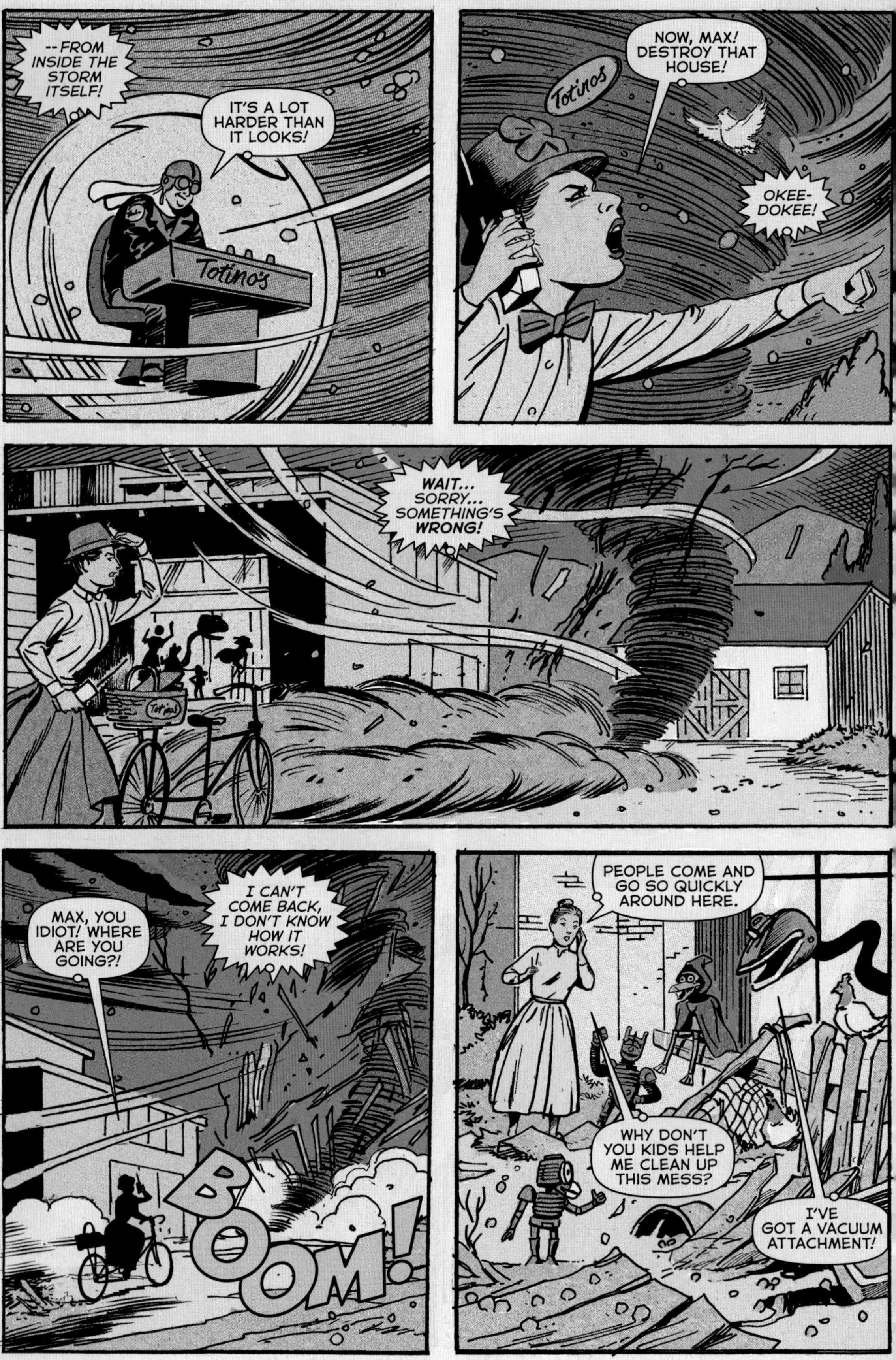
--FROM INSIDE THE STORM ITSELF!
IT'S A LOT HARDER THAN IT LOOKS!
Totino's
Totinos
NOW, MAX! DESTROY THAT HOUSE!
OKEE-DOKEE!
WAIT... SORRY... SOMETHING'S WRONG!
MAX, YOU IDIOT! WHERE ARE YOU GOING?!
I CAN'T COME BACK, I DON'T KNOW HOW IT WORKS!
BOOM!
PEOPLE COME AND GO SO QUICKLY AROUND HERE.
WHY DON'T YOU KIDS HELP ME CLEAN UP THIS MESS?
I'VE GOT A VACUUM ATTACHMENT!

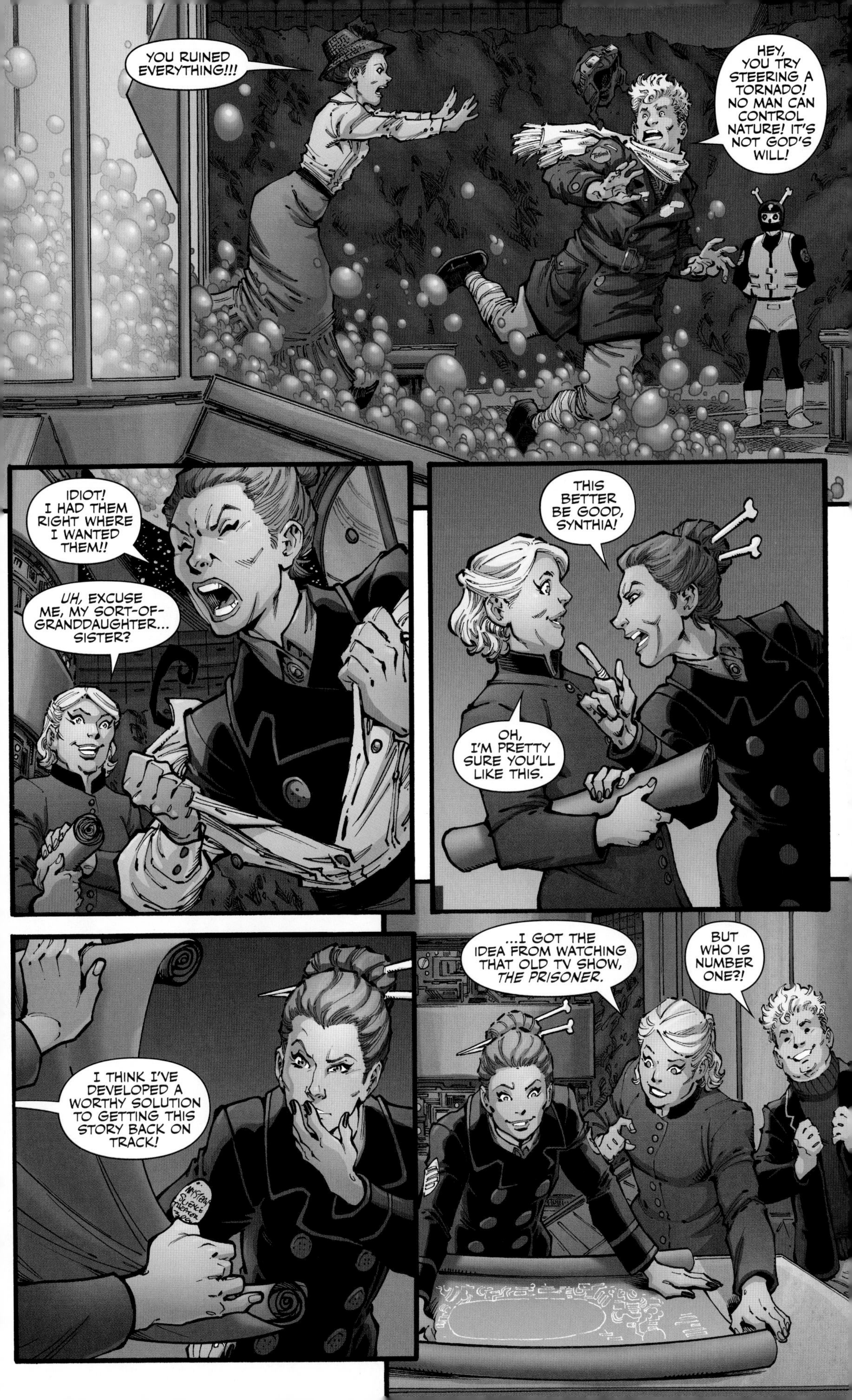
YOU RUINED EVERYTHING!!!
HEY, YOU TRY STEERING A TORNADO! NO MAN CAN CONTROL NATURE! IT'S NOT GOD'S WILL!
IDIOT! I HAD THEM RIGHT WHERE I WANTED THEM!!
UH, EXCUSE ME, MY SORT-OF-GRANDDAUGHTER... SISTER?
THIS BETTER BE GOOD, SYNTHIA!
OH, I'M PRETTY SURE YOU'LL LIKE THIS.
I THINK I'VE DEVELOPED A WORTHY SOLUTION TO GETTING THIS STORY BACK ON TRACK!
...I GOT THE IDEA FROM WATCHING THAT OLD TV SHOW, *THE PRISONER*.
BUT WHO IS NUMBER ONE?!

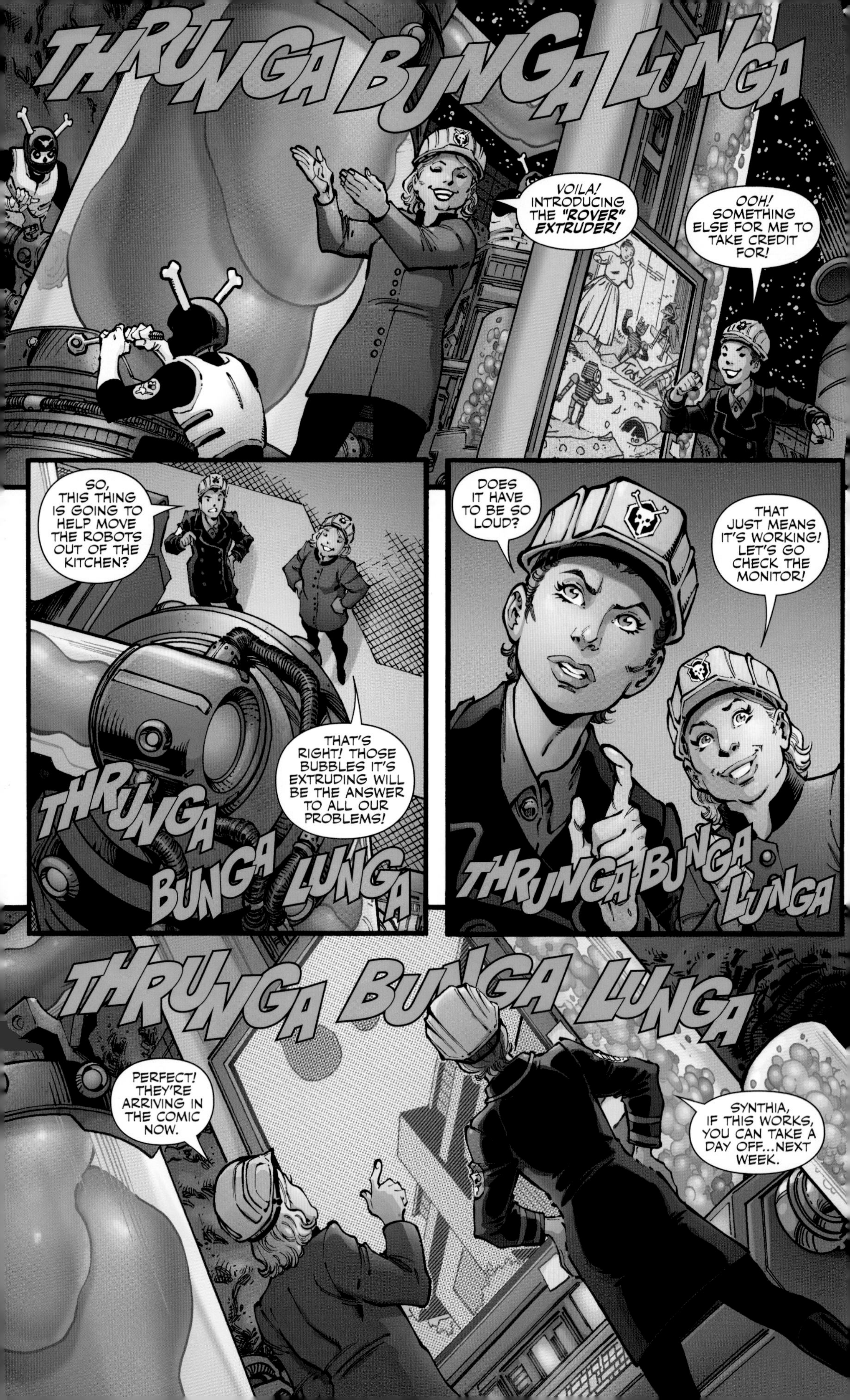
THRUNGA BUNGA LUNGA
VOILA! INTRODUCING THE "ROVER" EXTRUDER!
OOH! SOMETHING ELSE FOR ME TO TAKE CREDIT FOR!
SO, THIS THING IS GOING TO HELP MOVE THE ROBOTS OUT OF THE KITCHEN?
THAT'S RIGHT! THOSE BUBBLES IT'S EXTRUDING WILL BE THE ANSWER TO ALL OUR PROBLEMS!
THRUNGA BUNGA LUNGA
DOES IT HAVE TO BE SO LOUD?
THAT JUST MEANS IT'S WORKING! LET'S GO CHECK THE MONITOR!
THRUNGA BUNGA LUNGA
THRUNGA BUNGA LUNGA
PERFECT! THEY'RE ARRIVING IN THE COMIC NOW.
SYNTHIA, IF THIS WORKS, YOU CAN TAKE A DAY OFF...NEXT WEEK.

WHAT IN THE --?

IT'S THE *END TIMES!* RUN, KIDS, *RUN!!*

RUNNING FROM BUBBLES? I'M EXPERIENCING *DEJA VU.*

I'M GETTING CARRIED AWAY IN A BUBBLE AGAINST MY WILL! AND YOU KNOW WHAT? I KINDA LIKE IT!

HEY, WAVERLY, YOU WANNA LINK BUBBLES?

NAH, I'M NOT LOOKING FOR A ROOMMATE.

WAIT, I'M AFRAID OF HEIGHTS!

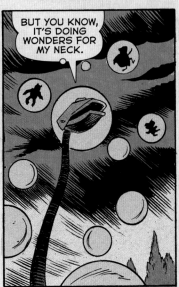

BUT YOU KNOW, IT'S DOING WONDERS FOR MY NECK.

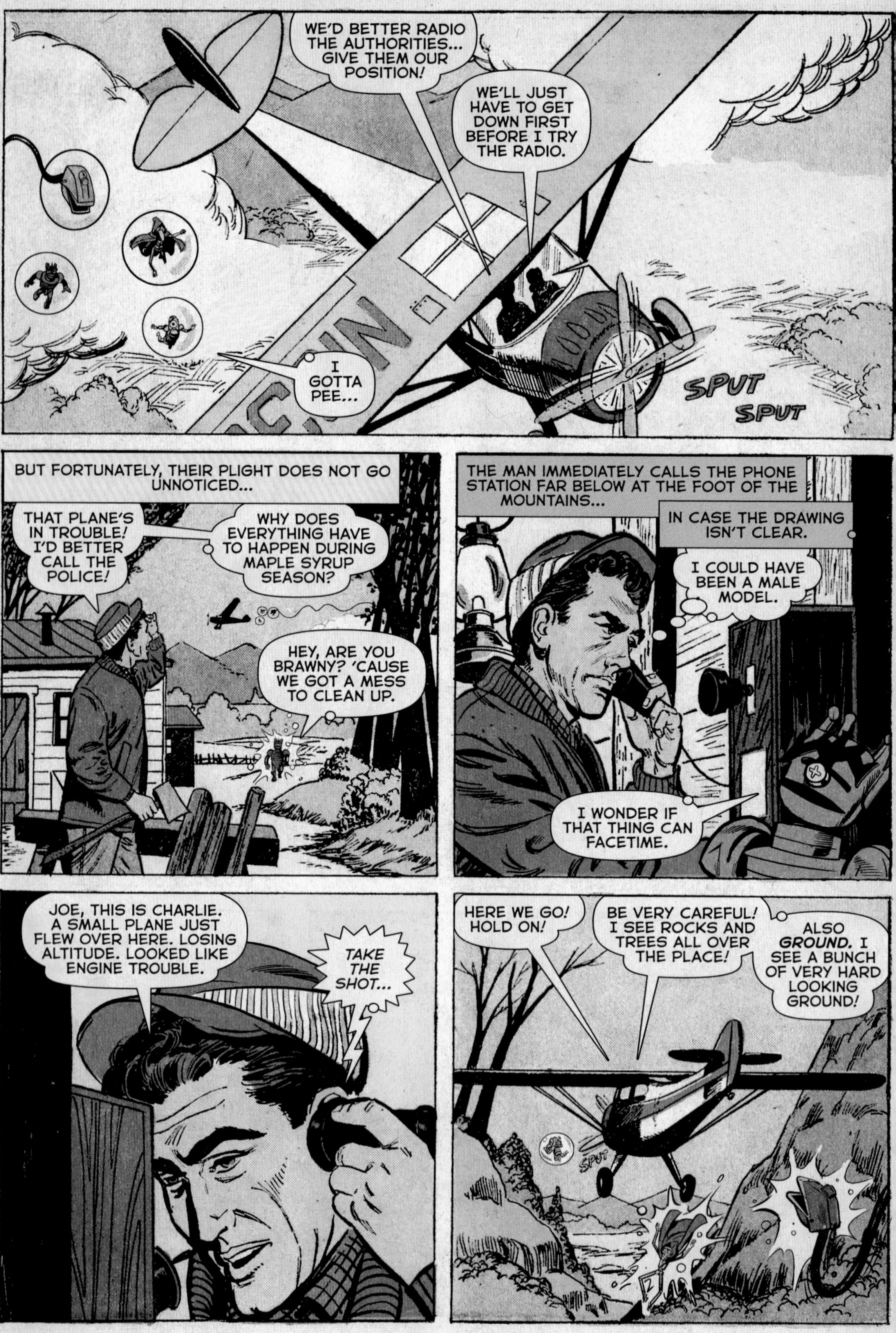
WE'D BETTER RADIO THE AUTHORITIES... GIVE THEM OUR POSITION!
WE'LL JUST HAVE TO GET DOWN FIRST BEFORE I TRY THE RADIO.
I GOTTA PEE...
SPUT SPUT
BUT FORTUNATELY, THEIR PLIGHT DOES NOT GO UNNOTICED...
THAT PLANE'S IN TROUBLE! I'D BETTER CALL THE POLICE!
WHY DOES EVERYTHING HAVE TO HAPPEN DURING MAPLE SYRUP SEASON?
HEY, ARE YOU BRAWNY? 'CAUSE WE GOT A MESS TO CLEAN UP.
THE MAN IMMEDIATELY CALLS THE PHONE STATION FAR BELOW AT THE FOOT OF THE MOUNTAINS...
IN CASE THE DRAWING ISN'T CLEAR.
I COULD HAVE BEEN A MALE MODEL.
I WONDER IF THAT THING CAN FACETIME.
JOE, THIS IS CHARLIE. A SMALL PLANE JUST FLEW OVER HERE. LOSING ALTITUDE. LOOKED LIKE ENGINE TROUBLE.
TAKE THE SHOT...
HERE WE GO! HOLD ON!
BE VERY CAREFUL! I SEE ROCKS AND TREES ALL OVER THE PLACE!
ALSO GROUND. I SEE A BUNCH OF VERY HARD LOOKING GROUND!
SPUT

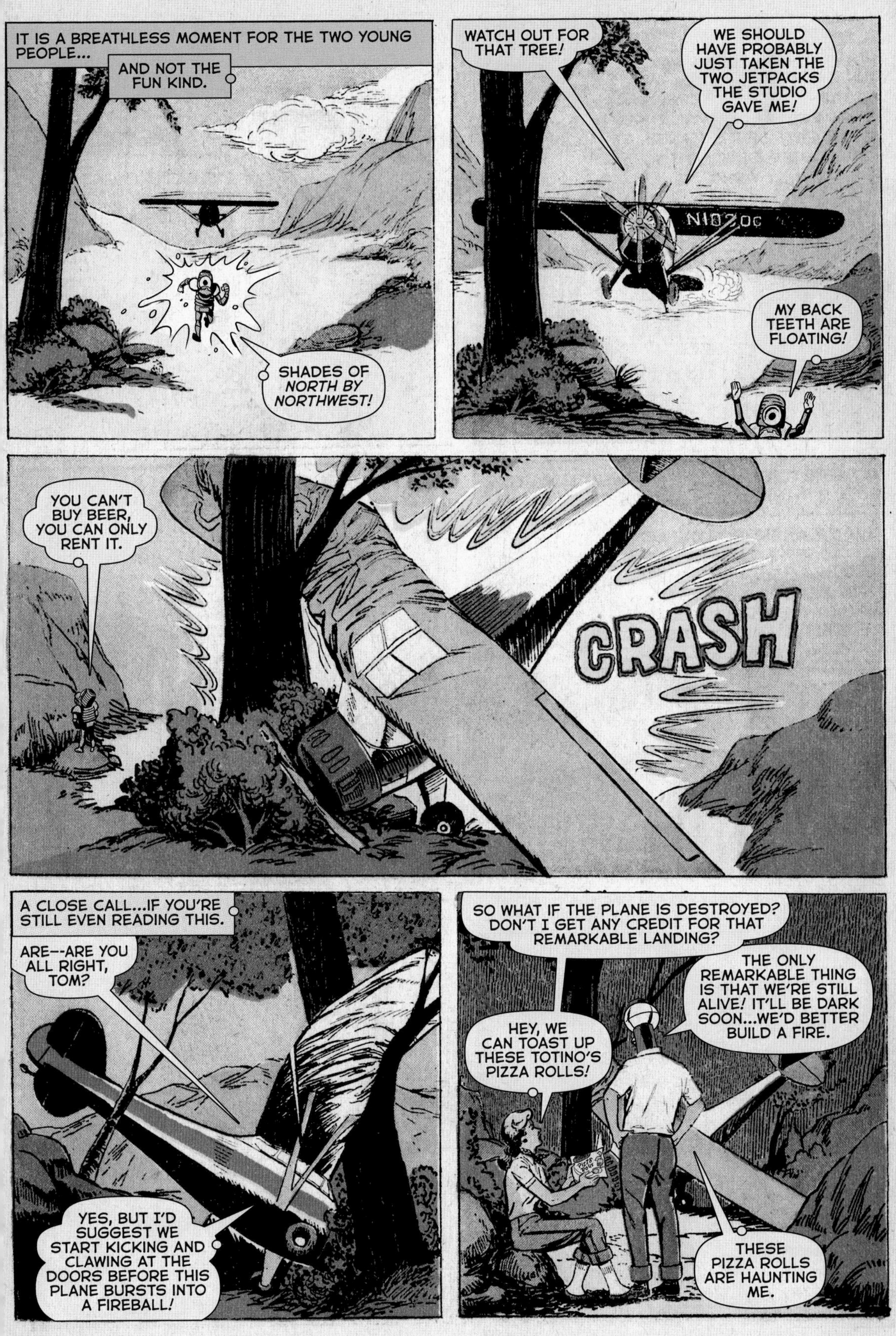

IT IS A BREATHLESS MOMENT FOR THE TWO YOUNG PEOPLE...
AND NOT THE FUN KIND.
SHADES OF *NORTH BY NORTHWEST!*
WATCH OUT FOR THAT TREE!
WE SHOULD HAVE PROBABLY JUST TAKEN THE TWO JETPACKS THE STUDIO GAVE ME!
N1020C
MY BACK TEETH ARE FLOATING!
YOU CAN'T BUY BEER, YOU CAN ONLY RENT IT.
CRASH
A CLOSE CALL...IF YOU'RE STILL EVEN READING THIS.
ARE--ARE YOU ALL RIGHT, TOM?
YES, BUT I'D SUGGEST WE START KICKING AND CLAWING AT THE DOORS BEFORE THIS PLANE BURSTS INTO A FIREBALL!
SO WHAT IF THE PLANE IS DESTROYED? DON'T I GET ANY CREDIT FOR THAT REMARKABLE LANDING?
THE ONLY REMARKABLE THING IS THAT WE'RE STILL ALIVE! IT'LL BE DARK SOON...WE'D BETTER BUILD A FIRE.
HEY, WE CAN TOAST UP THESE TOTINO'S PIZZA ROLLS!
Pizza Rolls
THESE PIZZA ROLLS ARE HAUNTING ME.

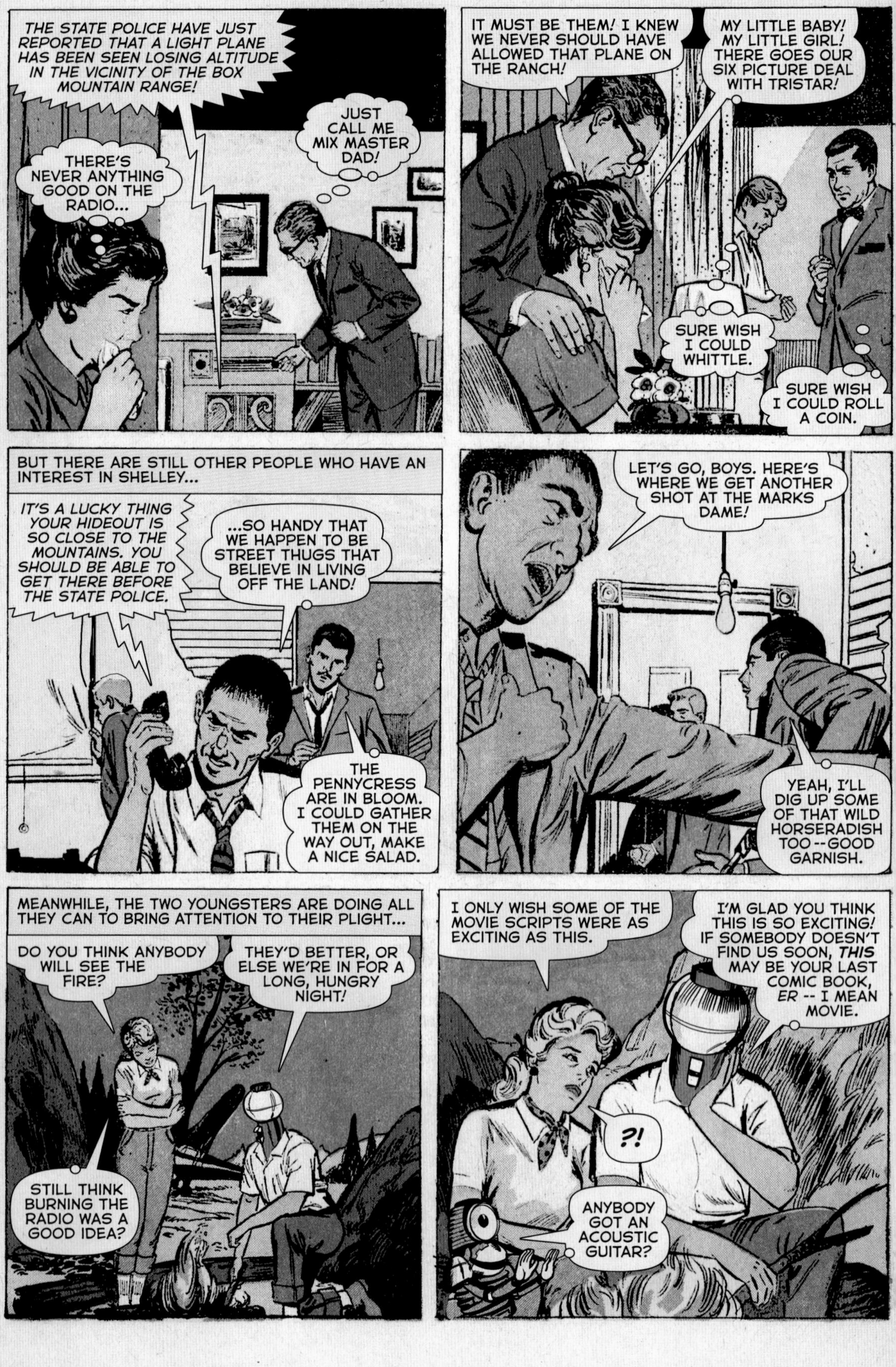
THE STATE POLICE HAVE JUST REPORTED THAT A LIGHT PLANE HAS BEEN SEEN LOSING ALTITUDE IN THE VICINITY OF THE BOX MOUNTAIN RANGE!
THERE'S NEVER ANYTHING GOOD ON THE RADIO...
JUST CALL ME MIX MASTER DAD!
IT MUST BE THEM! I KNEW WE NEVER SHOULD HAVE ALLOWED THAT PLANE ON THE RANCH!
MY LITTLE BABY! MY LITTLE GIRL! THERE GOES OUR SIX PICTURE DEAL WITH TRISTAR!
SURE WISH I COULD WHITTLE.
SURE WISH I COULD ROLL A COIN.
BUT THERE ARE STILL OTHER PEOPLE WHO HAVE AN INTEREST IN SHELLEY...
IT'S A LUCKY THING YOUR HIDEOUT IS SO CLOSE TO THE MOUNTAINS. YOU SHOULD BE ABLE TO GET THERE BEFORE THE STATE POLICE.
...SO HANDY THAT WE HAPPEN TO BE STREET THUGS THAT BELIEVE IN LIVING OFF THE LAND!
THE PENNYCRESS ARE IN BLOOM. I COULD GATHER THEM ON THE WAY OUT, MAKE A NICE SALAD.
LET'S GO, BOYS. HERE'S WHERE WE GET ANOTHER SHOT AT THE MARKS DAME!
YEAH, I'LL DIG UP SOME OF THAT WILD HORSERADISH TOO -- GOOD GARNISH.
MEANWHILE, THE TWO YOUNGSTERS ARE DOING ALL THEY CAN TO BRING ATTENTION TO THEIR PLIGHT...
DO YOU THINK ANYBODY WILL SEE THE FIRE?
THEY'D BETTER, OR ELSE WE'RE IN FOR A LONG, HUNGRY NIGHT!
STILL THINK BURNING THE RADIO WAS A GOOD IDEA?
I ONLY WISH SOME OF THE MOVIE SCRIPTS WERE AS EXCITING AS THIS.
I'M GLAD YOU THINK THIS IS SO EXCITING! IF SOMEBODY DOESN'T FIND US SOON, THIS MAY BE YOUR LAST COMIC BOOK, ER -- I MEAN MOVIE.
?!
ANYBODY GOT AN ACOUSTIC GUITAR?

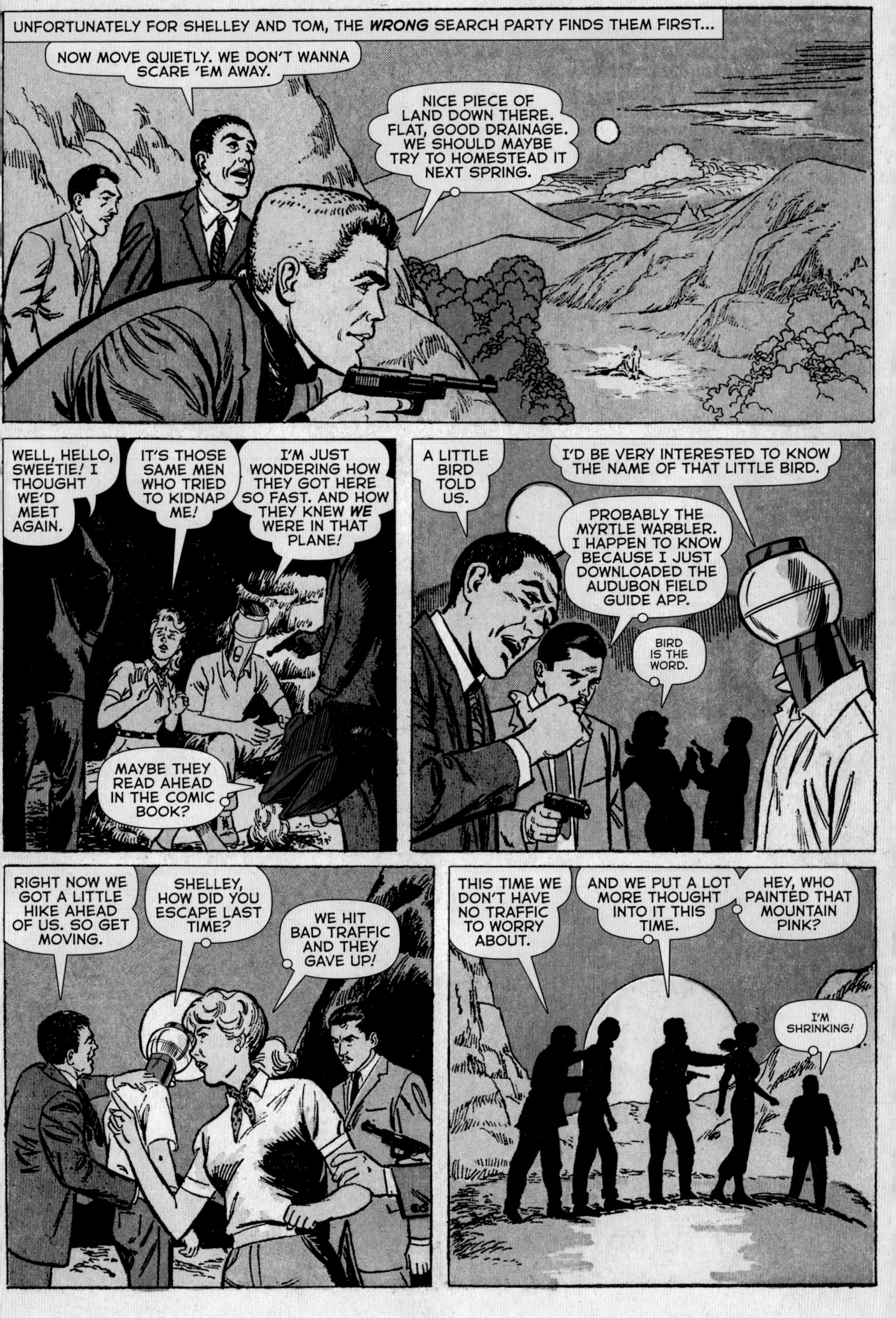
UNFORTUNATELY FOR SHELLEY AND TOM, THE *WRONG* SEARCH PARTY FINDS THEM FIRST...
NOW MOVE QUIETLY. WE DON'T WANNA SCARE 'EM AWAY.
NICE PIECE OF LAND DOWN THERE. FLAT, GOOD DRAINAGE. WE SHOULD MAYBE TRY TO HOMESTEAD IT NEXT SPRING.
WELL, HELLO, SWEETIE! I THOUGHT WE'D MEET AGAIN.
IT'S THOSE SAME MEN WHO TRIED TO KIDNAP ME!
I'M JUST WONDERING HOW THEY GOT HERE SO FAST. AND HOW THEY KNEW *WE* WERE IN THAT PLANE!
MAYBE THEY READ AHEAD IN THE COMIC BOOK?
A LITTLE BIRD TOLD US.
I'D BE VERY INTERESTED TO KNOW THE NAME OF THAT LITTLE BIRD.
PROBABLY THE MYRTLE WARBLER. I HAPPEN TO KNOW BECAUSE I JUST DOWNLOADED THE AUDUBON FIELD GUIDE APP.
BIRD IS THE WORD.
RIGHT NOW WE GOT A LITTLE HIKE AHEAD OF US. SO GET MOVING.
SHELLEY, HOW DID YOU ESCAPE LAST TIME?
WE HIT BAD TRAFFIC AND THEY GAVE UP!
THIS TIME WE DON'T HAVE NO TRAFFIC TO WORRY ABOUT.
AND WE PUT A LOT MORE THOUGHT INTO IT THIS TIME.
HEY, WHO PAINTED THAT MOUNTAIN PINK?
I'M SHRINKING!

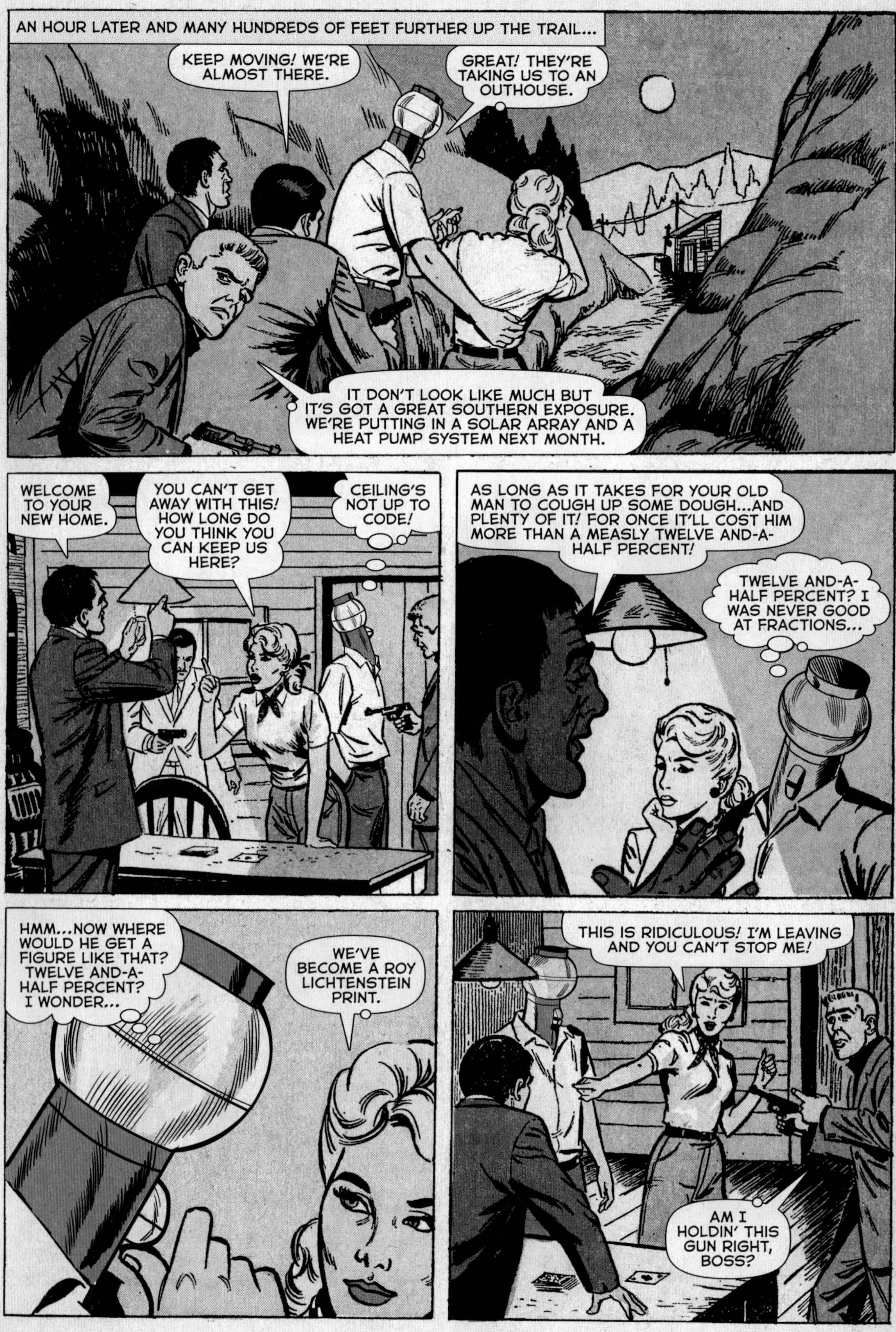
AN HOUR LATER AND MANY HUNDREDS OF FEET FURTHER UP THE TRAIL...
KEEP MOVING! WE'RE ALMOST THERE.
GREAT! THEY'RE TAKING US TO AN OUTHOUSE.
IT DON'T LOOK LIKE MUCH BUT IT'S GOT A GREAT SOUTHERN EXPOSURE. WE'RE PUTTING IN A SOLAR ARRAY AND A HEAT PUMP SYSTEM NEXT MONTH.
WELCOME TO YOUR NEW HOME.
YOU CAN'T GET AWAY WITH THIS! HOW LONG DO YOU THINK YOU CAN KEEP US HERE?
CEILING'S NOT UP TO CODE!
AS LONG AS IT TAKES FOR YOUR OLD MAN TO COUGH UP SOME DOUGH...AND PLENTY OF IT! FOR ONCE IT'LL COST HIM MORE THAN A MEASLY TWELVE AND-A-HALF PERCENT!
TWELVE AND-A-HALF PERCENT? I WAS NEVER GOOD AT FRACTIONS...
HMM...NOW WHERE WOULD HE GET A FIGURE LIKE THAT? TWELVE AND-A-HALF PERCENT? I WONDER...
WE'VE BECOME A ROY LICHTENSTEIN PRINT.
THIS IS RIDICULOUS! I'M LEAVING AND YOU CAN'T STOP ME!
AM I HOLDIN' THIS GUN RIGHT, BOSS?

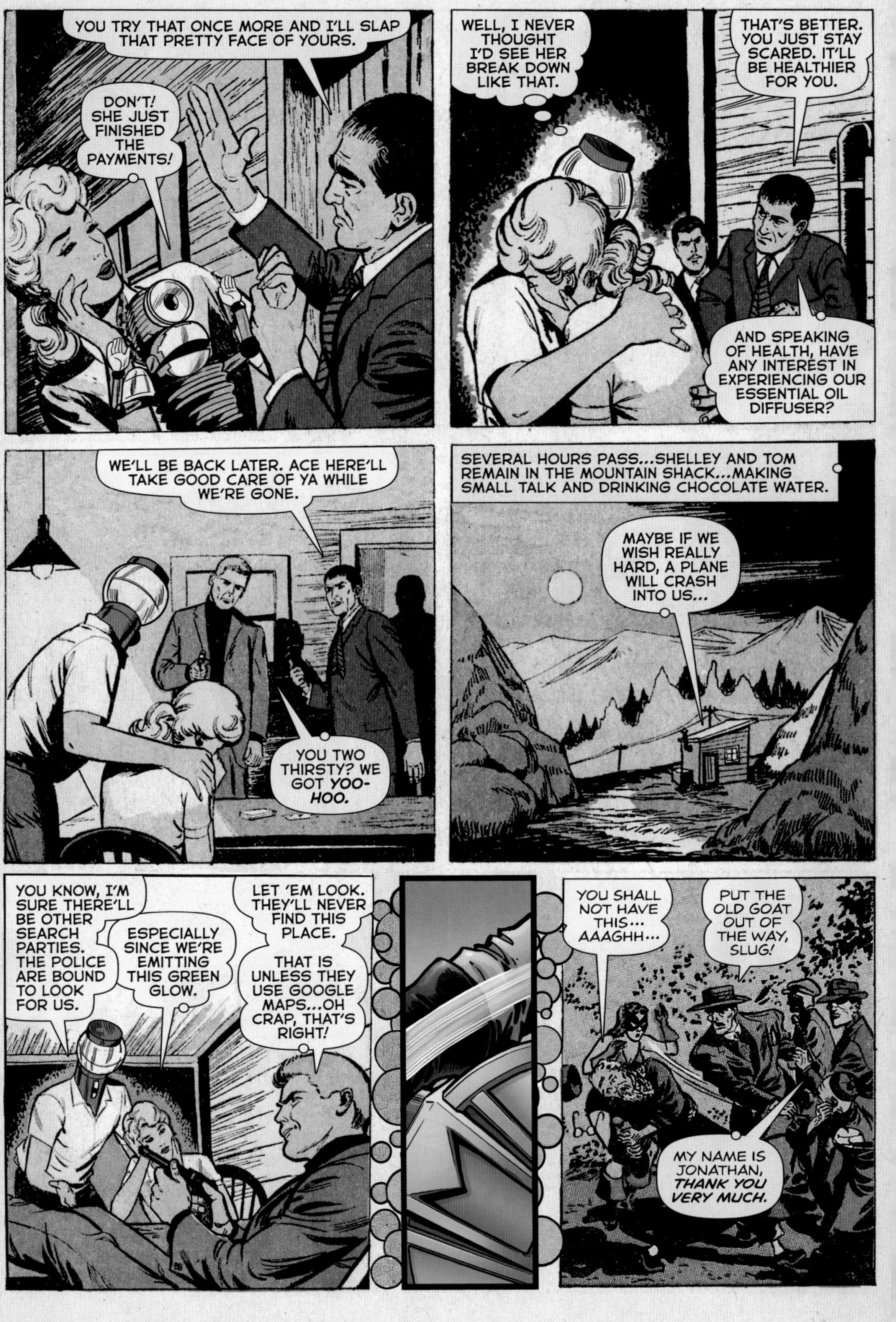

YOU TRY THAT ONCE MORE AND I'LL SLAP THAT PRETTY FACE OF YOURS.
DON'T! SHE JUST FINISHED THE PAYMENTS!
WELL, I NEVER THOUGHT I'D SEE HER BREAK DOWN LIKE THAT.
THAT'S BETTER. YOU JUST STAY SCARED. IT'LL BE HEALTHIER FOR YOU.
AND SPEAKING OF HEALTH, HAVE ANY INTEREST IN EXPERIENCING OUR ESSENTIAL OIL DIFFUSER?
WE'LL BE BACK LATER. ACE HERE'LL TAKE GOOD CARE OF YA WHILE WE'RE GONE.
YOU TWO THIRSTY? WE GOT *YOO-HOO.*
SEVERAL HOURS PASS...SHELLEY AND TOM REMAIN IN THE MOUNTAIN SHACK...MAKING SMALL TALK AND DRINKING CHOCOLATE WATER.
MAYBE IF WE WISH REALLY HARD, A PLANE WILL CRASH INTO US...
YOU KNOW, I'M SURE THERE'LL BE OTHER SEARCH PARTIES. THE POLICE ARE BOUND TO LOOK FOR US.
ESPECIALLY SINCE WE'RE EMITTING THIS GREEN GLOW.
LET 'EM LOOK. THEY'LL NEVER FIND THIS PLACE.
THAT IS UNLESS THEY USE GOOGLE MAPS...OH CRAP, THAT'S RIGHT!
YOU SHALL NOT HAVE THIS... AAAGHH...
PUT THE OLD GOAT OUT OF THE WAY, SLUG!
MY NAME IS JONATHAN, *THANK YOU VERY MUCH.*

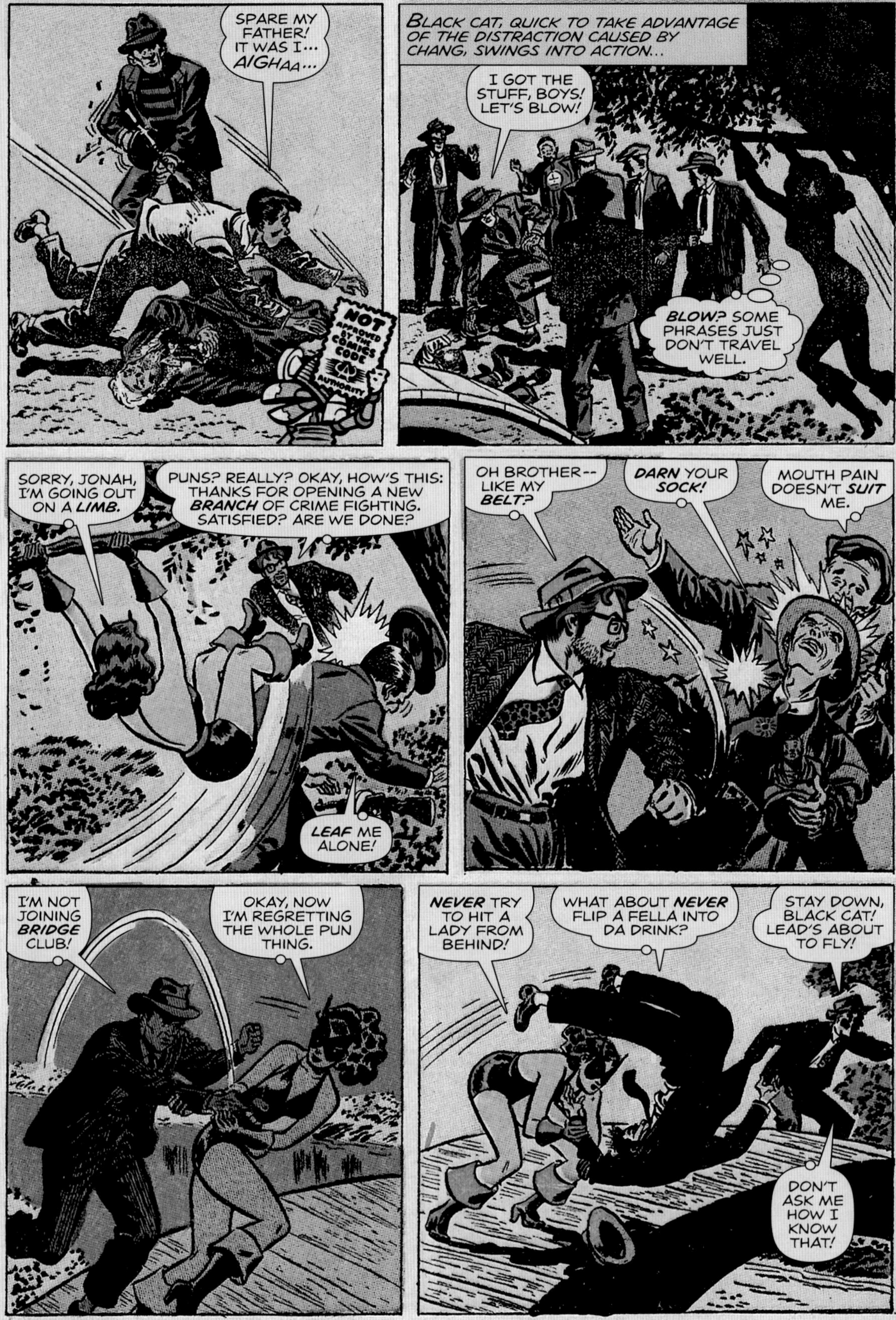
SPARE MY FATHER! IT WAS I... AIGHAA...
NOT APPROVED BY THE COMICS CODE AUTHORITY
BLACK CAT, QUICK TO TAKE ADVANTAGE OF THE DISTRACTION CAUSED BY CHANG, SWINGS INTO ACTION...
I GOT THE STUFF, BOYS! LET'S BLOW!
BLOW? SOME PHRASES JUST DON'T TRAVEL WELL.
SORRY, JONAH, I'M GOING OUT ON A LIMB.
PUNS? REALLY? OKAY, HOW'S THIS: THANKS FOR OPENING A NEW BRANCH OF CRIME FIGHTING. SATISFIED? ARE WE DONE?
LEAF ME ALONE!
OH BROTHER-- LIKE MY BELT?
DARN YOUR SOCK!
MOUTH PAIN DOESN'T SUIT ME.
I'M NOT JOINING BRIDGE CLUB!
OKAY, NOW I'M REGRETTING THE WHOLE PUN THING.
NEVER TRY TO HIT A LADY FROM BEHIND!
WHAT ABOUT NEVER FLIP A FELLA INTO DA DRINK?
STAY DOWN, BLACK CAT! LEAD'S ABOUT TO FLY!
DON'T ASK ME HOW I KNOW THAT!

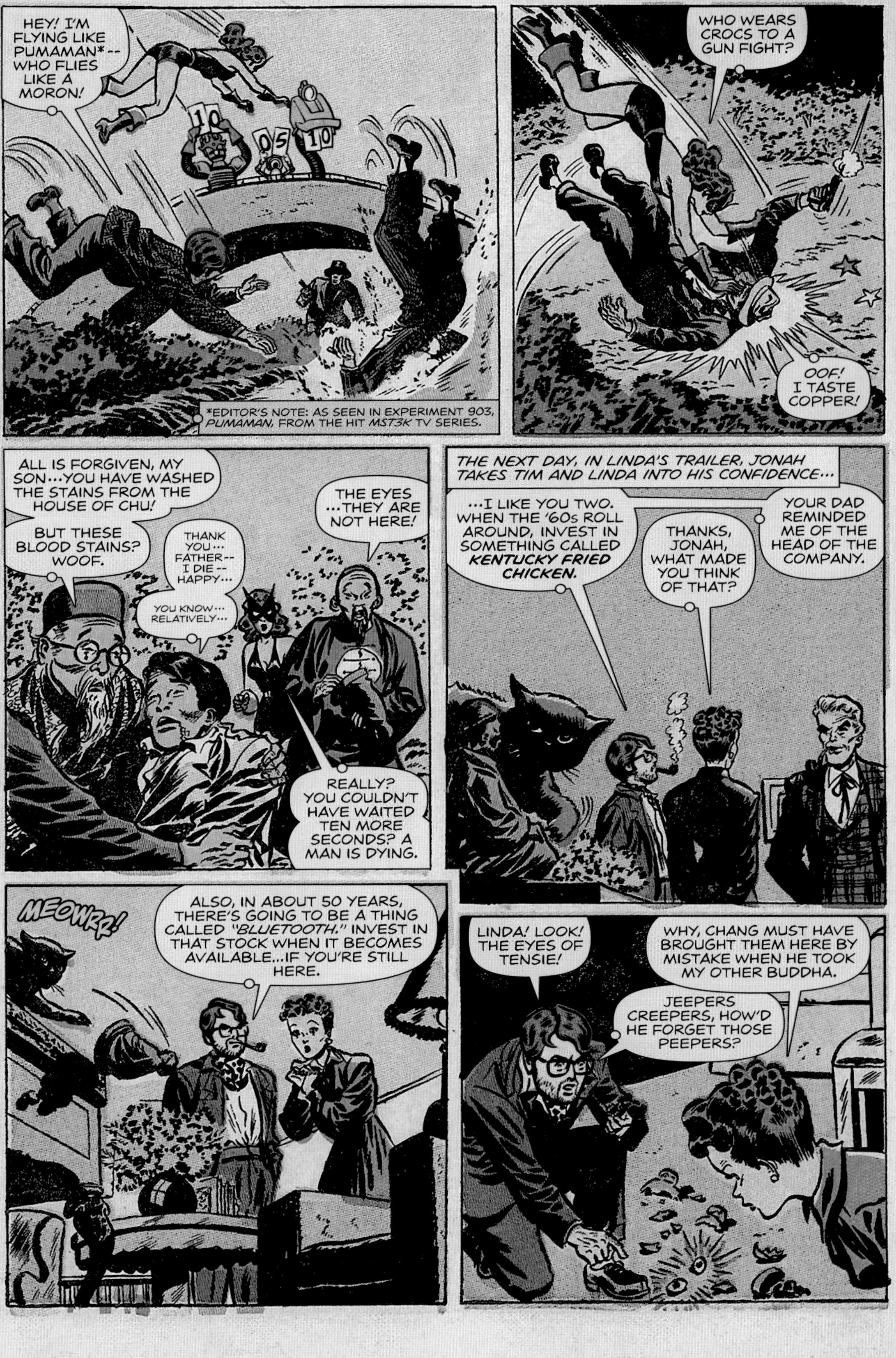
HEY! I'M FLYING LIKE PUMAMAN*-- WHO FLIES LIKE A MORON!
10
05
10
*EDITOR'S NOTE: AS SEEN IN EXPERIMENT 903, PUMAMAN, FROM THE HIT MST3K TV SERIES.
WHO WEARS CROCS TO A GUN FIGHT?
OOF! I TASTE COPPER!
ALL IS FORGIVEN, MY SON...YOU HAVE WASHED THE STAINS FROM THE HOUSE OF CHU!
BUT THESE BLOOD STAINS? WOOF.
THANK YOU... FATHER-- I DIE-- HAPPY...
YOU KNOW... RELATIVELY...
THE EYES ...THEY ARE NOT HERE!
REALLY? YOU COULDN'T HAVE WAITED TEN MORE SECONDS? A MAN IS DYING.
THE NEXT DAY, IN LINDA'S TRAILER, JONAH TAKES TIM AND LINDA INTO HIS CONFIDENCE...
...I LIKE YOU TWO. WHEN THE '60s ROLL AROUND, INVEST IN SOMETHING CALLED KENTUCKY FRIED CHICKEN.
THANKS, JONAH, WHAT MADE YOU THINK OF THAT?
YOUR DAD REMINDED ME OF THE HEAD OF THE COMPANY.
MEOWRR!
ALSO, IN ABOUT 50 YEARS, THERE'S GOING TO BE A THING CALLED "BLUETOOTH." INVEST IN THAT STOCK WHEN IT BECOMES AVAILABLE...IF YOU'RE STILL HERE.
LINDA! LOOK! THE EYES OF TENSIE!
WHY, CHANG MUST HAVE BROUGHT THEM HERE BY MISTAKE WHEN HE TOOK MY OTHER BUDDHA.
JEEPERS CREEPERS, HOW'D HE FORGET THOSE PEEPERS?

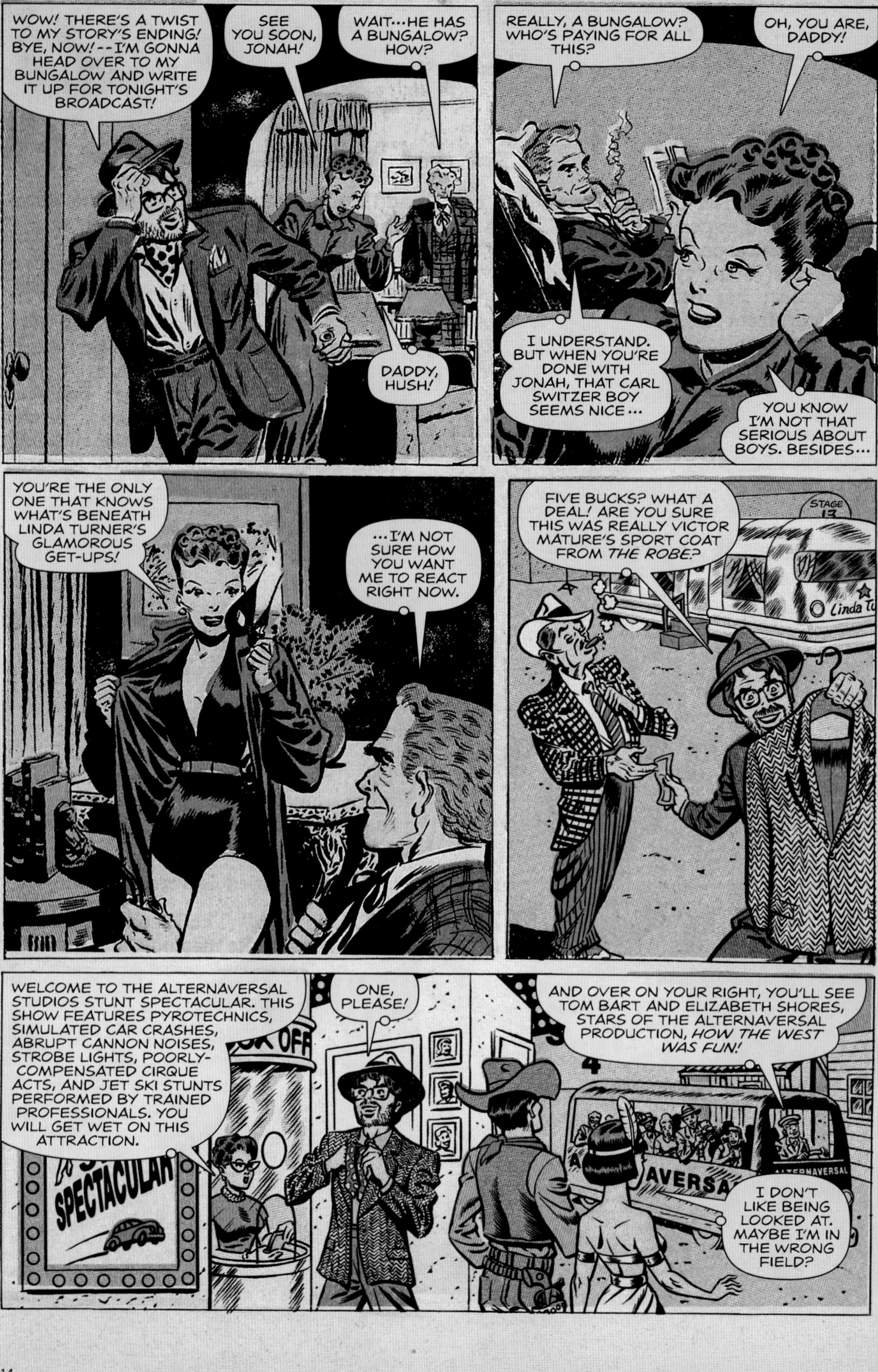
WOW! THERE'S A TWIST TO MY STORY'S ENDING! BYE, NOW! --I'M GONNA HEAD OVER TO MY BUNGALOW AND WRITE IT UP FOR TONIGHT'S BROADCAST!
SEE YOU SOON, JONAH!
WAIT...HE HAS A BUNGALOW? HOW?
DADDY, HUSH!
REALLY, A BUNGALOW? WHO'S PAYING FOR ALL THIS?
OH, YOU ARE, DADDY!
I UNDERSTAND. BUT WHEN YOU'RE DONE WITH JONAH, THAT CARL SWITZER BOY SEEMS NICE...
YOU KNOW I'M NOT THAT SERIOUS ABOUT BOYS. BESIDES...
YOU'RE THE ONLY ONE THAT KNOWS WHAT'S BENEATH LINDA TURNER'S GLAMOROUS GET-UPS!
...I'M NOT SURE HOW YOU WANT ME TO REACT RIGHT NOW.
FIVE BUCKS? WHAT A DEAL! ARE YOU SURE THIS WAS REALLY VICTOR MATURE'S SPORT COAT FROM *THE ROBE*?
STAGE 13
Linda Tu
WELCOME TO THE ALTERNAVERSAL STUDIOS STUNT SPECTACULAR. THIS SHOW FEATURES PYROTECHNICS, SIMULATED CAR CRASHES, ABRUPT CANNON NOISES, STROBE LIGHTS, POORLY-COMPENSATED CIRQUE ACTS, AND JET SKI STUNTS PERFORMED BY TRAINED PROFESSIONALS. YOU WILL GET WET ON THIS ATTRACTION.
ONE, PLEASE!
AND OVER ON YOUR RIGHT, YOU'LL SEE TOM BART AND ELIZABETH SHORES, STARS OF THE ALTERNAVERSAL PRODUCTION, *HOW THE WEST WAS FUN!*
SPECTACULAR
ALTERNAVERSAL
I DON'T LIKE BEING LOOKED AT. MAYBE I'M IN THE WRONG FIELD?

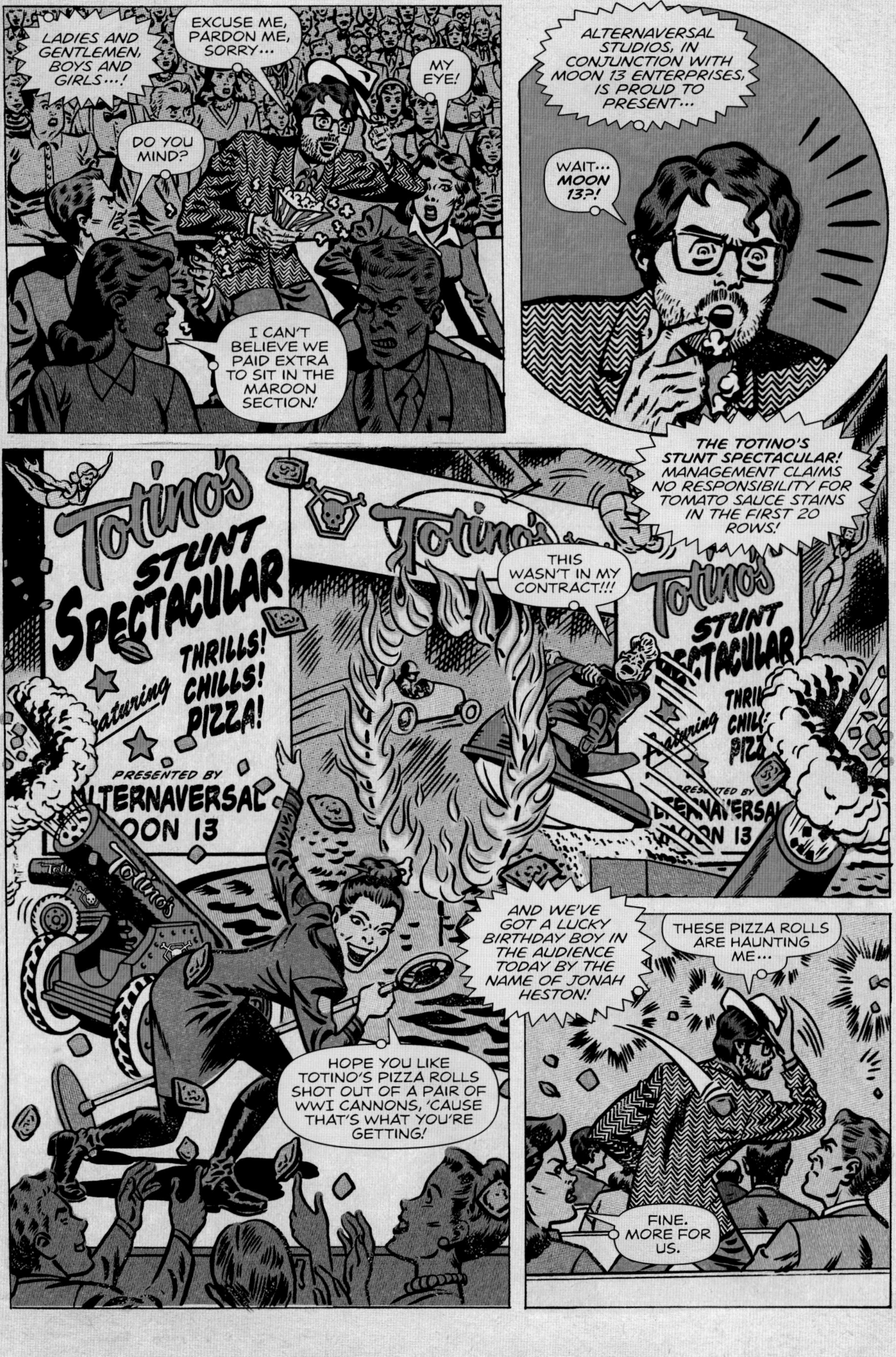
LADIES AND GENTLEMEN, BOYS AND GIRLS...!
EXCUSE ME, PARDON ME, SORRY...
MY EYE!
DO YOU MIND?
I CAN'T BELIEVE WE PAID EXTRA TO SIT IN THE MAROON SECTION!
ALTERNAVERSAL STUDIOS, IN CONJUNCTION WITH MOON 13 ENTERPRISES, IS PROUD TO PRESENT...
WAIT... MOON 13?!
THE TOTINO'S STUNT SPECTACULAR! MANAGEMENT CLAIMS NO RESPONSIBILITY FOR TOMATO SAUCE STAINS IN THE FIRST 20 ROWS!
Totino's
STUNT SPECTACULAR
featuring THRILLS! CHILLS! PIZZA!
PRESENTED BY
LTERNAVERSAL
OON 13
Totino's
THIS WASN'T IN MY CONTRACT!!!
AND WE'VE GOT A LUCKY BIRTHDAY BOY IN THE AUDIENCE TODAY BY THE NAME OF JONAH HESTON!
HOPE YOU LIKE TOTINO'S PIZZA ROLLS SHOT OUT OF A PAIR OF WWI CANNONS, 'CAUSE THAT'S WHAT YOU'RE GETTING!
THESE PIZZA ROLLS ARE HAUNTING ME...
FINE. MORE FOR US.

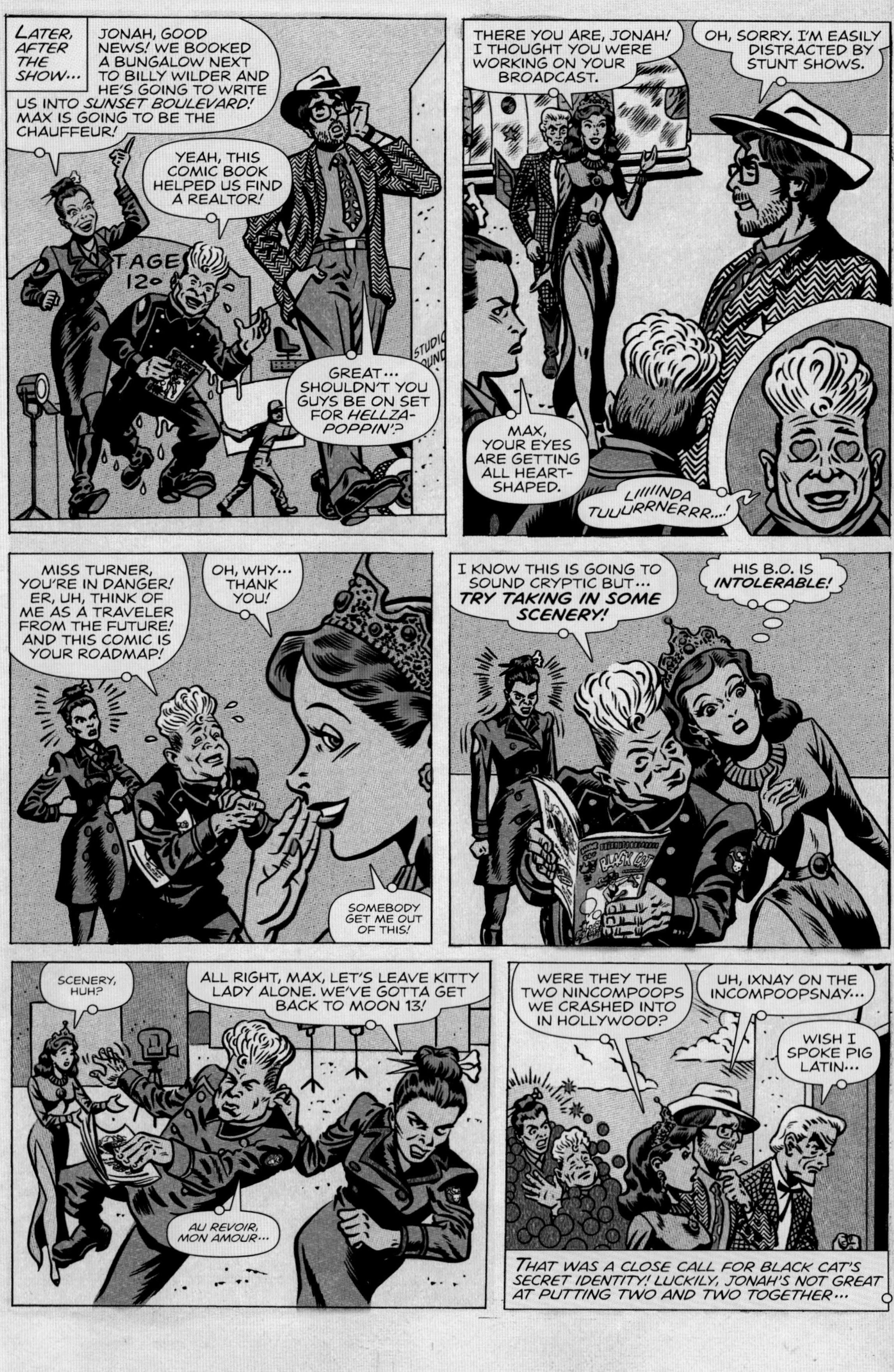

LATER, AFTER THE SHOW...
JONAH, GOOD NEWS! WE BOOKED A BUNGALOW NEXT TO BILLY WILDER AND HE'S GOING TO WRITE US INTO SUNSET BOULEVARD! MAX IS GOING TO BE THE CHAUFFEUR!
YEAH, THIS COMIC BOOK HELPED US FIND A REALTOR!
GREAT... SHOULDN'T YOU GUYS BE ON SET FOR HELLZA-POPPIN'?
THERE YOU ARE, JONAH! I THOUGHT YOU WERE WORKING ON YOUR BROADCAST.
OH, SORRY. I'M EASILY DISTRACTED BY STUNT SHOWS.
MAX, YOUR EYES ARE GETTING ALL HEART-SHAPED.
LIIIIINDA TUUURRNERRR...!
MISS TURNER, YOU'RE IN DANGER! ER, UH, THINK OF ME AS A TRAVELER FROM THE FUTURE! AND THIS COMIC IS YOUR ROADMAP!
OH, WHY... THANK YOU!
SOMEBODY GET ME OUT OF THIS!
I KNOW THIS IS GOING TO SOUND CRYPTIC BUT... TRY TAKING IN SOME SCENERY!
HIS B.O. IS INTOLERABLE!
SCENERY, HUH?
ALL RIGHT, MAX, LET'S LEAVE KITTY LADY ALONE. WE'VE GOTTA GET BACK TO MOON 13!
AU REVOIR, MON AMOUR...
WERE THEY THE TWO NINCOMPOOPS WE CRASHED INTO IN HOLLYWOOD?
UH, IXNAY ON THE INCOMPOOPSNAY...
WISH I SPOKE PIG LATIN...
THAT WAS A CLOSE CALL FOR BLACK CAT'S SECRET IDENTITY! LUCKILY, JONAH'S NOT GREAT AT PUTTING TWO AND TWO TOGETHER...

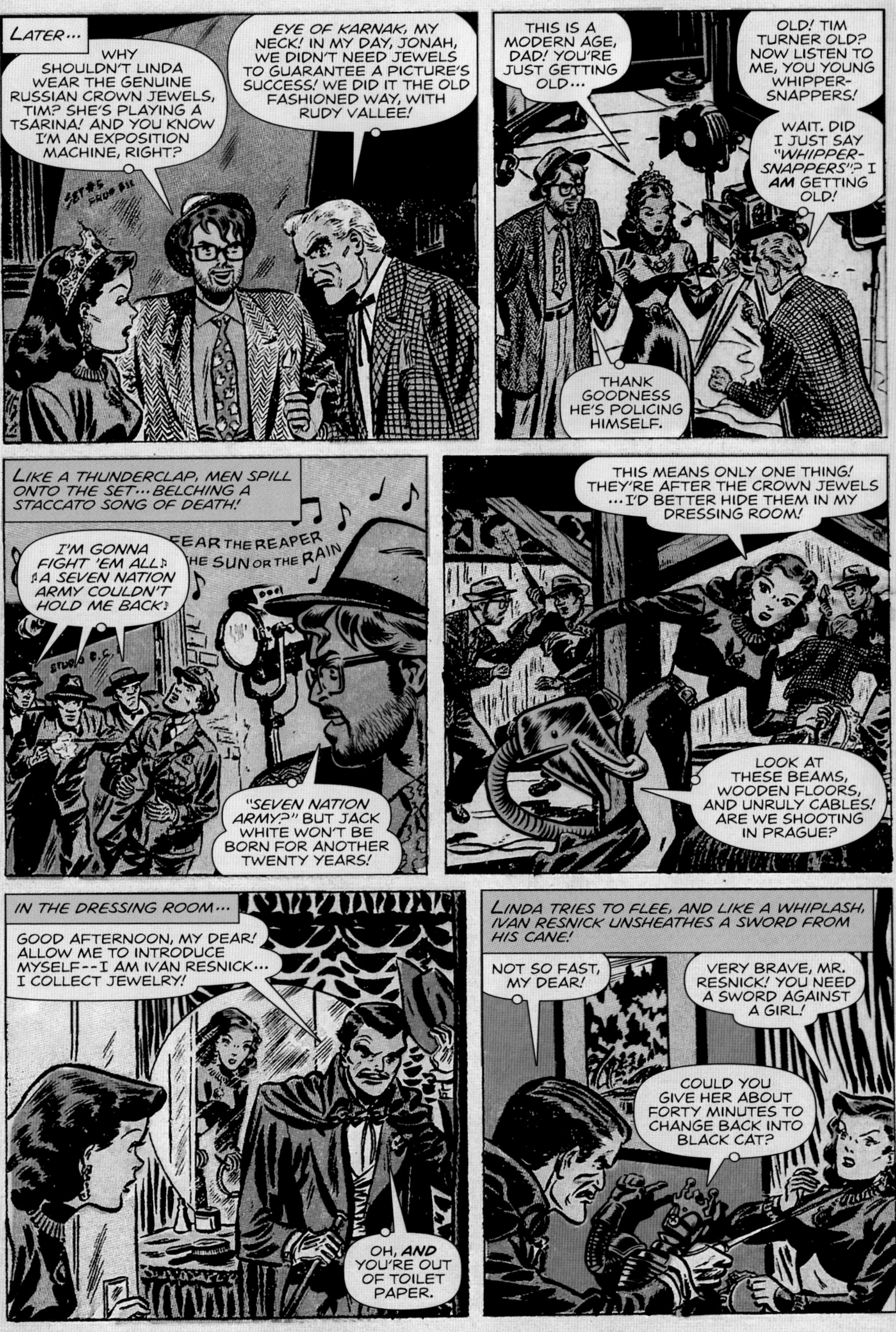
LATER...
WHY SHOULDN'T LINDA WEAR THE GENUINE RUSSIAN CROWN JEWELS, TIM? SHE'S PLAYING A TSARINA! AND YOU KNOW I'M AN EXPOSITION MACHINE, RIGHT?
EYE OF KARNAK, MY NECK! IN MY DAY, JONAH, WE DIDN'T NEED JEWELS TO GUARANTEE A PICTURE'S SUCCESS! WE DID IT THE OLD FASHIONED WAY, WITH RUDY VALLEE!
THIS IS A MODERN AGE, DAD! YOU'RE JUST GETTING OLD...
OLD! TIM TURNER OLD? NOW LISTEN TO ME, YOU YOUNG WHIPPER-SNAPPERS!
WAIT. DID I JUST SAY "WHIPPER-SNAPPERS"? I AM GETTING OLD!
THANK GOODNESS HE'S POLICING HIMSELF.
LIKE A THUNDERCLAP, MEN SPILL ONTO THE SET...BELCHING A STACCATO SONG OF DEATH!
FEAR THE REAPER
SUN OR THE RAIN
I'M GONNA FIGHT 'EM ALL♪ ♪A SEVEN NATION ARMY COULDN'T HOLD ME BACK♪
"SEVEN NATION ARMY?" BUT JACK WHITE WON'T BE BORN FOR ANOTHER TWENTY YEARS!
THIS MEANS ONLY ONE THING! THEY'RE AFTER THE CROWN JEWELS ...I'D BETTER HIDE THEM IN MY DRESSING ROOM!
LOOK AT THESE BEAMS, WOODEN FLOORS, AND UNRULY CABLES! ARE WE SHOOTING IN PRAGUE?
IN THE DRESSING ROOM...
GOOD AFTERNOON, MY DEAR! ALLOW ME TO INTRODUCE MYSELF--I AM IVAN RESNICK... I COLLECT JEWELRY!
OH, AND YOU'RE OUT OF TOILET PAPER.
LINDA TRIES TO FLEE, AND LIKE A WHIPLASH, IVAN RESNICK UNSHEATHES A SWORD FROM HIS CANE!
NOT SO FAST, MY DEAR!
VERY BRAVE, MR. RESNICK! YOU NEED A SWORD AGAINST A GIRL!
COULD YOU GIVE HER ABOUT FORTY MINUTES TO CHANGE BACK INTO BLACK CAT?

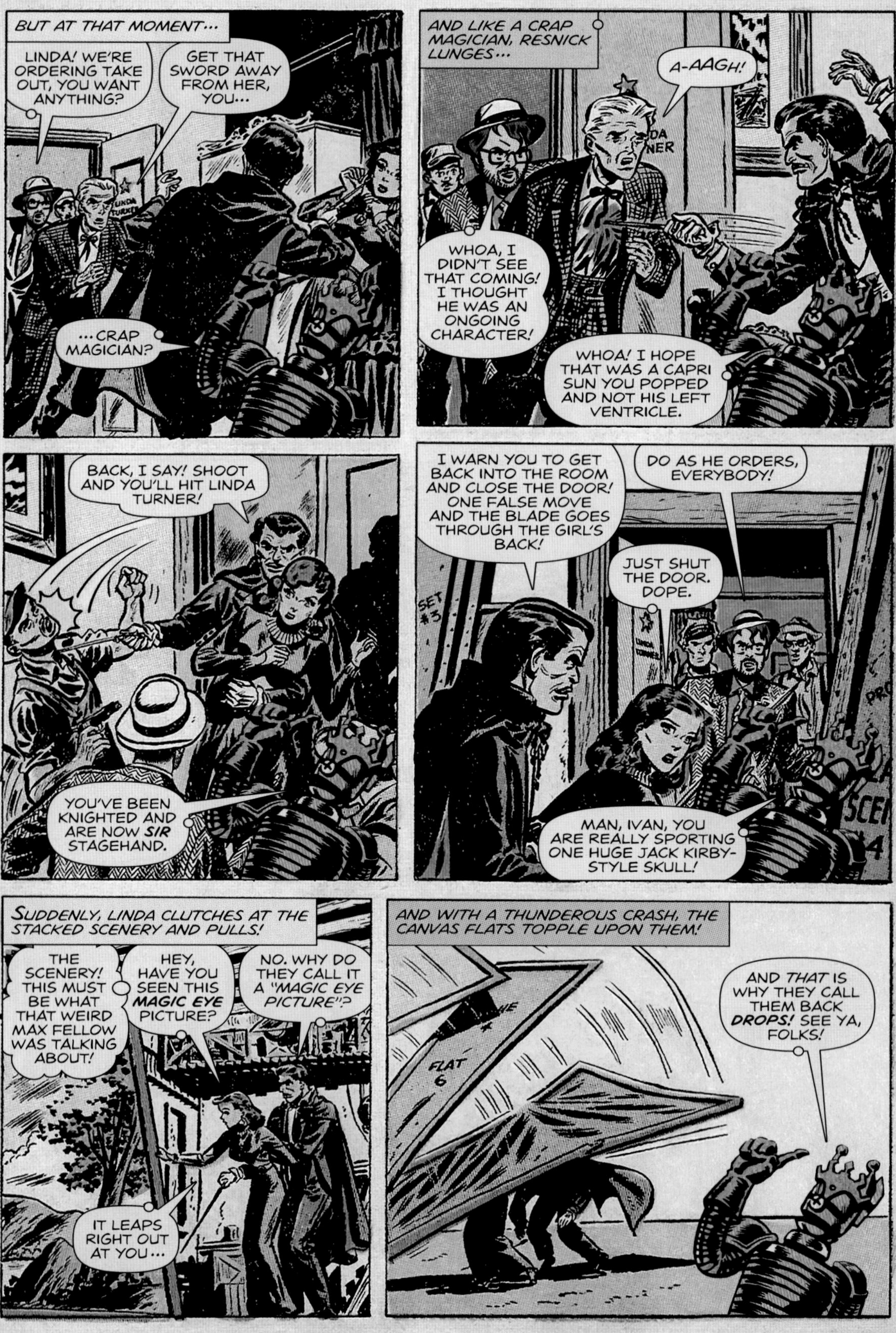
BUT AT THAT MOMENT...
LINDA! WE'RE ORDERING TAKE OUT, YOU WANT ANYTHING?
GET THAT SWORD AWAY FROM HER, YOU...
LINDA TURNER
...CRAP MAGICIAN?
AND LIKE A CRAP MAGICIAN, RESNICK LUNGES...
A-AAGH!
WHOA, I DIDN'T SEE THAT COMING! I THOUGHT HE WAS AN ONGOING CHARACTER!
WHOA! I HOPE THAT WAS A CAPRI SUN YOU POPPED AND NOT HIS LEFT VENTRICLE.
BACK, I SAY! SHOOT AND YOU'LL HIT LINDA TURNER!
YOU'VE BEEN KNIGHTED AND ARE NOW *SIR* STAGEHAND.
I WARN YOU TO GET BACK INTO THE ROOM AND CLOSE THE DOOR! ONE FALSE MOVE AND THE BLADE GOES THROUGH THE GIRL'S BACK!
DO AS HE ORDERS, EVERYBODY!
JUST SHUT THE DOOR. DOPE.
SET #3
MAN, IVAN, YOU ARE REALLY SPORTING ONE HUGE JACK KIRBY-STYLE SKULL!
SUDDENLY, LINDA CLUTCHES AT THE STACKED SCENERY AND PULLS!
THE SCENERY! THIS MUST BE WHAT THAT WEIRD MAX FELLOW WAS TALKING ABOUT!
HEY, HAVE YOU SEEN THIS ***MAGIC EYE*** PICTURE?
NO. WHY DO THEY CALL IT A *"MAGIC EYE PICTURE"*?
IT LEAPS RIGHT OUT AT YOU...
AND WITH A THUNDEROUS CRASH, THE CANVAS FLATS TOPPLE UPON THEM!
FLAT 6
AND *THAT* IS WHY THEY CALL THEM BACK ***DROPS!*** SEE YA, FOLKS!

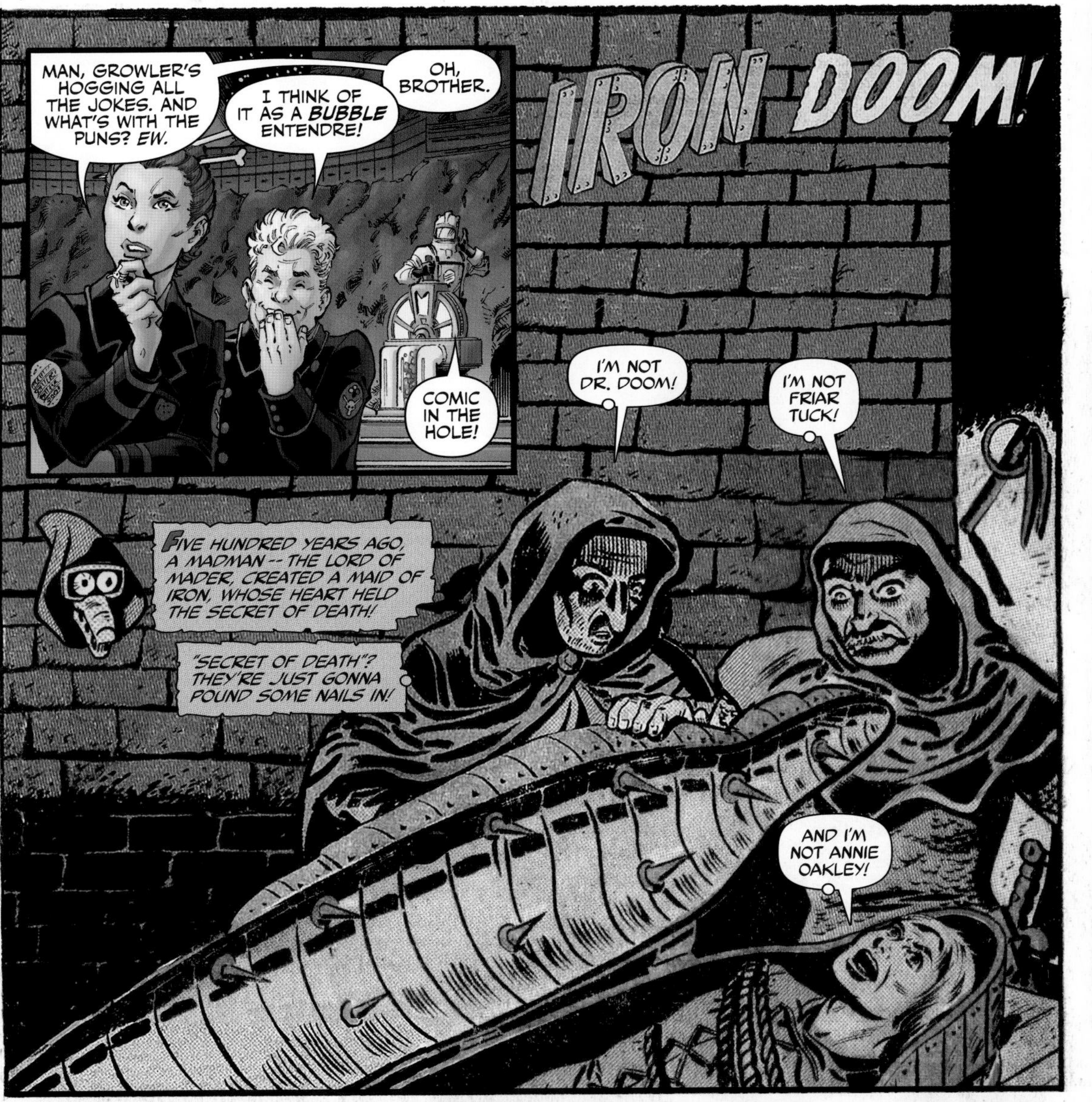
MAN, GROWLER'S HOGGING ALL THE JOKES. AND WHAT'S WITH THE PUNS? EW.
I THINK OF IT AS A BUBBLE ENTENDRE!
OH, BROTHER.
COMIC IN THE HOLE!
IRON DOOM!
I'M NOT DR. DOOM!
I'M NOT FRIAR TUCK!
FIVE HUNDRED YEARS AGO, A MADMAN -- THE LORD OF MADER, CREATED A MAID OF IRON, WHOSE HEART HELD THE SECRET OF DEATH!
"SECRET OF DEATH"? THEY'RE JUST GONNA POUND SOME NAILS IN!
AND I'M NOT ANNIE OAKLEY!

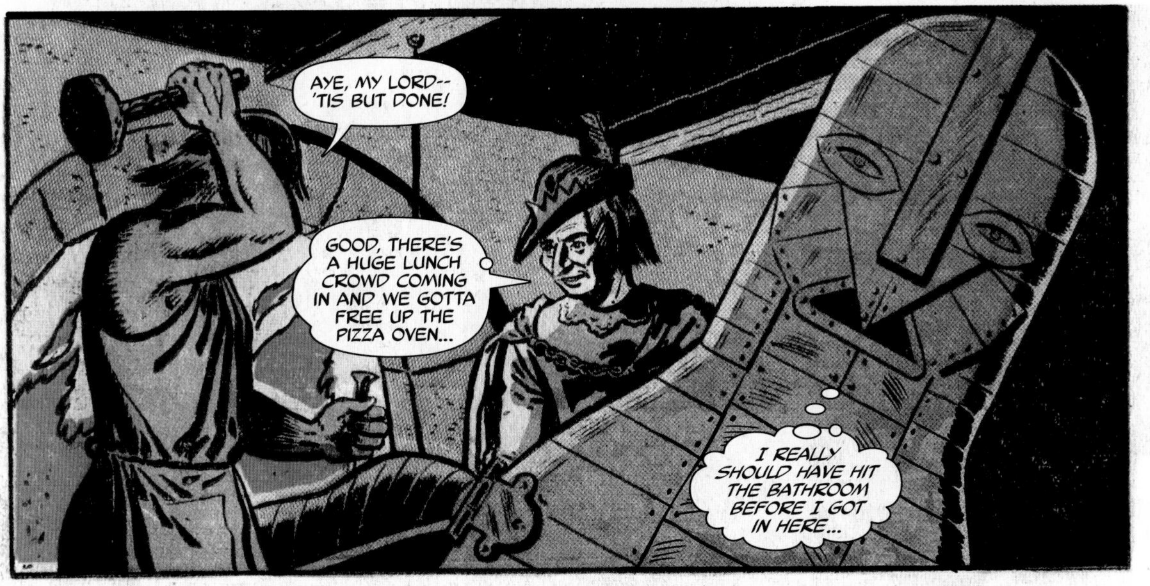
AYE, MY LORD-- 'TIS BUT DONE!
GOOD, THERE'S A HUGE LUNCH CROWD COMING IN AND WE GOTTA FREE UP THE PIZZA OVEN...
I REALLY SHOULD HAVE HIT THE BATHROOM BEFORE I GOT IN HERE...

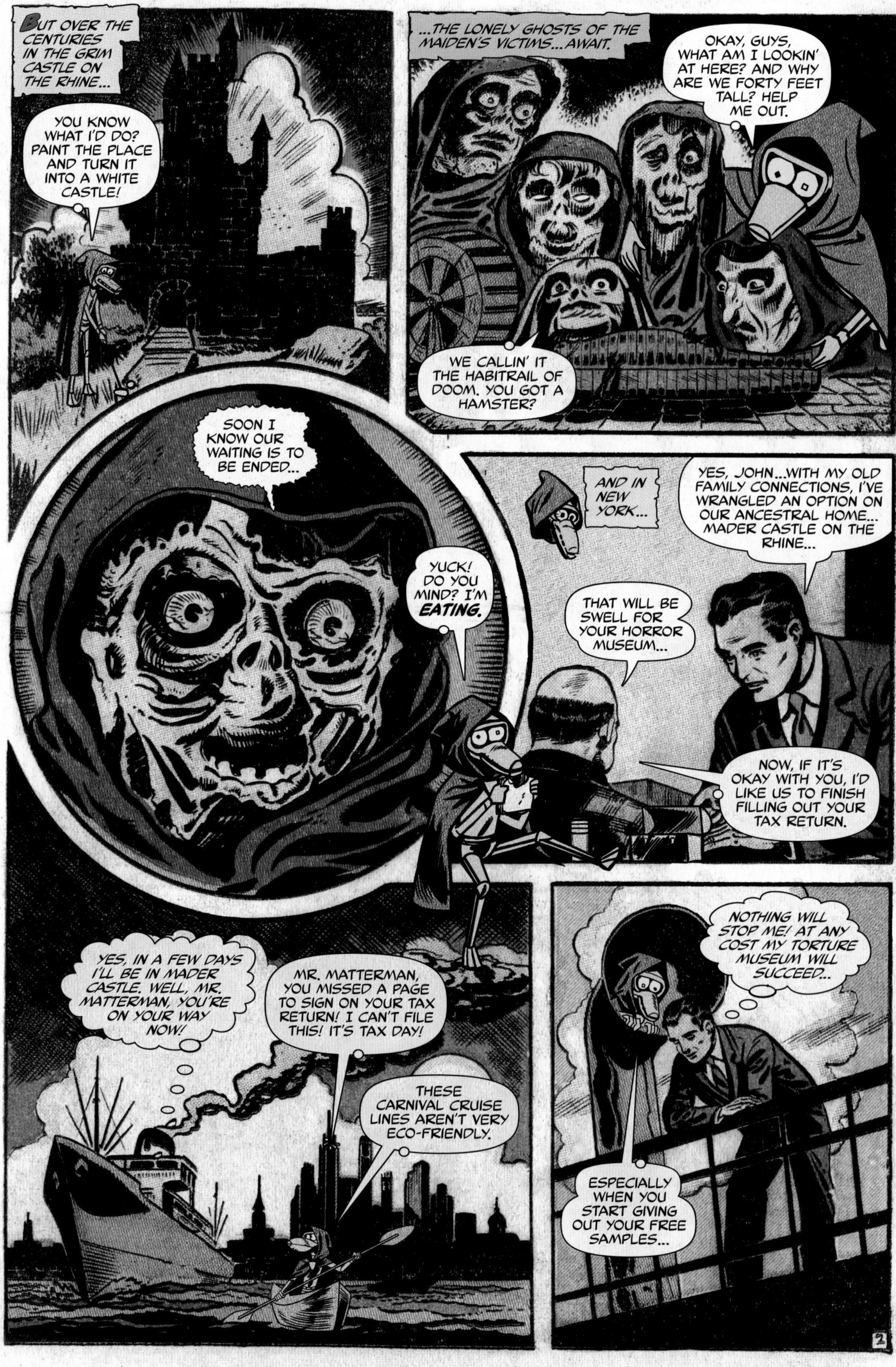
BUT OVER THE CENTURIES IN THE GRIM CASTLE ON THE RHINE...
YOU KNOW WHAT I'D DO? PAINT THE PLACE AND TURN IT INTO A WHITE CASTLE!
...THE LONELY GHOSTS OF THE MAIDEN'S VICTIMS...AWAIT.
OKAY, GUYS, WHAT AM I LOOKIN' AT HERE? AND WHY ARE WE FORTY FEET TALL? HELP ME OUT.
WE CALLIN' IT THE HABITRAIL OF DOOM. YOU GOT A HAMSTER?
SOON I KNOW OUR WAITING IS TO BE ENDED...
YUCK! DO YOU MIND? I'M EATING.
AND IN NEW YORK...
YES, JOHN...WITH MY OLD FAMILY CONNECTIONS, I'VE WRANGLED AN OPTION ON OUR ANCESTRAL HOME... MADER CASTLE ON THE RHINE...
THAT WILL BE SWELL FOR YOUR HORROR MUSEUM...
NOW, IF IT'S OKAY WITH YOU, I'D LIKE US TO FINISH FILLING OUT YOUR TAX RETURN.
YES, IN A FEW DAYS I'LL BE IN MADER CASTLE. WELL, MR. MATTERMAN, YOU'RE ON YOUR WAY NOW!
MR. MATTERMAN, YOU MISSED A PAGE TO SIGN ON YOUR TAX RETURN! I CAN'T FILE THIS! IT'S TAX DAY!
THESE CARNIVAL CRUISE LINES AREN'T VERY ECO-FRIENDLY.
NOTHING WILL STOP ME! AT ANY COST MY TORTURE MUSEUM WILL SUCCEED...
ESPECIALLY WHEN YOU START GIVING OUT YOUR FREE SAMPLES...
2

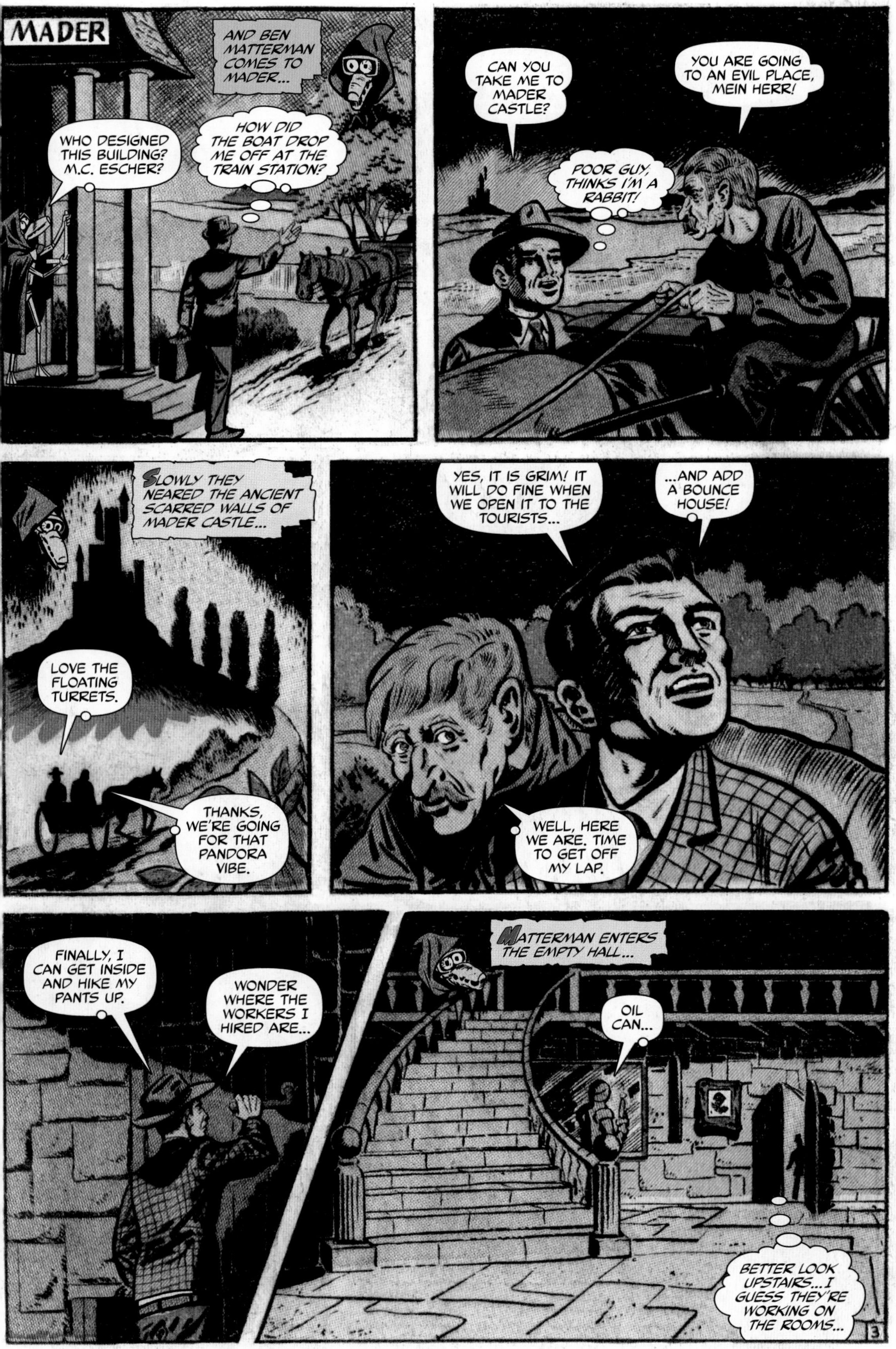
MADER
AND BEN MATTERMAN COMES TO MADER...
WHO DESIGNED THIS BUILDING? M.C. ESCHER?
HOW DID THE BOAT DROP ME OFF AT THE TRAIN STATION?
CAN YOU TAKE ME TO MADER CASTLE?
YOU ARE GOING TO AN EVIL PLACE, MEIN HERR!
POOR GUY, THINKS I'M A RABBIT!
SLOWLY THEY NEARED THE ANCIENT SCARRED WALLS OF MADER CASTLE...
LOVE THE FLOATING TURRETS.
THANKS, WE'RE GOING FOR THAT PANDORA VIBE.
YES, IT IS GRIM! IT WILL DO FINE WHEN WE OPEN IT TO THE TOURISTS...
...AND ADD A BOUNCE HOUSE!
WELL, HERE WE ARE. TIME TO GET OFF MY LAP.
FINALLY, I CAN GET INSIDE AND HIKE MY PANTS UP.
WONDER WHERE THE WORKERS I HIRED ARE...
MATTERMAN ENTERS THE EMPTY HALL...
OIL CAN...
BETTER LOOK UPSTAIRS...I GUESS THEY'RE WORKING ON THE ROOMS...
3

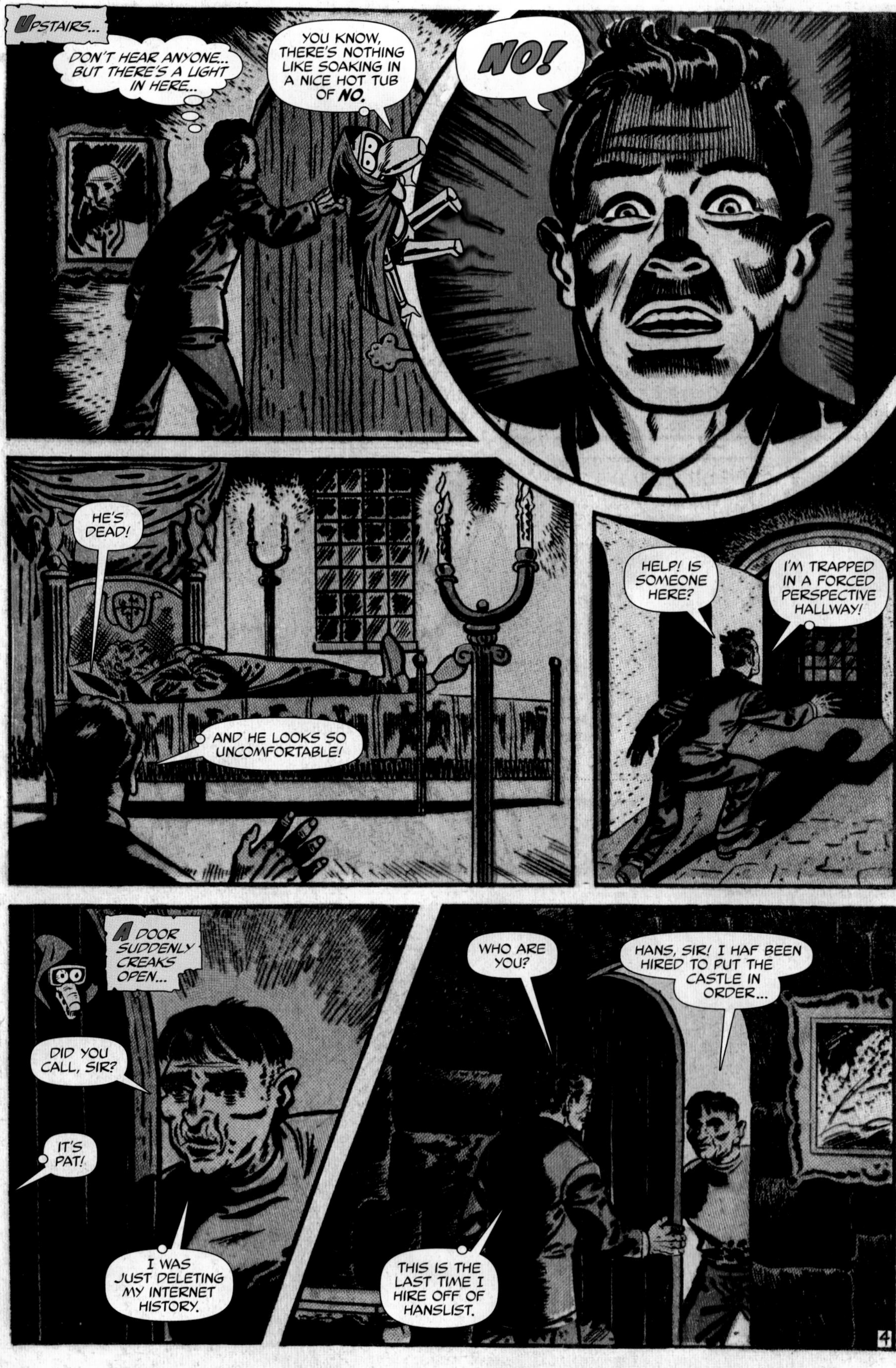
UPSTAIRS...
DON'T HEAR ANYONE... BUT THERE'S A LIGHT IN HERE...
YOU KNOW, THERE'S NOTHING LIKE SOAKING IN A NICE HOT TUB OF NO.
NO!
HE'S DEAD!
AND HE LOOKS SO UNCOMFORTABLE!
HELP! IS SOMEONE HERE?
I'M TRAPPED IN A FORCED PERSPECTIVE HALLWAY!
A DOOR SUDDENLY CREAKS OPEN...
DID YOU CALL, SIR?
IT'S PAT!
I WAS JUST DELETING MY INTERNET HISTORY.
WHO ARE YOU?
HANS, SIR! I HAF BEEN HIRED TO PUT THE CASTLE IN ORDER...
THIS IS THE LAST TIME I HIRE OFF OF HANSLIST.
4

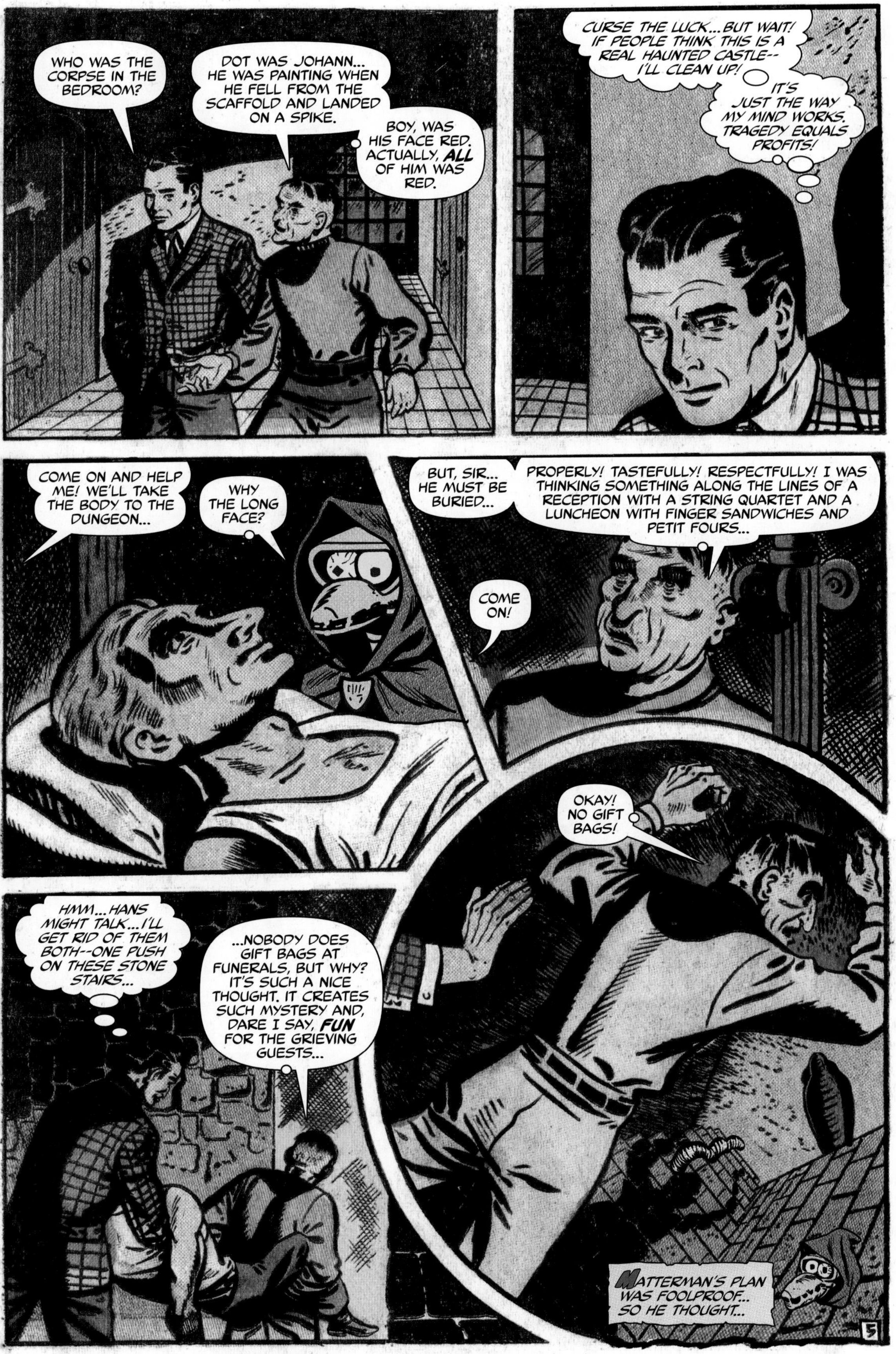
WHO WAS THE CORPSE IN THE BEDROOM?
DOT WAS JOHANN... HE WAS PAINTING WHEN HE FELL FROM THE SCAFFOLD AND LANDED ON A SPIKE.
BOY, WAS HIS FACE RED. ACTUALLY, ALL OF HIM WAS RED.
CURSE THE LUCK... BUT WAIT! IF PEOPLE THINK THIS IS A REAL HAUNTED CASTLE-- I'LL CLEAN UP!
IT'S JUST THE WAY MY MIND WORKS. TRAGEDY EQUALS PROFITS!
COME ON AND HELP ME! WE'LL TAKE THE BODY TO THE DUNGEON...
WHY THE LONG FACE?
BUT, SIR... HE MUST BE BURIED...
PROPERLY! TASTEFULLY! RESPECTFULLY! I WAS THINKING SOMETHING ALONG THE LINES OF A RECEPTION WITH A STRING QUARTET AND A LUNCHEON WITH FINGER SANDWICHES AND PETIT FOURS...
COME ON!
OKAY! NO GIFT BAGS!
HMM... HANS MIGHT TALK... I'LL GET RID OF THEM BOTH--ONE PUSH ON THESE STONE STAIRS...
...NOBODY DOES GIFT BAGS AT FUNERALS, BUT WHY? IT'S SUCH A NICE THOUGHT. IT CREATES SUCH MYSTERY AND, DARE I SAY, FUN FOR THE GRIEVING GUESTS...
MATTERMAN'S PLAN WAS FOOLPROOF.. SO HE THOUGHT...
5

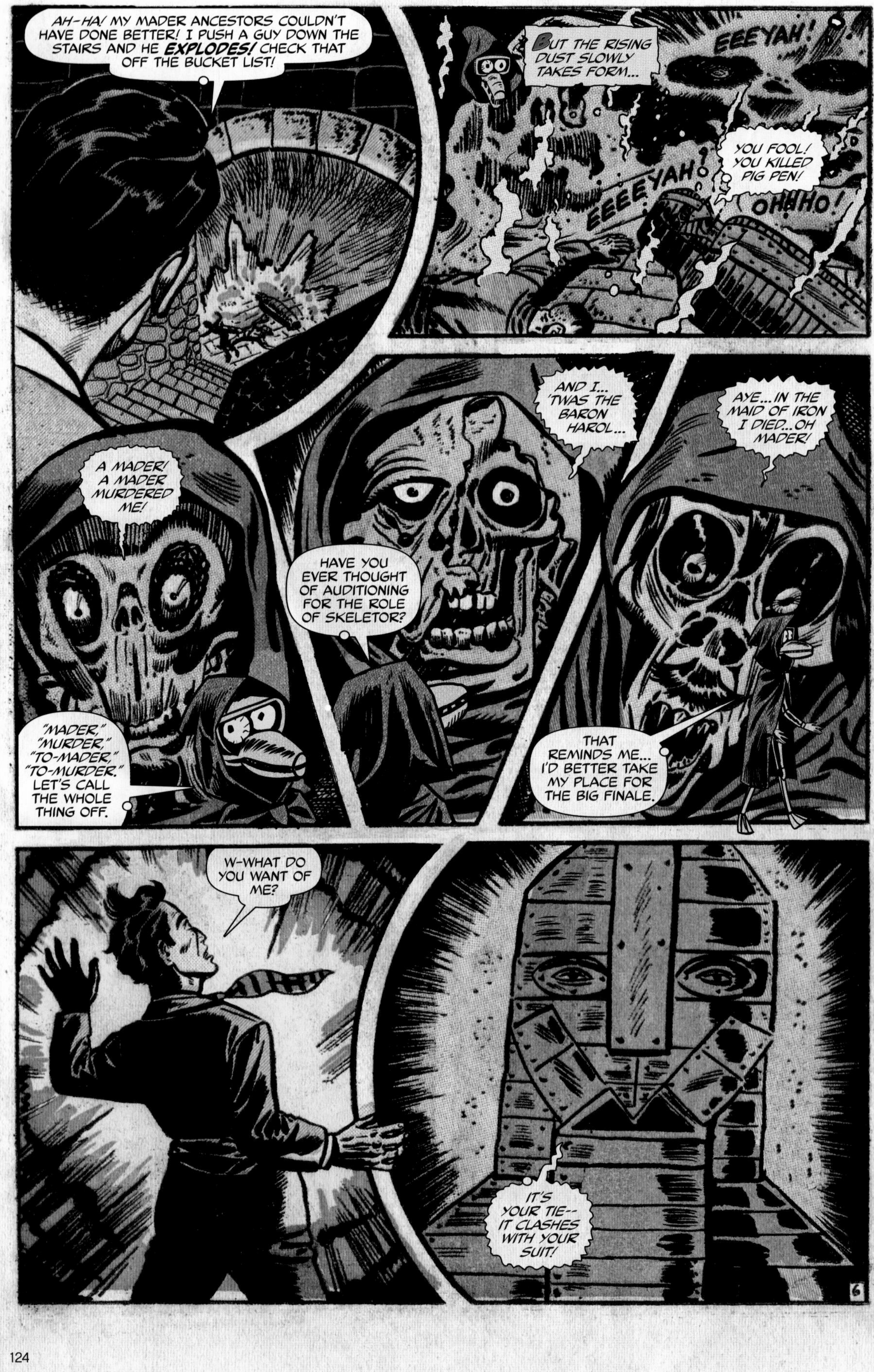
AH-HA! MY MADER ANCESTORS COULDN'T HAVE DONE BETTER! I PUSH A GUY DOWN THE STAIRS AND HE EXPLODES! CHECK THAT OFF THE BUCKET LIST!
BUT THE RISING DUST SLOWLY TAKES FORM...
EEEYAH!
YOU FOOL! YOU KILLED PIG PEN!
EEEEYAH!
OHHHO!
A MADER! A MADER MURDERED ME!
AND I... 'TWAS THE BARON HAROL...
AYE...IN THE MAID OF IRON I DIED...OH MADER!
HAVE YOU EVER THOUGHT OF AUDITIONING FOR THE ROLE OF SKELETOR?
"MADER," "MURDER," "TO-MADER," "TO-MURDER." LET'S CALL THE WHOLE THING OFF.
THAT REMINDS ME... I'D BETTER TAKE MY PLACE FOR THE BIG FINALE.
W-WHAT DO YOU WANT OF ME?
IT'S YOUR TIE-- IT CLASHES WITH YOUR SUIT!
6

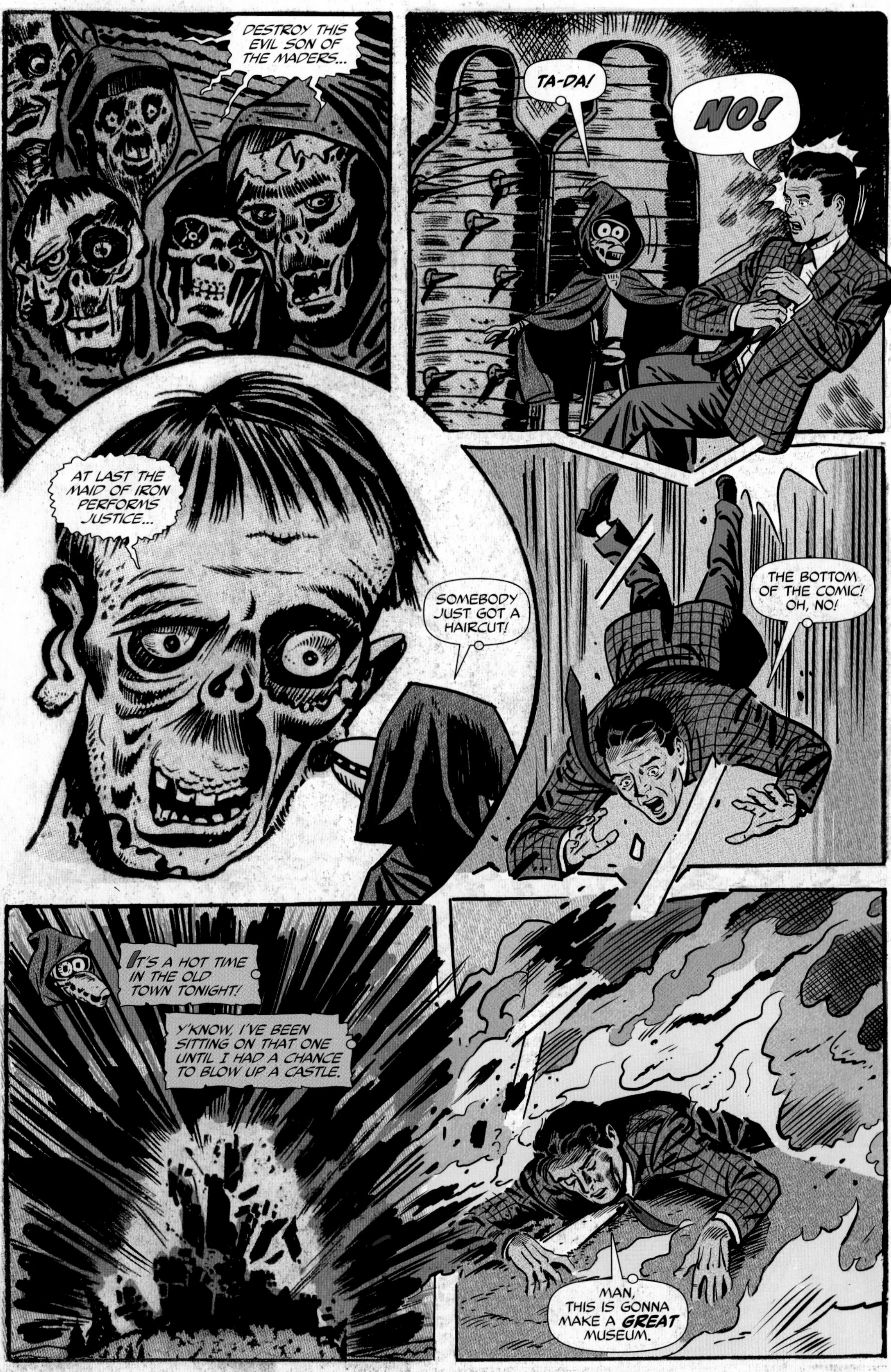
DESTROY THIS EVIL SON OF THE MADERS...
TA-DA!
NO!
AT LAST THE MAID OF IRON PERFORMS JUSTICE...
SOMEBODY JUST GOT A HAIRCUT!
THE BOTTOM OF THE COMIC! OH, NO!
IT'S A HOT TIME IN THE OLD TOWN TONIGHT!
Y'KNOW, I'VE BEEN SITTING ON THAT ONE UNTIL I HAD A CHANCE TO BLOW UP A CASTLE.
MAN, THIS IS GONNA MAKE A **GREAT** MUSEUM.

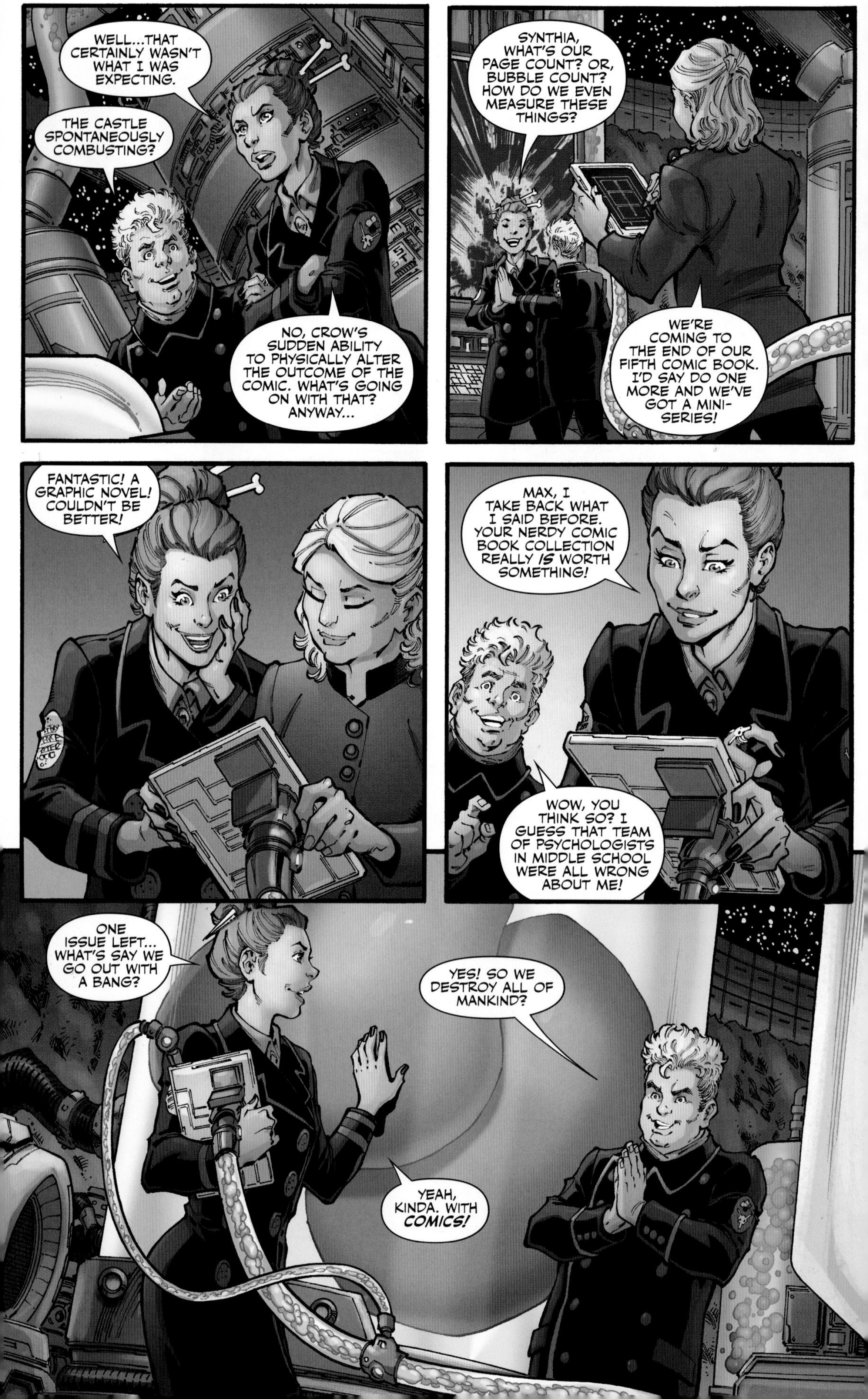
WELL...THAT CERTAINLY WASN'T WHAT I WAS EXPECTING.
THE CASTLE SPONTANEOUSLY COMBUSTING?
NO, CROW'S SUDDEN ABILITY TO PHYSICALLY ALTER THE OUTCOME OF THE COMIC. WHAT'S GOING ON WITH THAT? ANYWAY...
SYNTHIA, WHAT'S OUR PAGE COUNT? OR, BUBBLE COUNT? HOW DO WE EVEN MEASURE THESE THINGS?
WE'RE COMING TO THE END OF OUR FIFTH COMIC BOOK. I'D SAY DO ONE MORE AND WE'VE GOT A MINI-SERIES!
FANTASTIC! A GRAPHIC NOVEL! COULDN'T BE BETTER!
MAX, I TAKE BACK WHAT I SAID BEFORE. YOUR NERDY COMIC BOOK COLLECTION REALLY *IS* WORTH SOMETHING!
WOW, YOU THINK SO? I GUESS THAT TEAM OF PSYCHOLOGISTS IN MIDDLE SCHOOL WERE ALL WRONG ABOUT ME!
ONE ISSUE LEFT... WHAT'S SAY WE GO OUT WITH A BANG?
YES! SO WE DESTROY ALL OF MANKIND?
YEAH, KINDA. WITH ***COMICS!***

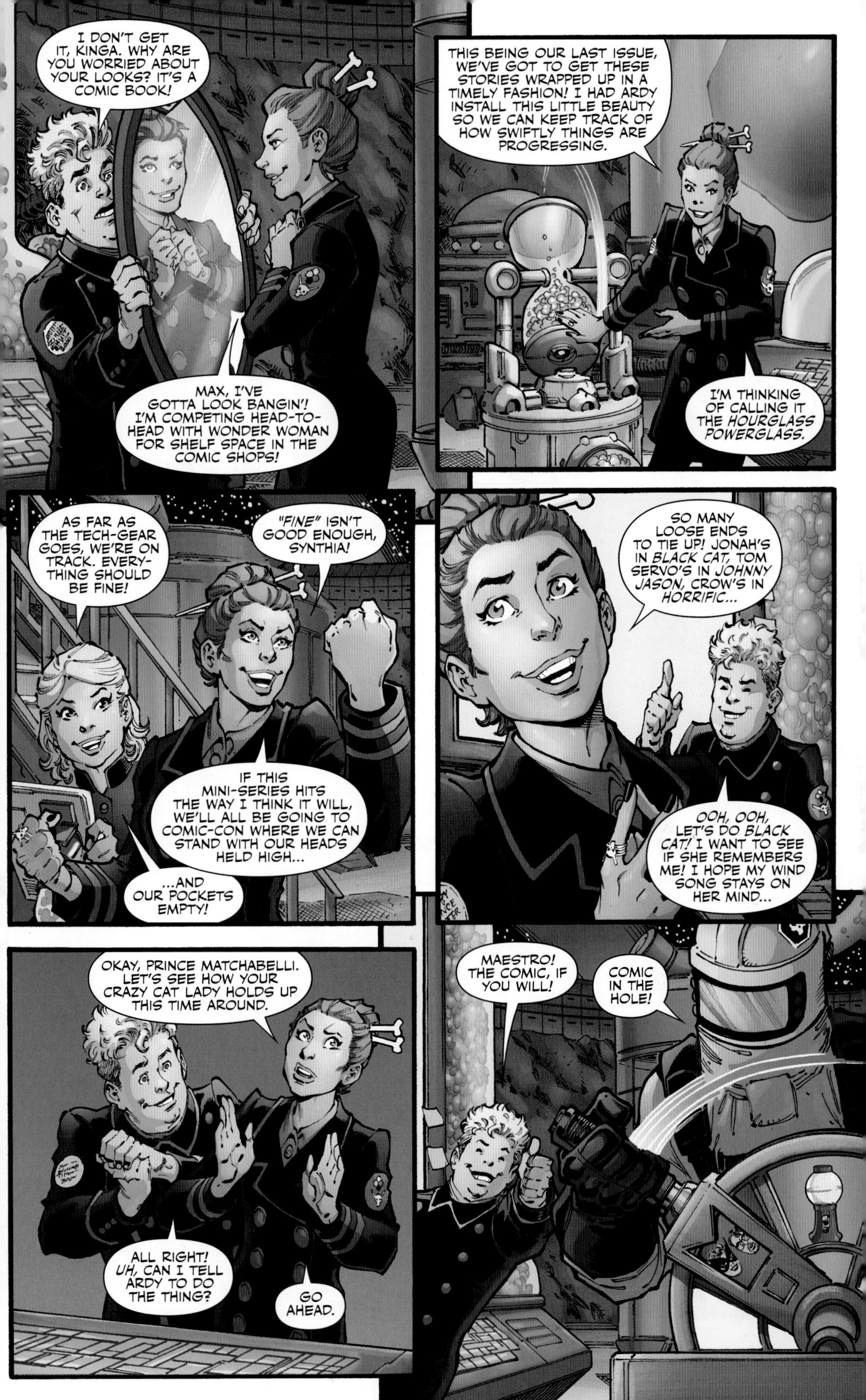
I DON'T GET IT, KINGA. WHY ARE YOU WORRIED ABOUT YOUR LOOKS? IT'S A COMIC BOOK!
MAX, I'VE GOTTA LOOK BANGIN'! I'M COMPETING HEAD-TO-HEAD WITH WONDER WOMAN FOR SHELF SPACE IN THE COMIC SHOPS!
THIS BEING OUR LAST ISSUE, WE'VE GOT TO GET THESE STORIES WRAPPED UP IN A TIMELY FASHION! I HAD ARDY INSTALL THIS LITTLE BEAUTY SO WE CAN KEEP TRACK OF HOW SWIFTLY THINGS ARE PROGRESSING.
I'M THINKING OF CALLING IT THE *HOURGLASS POWERGLASS.*
AS FAR AS THE TECH-GEAR GOES, WE'RE ON TRACK. EVERY-THING SHOULD BE FINE!
"FINE" ISN'T GOOD ENOUGH, SYNTHIA!
IF THIS MINI-SERIES HITS THE WAY I THINK IT WILL, WE'LL ALL BE GOING TO COMIC-CON WHERE WE CAN STAND WITH OUR HEADS HELD HIGH...
...AND OUR POCKETS EMPTY!
SO MANY LOOSE ENDS TO TIE UP! JONAH'S IN *BLACK CAT*, TOM SERVO'S IN *JOHNNY JASON*, CROW'S IN *HORRIFIC*...
OOH, OOH, LET'S DO *BLACK CAT!* I WANT TO SEE IF SHE REMEMBERS ME! I HOPE MY WIND SONG STAYS ON HER MIND...
OKAY, PRINCE MATCHABELLI. LET'S SEE HOW YOUR CRAZY CAT LADY HOLDS UP THIS TIME AROUND.
ALL RIGHT! *UH,* CAN I TELL ARDY TO DO THE THING?
GO AHEAD.
MAESTRO! THE COMIC, IF YOU WILL!
COMIC IN THE HOLE!

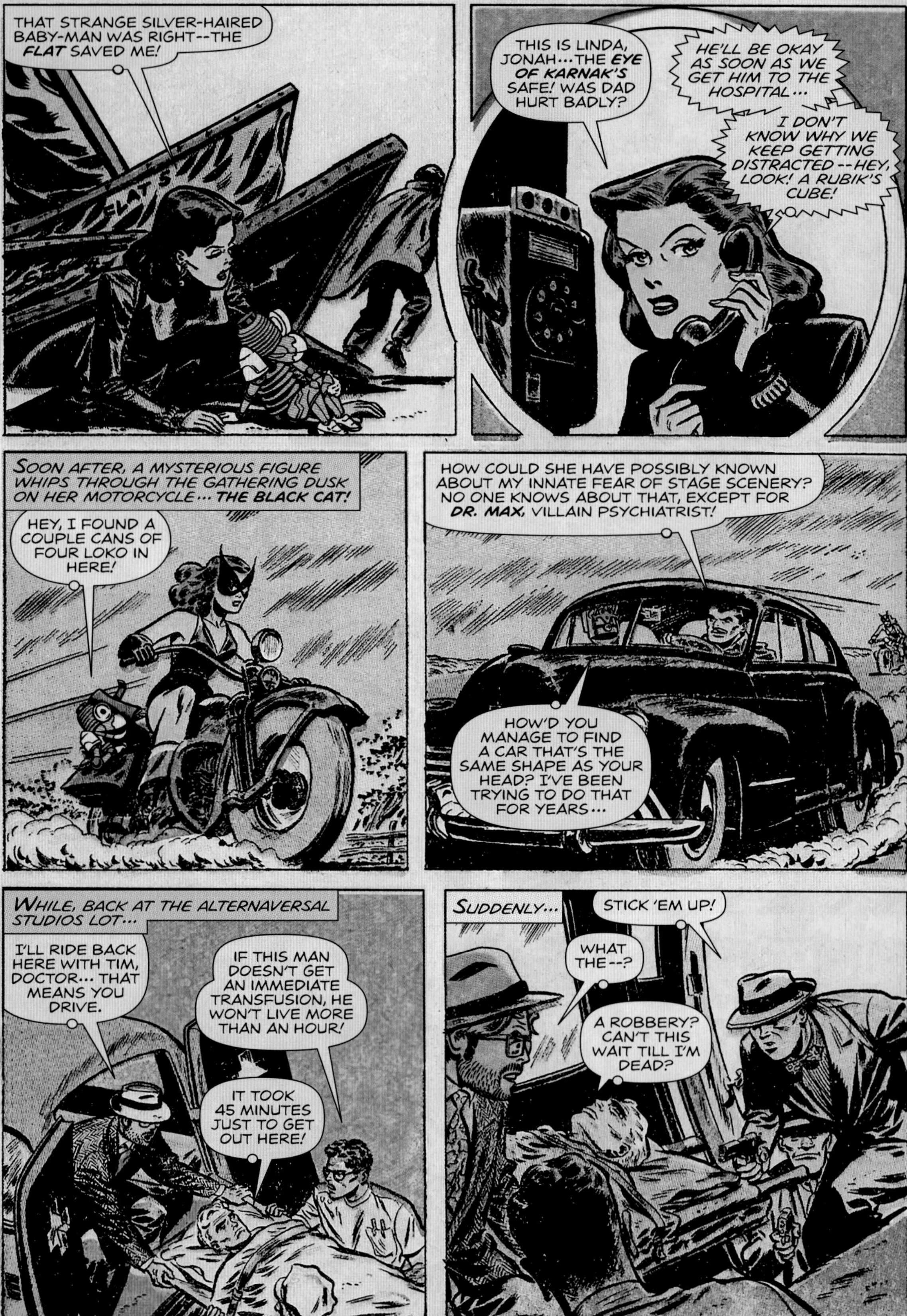
THAT STRANGE SILVER-HAIRED BABY-MAN WAS RIGHT--THE FLAT SAVED ME!
THIS IS LINDA, JONAH…THE EYE OF KARNAK'S SAFE! WAS DAD HURT BADLY?
HE'LL BE OKAY AS SOON AS WE GET HIM TO THE HOSPITAL…
I DON'T KNOW WHY WE KEEP GETTING DISTRACTED--HEY, LOOK! A RUBIK'S CUBE!
SOON AFTER, A MYSTERIOUS FIGURE WHIPS THROUGH THE GATHERING DUSK ON HER MOTORCYCLE…THE BLACK CAT!
HEY, I FOUND A COUPLE CANS OF FOUR LOKO IN HERE!
HOW COULD SHE HAVE POSSIBLY KNOWN ABOUT MY INNATE FEAR OF STAGE SCENERY? NO ONE KNOWS ABOUT THAT, EXCEPT FOR DR. MAX, VILLAIN PSYCHIATRIST!
HOW'D YOU MANAGE TO FIND A CAR THAT'S THE SAME SHAPE AS YOUR HEAD? I'VE BEEN TRYING TO DO THAT FOR YEARS…
WHILE, BACK AT THE ALTERNAVERSAL STUDIOS LOT…
I'LL RIDE BACK HERE WITH TIM, DOCTOR…THAT MEANS YOU DRIVE.
IF THIS MAN DOESN'T GET AN IMMEDIATE TRANSFUSION, HE WON'T LIVE MORE THAN AN HOUR!
IT TOOK 45 MINUTES JUST TO GET OUT HERE!
SUDDENLY…
STICK 'EM UP!
WHAT THE--?
A ROBBERY? CAN'T THIS WAIT TILL I'M DEAD?

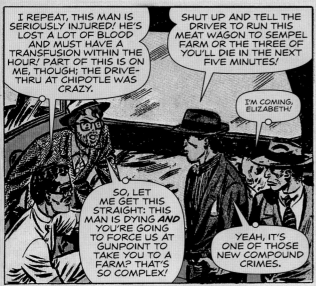

I REPEAT, THIS MAN IS SERIOUSLY INJURED! HE'S LOST A LOT OF BLOOD AND MUST HAVE A TRANSFUSION WITHIN THE HOUR! PART OF THIS IS ON ME, THOUGH; THE DRIVE-THRU AT CHIPOTLE WAS CRAZY.

SHUT UP AND TELL THE DRIVER TO RUN THIS MEAT WAGON TO SEMPEL FARM OR THE THREE OF YOU'LL DIE IN THE NEXT FIVE MINUTES!

I'M COMING, ELIZABETH!

SO, LET ME GET THIS STRAIGHT: THIS MAN IS DYING AND YOU'RE GOING TO FORCE US AT GUNPOINT TO TAKE YOU TO A FARM? THAT'S SO COMPLEX!

YEAH, IT'S ONE OF THOSE NEW COMPOUND CRIMES.

LATER AT THE SEMPEL FARM...

IT SURE TOOK RESNICK A LONG TIME TO GET HERE. HOW DOES A MAN SPEND HIS WHOLE EVENING IN A BURLINGTON COAT FACTORY?

THIS IS LUCK...ROOM DARK AND UNOCCUPIED!

AND I GET TO DO MY SIGNATURE POSE!

ALL I SEE IS A BUNCH OF BLACKLIGHT POSTERS.

WHAT ARE YOU, A CPA? OR SOME KIND OF INSURANCE BROKER?

OH, THIS? YEAH, I DO A BUNCH OF MY THINKING HERE: WRITE FAN FICTION, DO MY BEAD WORK. EVENTUALLY THIS WHOLE WALL WILL BE COVERED WITH SWORDS.

WITH FELINE SWIFTNESS, BLACK CAT LEAPS, AND WITH A TRICK OF JUDO...

LET ME SHOW YOU WHAT I LEARNED FROM THE ARMY!

MY HAIKUS!

BUT WITH EQUAL SPEED, RESNICK RECOVERS AND...

IF YOU DON'T WANT TO BE MY FRIEND, THEN WHY DID YOU COME OVER?!

THIS PANEL HAS A TEMPORARY TATTOO VIBE.

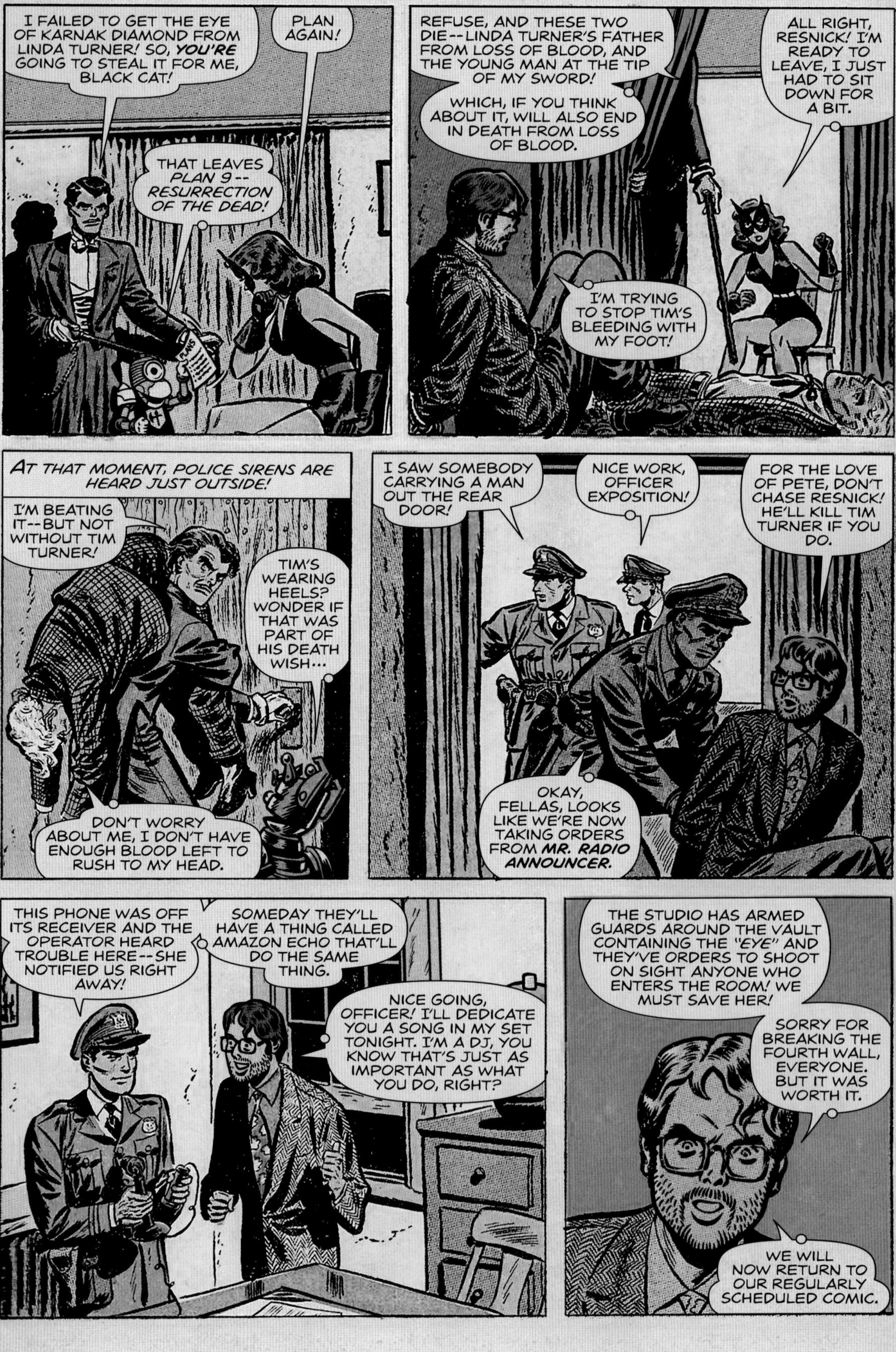
I FAILED TO GET THE EYE OF KARNAK DIAMOND FROM LINDA TURNER! SO, YOU'RE GOING TO STEAL IT FOR ME, BLACK CAT!
PLAN AGAIN!
THAT LEAVES PLAN 9 -- RESURRECTION OF THE DEAD!
PLANS
REFUSE, AND THESE TWO DIE--LINDA TURNER'S FATHER FROM LOSS OF BLOOD, AND THE YOUNG MAN AT THE TIP OF MY SWORD!
WHICH, IF YOU THINK ABOUT IT, WILL ALSO END IN DEATH FROM LOSS OF BLOOD.
ALL RIGHT, RESNICK! I'M READY TO LEAVE, I JUST HAD TO SIT DOWN FOR A BIT.
I'M TRYING TO STOP TIM'S BLEEDING WITH MY FOOT!
AT THAT MOMENT, POLICE SIRENS ARE HEARD JUST OUTSIDE!
I'M BEATING IT--BUT NOT WITHOUT TIM TURNER!
TIM'S WEARING HEELS? WONDER IF THAT WAS PART OF HIS DEATH WISH...
DON'T WORRY ABOUT ME, I DON'T HAVE ENOUGH BLOOD LEFT TO RUSH TO MY HEAD.
I SAW SOMEBODY CARRYING A MAN OUT THE REAR DOOR!
NICE WORK, OFFICER EXPOSITION!
FOR THE LOVE OF PETE, DON'T CHASE RESNICK! HE'LL KILL TIM TURNER IF YOU DO.
OKAY, FELLAS, LOOKS LIKE WE'RE NOW TAKING ORDERS FROM MR. RADIO ANNOUNCER.
THIS PHONE WAS OFF ITS RECEIVER AND THE OPERATOR HEARD TROUBLE HERE--SHE NOTIFIED US RIGHT AWAY!
SOMEDAY THEY'LL HAVE A THING CALLED AMAZON ECHO THAT'LL DO THE SAME THING.
NICE GOING, OFFICER! I'LL DEDICATE YOU A SONG IN MY SET TONIGHT. I'M A DJ, YOU KNOW THAT'S JUST AS IMPORTANT AS WHAT YOU DO, RIGHT?
THE STUDIO HAS ARMED GUARDS AROUND THE VAULT CONTAINING THE "EYE" AND THEY'VE ORDERS TO SHOOT ON SIGHT ANYONE WHO ENTERS THE ROOM! WE MUST SAVE HER!
SORRY FOR BREAKING THE FOURTH WALL, EVERYONE. BUT IT WAS WORTH IT.
WE WILL NOW RETURN TO OUR REGULARLY SCHEDULED COMIC.

MEANWHILE, THE BLACK CAT MAKES HER STEALTHY WAY UP TO THE ROOM WHERE THE EYE OF KARNAK IS KEPT...

MAN, MY KUDZU ALLERGY IS REALLY ACTING UP...

NO TRESPASSING

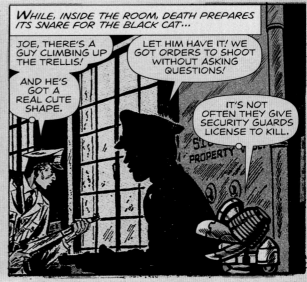

WHILE, INSIDE THE ROOM, DEATH PREPARES ITS SNARE FOR THE BLACK CAT...

JOE, THERE'S A GUY CLIMBING UP THE TRELLIS!

AND HE'S GOT A REAL CUTE SHAPE.

LET HIM HAVE IT! WE GOT ORDERS TO SHOOT WITHOUT ASKING QUESTIONS!

IT'S NOT OFTEN THEY GIVE SECURITY GUARDS LICENSE TO KILL.

PROPERTY

AND AT THAT INSTANT...

LIGHTS! I MUSTN'T BE CAUGHT!

NO TRESPASSIN

BUT I'M STRUGGLING AGAINST MY CATLIKE INSTINCTS TO CHASE ANY MOVING LIGHT!

LIKE A BLACK STREAK, THE BLACK CAT PLUMMETS EARTHWARD!

THOSE BUSHES BELOW WILL SCREEN MY ESCAPE!

NO TR SPASSING

YOU KNOW I'M NUDE!

BUT SOMEONE INTRUDES ON BLACK CAT'S "BUSINESS!"

BLACK CAT! AM I GLAD I FOUND YOU!

OCCUPADO!

PFEW! WE GOT HERE IN TIME! IF YOU'D STUCK YOUR HEAD IN THAT WINDOW YOU'D'VE BEEN A DEAD DUCK!

DEAD DUCK? IS IT TOO LATE TO MAKE THAT MY SUPERHERO NAME?

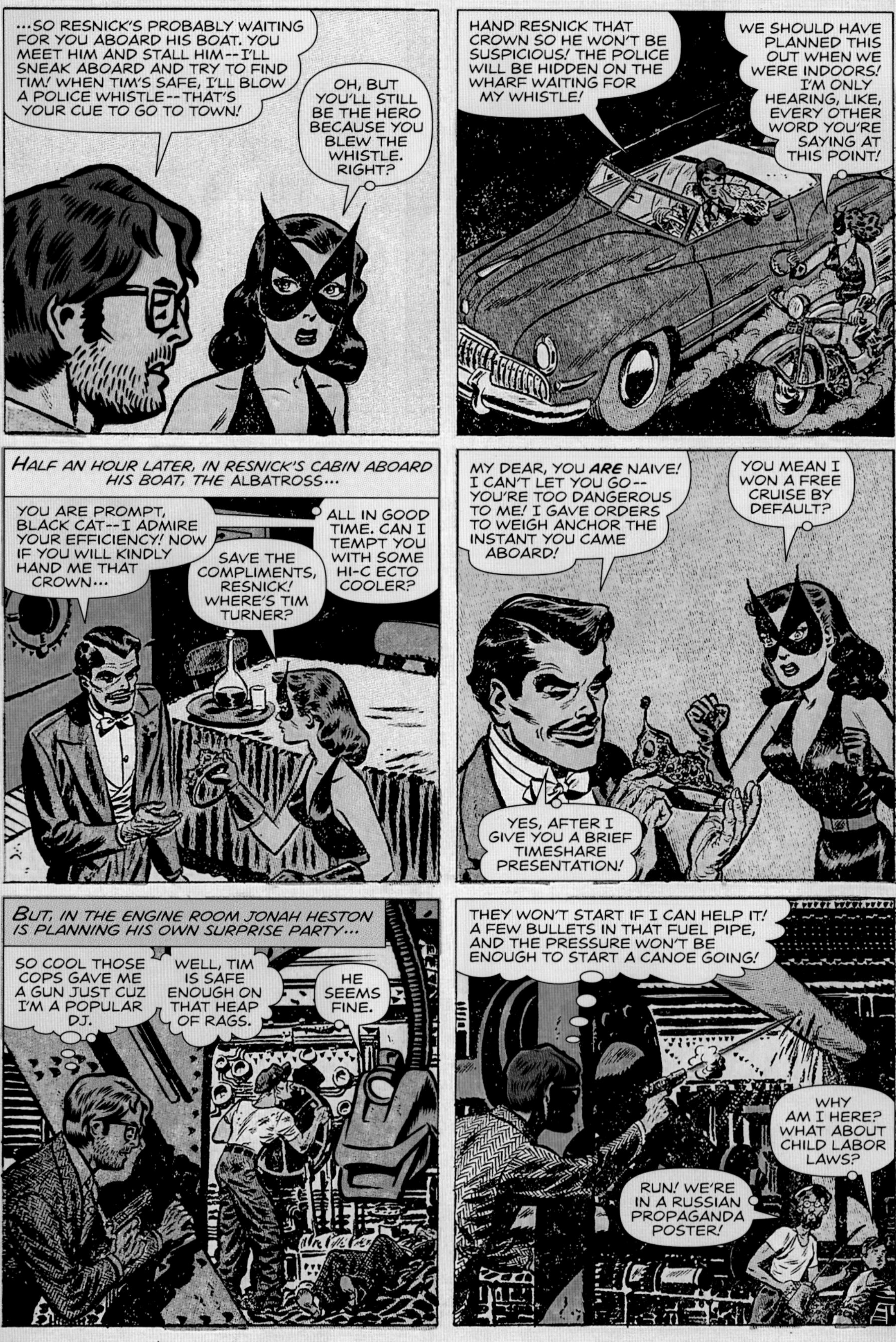
...SO RESNICK'S PROBABLY WAITING FOR YOU ABOARD HIS BOAT. YOU MEET HIM AND STALL HIM--I'LL SNEAK ABOARD AND TRY TO FIND TIM! WHEN TIM'S SAFE, I'LL BLOW A POLICE WHISTLE--THAT'S YOUR CUE TO GO TO TOWN!
OH, BUT YOU'LL STILL BE THE HERO BECAUSE YOU BLEW THE WHISTLE. RIGHT?
HAND RESNICK THAT CROWN SO HE WON'T BE SUSPICIOUS! THE POLICE WILL BE HIDDEN ON THE WHARF WAITING FOR MY WHISTLE!
WE SHOULD HAVE PLANNED THIS OUT WHEN WE WERE INDOORS! I'M ONLY HEARING, LIKE, EVERY OTHER WORD YOU'RE SAYING AT THIS POINT!
HALF AN HOUR LATER, IN RESNICK'S CABIN ABOARD HIS BOAT, THE ALBATROSS...
YOU ARE PROMPT, BLACK CAT--I ADMIRE YOUR EFFICIENCY! NOW IF YOU WILL KINDLY HAND ME THAT CROWN...
SAVE THE COMPLIMENTS, RESNICK! WHERE'S TIM TURNER?
ALL IN GOOD TIME. CAN I TEMPT YOU WITH SOME HI-C ECTO COOLER?
MY DEAR, YOU ARE NAIVE! I CAN'T LET YOU GO--YOU'RE TOO DANGEROUS TO ME! I GAVE ORDERS TO WEIGH ANCHOR THE INSTANT YOU CAME ABOARD!
YOU MEAN I WON A FREE CRUISE BY DEFAULT?
YES, AFTER I GIVE YOU A BRIEF TIMESHARE PRESENTATION!
BUT, IN THE ENGINE ROOM JONAH HESTON IS PLANNING HIS OWN SURPRISE PARTY...
SO COOL THOSE COPS GAVE ME A GUN JUST CUZ I'M A POPULAR DJ.
WELL, TIM IS SAFE ENOUGH ON THAT HEAP OF RAGS.
HE SEEMS FINE.
THEY WON'T START IF I CAN HELP IT! A FEW BULLETS IN THAT FUEL PIPE, AND THE PRESSURE WON'T BE ENOUGH TO START A CANOE GOING!
WHY AM I HERE? WHAT ABOUT CHILD LABOR LAWS?
RUN! WE'RE IN A RUSSIAN PROPAGANDA POSTER!

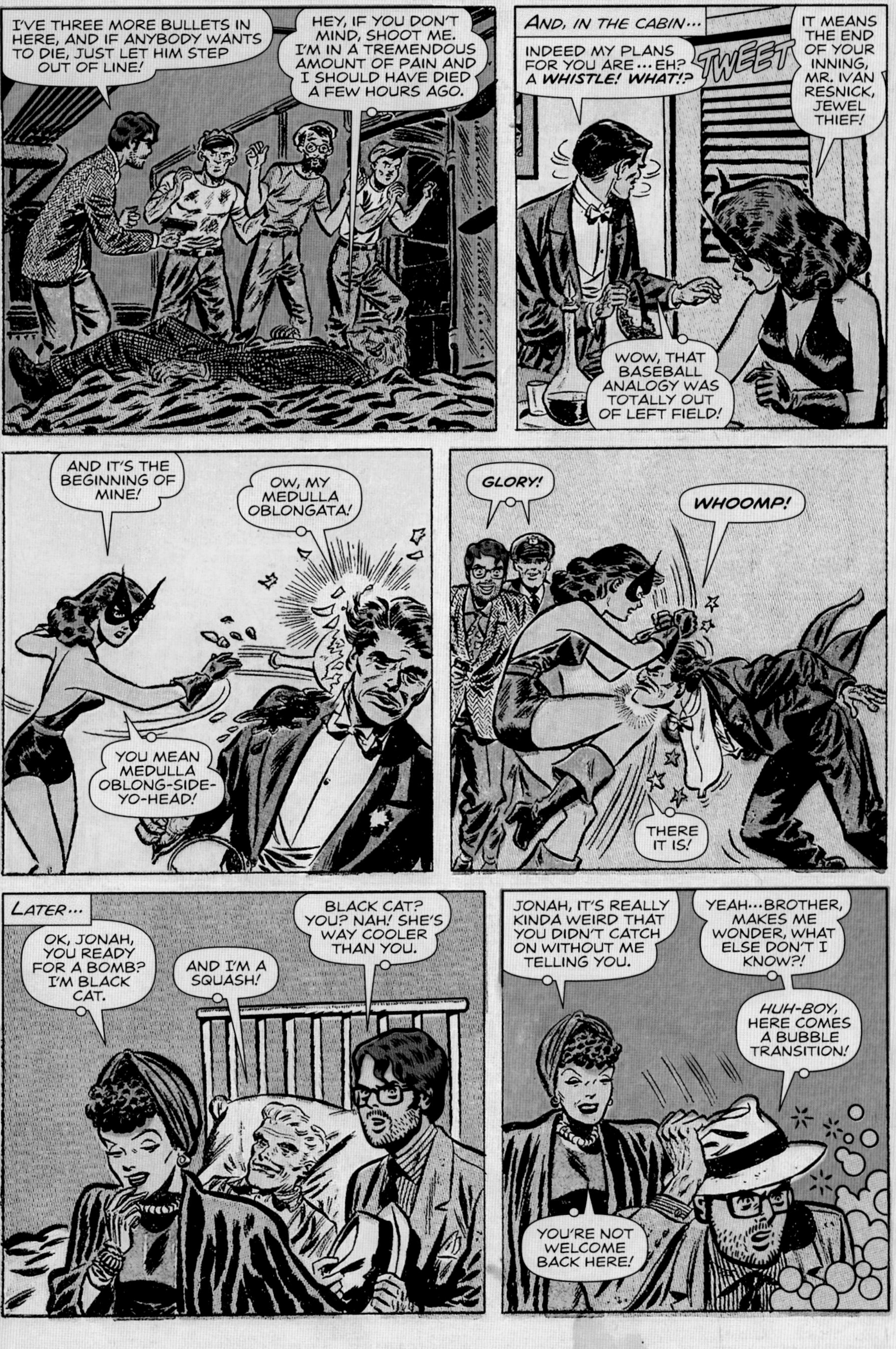
I'VE THREE MORE BULLETS IN HERE, AND IF ANYBODY WANTS TO DIE, JUST LET HIM STEP OUT OF LINE!
HEY, IF YOU DON'T MIND, SHOOT ME. I'M IN A TREMENDOUS AMOUNT OF PAIN AND I SHOULD HAVE DIED A FEW HOURS AGO.
AND, IN THE CABIN...
INDEED MY PLANS FOR YOU ARE... EH? A WHISTLE! WHAT!?
TWEET
IT MEANS THE END OF YOUR INNING, MR. IVAN RESNICK, JEWEL THIEF!
WOW, THAT BASEBALL ANALOGY WAS TOTALLY OUT OF LEFT FIELD!
AND IT'S THE BEGINNING OF MINE!
OW, MY MEDULLA OBLONGATA!
YOU MEAN MEDULLA OBLONG-SIDE-YO-HEAD!
GLORY!
WHOOMP!
THERE IT IS!
LATER...
OK, JONAH, YOU READY FOR A BOMB? I'M BLACK CAT.
AND I'M A SQUASH!
BLACK CAT? YOU? NAH! SHE'S WAY COOLER THAN YOU.
JONAH, IT'S REALLY KINDA WEIRD THAT YOU DIDN'T CATCH ON WITHOUT ME TELLING YOU.
YEAH...BROTHER, MAKES ME WONDER, WHAT ELSE DON'T I KNOW?!
HUH-BOY, HERE COMES A BUBBLE TRANSITION!
YOU'RE NOT WELCOME BACK HERE!

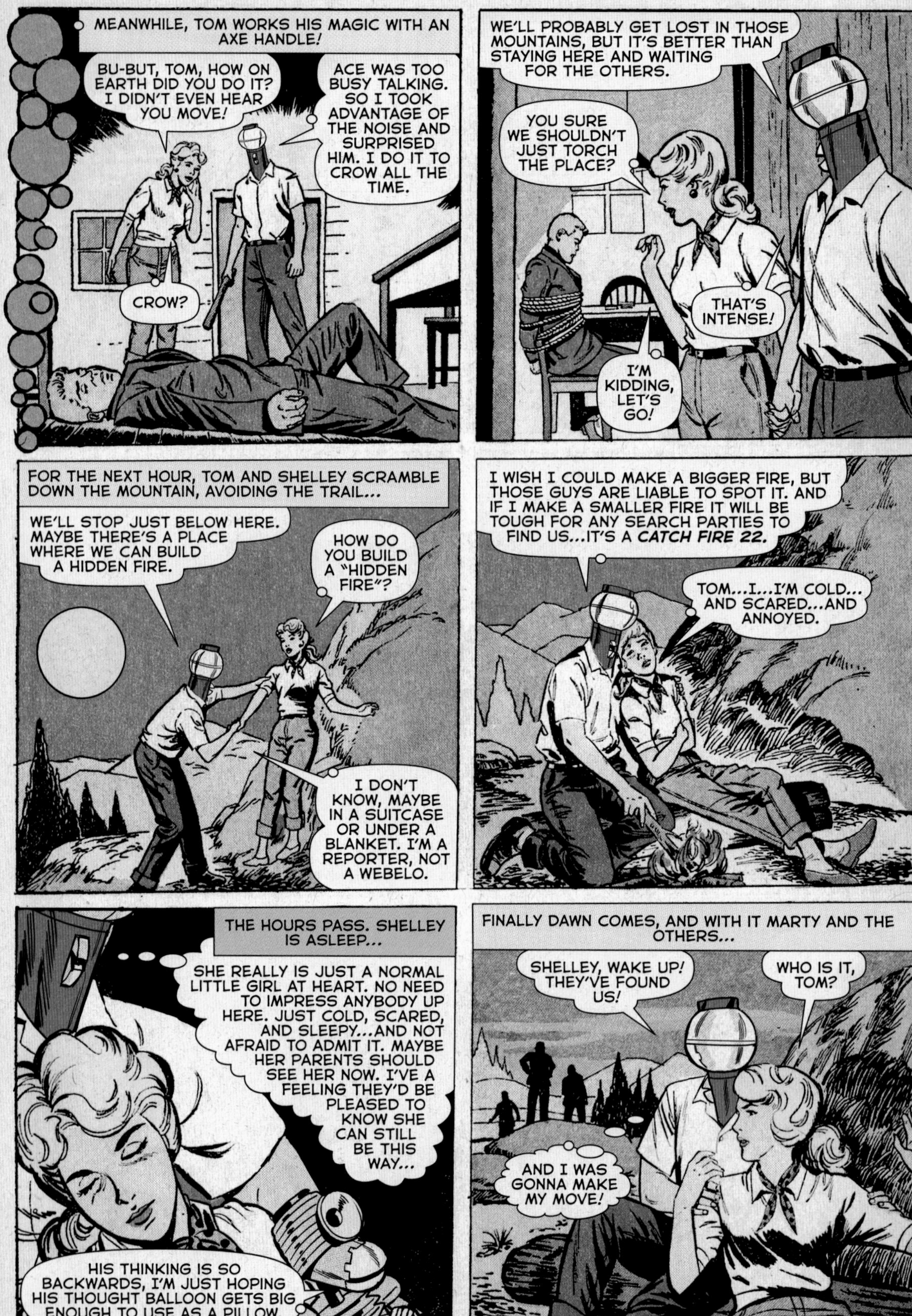

MEANWHILE, TOM WORKS HIS MAGIC WITH AN AXE HANDLE!
BU-BUT, TOM, HOW ON EARTH DID YOU DO IT? I DIDN'T EVEN HEAR YOU MOVE!
ACE WAS TOO BUSY TALKING. SO I TOOK ADVANTAGE OF THE NOISE AND SURPRISED HIM. I DO IT TO CROW ALL THE TIME.
CROW?
WE'LL PROBABLY GET LOST IN THOSE MOUNTAINS, BUT IT'S BETTER THAN STAYING HERE AND WAITING FOR THE OTHERS.
YOU SURE WE SHOULDN'T JUST TORCH THE PLACE?
THAT'S INTENSE!
I'M KIDDING, LET'S GO!
FOR THE NEXT HOUR, TOM AND SHELLEY SCRAMBLE DOWN THE MOUNTAIN, AVOIDING THE TRAIL...
WE'LL STOP JUST BELOW HERE. MAYBE THERE'S A PLACE WHERE WE CAN BUILD A HIDDEN FIRE.
HOW DO YOU BUILD A "HIDDEN FIRE"?
I DON'T KNOW, MAYBE IN A SUITCASE OR UNDER A BLANKET. I'M A REPORTER, NOT A WEBELO.
I WISH I COULD MAKE A BIGGER FIRE, BUT THOSE GUYS ARE LIABLE TO SPOT IT. AND IF I MAKE A SMALLER FIRE IT WILL BE TOUGH FOR ANY SEARCH PARTIES TO FIND US...IT'S A *CATCH FIRE 22.*
TOM...I...I'M COLD... AND SCARED...AND ANNOYED.
THE HOURS PASS. SHELLEY IS ASLEEP...
SHE REALLY IS JUST A NORMAL LITTLE GIRL AT HEART. NO NEED TO IMPRESS ANYBODY UP HERE. JUST COLD, SCARED, AND SLEEPY...AND NOT AFRAID TO ADMIT IT. MAYBE HER PARENTS SHOULD SEE HER NOW. I'VE A FEELING THEY'D BE PLEASED TO KNOW SHE CAN STILL BE THIS WAY...
HIS THINKING IS SO BACKWARDS, I'M JUST HOPING HIS THOUGHT BALLOON GETS BIG ENOUGH TO USE AS A PILLOW.
FINALLY DAWN COMES, AND WITH IT MARTY AND THE OTHERS...
SHELLEY, WAKE UP! THEY'VE FOUND US!
WHO IS IT, TOM?
AND I WAS GONNA MAKE MY MOVE!

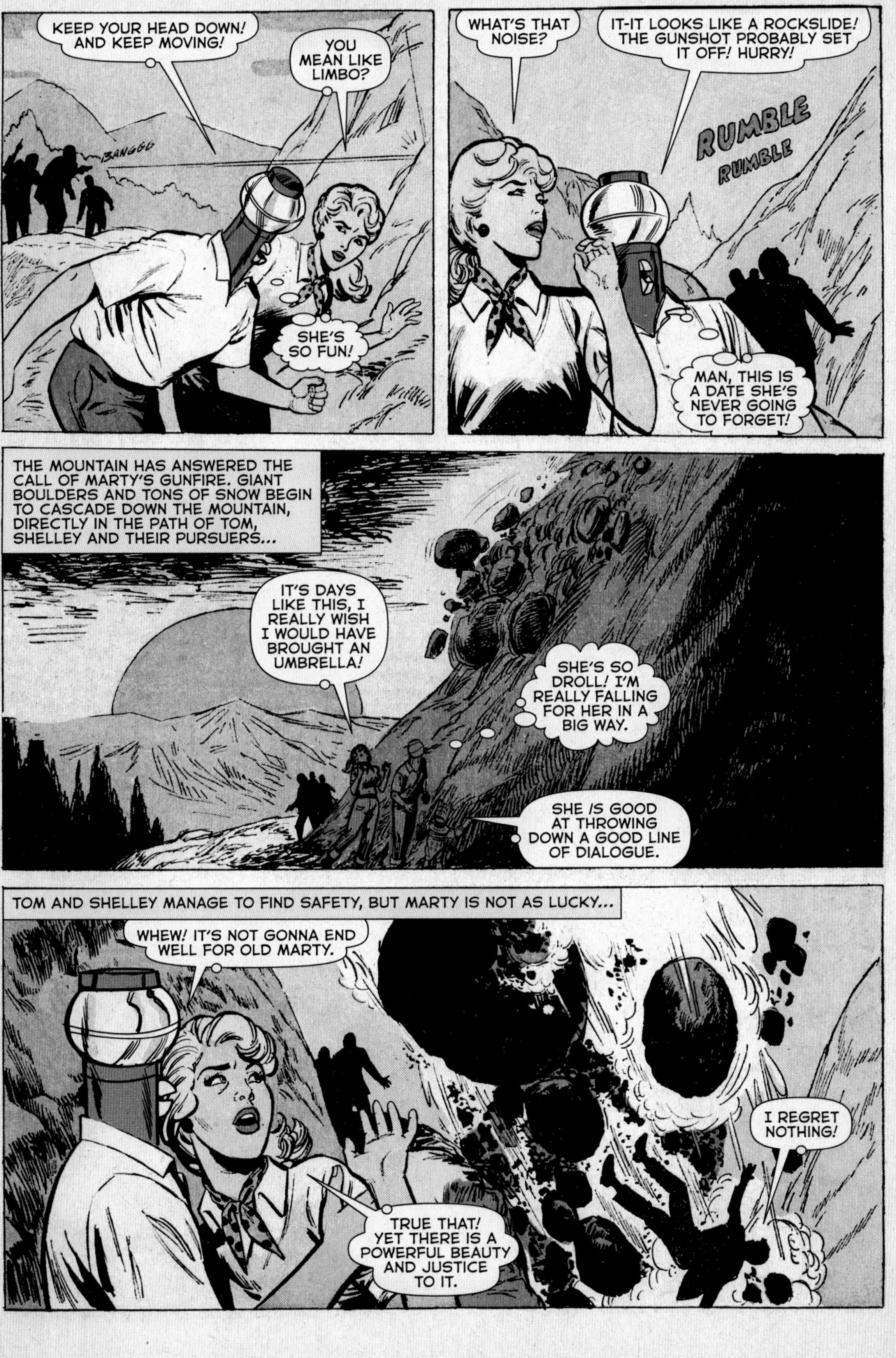

KEEP YOUR HEAD DOWN! AND KEEP MOVING!
YOU MEAN LIKE LIMBO?
BANGGG
SHE'S SO FUN!
WHAT'S THAT NOISE?
IT-IT LOOKS LIKE A ROCKSLIDE! THE GUNSHOT PROBABLY SET IT OFF! HURRY!
RUMBLE
RUMBLE
MAN, THIS IS A DATE SHE'S NEVER GOING TO FORGET!
THE MOUNTAIN HAS ANSWERED THE CALL OF MARTY'S GUNFIRE. GIANT BOULDERS AND TONS OF SNOW BEGIN TO CASCADE DOWN THE MOUNTAIN, DIRECTLY IN THE PATH OF TOM, SHELLEY AND THEIR PURSUERS...
IT'S DAYS LIKE THIS, I REALLY WISH I WOULD HAVE BROUGHT AN UMBRELLA!
SHE'S SO DROLL! I'M REALLY FALLING FOR HER IN A BIG WAY.
SHE *IS* GOOD AT THROWING DOWN A GOOD LINE OF DIALOGUE.
TOM AND SHELLEY MANAGE TO FIND SAFETY, BUT MARTY IS NOT AS LUCKY...
WHEW! IT'S NOT GONNA END WELL FOR OLD MARTY.
TRUE THAT! YET THERE IS A POWERFUL BEAUTY AND JUSTICE TO IT.
I REGRET NOTHING!

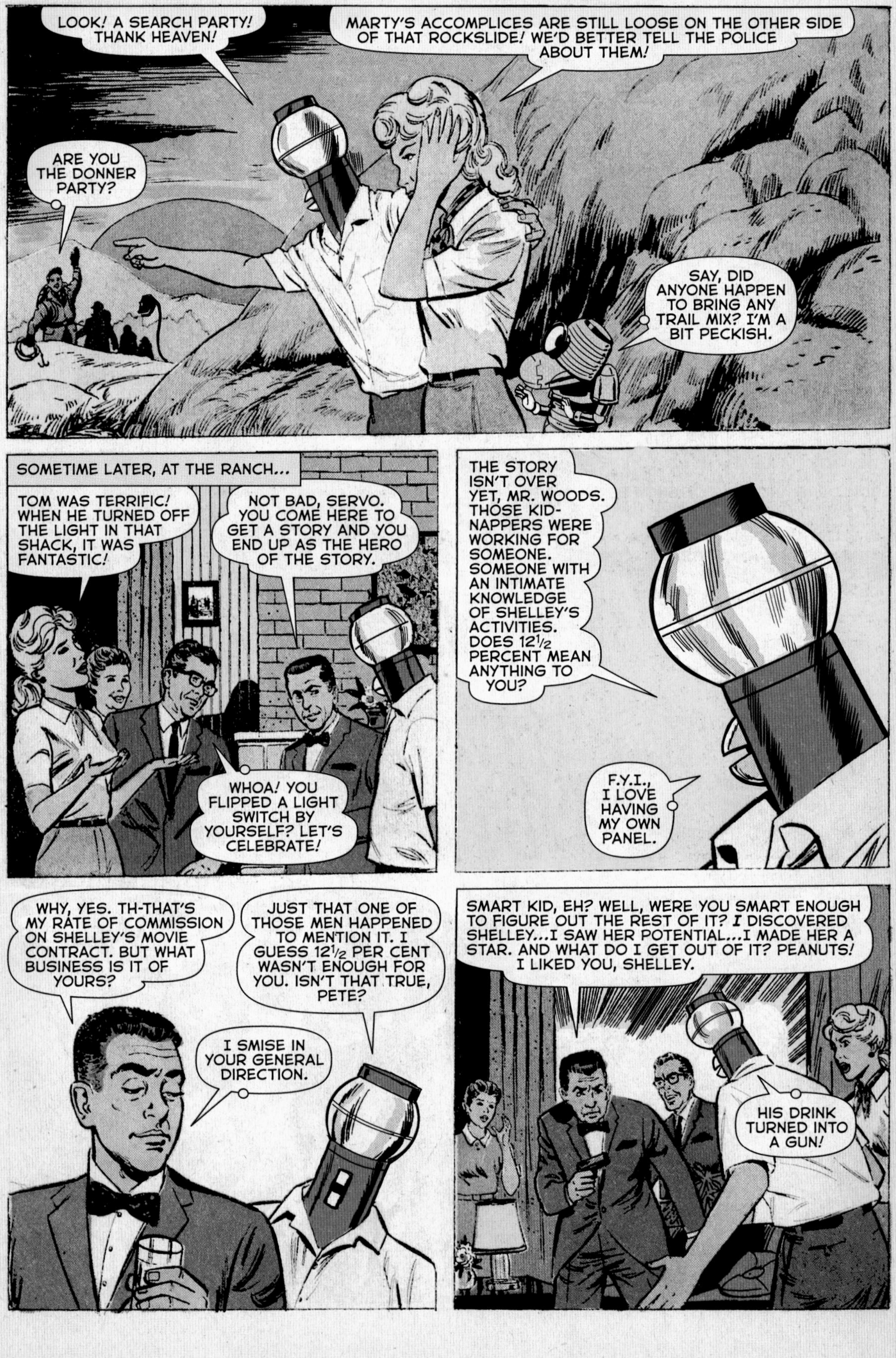
LOOK! A SEARCH PARTY! THANK HEAVEN!
MARTY'S ACCOMPLICES ARE STILL LOOSE ON THE OTHER SIDE OF THAT ROCKSLIDE! WE'D BETTER TELL THE POLICE ABOUT THEM!
ARE YOU THE DONNER PARTY?
SAY, DID ANYONE HAPPEN TO BRING ANY TRAIL MIX? I'M A BIT PECKISH.
SOMETIME LATER, AT THE RANCH...
TOM WAS TERRIFIC! WHEN HE TURNED OFF THE LIGHT IN THAT SHACK, IT WAS FANTASTIC!
NOT BAD, SERVO. YOU COME HERE TO GET A STORY AND YOU END UP AS THE HERO OF THE STORY.
WHOA! YOU FLIPPED A LIGHT SWITCH BY YOURSELF? LET'S CELEBRATE!
THE STORY ISN'T OVER YET, MR. WOODS. THOSE KID-NAPPERS WERE WORKING FOR SOMEONE. SOMEONE WITH AN INTIMATE KNOWLEDGE OF SHELLEY'S ACTIVITIES. DOES 12½ PERCENT MEAN ANYTHING TO YOU?
F.Y.I., I LOVE HAVING MY OWN PANEL.
WHY, YES. TH-THAT'S MY RATE OF COMMISSION ON SHELLEY'S MOVIE CONTRACT. BUT WHAT BUSINESS IS IT OF YOURS?
JUST THAT ONE OF THOSE MEN HAPPENED TO MENTION IT. I GUESS 12½ PER CENT WASN'T ENOUGH FOR YOU. ISN'T THAT TRUE, PETE?
I SMISE IN YOUR GENERAL DIRECTION.
SMART KID, EH? WELL, WERE YOU SMART ENOUGH TO FIGURE OUT THE REST OF IT? I DISCOVERED SHELLEY...I SAW HER POTENTIAL...I MADE HER A STAR. AND WHAT DO I GET OUT OF IT? PEANUTS! I LIKED YOU, SHELLEY.
HIS DRINK TURNED INTO A GUN!

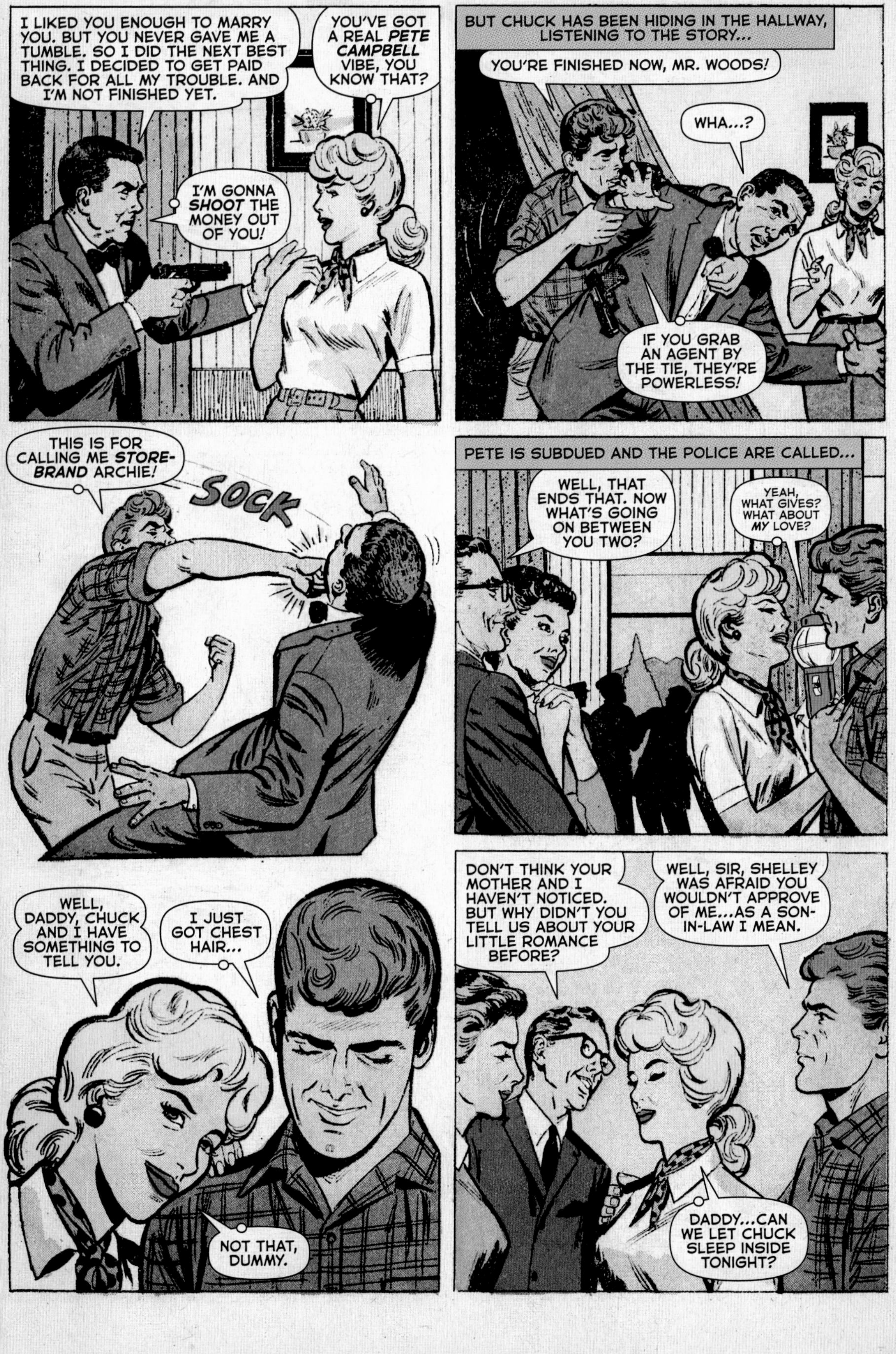

I LIKED YOU ENOUGH TO MARRY YOU. BUT YOU NEVER GAVE ME A TUMBLE. SO I DID THE NEXT BEST THING. I DECIDED TO GET PAID BACK FOR ALL MY TROUBLE. AND I'M NOT FINISHED YET.
YOU'VE GOT A REAL PETE CAMPBELL VIBE, YOU KNOW THAT?
I'M GONNA SHOOT THE MONEY OUT OF YOU!
BUT CHUCK HAS BEEN HIDING IN THE HALLWAY, LISTENING TO THE STORY...
YOU'RE FINISHED NOW, MR. WOODS!
WHA...?
IF YOU GRAB AN AGENT BY THE TIE, THEY'RE POWERLESS!
THIS IS FOR CALLING ME STORE-BRAND ARCHIE!
SOCK
PETE IS SUBDUED AND THE POLICE ARE CALLED...
WELL, THAT ENDS THAT. NOW WHAT'S GOING ON BETWEEN YOU TWO?
YEAH, WHAT GIVES? WHAT ABOUT MY LOVE?
WELL, DADDY, CHUCK AND I HAVE SOMETHING TO TELL YOU.
I JUST GOT CHEST HAIR...
NOT THAT, DUMMY.
DON'T THINK YOUR MOTHER AND I HAVEN'T NOTICED. BUT WHY DIDN'T YOU TELL US ABOUT YOUR LITTLE ROMANCE BEFORE?
WELL, SIR, SHELLEY WAS AFRAID YOU WOULDN'T APPROVE OF ME...AS A SON-IN-LAW I MEAN.
DADDY...CAN WE LET CHUCK SLEEP INSIDE TONIGHT?

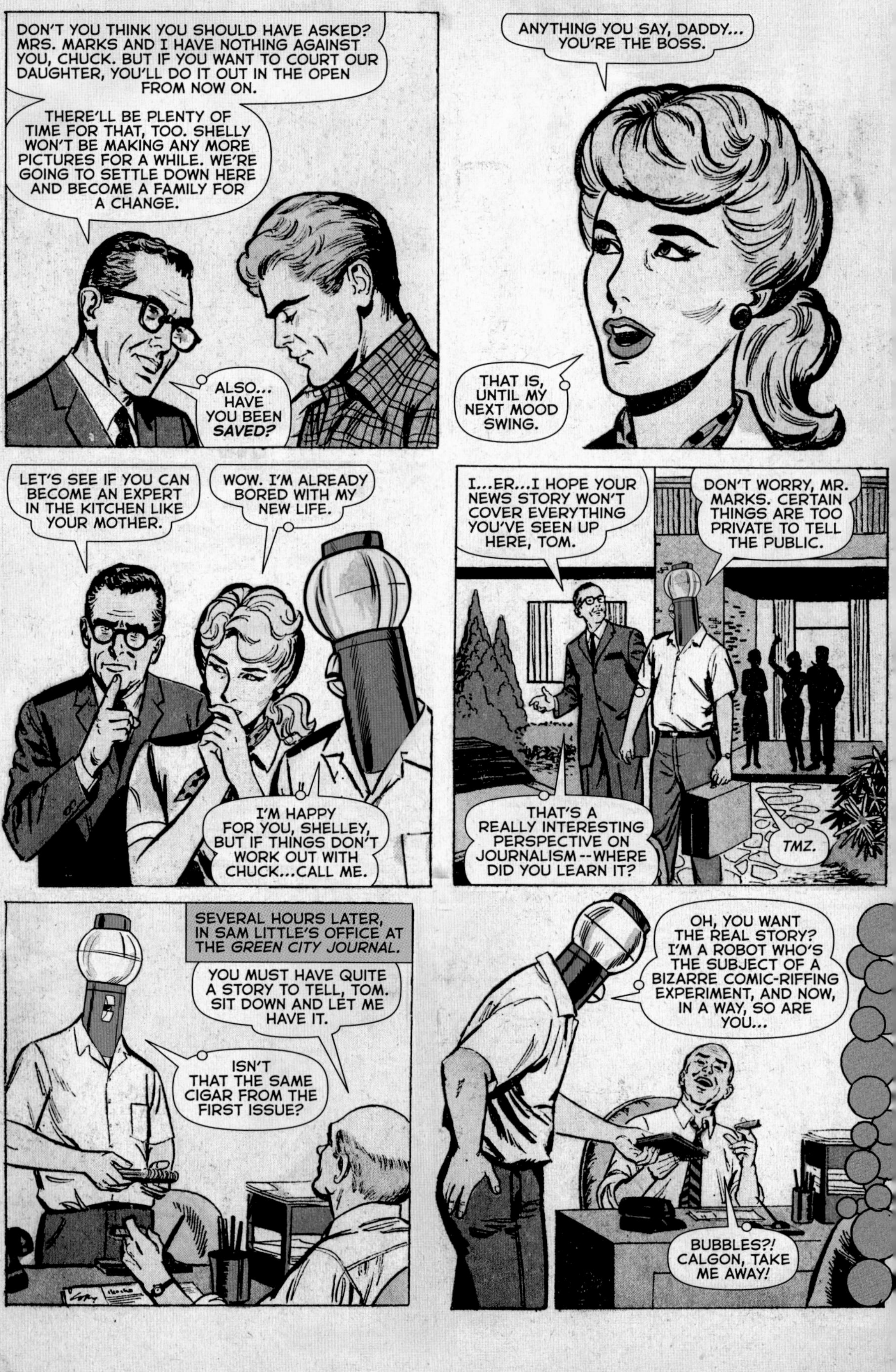
DON'T YOU THINK YOU SHOULD HAVE ASKED? MRS. MARKS AND I HAVE NOTHING AGAINST YOU, CHUCK. BUT IF YOU WANT TO COURT OUR DAUGHTER, YOU'LL DO IT OUT IN THE OPEN FROM NOW ON.
THERE'LL BE PLENTY OF TIME FOR THAT, TOO. SHELLY WON'T BE MAKING ANY MORE PICTURES FOR A WHILE. WE'RE GOING TO SETTLE DOWN HERE AND BECOME A FAMILY FOR A CHANGE.
ALSO... HAVE YOU BEEN *SAVED?*
ANYTHING YOU SAY, DADDY... YOU'RE THE BOSS.
THAT IS, UNTIL MY NEXT MOOD SWING.
LET'S SEE IF YOU CAN BECOME AN EXPERT IN THE KITCHEN LIKE YOUR MOTHER.
WOW. I'M ALREADY BORED WITH MY NEW LIFE.
I'M HAPPY FOR YOU, SHELLEY, BUT IF THINGS DON'T WORK OUT WITH CHUCK...CALL ME.
I...ER...I HOPE YOUR NEWS STORY WON'T COVER EVERYTHING YOU'VE SEEN UP HERE, TOM.
DON'T WORRY, MR. MARKS. CERTAIN THINGS ARE TOO PRIVATE TO TELL THE PUBLIC.
THAT'S A REALLY INTERESTING PERSPECTIVE ON JOURNALISM --WHERE DID YOU LEARN IT?
TMZ.
SEVERAL HOURS LATER, IN SAM LITTLE'S OFFICE AT THE *GREEN CITY JOURNAL.*
YOU MUST HAVE QUITE A STORY TO TELL, TOM. SIT DOWN AND LET ME HAVE IT.
ISN'T THAT THE SAME CIGAR FROM THE FIRST ISSUE?
OH, YOU WANT THE REAL STORY? I'M A ROBOT WHO'S THE SUBJECT OF A BIZARRE COMIC-RIFFING EXPERIMENT, AND NOW, IN A WAY, SO ARE YOU...
BUBBLES?! CALGON, TAKE ME AWAY!

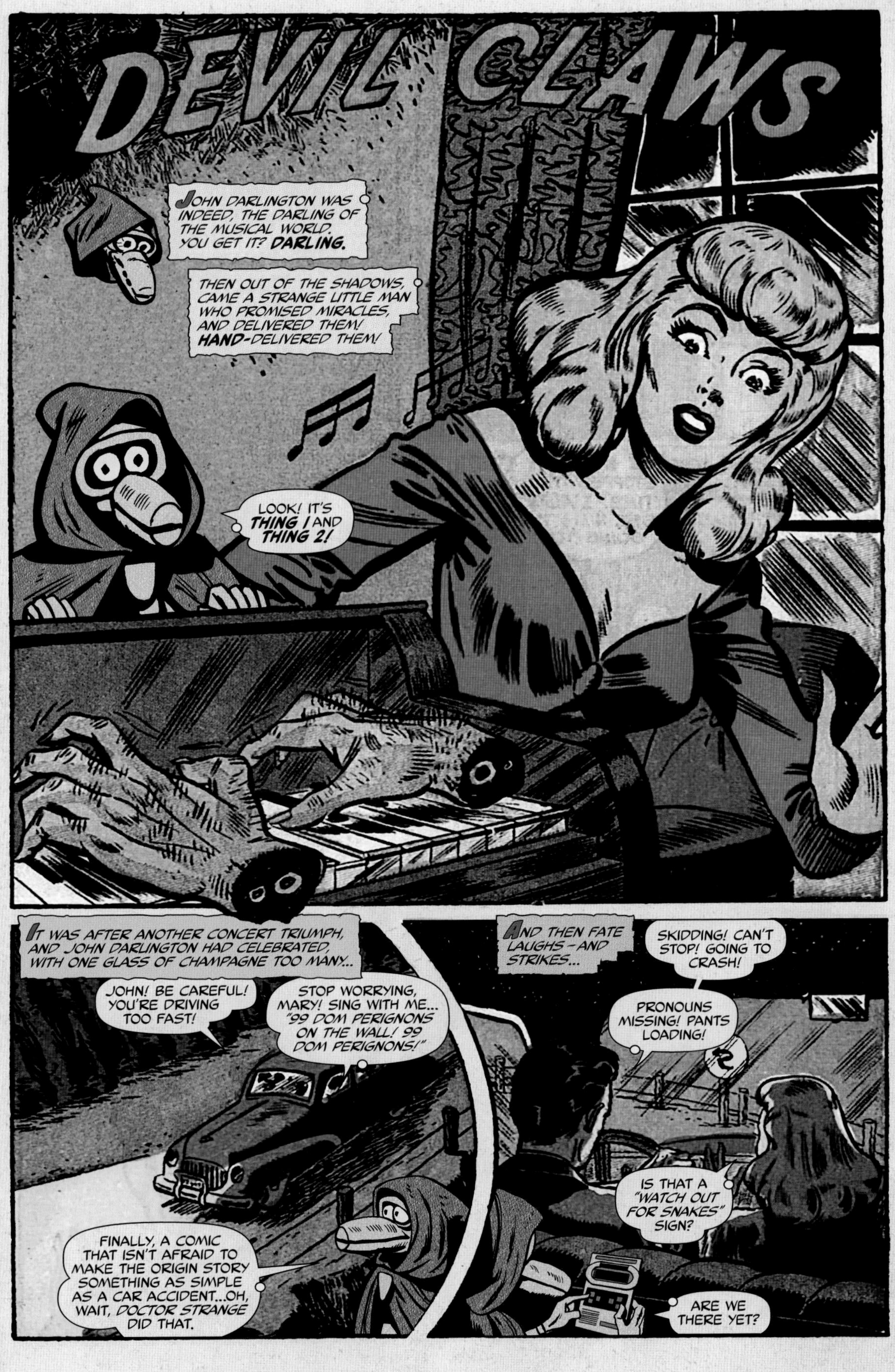

DEVIL CLAWS
JOHN DARLINGTON WAS INDEED, THE DARLING OF THE MUSICAL WORLD. YOU GET IT? DARLING.
THEN OUT OF THE SHADOWS, CAME A STRANGE LITTLE MAN WHO PROMISED MIRACLES, AND DELIVERED THEM! HAND-DELIVERED THEM!
LOOK! IT'S THING 1 AND THING 2!
IT WAS AFTER ANOTHER CONCERT TRIUMPH, AND JOHN DARLINGTON HAD CELEBRATED, WITH ONE GLASS OF CHAMPAGNE TOO MANY...
JOHN! BE CAREFUL! YOU'RE DRIVING TOO FAST!
STOP WORRYING, MARY! SING WITH ME... "99 DOM PERIGNONS ON THE WALL! 99 DOM PERIGNONS!"
FINALLY, A COMIC THAT ISN'T AFRAID TO MAKE THE ORIGIN STORY SOMETHING AS SIMPLE AS A CAR ACCIDENT...OH, WAIT, DOCTOR STRANGE DID THAT.
AND THEN FATE LAUGHS—AND STRIKES...
SKIDDING! CAN'T STOP! GOING TO CRASH!
PRONOUNS MISSING! PANTS LOADING!
IS THAT A "WATCH OUT FOR SNAKES" SIGN?
ARE WE THERE YET?

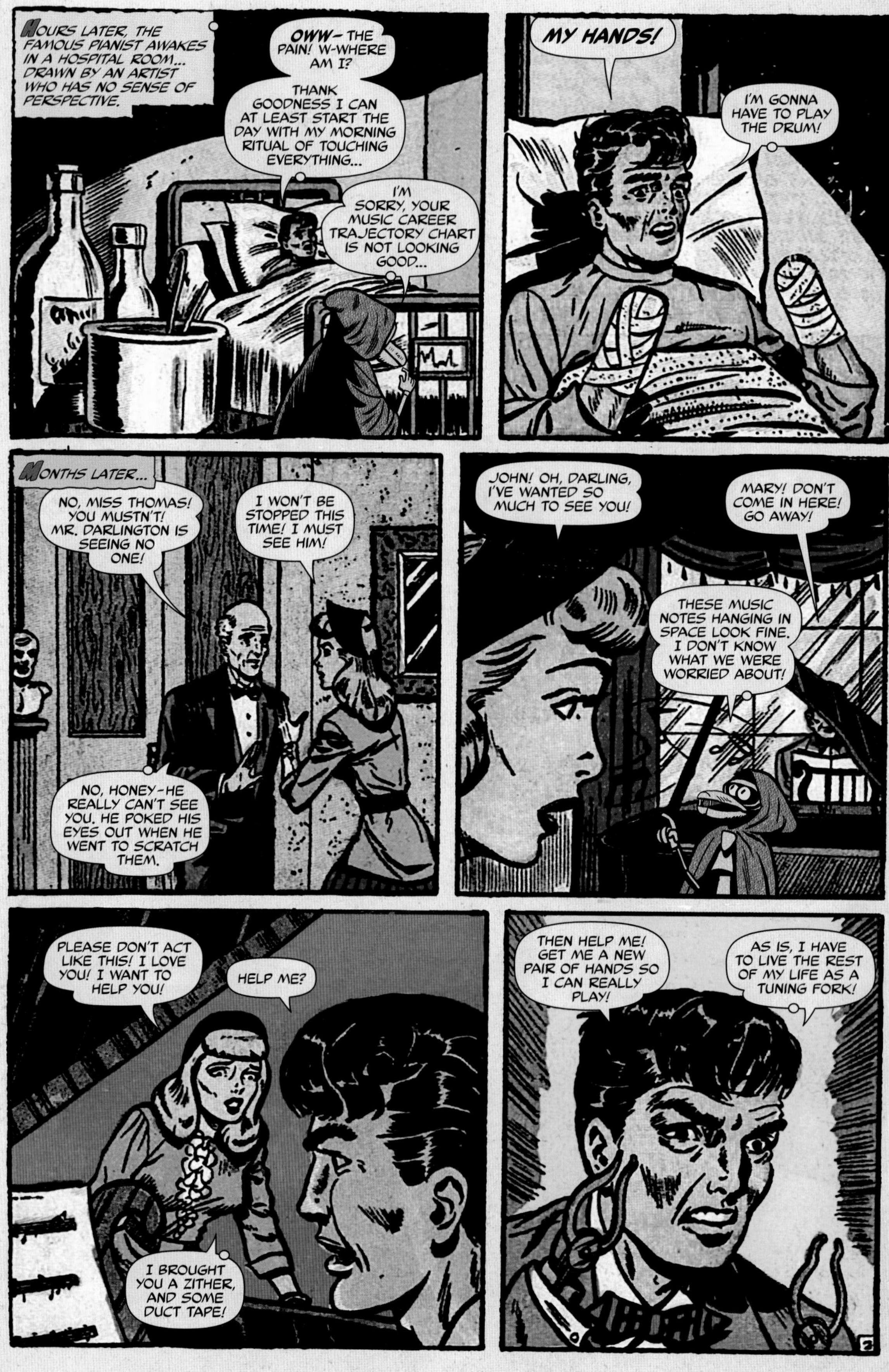
HOURS LATER, THE FAMOUS PIANIST AWAKES IN A HOSPITAL ROOM... DRAWN BY AN ARTIST WHO HAS NO SENSE OF PERSPECTIVE.
OWW- THE PAIN! W-WHERE AM I?
THANK GOODNESS I CAN AT LEAST START THE DAY WITH MY MORNING RITUAL OF TOUCHING EVERYTHING...
I'M SORRY, YOUR MUSIC CAREER TRAJECTORY CHART IS NOT LOOKING GOOD...
MY HANDS!
I'M GONNA HAVE TO PLAY THE DRUM!
MONTHS LATER...
NO, MISS THOMAS! YOU MUSTN'T! MR. DARLINGTON IS SEEING NO ONE!
I WON'T BE STOPPED THIS TIME! I MUST SEE HIM!
NO, HONEY-HE REALLY CAN'T SEE YOU. HE POKED HIS EYES OUT WHEN HE WENT TO SCRATCH THEM.
JOHN! OH, DARLING, I'VE WANTED SO MUCH TO SEE YOU!
MARY! DON'T COME IN HERE! GO AWAY!
THESE MUSIC NOTES HANGING IN SPACE LOOK FINE. I DON'T KNOW WHAT WE WERE WORRIED ABOUT!
PLEASE DON'T ACT LIKE THIS! I LOVE YOU! I WANT TO HELP YOU!
HELP ME?
I BROUGHT YOU A ZITHER, AND SOME DUCT TAPE!
THEN HELP ME! GET ME A NEW PAIR OF HANDS SO I CAN REALLY PLAY!
AS IS, I HAVE TO LIVE THE REST OF MY LIFE AS A TUNING FORK!
2

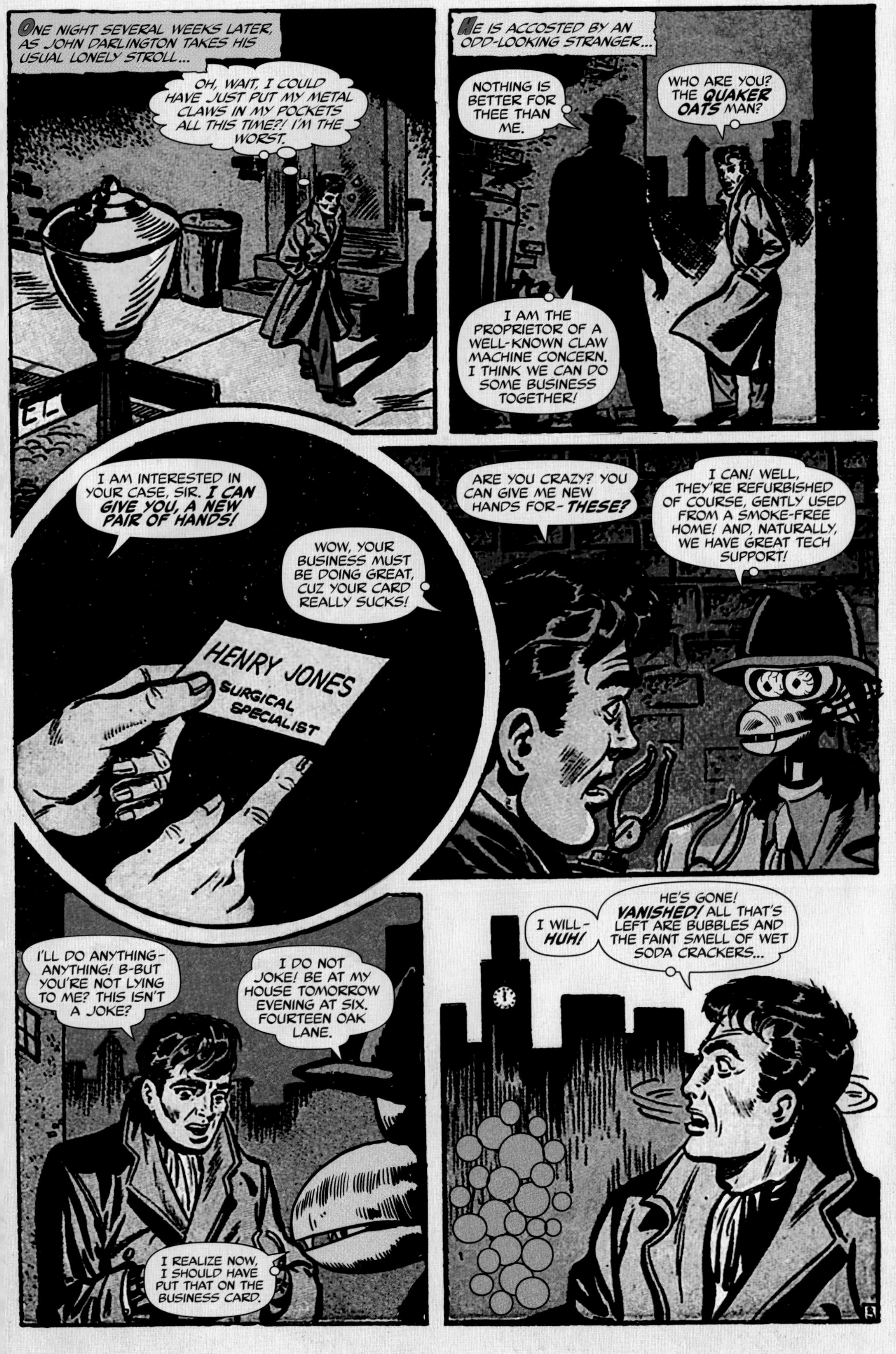
ONE NIGHT SEVERAL WEEKS LATER, AS JOHN DARLINGTON TAKES HIS USUAL LONELY STROLL...
OH, WAIT, I COULD HAVE JUST PUT MY METAL CLAWS IN MY POCKETS ALL THIS TIME?! I'M THE WORST.
HE IS ACCOSTED BY AN ODD-LOOKING STRANGER...
NOTHING IS BETTER FOR THEE THAN ME.
WHO ARE YOU? THE QUAKER OATS MAN?
I AM THE PROPRIETOR OF A WELL-KNOWN CLAW MACHINE CONCERN. I THINK WE CAN DO SOME BUSINESS TOGETHER!
I AM INTERESTED IN YOUR CASE, SIR. I CAN GIVE YOU, A NEW PAIR OF HANDS!
WOW, YOUR BUSINESS MUST BE DOING GREAT, CUZ YOUR CARD REALLY SUCKS!
HENRY JONES
SURGICAL SPECIALIST
ARE YOU CRAZY? YOU CAN GIVE ME NEW HANDS FOR- THESE?
I CAN! WELL, THEY'RE REFURBISHED OF COURSE, GENTLY USED FROM A SMOKE-FREE HOME! AND, NATURALLY, WE HAVE GREAT TECH SUPPORT!
I'LL DO ANYTHING- ANYTHING! B-BUT YOU'RE NOT LYING TO ME? THIS ISN'T A JOKE?
I DO NOT JOKE! BE AT MY HOUSE TOMORROW EVENING AT SIX. FOURTEEN OAK LANE.
I REALIZE NOW, I SHOULD HAVE PUT THAT ON THE BUSINESS CARD.
I WILL- HUH!
HE'S GONE! VANISHED! ALL THAT'S LEFT ARE BUBBLES AND THE FAINT SMELL OF WET SODA CRACKERS...

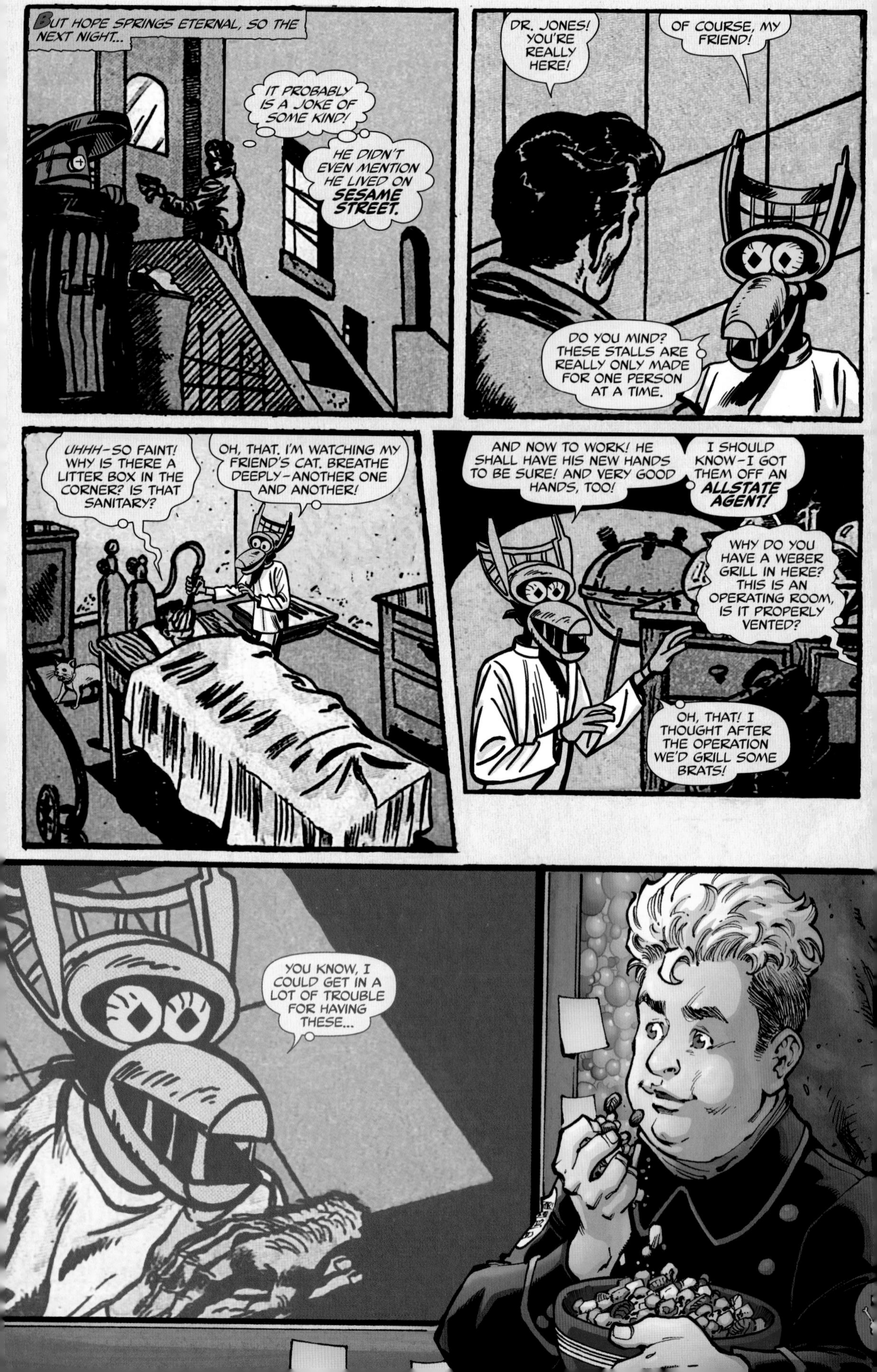
BUT HOPE SPRINGS ETERNAL, SO THE NEXT NIGHT...
IT PROBABLY IS A JOKE OF SOME KIND!
HE DIDN'T EVEN MENTION HE LIVED ON SESAME STREET.
DR. JONES! YOU'RE REALLY HERE!
OF COURSE, MY FRIEND!
DO YOU MIND? THESE STALLS ARE REALLY ONLY MADE FOR ONE PERSON AT A TIME.
UHHH—SO FAINT! WHY IS THERE A LITTER BOX IN THE CORNER? IS THAT SANITARY?
OH, THAT. I'M WATCHING MY FRIEND'S CAT. BREATHE DEEPLY—ANOTHER ONE AND ANOTHER!
AND NOW TO WORK! HE SHALL HAVE HIS NEW HANDS TO BE SURE! AND VERY GOOD HANDS, TOO!
I SHOULD KNOW—I GOT THEM OFF AN ALLSTATE AGENT!
WHY DO YOU HAVE A WEBER GRILL IN HERE? THIS IS AN OPERATING ROOM, IS IT PROPERLY VENTED?
OH, THAT! I THOUGHT AFTER THE OPERATION WE'D GRILL SOME BRATS!
YOU KNOW, I COULD GET IN A LOT OF TROUBLE FOR HAVING THESE...

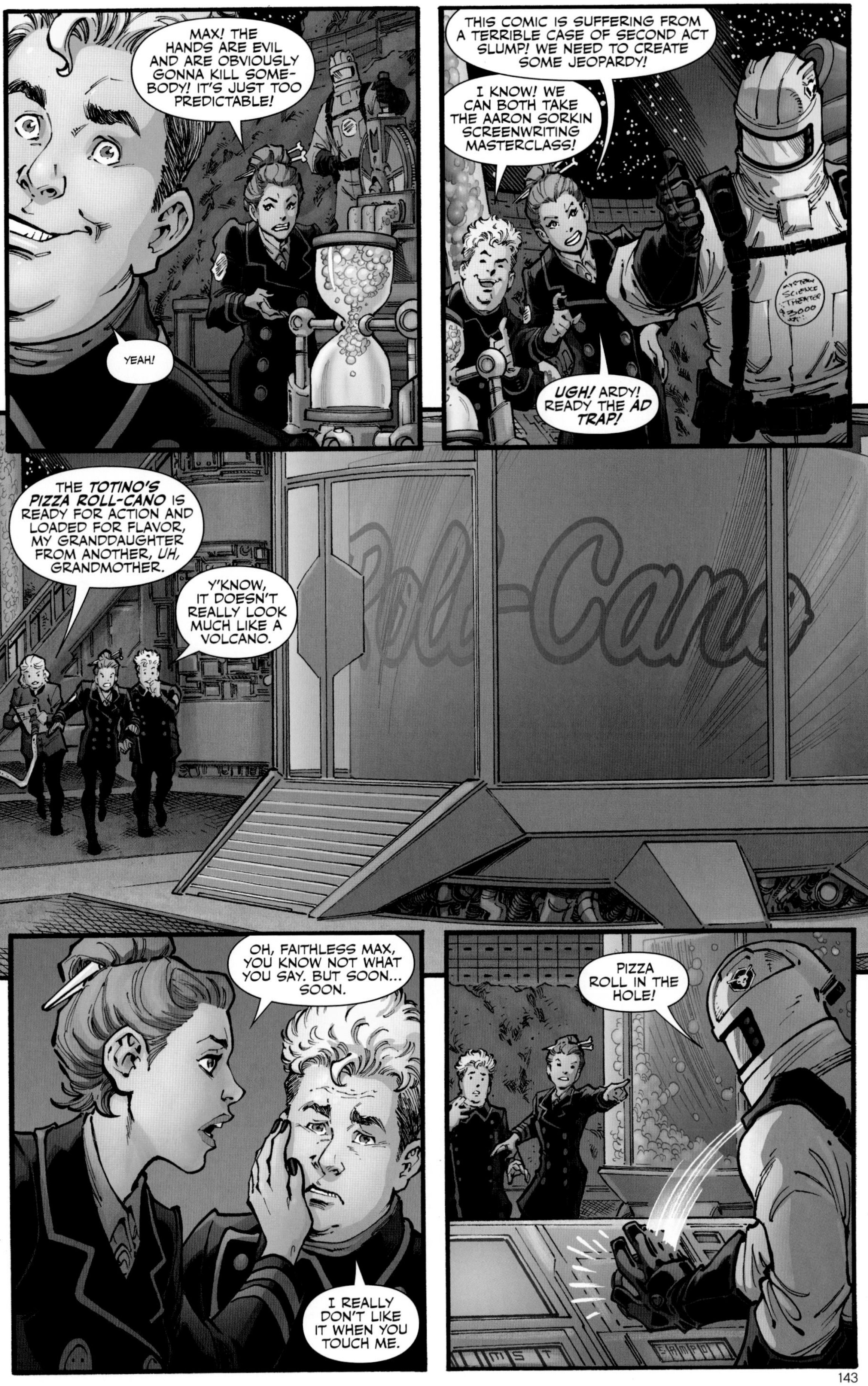

MAX! THE HANDS ARE EVIL AND ARE OBVIOUSLY GONNA KILL SOME-BODY! IT'S JUST TOO PREDICTABLE!
YEAH!
THIS COMIC IS SUFFERING FROM A TERRIBLE CASE OF SECOND ACT SLUMP! WE NEED TO CREATE SOME JEOPARDY!
I KNOW! WE CAN BOTH TAKE THE AARON SORKIN SCREENWRITING MASTERCLASS!
UGH! ARDY! READY THE AD TRAP!
THE TOTINO'S PIZZA ROLL-CANO IS READY FOR ACTION AND LOADED FOR FLAVOR, MY GRANDDAUGHTER FROM ANOTHER, UH, GRANDMOTHER.
Y'KNOW, IT DOESN'T REALLY LOOK MUCH LIKE A VOLCANO.
OH, FAITHLESS MAX, YOU KNOW NOT WHAT YOU SAY. BUT SOON... SOON.
I REALLY DON'T LIKE IT WHEN YOU TOUCH ME.
PIZZA ROLL IN THE HOLE!

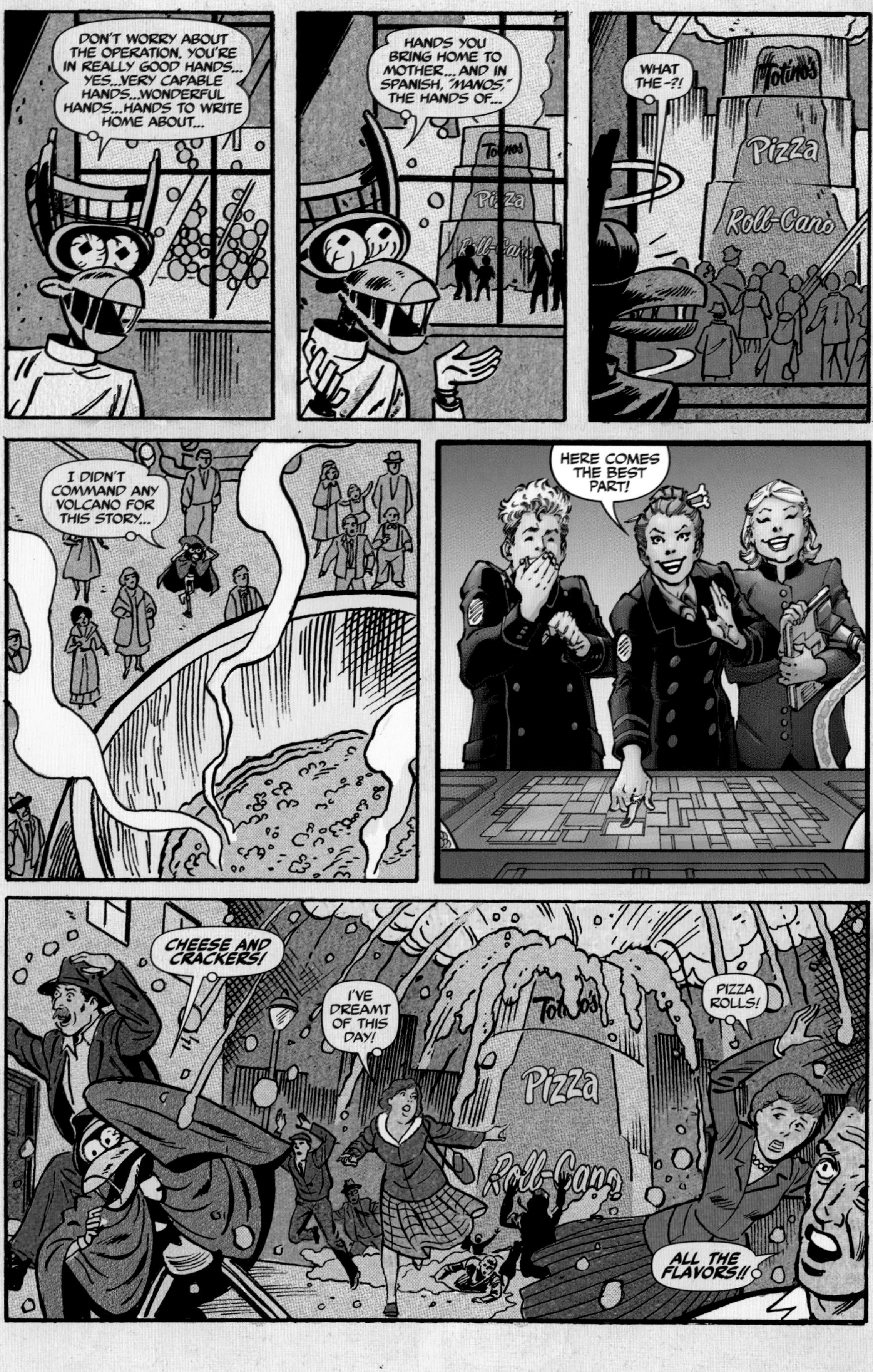
DON'T WORRY ABOUT THE OPERATION. YOU'RE IN REALLY GOOD HANDS... YES...VERY CAPABLE HANDS...WONDERFUL HANDS...HANDS TO WRITE HOME ABOUT...
HANDS YOU BRING HOME TO MOTHER...AND IN SPANISH, "MANOS," THE HANDS OF...
Totino's
Pizza
Roll-Cano
WHAT THE-?!
Totino's
Pizza
Roll-Cano
I DIDN'T COMMAND ANY VOLCANO FOR THIS STORY...
HERE COMES THE BEST PART!
CHEESE AND CRACKERS!
I'VE DREAMT OF THIS DAY!
Totino's
Pizza
Roll-Cano
PIZZA ROLLS!
ALL THE FLAVORS!!

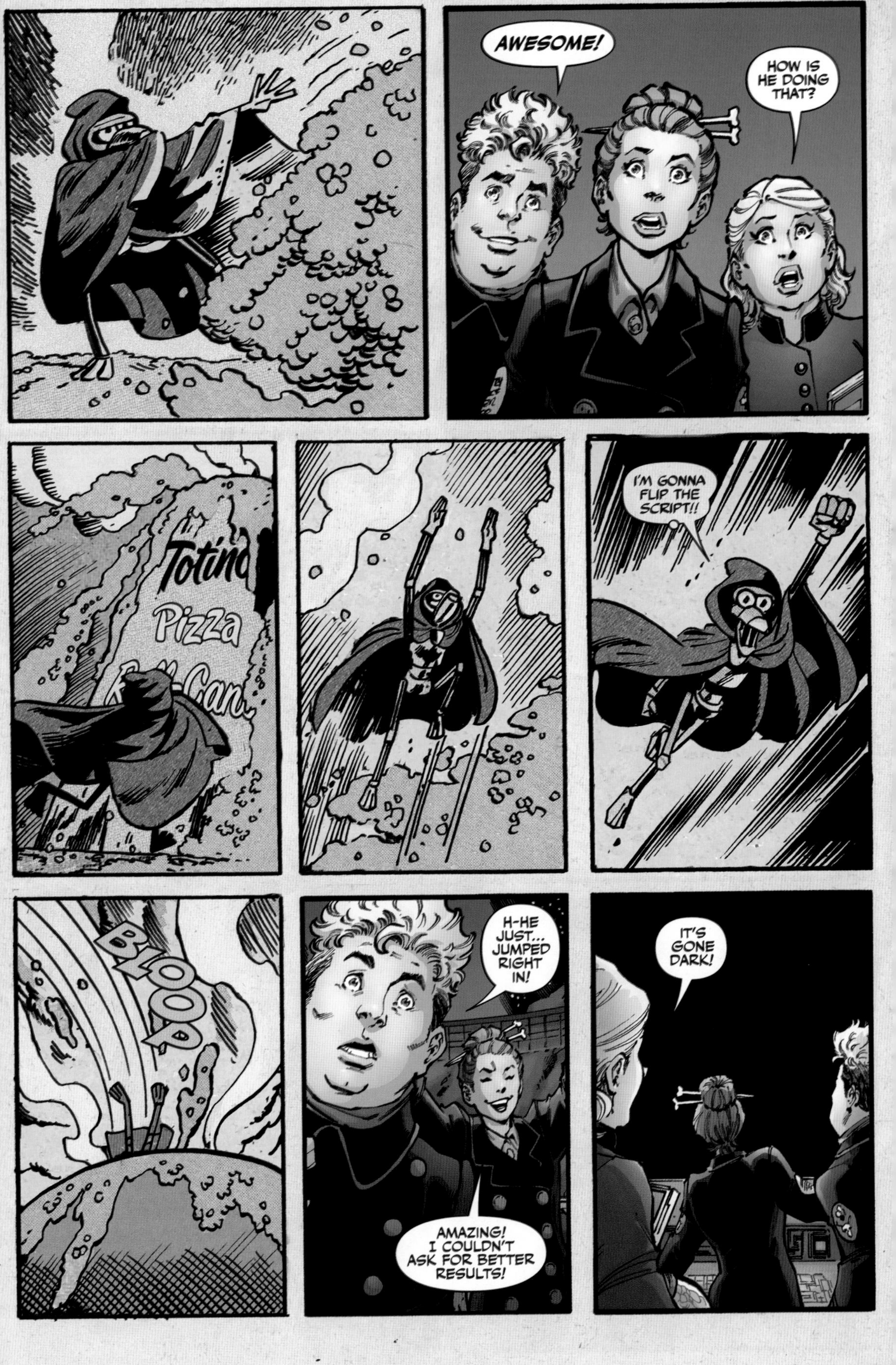
AWESOME!
HOW IS HE DOING THAT?
Totino
Pizza
I'M GONNA FLIP THE SCRIPT!!
BLOOP
H-HE JUST... JUMPED RIGHT IN!
AMAZING! I COULDN'T ASK FOR BETTER RESULTS!
IT'S GONE DARK!

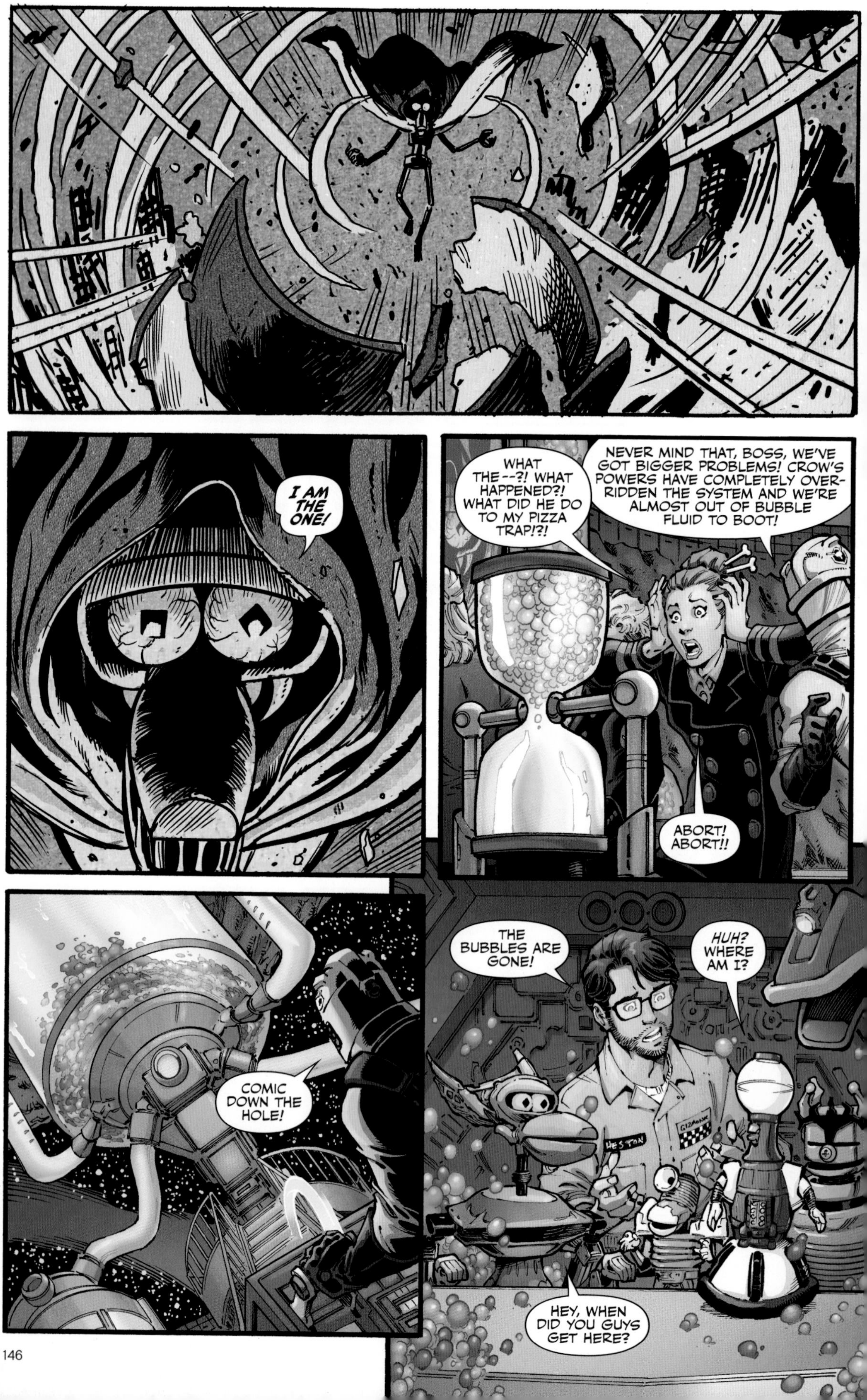
I AM THE ONE!
WHAT THE--?! WHAT HAPPENED?! WHAT DID HE DO TO MY PIZZA TRAP!?!
NEVER MIND THAT, BOSS, WE'VE GOT BIGGER PROBLEMS! CROW'S POWERS HAVE COMPLETELY OVERRIDDEN THE SYSTEM AND WE'RE ALMOST OUT OF BUBBLE FLUID TO BOOT!
ABORT! ABORT!!
COMIC DOWN THE HOLE!
THE BUBBLES ARE GONE!
HUH? WHERE AM I?
HEY, WHEN DID YOU GUYS GET HERE?

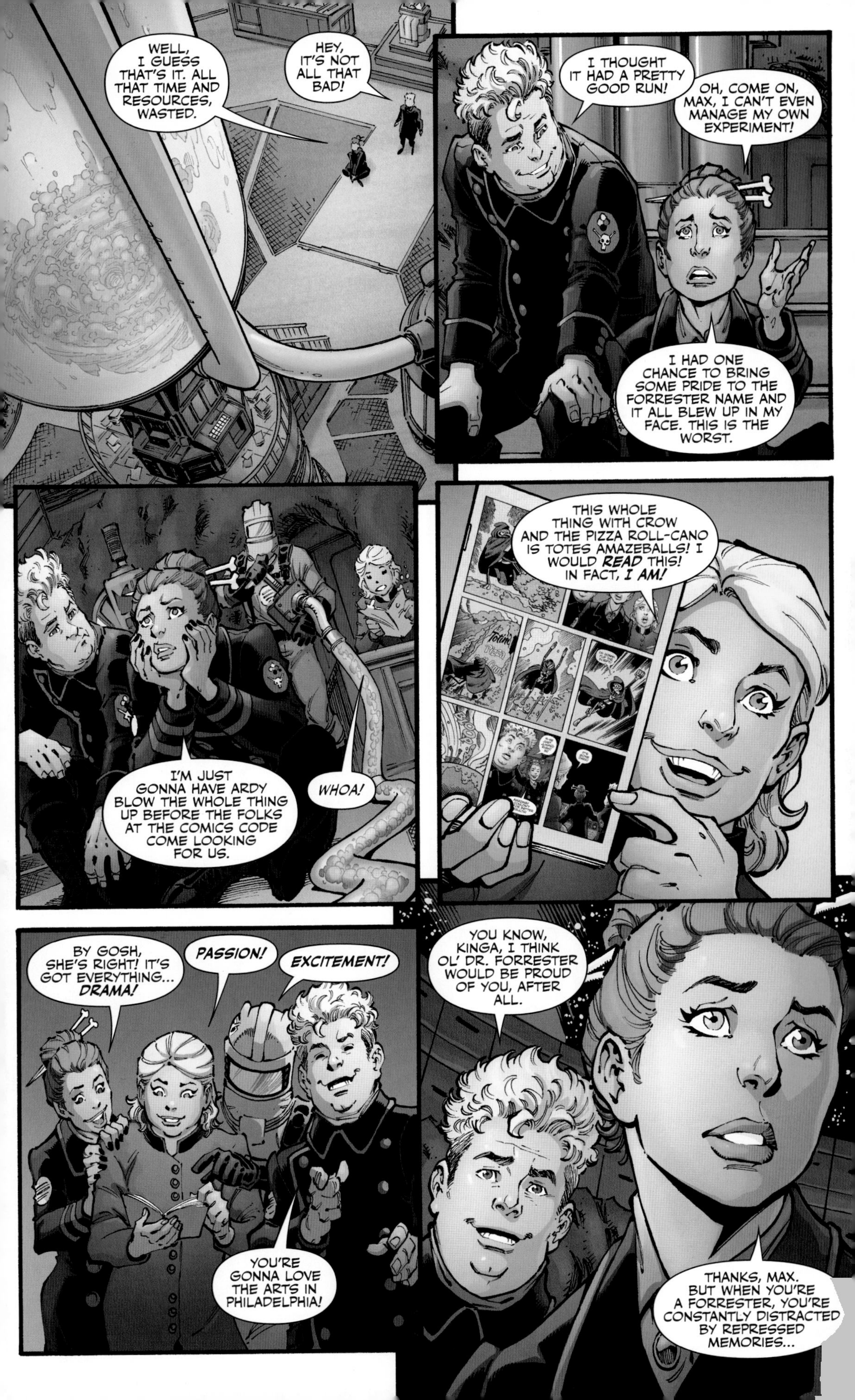
WELL, I GUESS THAT'S IT. ALL THAT TIME AND RESOURCES, WASTED.
HEY, IT'S NOT ALL THAT BAD!
I THOUGHT IT HAD A PRETTY GOOD RUN!
OH, COME ON, MAX, I CAN'T EVEN MANAGE MY OWN EXPERIMENT!
I HAD ONE CHANCE TO BRING SOME PRIDE TO THE FORRESTER NAME AND IT ALL BLEW UP IN MY FACE. THIS IS THE WORST.
I'M JUST GONNA HAVE ARDY BLOW THE WHOLE THING UP BEFORE THE FOLKS AT THE COMICS CODE COME LOOKING FOR US.
WHOA!
THIS WHOLE THING WITH CROW AND THE PIZZA ROLL-CANO IS TOTES AMAZEBALLS! I WOULD *READ* THIS! IN FACT, *I AM!*
BY GOSH, SHE'S RIGHT! IT'S GOT EVERYTHING... *DRAMA!*
PASSION!
EXCITEMENT!
YOU'RE GONNA LOVE THE ARTS IN PHILADELPHIA!
YOU KNOW, KINGA, I THINK OL' DR. FORRESTER WOULD BE PROUD OF YOU, AFTER ALL.
THANKS, MAX. BUT WHEN YOU'RE A FORRESTER, YOU'RE CONSTANTLY DISTRACTED BY REPRESSED MEMORIES...

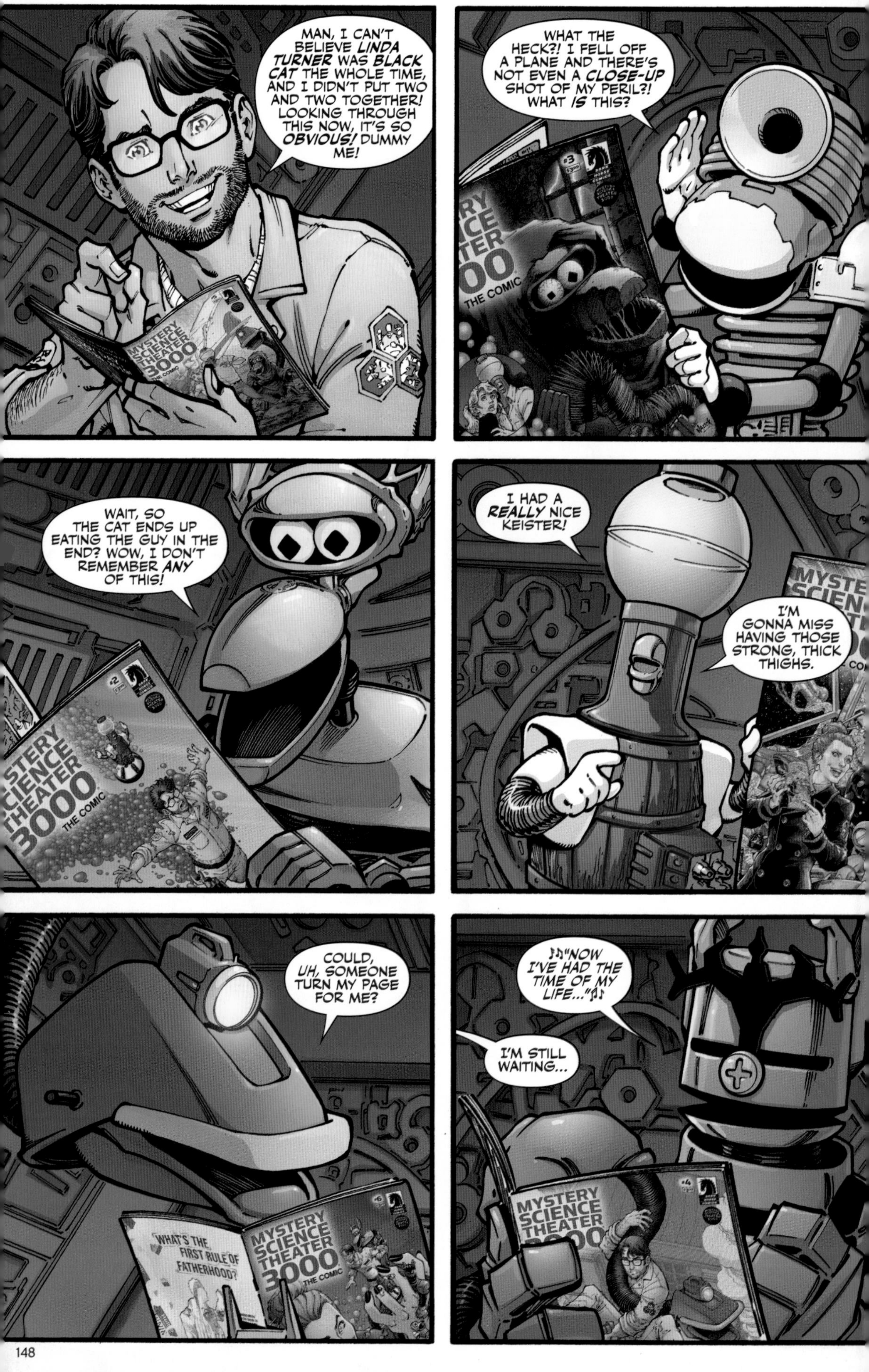
MAN, I CAN'T BELIEVE *LINDA TURNER* WAS *BLACK CAT* THE WHOLE TIME, AND I DIDN'T PUT TWO AND TWO TOGETHER! LOOKING THROUGH THIS NOW, IT'S SO *OBVIOUS!* DUMMY ME!
MYSTERY SCIENCE THEATER 3000 THE COMIC
WHAT THE HECK?! I FELL OFF A PLANE AND THERE'S NOT EVEN A *CLOSE-UP* SHOT OF MY PERIL?! WHAT *IS* THIS?
MYSTERY SCIENCE THEATER 3000 THE COMIC
WAIT, SO THE CAT ENDS UP EATING THE GUY IN THE END? WOW, I DON'T REMEMBER *ANY* OF THIS!
MYSTERY SCIENCE THEATER 3000 THE COMIC
I HAD A *REALLY* NICE KEISTER!
I'M GONNA MISS HAVING THOSE STRONG, THICK THIGHS.
COULD, *UH,* SOMEONE TURN MY PAGE FOR ME?
WHAT'S THE FIRST RULE OF FATHERHOOD?
MYSTERY SCIENCE THEATER 3000 THE COMIC
♪♫"*NOW I'VE HAD THE TIME OF MY LIFE...*"♫♪
I'M STILL WAITING...
MYSTERY SCIENCE THEATER 3000

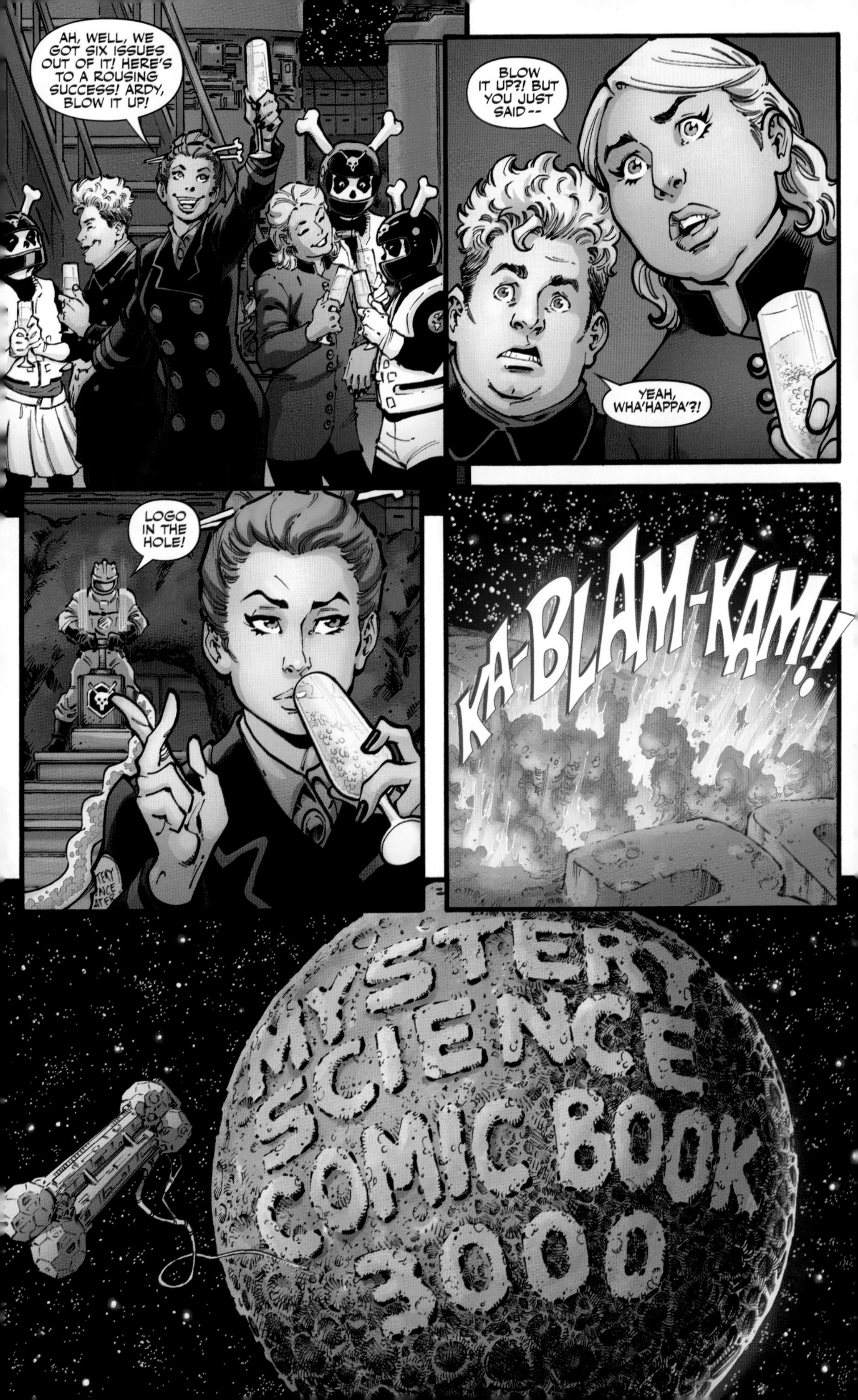
AH, WELL, WE GOT SIX ISSUES OUT OF IT! HERE'S TO A ROUSING SUCCESS! ARDY, BLOW IT UP!
BLOW IT UP?! BUT YOU JUST SAID --
YEAH, WHA'HAPPA'?!
LOGO IN THE HOLE!
KA-BLAM-KAM!!
MYSTERY SCIENCE COMIC BOOK 3000

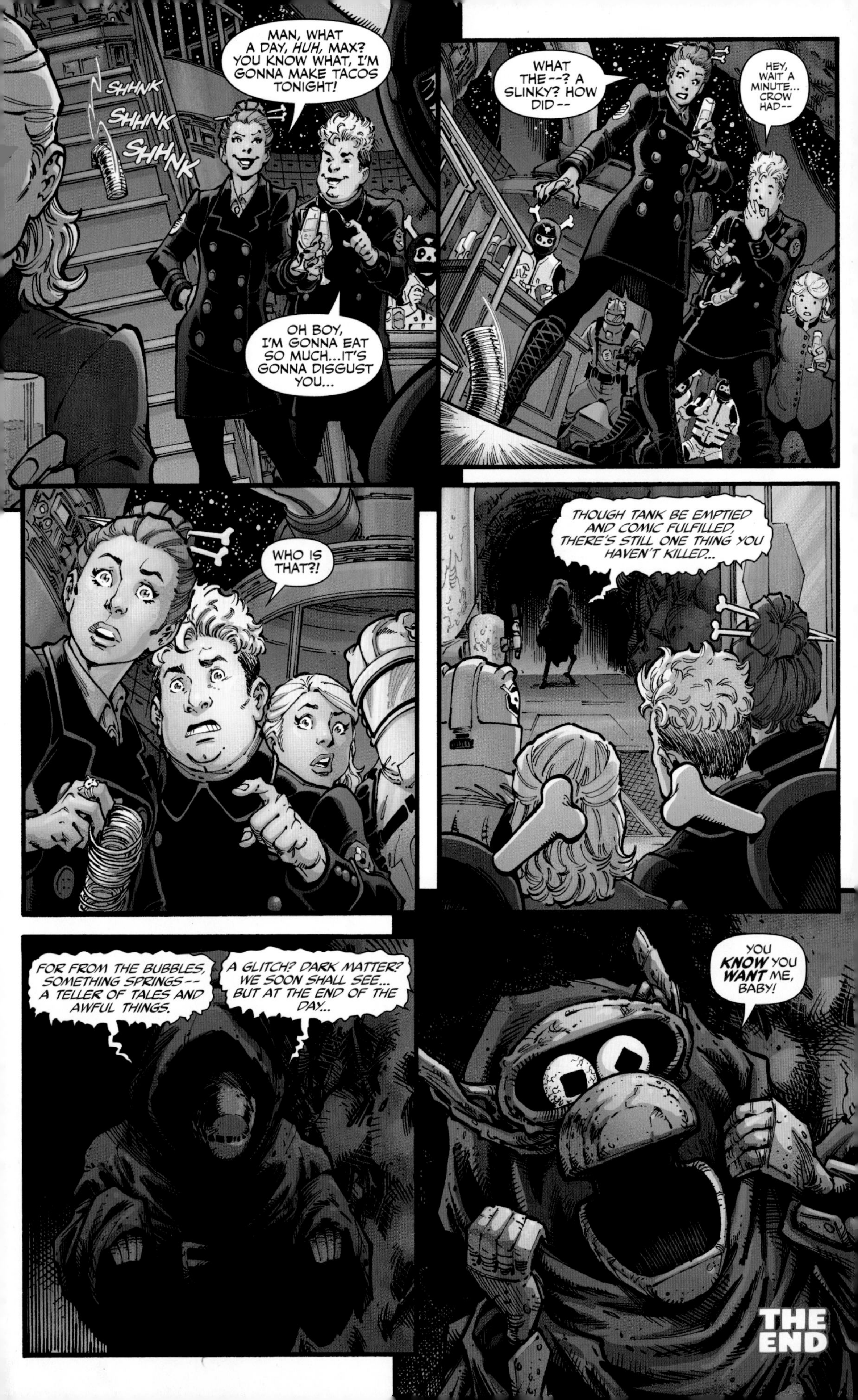
SHHNK
SHHNK
SHHNK
MAN, WHAT A DAY, HUH, MAX? YOU KNOW WHAT, I'M GONNA MAKE TACOS TONIGHT!
OH BOY, I'M GONNA EAT SO MUCH...IT'S GONNA DISGUST YOU...
WHAT THE--? A SLINKY? HOW DID--
HEY, WAIT A MINUTE... CROW HAD--
WHO IS THAT?!
THOUGH TANK BE EMPTIED AND COMIC FULFILLED, THERE'S STILL ONE THING YOU HAVEN'T KILLED...
FOR FROM THE BUBBLES, SOMETHING SPRINGS-- A TELLER OF TALES AND AWFUL THINGS.
A GLITCH? DARK MATTER? WE SOON SHALL SEE... BUT AT THE END OF THE DAY...
YOU KNOW YOU WANT ME, BABY!
THE END

AFTERWORD
by HAROLD BUCHHOLZ

I hope you've enjoyed the *Mystery Science Theater 3000* graphic novel. My journey with this project has been full of surprises. It all began over twenty-five years ago.

Like so many others, my wife, Diane Cooke, and I discovered *MST3K* on Comedy Central around 1992. Diane and I had met in film school and were recently married. I'd long been interested in old movies, particularly the type of low-grade films featured in the Medved brothers' *Golden Turkey Awards* book. All of a sudden so many of these films that had been unavailable to view were now on *MST3K*—with the added bonus of a humorous overlay. We quickly fell in love with the show's smart, loose style and the laid-back, good-natured mid-western comic flair of Joel Hodgson, the shows' creator and host. There had never been anything quite like this on television before, and Diane and I were hooked.

When Joel left the show in 1993 midway through its ten-year cable run, Diane and I were deeply disappointed. We talked about him, prayed for him, searched on the fledgling internet for what he might be doing next. We never stopped thinking about Joel.

In 1995, I got the fantastic opportunity to write and draw my own comic book for Don Chin's Entity Comics. It was a unique funny animal title called *Apathy Kat*.

For its third issue, I created a story where the characters entered a virtual reality world of old public domain comic books. The main event in this issue featured a 1950s Robin Hood comic, where Apathy Kat replaced brave Sir Robin, playing off of the villagers and villains just as they were in the original comic. This was certainly inspired in part by my love for *MST3K*.

After *Apathy Kat*'s run, in 1997 I started a business to help creators of kid-friendly comics get their books printed and distributed.

About six years later, with the brilliant Jimmy Gownley, soon-to-be *New York Times* best-selling author of the classic *Amelia Rules!* graphic novel series, I helped establish an organization called Kids Love Comics to promote comics for younger audiences. Through Kids Love Comics, I met networker-extraordinaire and current President of Archie Comics Mike Pellerito, who was working hard to connect Archie Comics to the outside art and publishing world. In 2010, Mike brought me to New York to work under the innovative CEO Jon Goldwater, who was busy updating the company with Mike and long-time editor and co-President Victor Gorelick with the talented staff at Archie. It was a dream job for me—as Senior Vice President of Publishing and Operations, I was charged with growing their graphic novel business, which we did quite successfully over the next six years.

When Joel reemerged in the 2000s, riffing on movies with former *MST3K* cast members live on stage across the country as *Cinematic Titanic*, Diane and I were thrilled. In 2012 we attended a show in New Jersey. Diane said, "You should bring your Archie business cards. Maybe they'd like to do a comic book version of *Cinematic Titanic*." I handed out cards to the cast, and the next day Joel was in touch.

We met for lunch at the Skylark Diner in Edison, New Jersey, where Joel had recently filmed an episode of *Comedians in Cars Getting Coffee* with Jerry Seinfeld. That lunch lasted five hours.

Joel informed me that he wasn't as interested in doing a *Cinematic Titanic* comic as he was an *MST3K* comic—as a path toward reengaging with the brand. With the possibility that new episodes might come of that, I suggested that a Kickstarter campaign would be an excellent way to launch them, given the massive goodwill the classic series had engendered and the amazing story that its creator would be returning to bring the show back after a twenty-plus year hiatus. As a fan, I knew I'd certainly contribute to such an effort.

Robin Katt
THERE WAS NO REJOICING IN SHERWOOD FOREST! ONE BY ONE, ROBIN HOOD'S MERRY MEN WERE BECOMING UNMERRY! FOR A MIRTHLESS SITUATION CONFRONTED THEM ALL! AS IF THEY WERE MARKED FOR DOOM, ONE BOLD FORESTER AFTER THE OTHER VANISHED INTO NOWHERE! THE SITUATION MOCKED EVERY EFFORT ROBIN HOOD MADE TO SOLVE IT! WAS SOME EVIL MAGICIAN WORKING THE DESTRUCTION OF HIS BAND? HAD EACH MEMBER TURNED TRAITOR AND DESERTED? SOME NEFARIOUS POWER LAY BEHIND THE CONTINUOUS AND DESTRUCTIVE...
AMBUSH OF THE MERRY MEN
PRITHEE, PULLEST UP THINE HAMMOCK FOR A JIGGER O' 'NIP, DADDY-O!
THOU ART EVEN BOLDER THAN I'D HEARD! STORMING WESSEX CASTLE BY YOURSELF! ART THOU MAD, ROGUE, OR DOST THOU STUPIDLY EXAGGERATE THINE OWN MIGHT?

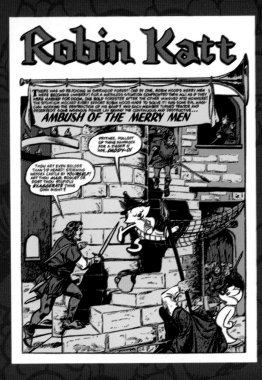

For the next three years in my spare time I worked with Joel to achieve this dream. To me, it was all about helping Joel get his unique voice back out into the world. We partnered with the great long-time *MST3K* DVD distributor Shout! Factory to obtain the rights to *MST3K* and planned for the creation of new episodes.

The Kickstarter happened in late 2015—under the guidance of crowdfunding master Ivan Askwith—breaking all records for movie and TV crowdfunding, and two months later I was running Joel's fledgling company, Alternaversal.

One of our co-ventures with Shout! was licensing *MST3K*. For years Dark Horse VP of Publishing Randy Stradley had enthusiastically been talking with Joel about doing a project together, so giving Dark Horse the license to make a comic seemed a perfect fit.

Now, normally a licensed comic book is not written by its creator, but Joel wanted to develop the scope of *MST3K* and thought engaging with the comic directly would be beneficial on multiple levels.

So next came the obvious question: how do you translate such a quirky TV show to this new medium?

Because of my past experience with comics, I had plenty of ideas, but I happily took a back seat to Joel's unique holistic creative process and watched him engage with the comic from the ground up, giving input where it was helpful to him. To my delight, what emerged contained many elements that had mirrored my own approach back in 1996 with *Apathy Kat*, but with additional layers of creativity typical of Joel that created a rich, freewheeling world.

Joel's creative process is collaborative, and he engaged his "vision team" at Alternaversal to develop and write the comic, and through the able coordination of team member Matt McGinnis, we joined forces with the incredibly talented team at Dark Horse in a process that contained significantly more back-and-forth between writing and art than is typically seen in comics, which by necessity tends toward a more orderly assembly-line approach. We were thrilled with the results.

Thanks to Joel, Matt, Sharyl Volpe, Seth and Mary Robinson, Randy Stradley, Todd Nauck, Mike Manley, Jack Pollock, Mimi Simon, Wes Dzioba, Michael Heisler, Steve Vance, Ethan Kimberling, Patrick Satterfield, Adam Pruett, Judy Khuu, and Mike Richardson for making this project such a joy to work on.

It's been quite a journey, and I couldn't be happier with where it's led.

Illustration by STEVE VANCE

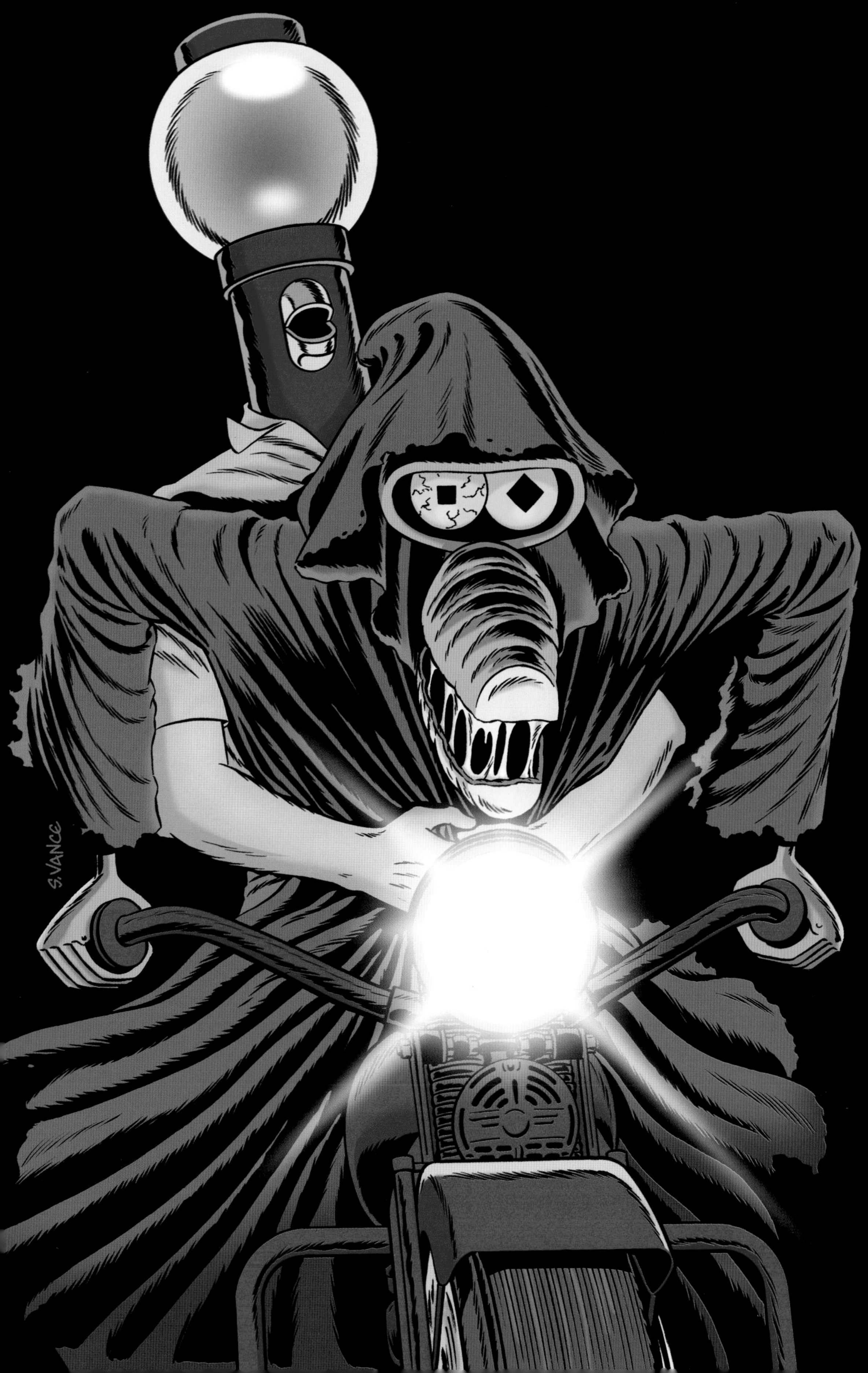
S.VANCE

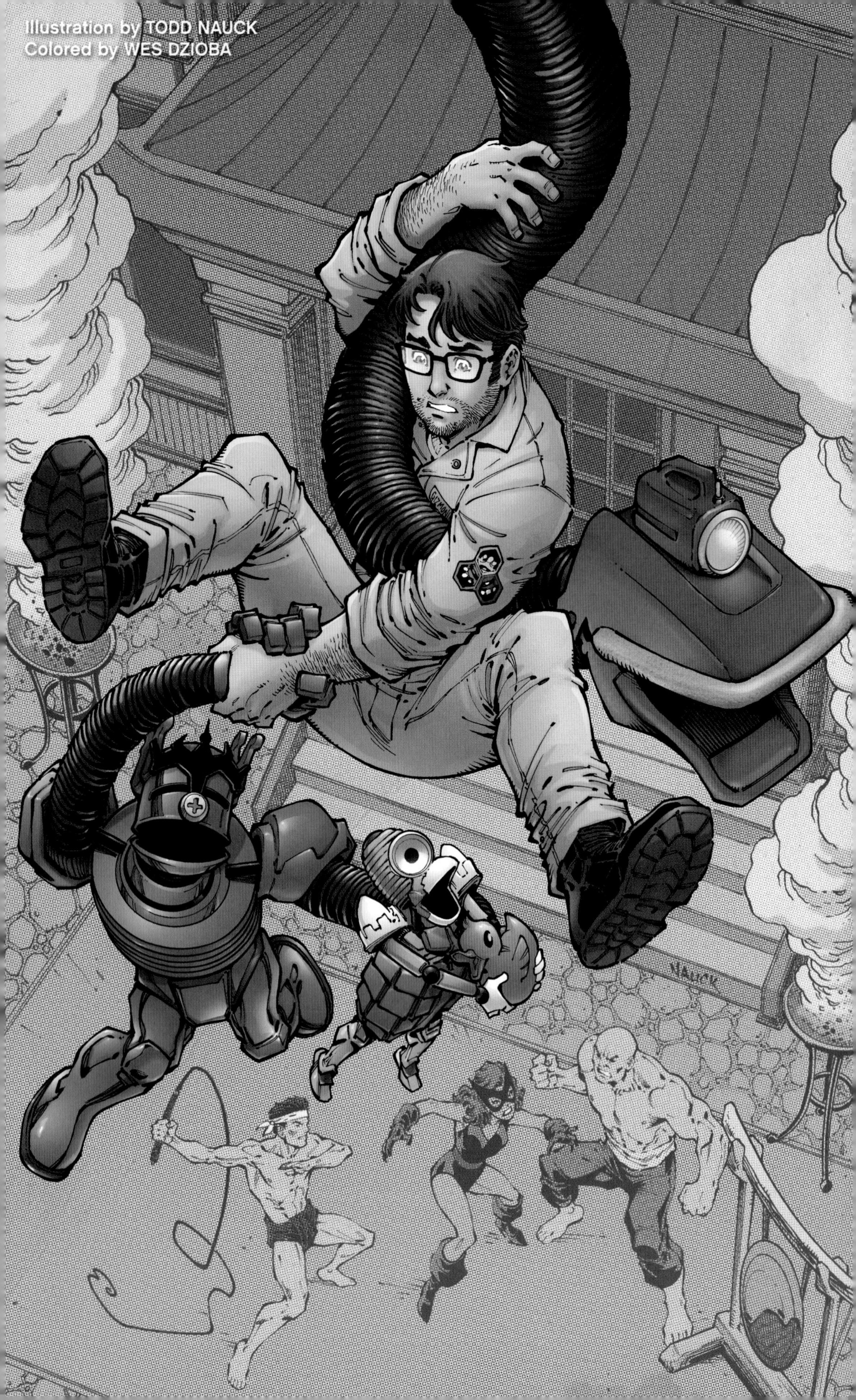
NAUCK

Illustration by TODD NAUCK
Colored by WES DZIOBA

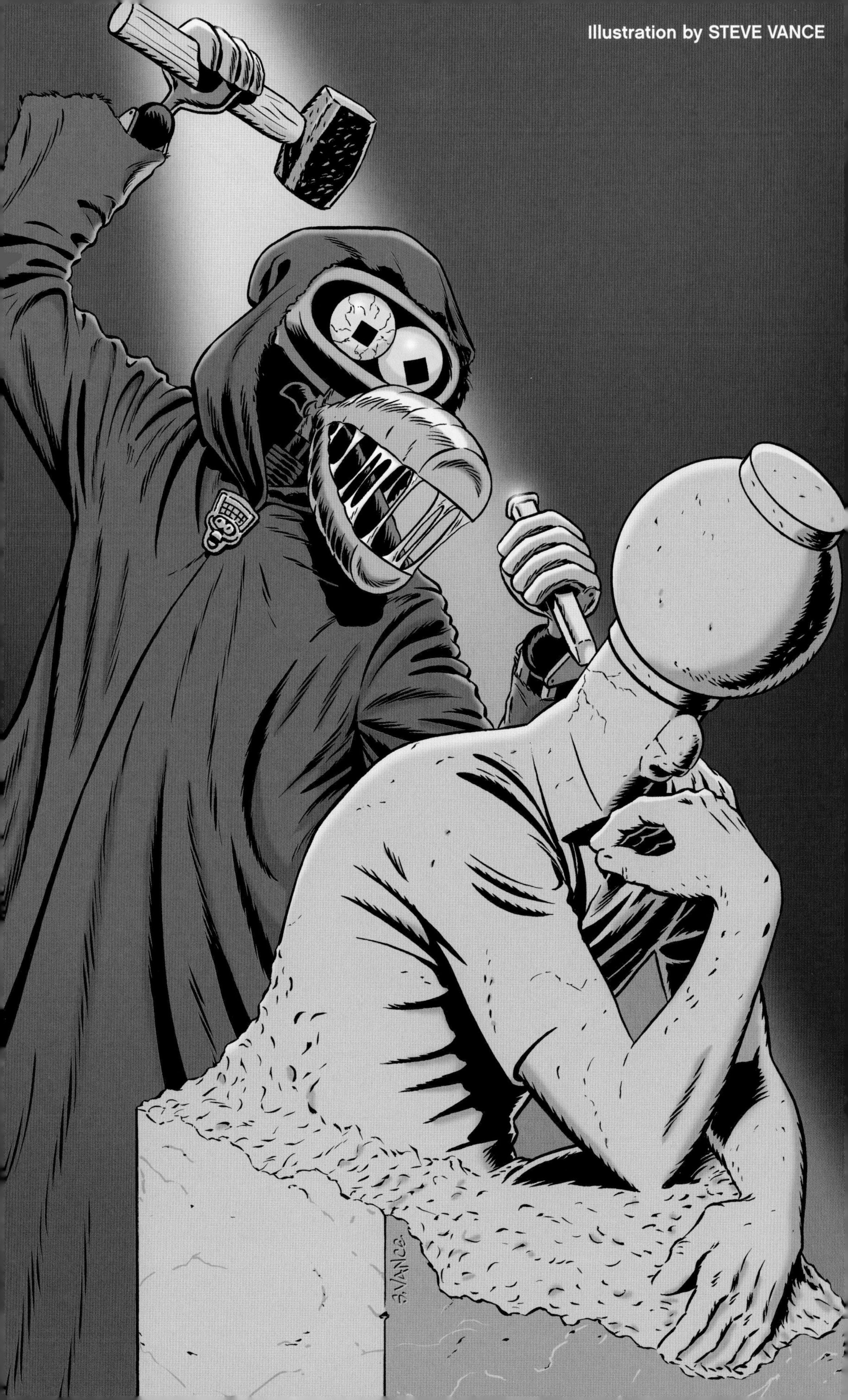

Illustration by STEVE VANCE

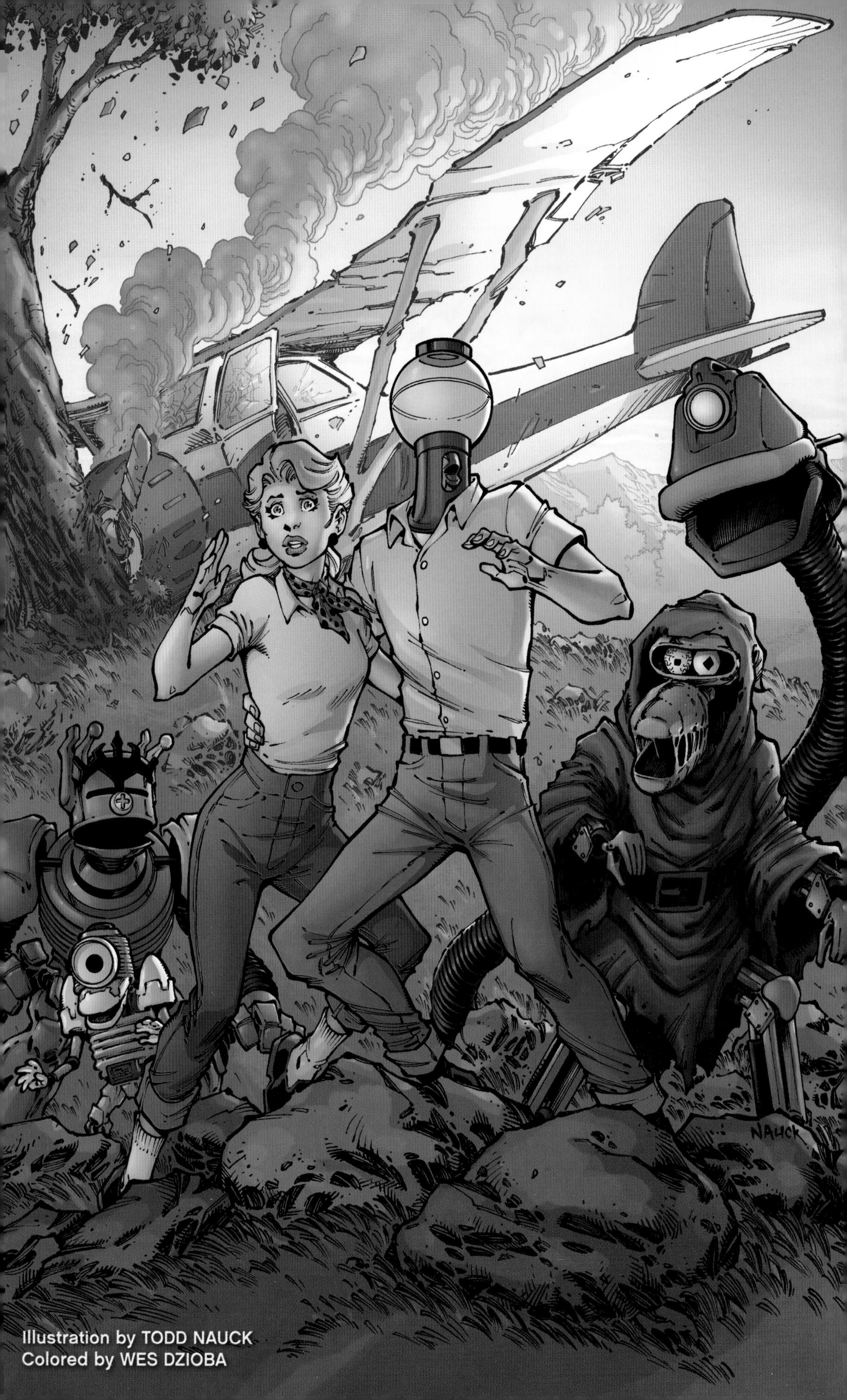
NAUCK

Illustration by TODD NAUCK
Colored by WES DZIOBA

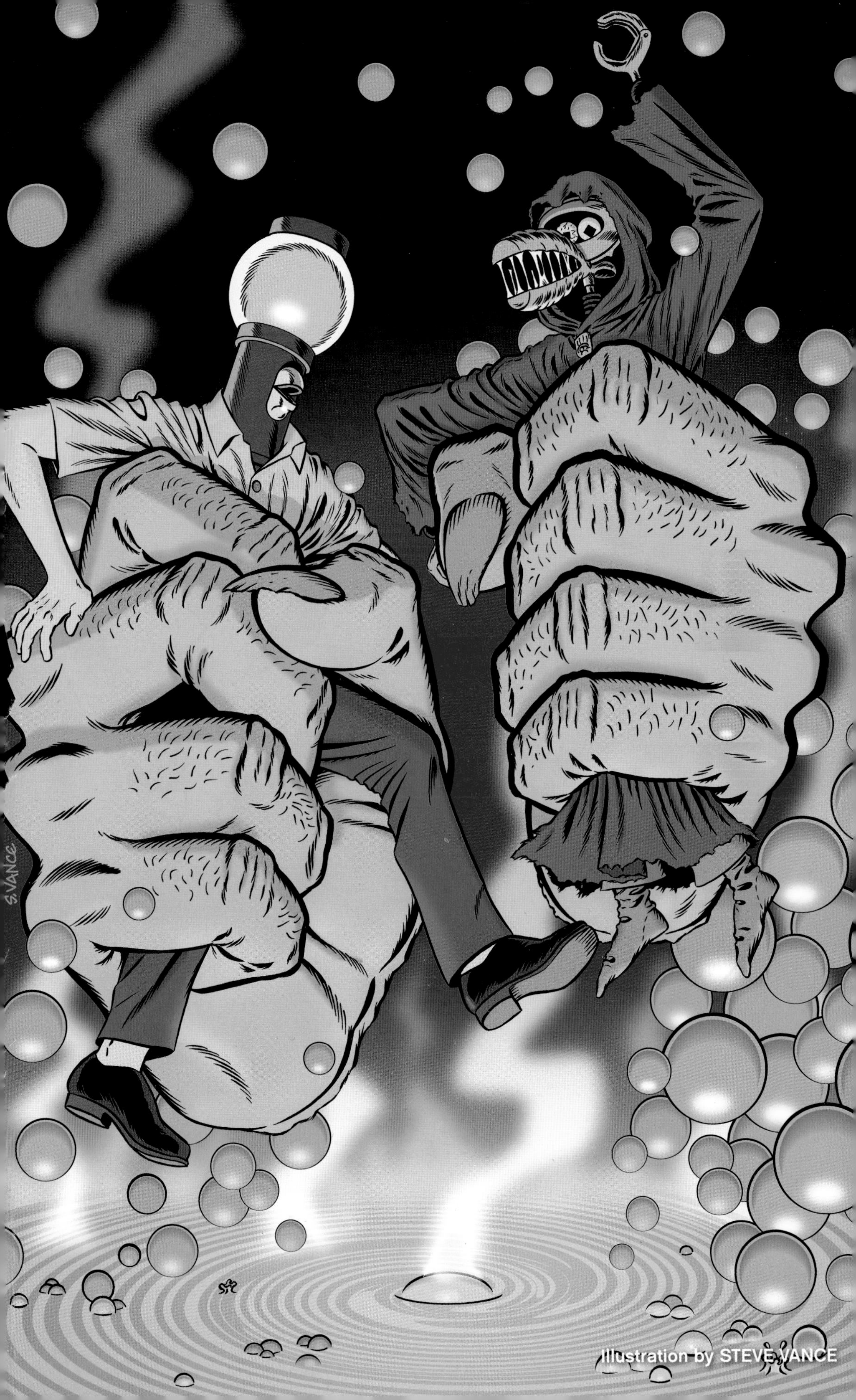
S.VANCE
Illustration by STEVE VANCE

Illustration by TODD NAUCK
Colored by WES DZIOBA

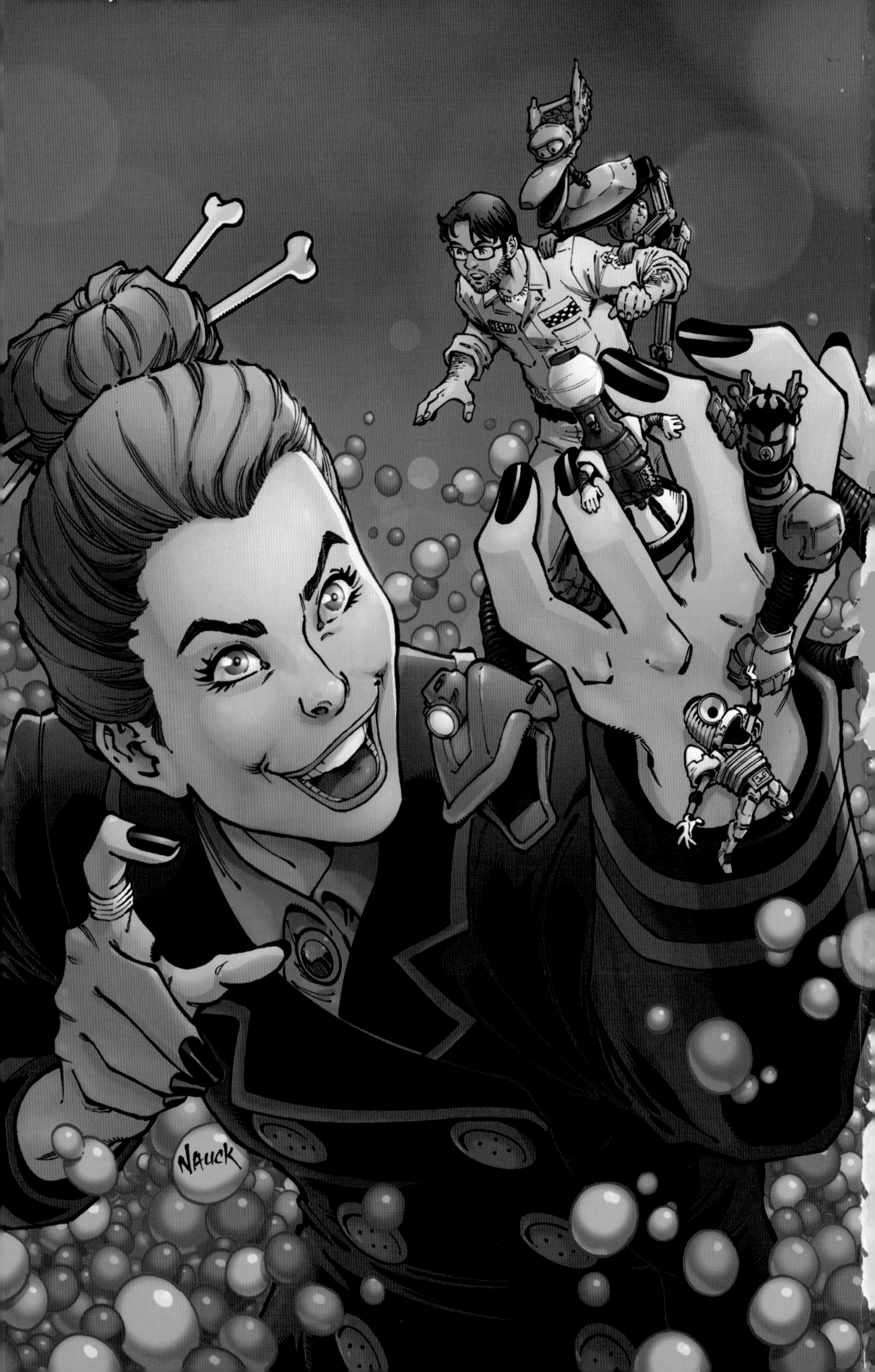
NAUCK